BOOKS BY JORDAN DUGDALE

The Whispered Tales Series

The Tidings of Misfits
A Waltz Through Flames
A Song of Hope

A SONG OF HOPE

JORDAN DUGDALE

When everything feels hopeless, remember the wise words of Aragorn, son of Arathorn:

There is always hope.

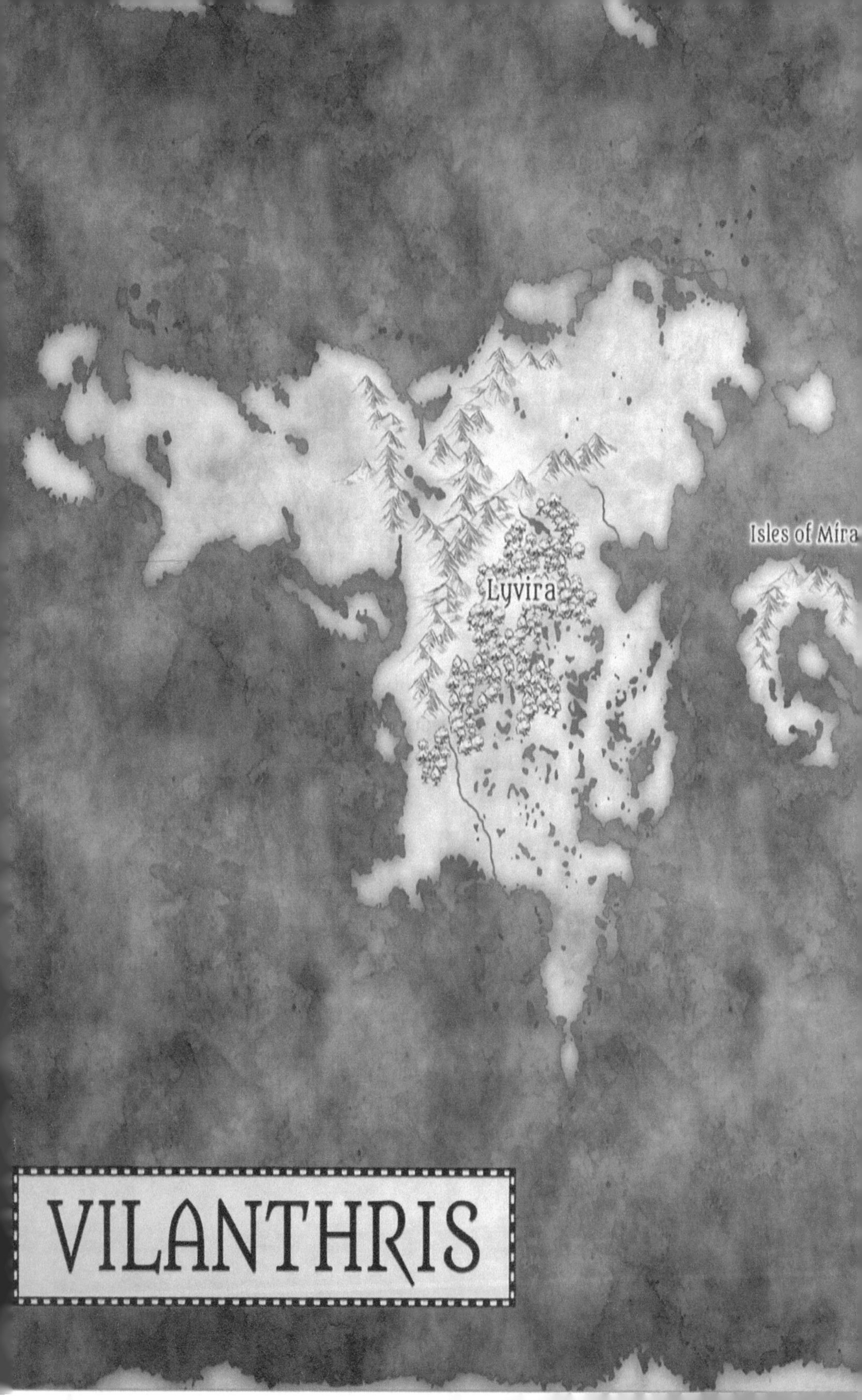

Isles of Mira
Lyvira
VILANTHRIS

Kreznov
Volreya
Spine Mountains
Volendam
Amajin
Wolstadt
Fraheim
Nantielle
Rovania
Wilhaven
Halvðarc
Hestia
Kythera
Daesthara
Shoma
Dalasae

CONTENT WARNINGS

Rats – these rats are a giant, mutated, intelligent race that are a main presence in the series

Cults – this includes cult activity and cult sacrifice but it is brief in this book

Child death – this is briefly described in a flashback

Fantasy violence - gore, battle horror, body horror, death, murder, one scene where a character blows up an area with magic

Family trauma – brief / one chapter

Brief moments of PTSD

Torture – includes whipping and slowly burning someone over a fire / brief – two chapters

WHAT CAME BEFORE...

<u>The Tidings of Misfits</u>

At the beginning of their journey, the vampire Cassius finds himself woken from a tomb he's been imprisoned inside of for the last five years. Fleeing back to his estate, he's only given a short time to collect himself before he discovers a magical gun has been placed inside his arm, and with it, a shadowy woman who urges him to Volendam where he may collect another piece of such magical armory.

His journey takes him through the Spine Mountains, where he is eventually captured by Shoma'kah, slavers of the sands. During his imprisonment, he meets Rooster, a human man with no recollection of his past, Helai, a woman from Shoma, and two drikoty, lizardfolk from Lyvira named Intoh and Linda.

Their journey is forever changed when they fall through a crack in the ground and land inside the mountain, where giant, mutated rats called the rakken intercept the slaver's caravans and mark the five of them with a dark brand. As they fight their way out of the mountain with the help of dwarves they meet along the way, their brand calls to something in Volendam.

After many trials, they find themselves inside the port trading city, where they meet Velius, an eldrasi blacksmith on board a ship called the Firebrand. There, he offers them aid. The only price is to infiltrate an exclusive club in the wealthy district and steal a few gems and a mysterious locket. After meeting Velius, they make their way to the nearest inn, The Broken Arrow, where they're received warmly by inn workers Felix, Patrina, and Hilde.

Meanwhile, Cassius discovers that the woman in his arm has been pulling him towards an abandoned opera house, where something calls him inside. With no weapons to speak of, Cassius refrains from entering just yet, and the ragtag team sets out to retrieve what Velius asked for to have their weapons made. They end up fighting mermaids to gain entry into the exclusive club, where they successfully retrieve the gems and locket for Velius. Upon touching said locket, Rooster has a vision of his past, and of a woman with fiery red hair. He knows it has some tie to his past so he keeps it for himself and tells Velius that it has been lost.

After receiving their newly forged weapons from Velius, they make their way to the opera house, where they discover a group of vampires standing in the way of the object Cassius has been sent to retrieve. It's a hard battle but a battle won nonetheless, and as the Misfits move to leave, they're called out to by a strange door. Inside they discover a ritual being performed by rakken and dyrvak, large woodland creatures similar to centaurs (only deer instead of horses) as they surround a dragon tooth. Their attempts to resurrect the dragon are foiled by the Misfits who stumble back out into the streets of Volendam and they discover that the city has been surrounded by an army of dyrvak and they must prepare themselves:

War is upon them.

<u>A Waltz Through Flames</u>

The second book in the *Whispered Tales* series opens up with a lone rakken scuttling through the sewers as he tails the Misfits from below the city of Volendam. There, he finds a small cult of rakken worshiping the dragon god Gorvayne, the same god whose sigil brands each of the Misfits. The chapter ends with that lone rakken branding himself with the same sigil, eager to find someone called *Carter*.

Above, the city of Volendam is being sieged by the horrific dyrvak, a woodland deer-centaurian race that worships the lost dragon gods. The Misfits fight valiantly to hold the city's walls, but it appears the dyrvak have teamed up with the Spine Mountain's rakken, who use their vile magic to blow up the city's walls. With the wall lost, Cassius, Helai, and Rooster retreat to the docks, where Linda and Intoh are fighting a massive, dead deer in Volendam's bay. It is at the docks where they make their final stand and manage to keep claim over their city. But it is not without major loss, one nearly being the vampire Cassius, who narrowly survives a grievous wound. He makes his recovery on the eldrasi blacksmith Velius' ship, the *Firebrand*, where some romantic tension begins to flourish. He also gets another visit from Ahma, the daughter of Emporer Aikawa from Amajin and the woman who possesses his blood. She tells him of the next piece in the armory she is having him seek out: a cuirass in Halvdarc to the south. Halvdarc is in Rovania, the same place where Cassius' estate resides, and the brand urges them all there. They also find the Broken Arrow has been utterly destroyed but to be rebuilt with the aid of the dwarves, who had come to offer their aid during the siege. Helai receives a cryptic letter from one of her Ghosts, who claims he is in Halvdarc and wishes to speak with her. Rooster manages to secure safe passage on a trade ship that will take them to Halvdarc, and soon, the Misfits leave Volendam for the first time since they've arrived.

As they're sailing down the coast, the ship they've taken passage on is attacked by Vykra, a northern people of the bitter north that seeks to claim their ship. Much seems lost as they begin to get overwhelmed, only for their savior to be of the strangest kind: a ship of vampire pirates accompanied by a hydra, a dragon-like sea beast with several heads. Even stranger? They know Rooster, or rather, Carter Wingman. Their captain is Delroy Greaves, who speaks of cults attempting to wake a dragon in the far west, and they only have so much time to find a tome that could possibly house information on keeping it asleep. He tells the Misfits that he will be in touch as he discovers more and that they are to obtain this tome if they wish for their beloved Volendam to remain untouched. Rooster wrangles with his rediscovered name, still frustrated that his amnesia holds strong. Cassius fights with his own demons.

The rest of the trip is uneventful, and they arrive in Halvdarc to find it strange. The people of the town are nowhere to be seen, hidden away in their homes. Cassius believes the cuirass they seek is in the Welker Estate, the estate of a noble family that lives on a cliffside and is known for their flower trade. He is familiar with their adviser, who meets them at the local inn to arrange a meeting. Before his arrival, two greka come into the inn searching for Intoh, who isn't discovered purely by the fact that he is wearing his illusion ring. The innkeeper kicks the greka out, but Cassius finds them to arrange a meeting with them after Intoh agrees they could have something important to say.

The adviser arrives and agrees that a meeting could be arranged if they can find Welker's missing son, Rembrandt. The Misfits agree and spend some time looking for clues on where he might have gone, but not before meeting with the greka who sought out Intoh's company. They pledge themselves to Intoh, claiming he is a prophet of their god. After, the Misfits split up to look for trails of Rembrandt. Rooster heads to the docks, but before he can arrive, he's attacked by a cultist and saved by a strange dwarf who claims to know of Rooster's past and bears the same burning brand as the Misfits. He calls himself Rackjack, and refuses to then leave Rooster's side. On the other side of town, Cassius is forced to feed and finds a father beating a young man. Cassius saves him, and the young man, who Cassius comes to find as Itale, reveals that he noticed the young Rembrandt heading towards the town Wilhaven, which is where Cassius' estate resides. With several new companions, the Misfits set out to Wilhaven.

Rembrandt's trail leads them to a strange, abandoned winery, where they discover two grotesque women who are harvesting the blood of humans. Rembrandt is among them, and while they are successful in rescuing the young boy, Rooster is seriously injured. They rush him back to Cassius' estate, where they manage to heal him. During this time, Cassius also finds out Itale is a necromancer and needs a teacher if he is to survive the death magic.

They return Rembrandt safely to his parents. Emir and Alyse Welker are extremely thankful for their child's return and demand they host a masquerade ball in their honor. Helai accidentally runs into her Ghost, a man named Zamir, who is hiding among the servants as he attempts to seek out a lamp in Emir Welker's possession. The lamp is a jinn lamp, one capable of granting wishes. He also fills Helai in on Massoud's whereabouts and the fact that Shoma has declared war on Hestia, who have long since been at peace and in a trade agreement with one another.

The estate grows more unsettling the longer the Misfits remain, and Cassius soon finds that the cuirass he seeks is inside Emir Welker's personal collection. He will need to figure out a way to steal it before they leave.

The masquerade ball arrives, and the Misfits have a plan to steal both the cuirass and the lamp, which they found behind some magical lock in the library. Every plan falls apart as each Misfit is captured and rendered unconscious, only to wake up tied up beneath the estate. There, they are rescued by Rackjack, but in doing so he reveals himself to be a rakken. Though they've only been known as an enemy up until now, Rooster protects him, determined to know how Rackjack is linked to his past.

Emir Welker appears, and it is revealed he is a cultist of the dead dragons. They chase him to a room where cults surround a massive tooth. A woman stands before Rembrandt, who's tied to a wooden post. The Misfits are tied up, and Cassius is brought to the center of the room, where he is sacrificed, his blood smeared across the dragon tooth. A phoenix dragon is reborn; Rhavna is resurrected. In the darkness of death, Cassius speaks to Drausmírtus, the god of death. He binds himself to them and, in return, is brought back, reforged with wings and a lack of bloodlust, though his vampirism remains. Before Drausmírtus banishes Rhavna by wounding her and sending her north, she burns Rembrandt and his mother alive and eats the rest of the cultists. The Misfits then blink, and they're back at the ball, where the estate begins to burn, and they're forced to flee.

Once they get outside, they seek out Velius, whom Rackjack recognizes and calls Tantien. They seek shelter on his ship, and, using his portal, takes them back to The Broken Arrow, which has been rebuilt. A bathhouse, named in Cassius' honor, has been built, a gift from the dwarves for the Misfits' aid in the mountain all that time ago. It is then they realize two things: the brand that has been tying them together is no longer ailing them, and Velius is actually named Tantien, and he seeks the Misfits' aid in breaking his sister out of an eldrasi prison. Rooster discovers Tantien is Igraine's brother, the redhead in his memories. In order to save Igraine, they must travel south to the war-torn city of Alavae and rescue Massoud, one of Helai's ghosts. He is a master illusionist and can aid in the coming prison break.

MASSOUD

The moon illuminated the Shoman military camp as Massoud pulled back the fabric of the tent and stepped inside.

"Massoud?" a hushed voice called out through the darkness. Massoud was accustomed to moving through the shadows, having survived on the streets of Shoma for the last thirty years and having given his faith to Dalnor, the shadow god who'd gifted him his ability to manipulate the shadows. He stepped expertly through the tent, towards the bed and the male voice without so much as knocking into anything.

"Where did you go?" the voice asked.

"Shhh." Massoud sought out the other body in the darkness, the bed dipping as he pressed a knee onto the mattress. "You ask far too many questions for someone who is supposed to be up early for a meeting, Sarem. Why aren't you asleep?"

Sarem's hand reached out and tugged Massoud's shirt, pulling him down against him. Massoud relished the warmth that radiated off the other man, especially with the coming winter. He huddled closer, his fingers splaying across Sarem's chest as his face fell into the crook of his neck. Sarem smelled vaguely of sweat and bonfire smoke.

"I woke, and you were gone. I was worried we had a deserter on our hands."

Laughter rumbled deep in Massoud's throat as his fingers grazed gentle pathways across Sarem's chest. "No, no. You, ah…" He paused, his breathless laughter tickling Sarem's neck. "I slipped away to check the perimeter. With being so close to Alavae's walls, one can never be too careful. Hestian spies are ever the possibility." The lies came easily as he forced his gaze to meet Sarem's. In truth, he would always be a man from Shoma, but Shoma no longer had his loyalty. It had lost it long ago when he was no more than a child starving on the streets. Disgust echoed in the cavities of his chest every time he looked into Sarem's eyes, every time he heard a Shoman soldier laughing about what they planned to do to the Hestian women should they find them. Evil, disgusting men; they were a dishonor to his home, a once thriving, beautiful country full of thriving, beautiful people. Shoma was but a husk of that now. Mohalis, the current sultan of Shoma, had made sure of that when he bred hatred and love for only skaels and power. Massoud had lost hope in his home when he was an adolescent and had nearly lost his hand for stealing a loaf of bread from a rich merchant's cart.

It was Helai who had relit a small flame of hope within him. He'd found her small, tear-stained, and starving on the sandy streets of Dalasae. Since then, he'd made it his life to make sure she liberated herself from the pain and suffering of her home. She was sixteen winters when she came to him with the idea of finding like-minded people, people who wanted to see their home free from the corrupt that sat in power. Helai was his sister in all but blood, and his heart ached every time he thought of her. He missed her. Imagining her look of disgust where he was now, what he had had to do to ensure Sarem's trust so that he may act as a spy for Alavae's army...it had brought a smile to his face.

"Well... I'm up now." Sarem shifted in the dark, and Massoud blinked against the harshness of the sudden torchlight. Sarem pulled his hand away from the oil lamp near the bed, a satisfied smile on his face. The tent was illuminated in a soft glow, low enough to maintain their privacy but light enough that Massoud could look up and capture the dark gaze of Sarem's as he rose to hover over him. He was handsome for a general. Definitely Massoud's type, though he rarely got to indulge. The wealthy did not tend to give Massoud the time of day, not unless they mistook him for a whore. That usually worked in his favor, though; it granted his wishes for a distraction from the brutal survival of the streets and filled his pockets with a whore's wage.

"Sarem." Massoud laughed, attempting to calm his racing heart. He'd just told this Hestian contact about Shoma's intention to lay siege to the city of Alavae, and tensions were high. Massoud was confident in his ability to remain unnoticed, tucked behind the masquerade of a soldier, but it did not stop him from being weary. Not when he was right in the middle of a den of vipers. "If I never get my beauty sleep, how do you expect me to maintain myself for your pleasure?"

Sarem rumbled, his hand dancing between them to tug at the pants Massoud had slipped on to meet his contact. "I can feel your erection; sleep can come after."

Massoud batted his eyes at him; he wasn't wrong. His erection pressed against his pants as he held Sarem's gaze. "You are a persistent man, but I suppose that is why they made you general, hm?" He laughed.

Sarem did not join in on the laughter, but Massoud hadn't expected him to. The general was a stoic man. He reached down instead, grabbing Massoud's chin as he lowered himself to kiss him. A soft sigh pressed against Massoud's cheeks as he reached up to thread his fingers through Sarem's hair. A need built in his chest, desperate to tug Sarem closer as he hooked his leg over the small of Sarem's back and pulled him down.

"General."

Sarem pulled away, much to Massoud's displeasure, as three soldiers entered the tent. Massoud might have felt shameful about his state of undress had he not been with the most powerful man in the army. Instead, he teasingly danced his fingers across Sarem's jawline and said, "I didn't know we were having company joining us."

One of the soldiers stepped forward, his face covered by a thin layer of cream silk. Only his eyes were uncovered, and they stared at Sarem with intent. "We have confirmed your suspicions, general."

Massoud's panic flourished, his smile fading as the soldiers all looked at him. Sarem was slower to turn, his eyes burning with rage.

"What...what suspicions did you have?" Massoud asked, his earlier courage gone from his voice. *They know*, he thought. *Run while you can still move your hands.* He needed to be able to move his hands to shade step.

But as he pulled his hands away to slip into the shadows, Sarem grabbed his wrists and shoved them to his sides, preventing him from wielding his shadow magic. The general's cold fury fueled Massoud's panic as he laughed nervously. His eyes darted to the soldiers who stood near the flap of the tent, their expressions unreadable.

"Boys...I like it rough, but is this really necessary?"

"Take him," Sarem said.

No one spoke as the soldiers moved towards the bed. Sarem's hard expression was the last thing Massoud saw before they dragged him away.

Three days had passed, but the torture had never got any easier.

Clear mind, clear soul. A mantra Massoud had used to whisper to Helai when she'd been a terrified little girl, and the guards had been searching the houses nearby. "They will not catch us, little sister," he'd told her, guilt unfurling in his chest as she stared up at him with wide, round eyes. He'd wished he could find a better life for her.

"How do you know?" she had asked, her voice hoarse. He'd been unable to steal water, and his own dehydration had forced a headache at his temples. As the voices of the guards had grown louder, he'd shushed her whimpering and had gestured to a window behind her. It was high. He'd have to hoist her up, but if they were quick...

"Clear mind, clear soul," he'd said as he'd pushed her through the window, hoisting himself up and narrowly escaping the guards.

He'd been lucky to avoid being captured that day.

Now? Now he sat upon his knees before an open flame, his arms outstretched, his wrists tied to wooden pillars staked to the ground. His face ached from all the times they had struck him; one eye was swollen shut. He couldn't remember the last time he'd eaten, and they'd only been giving him water, and only a little because they still believed he had the information they could get from him.

They didn't know he'd forged his will stronger than steel.

"Tell us, brother. Were you born a street rat, or did you betray the will of the One?" Those around the fire sneered at him as they drank and smoked, their laughter mocking and loud. His mind was a haze from dehydration and the lack of food, but he still found the strength to smile, his teeth bloodied from a recent beating.

"Untie me, and I'll show you a time so mind-shattering, you will worship the ground I walk on." His voice turned low and seductive. "You won't even remember the One exists when my mouth is wrapped around your pretty little cock."

A young soldier spat on the ground at Massoud's feet before reaching up to strike him. Massoud refused to flinch as he jutted his chin upwards, ready to meet it, but it never came as one of the older guards stopped him.

"Wait."

Massoud had come to know the one speaking as Jarah.

The young soldier froze and lowered his head. Massoud had been watching these soldiers long enough to know that a lot of the others feared Jarah.

As Jarah approached, Massoud lowered his gaze, peering at him through his eyelashes. He knew better than to provoke Shoman soldiers, but he couldn't help himself. Not when his heart raced. Not when he knew deep down that they'd find no more use for him and murder him before the siege on the city of Alavae truly began.

"You first, big guy?" Massoud purred, his lips parting to a toothy grin as the soldier walked behind him. "You don't even have to untie me. I like a challenge. Just take off your pants..." His vision shuddered as the crack of a whip came down on his back, burning white-hot as the leather licked through his skin, clean as butter. Massoud cried out as his body shuddered forward against his will, desperate to escape the bite of the whip, but it came down on him again and again. The laughter of the Shoman soldiers filled his ears as he lost consciousness.

When he woke, it was nighttime. Most of the guards had retired, but there were still three that sat around an open flame near his shackles and many more that patrolled the camp. A soft whimper started to build, his lower lip quivering as he struggled to hold it back. He could not afford to show the soldiers any weakness. The moment he did so, he knew they would not hold back their attempts to pry information from him. Still, it was growing trickier and trickier.

The Shoma camp was nestled against the shores outside the eastern side of Alavae, some miles off from the walled city. The Shomans were waiting, taking time to muster their strength as the bulk of their forces were sailing from Dalasae. Kythera, ever bitter that Hestia had broken off to become their own kingdom, was aiding the Shoman cause for the promise of land. Massoud was certain it was only a matter of time before his use was bled dry and he was killed for his crimes against Shoma.

I'm sorry, Helai, he thought sadly. *I did not mean to abandon you, little sister.*

How he'd found himself amid two warring kingdoms was comical at best. How cruel that the one man intent on staying out of conflict had found himself in the center of it all.

He did not have the strength to raise his head; the wounds on his back screamed with pain as the wind caressed them. He struggled against the urge to shiver, knowing the movement would not aid his recovery, and he despaired. He should have fought harder against Sarem's men. He should have been more careful in the first place. He took comfort in knowing he'd been able to prepare Hestia for Shoma's intentions before he'd been caught. Perhaps that would turn the tide of the battle, at least.

A flicker of movement approached the fire, and Massoud watched through his good eye as Sarem approached, dressed for war. Shoman soldiers dressed lightly due to their time in the sands, and a mixture of leather and cloth clung to Sarem's skin as a beacon they were going to war soon. A khopesh, a sickle-shaped blade, hung from his hip, and the lines on his face were hard as he stared first at Massoud and then at the soldiers nestled around the flames.

"Bring him to the fire."

ONE
HELAI

Helai exhaled, circling Zamir, one of her Ghosts, in the empty tavern.

The Broken Arrow, the inn they'd been staying in on and off for the past year, had been empty all day. Helai had taken it upon herself to entertain her time by asking Zamir to spar with her, and the innkeepers Felix and Patrina had helped by pushing all the tables to the side to give them room.

Tantien (she still wasn't used to calling him that; the eldrasi blacksmith with the ship had been Velius to her up until a few days ago) had told them to stay put until he came back to ferry them south, and they'd been waiting ever since.

"You can do this, Helai!" Itale called out from their booth in the corner, his fingers drumming against the wood table as Intoh read an old, dusty tome beside him. The greka seemed annoyed with Itale's constant motion, and if he moved down any lower, he might slip entirely under the table.

Cassius had entered some moments earlier to grab a bottle of wine from behind the counter and disappear into the bathhouse. Ever since the dwarves had helped the Broken Arrow crew rebuild and added the bathhouse as a small gift to the Misfits for aiding them all that time ago in their mountain city, the vampire had made a home in his private bath. Helai had barely seen him since they got back to Volendam from Halvdarc. She didn't know where Rooster was either. Struggling with the knowledge that his beloved was locked away in some distant prison, most likely.

Helai rolled her shoulders and bounced from one foot to the other. It had been agonizing, waiting to leave. Ever since Zamir had told her Massoud was in Alavae, a small yarn ball of panic had sat mercilessly in her chest, refusing to untangle. Finding Zamir had been the start of her reunion with her ghosts. She still needed to find the others: Masika, Hosni, Ehsan, Aryan, but she didn't even know where to look for them. Aryan was most likely still in Lyvira, where Massoud had sent him all those years ago, but the others were simply ghosts. Just like the name for their merry band of thieves deemed them. She understood their delay; they meant to sail to war and had to prepare for the journey, but what if she was too late? What if something happened to Massoud? What if...

"Distractions will get you killed, Helai." Zamir clicked his tongue against the roof of his mouth as Helai pulled herself out of her spiral. She rubbed her chest, trying to curb the panic there, and then grinned, bending low to ready herself against her opponent.

"You'll need me distracted if you want to win, *asdiq*."

Zamir laughed deeply, pulling it from deep in the bowels of his belly to infect the room with. Felix and Patrina joined in as they cleaned mugs at the counter, and, for a bitter moment, there was nothing but lightness in the air. The troubles they all faced were washed away, and Helai was merely spending another day with the people she loved.

Zamir came at her without warning. He was quick, despite not being as trained in combat as she was, but she was a master of the shadow, her fingers drenched in inky darkness as her magic beckoned shadows from every corner of the room and pulled it to her, tucking her away from Zamir as she dodged his attack by rolling to the right. She was quick back on her feet, exhaling softly as she shot out of the shadows where Zamir had retreated and tackled him from the side, breathing hard when they both hit the ground.

"Careful, *asdi*," Zamir laughed, clutching the elbow he'd landed on. "I need to get back to my *amori* in one piece."

Helai's eyes flashed. "*Amori*?" She pushed herself to her feet and helped Zamir to his, stepping back to brush herself off and get back into a readied stance. The enemy did not wait for one to be prepared; they struck out without mercy, and Helai always prepared for such, even in sparring sessions. Build a wall and you save yourself from injury.

It paved way to only one path though, one of loneliness.

"You'll meet her when we enter the city. She's in charge of Alavae's spies."

Helai lashed out, but Zamir was ready and dodged her attack, his foot skirting along the floor as he danced around her outstretched hand and waved a hand. The shadowy visage of a crow burst from his fingers, cawing and flying towards the ceiling, and Helai blew a loose strand of hair out of her face.

Clear mind, clear soul.

"She has to be pretty special if she was able to convince the great Zamir to come down from his rooftops," Helai said. Where Massoud had always found himself in the bed of various men during Helai's adolescence, Zamir was the older brother figure preaching to push away idle distractions.

"No," Massoud had always said, accompanied by a simpering grin, "you are just hanging out with Masika too much. She's whispering chastity in your ear when you all go out on missions together. You can't convince me otherwise."

"She is," Zamir said, pulling Helai back to the present. There was a faraway look in his eye, a soft smile on his lips, and Helai's heart squeezed. She was happy for him.

It didn't mean she was going to be merciful.

She lashed out while he was distracted, keeping low to catch him off balance like she had before. He dodged out of the way of her attack, waving a hand as he nearly barreled into Rooster, who had come down from upstairs and was heading towards the bathhouse.

"Sorry, mate," Rooster said, offering a distracted smile.

"I can't believe her. Did you teach her these dirty tricks?" Zamir asked, jutting his thumb in Helai's direction. "No longer is there the young girl crying about fairness. That was a dirty move you did, trying to use the memory of my beloved against me."

Helai laughed. "I do want to know more about this elusive woman."

Zamir straightened, using both hands to brush his hair back from his temples. "After I beat you, we'll sit down and talk."

The end of Zamir's shoe changed into a murder of shadowy crows, and the rest of him followed as he disappeared into a trail of shadows. Felix and Patrina watched on with mild interest at the counter, and Helai closed her eyes, straining her ears to listen.

Behind you, Helai, Massoud's voice whispered in the back of her mind, much as it always had when he'd trained her in her youth. She ducked as the soft flutter of bird feathers sounded behind her right ear. *Now.*

Lashing out, her foot struck Zamir's ankle as he appeared. He hit the ground hard and grunted, his eyes flashing with surprise. Itale clapped softly from his spot at a booth. Steam curled off his tea as he pressed his fingers delicately to the porcelain of his cup.

"You really have gotten quicker," Zamir said, writhing on the floor as he nurtured the knee he'd fallen on. Still, laughter drenched his words, and he smiled as Helai reached out and offered her hand, pleased with the compliment. They were hard to get from Zamir.

A crow lunged from the rafters at Helai, and she tugged her hand back, scowling.

"Sadiki, *abibi*, it's alright. She isn't going to hurt me." Zamir cooed at the crow as she landed on his shoulder and glared at Helai. She'd never gotten along with Zamir's crow. He'd stolen it from one of the flocks in Shoma before they'd been separated, and she could never quite understand why the bird seemed to hate her. She'd suffered many injuries from that bird's beak.

"It has been quite some time since we've sparred together," Helai said, eyeing Sadiki as she pulled Zamir to his feet. "I have to admit—it feels nice to be quicker than you for once."

"Just once, perhaps," Zamir said. "I won't let you get me again."

"I could barely even keep track of you," Itale said, his fingers drumming against the table. "That was impressive, Helai."

Helai lowered her head in gratitude, a smile tugging at her lips. She felt lighter. Despite all that had transpired in the southern city of Halvdarc a few weeks ago, with Rhavna, the phoenix dragon, being resurrected and Rembrandt, the little boy of the Welker Estate, being sacrificed in her name, Helai was with one of her Ghosts and the brand the rakken had placed upon her skin had been removed. They were going to find Massoud soon; all was finally going their way for once.

"Everyone relies on sight when fighting. You have to remember—your other senses exist for a reason. I couldn't see him, but I could *hear* him," Helai said, tapping her ear.

"I will remember to work on holding my breath," Zamir retorted, earning laughter from everyone in the tavern as Sadiki returned to the shadows of the rafters above. "For now, it is time for a drink."

"Ah, you sound like Massoud," Helai said, waving her hand at him. "The sun has barely had a chance to be up, and you're already nursing the ale."

Zamir laughed, flipping her his middle finger. "You're not my mother, Helai."

He was right, of course, and Helai watched with the smallest of smiles as he approached Felix at the bar. The Broken Arrow was slowly returning to its familiar feeling of home, and despite Helai's best efforts, it had wormed its way into her heart. Patrina was laughing at something Zamir had said, and Itale had joined Intoh at the booth next to him, where he poured over whatever book Intoh was reading today.

"Go have bath?" Linda inquired, approaching Helai as they entered the tavern. "Saw Tantien. Said leave tomorrow." They gestured as Tantien, the eldrasi blacksmith they'd met when they first got to Volendam, entered the inn, his fingers pulling the door shut as quickly as he could to keep the chill of winter out. It still brushed against Helai relentlessly, and Helai shook her head, grinning at Linda.

"You go on without me. I want to talk with Tantien about the journey ahead." She turned away from Linda as they headed towards the door to the bathhouse, and Tantien approached, his eyes bright as he lowered his head in Helai's direction.

"Hello, dear Helai. I know you're anxious to leave. I've finished up the final preparations for the journey and came to let the Misfits know we'll leave on the morrow," Tantien said.

"Can't we leave now?" Helai's gut twisted anxiously. Now that she knew where Massoud was, she wanted to leave as quickly as possible. There was no telling if something would chase Massoud from Hestia, and she didn't want to lose his trail again.

"The journey down is long, I'm afraid. I'm having the rest of the supplies gathered now, but we'll leave as soon as we are able. I promise." Tantien's face expressed understanding as he leaned close. "I am anxious to get there too. The quicker we find your friend, the quicker we can begin the rescue mission for my sister." He shuddered. "I hate thinking about what they're doing to her in that prison. All eldrasi know of it; it's a vile place."

"We'll get them out," Helai said firmly. "Massoud is the best man for the task."

Tantien's eyes darkened. "Let us hope for his good health."

Helai's stomach twisted mercilessly, a maelstrom of worry that some unlucky fate had befallen her brother, who was also her oldest friend. Massoud was resourceful, the most resourceful person she'd ever met, but he wasn't invincible.

Tantien must have seen the look of distress cross her face because he moved to rest a hand on her shoulder. "Do not despair. Fear clouds judgment, and we need clear heads as we sail towards war." His fingers were warm to the touch, and Helai nodded, her mind thick with worry. When the time came, she would bind her fear, tucking it behind her determination, but now? Now that she knew where Massoud was and that he was possibly in trouble, she could not keep her fear at bay.

"Thank you, Tantien," was all she said, shrugging him away as she fled the confines of The Broken Arrow she felt trapped in. She ignored Zamir as he called out to her. The inn had become a home to her, but she couldn't handle being around anyone right now. Not even Zamir.

Winter had officially arrived at the city of Volendam, and Helai shivered despite bracing against the cold as she stepped out onto the street. Snow wasn't falling for the first time in days, but it blanketed the ground in a sense of deceitful calm as she made her way to a familiar alley.

It had been some time since Dalnor, the god of shadows, had spoken to her. His silence was jarring, and Helai's heart squeezed painfully.

"I could use your guidance now more than ever," she whispered, bending her head towards the shrine in the alley. Somehow it had remained safe from any danger during the siege, untouched by malice, but even as Helai stood here, willing her god to speak to her, she was met with nothing but silence.

Rage coursed through her, bubbling up from her stomach and reaching her throat, and it choked the air from her lungs.

"Helai." Zamir's voice sounded behind her as pain blossomed from her knuckles. She didn't remember lashing out, but her knuckles were pressed against the wall of the alley, and pain now radiated up her arm.

She hissed, pulling her hand away. She almost expected the brand on her back to burn before she remembered that it had been removed at the Welker Estate. After being branded by the rakken, giant, mutated rats, in the Spine Mountains, she'd grown used to the constant ache on her lower back, a reminder of its presence. Despite its removal, she often wondered if she was free of its burden or if she was doomed to be looking over her shoulder constantly. Rackjack, the rakken that had pledged his loyalty to Rooster, proved her time with the rakken was far from over, even if things had been silent.

A lump rose in her throat as she recalled Rembrandt, a mere child, being burned after having been sacrificed by his own parents. The stench of cooked flesh filling her nose, and the sight of the phoenix dragon rising to devour them all filled her mind. If it hadn't been for Cassius…

A sob lodged itself in her lungs, and she turned, letting Zamir embrace her. Her god was still silent, a watchful thief in the shadows who did not care for her trifles. Dalnor had never felt so far from Helai, her faith wavering in the cold alley of Volendam.

"Your strength is forged from iron, Helai," Zamir said, speaking quietly in Shoman, "It does not mean it does not falter from time to time. You are allowed to feel frightened for our friend."

"If Massoud is dead—"

"Do not speak of such tragedies. We don't know his fate. Do not weave it into his destiny. Worrying about it does not make it so; it only robs you of your sanity." Zamir pulled back slightly, his smile sad.

"When did you become so wise? Usually, it is Masika who speaks in such tongues." Masika was the only Ghost that remained faithful to the One instead of Dalnor, like the rest of them. She was always attempting to rein them in with her words of wisdom.

Zamir laughed, tucking Helai's hair behind her ear and clasping her shoulders, holding her at arm's length. "Out of all the Ghosts, I spent the most time with her. You learn a thing or two when information missions take days to scout out, and you only have Masika for company."

Gone were those days. Helai couldn't say she wished to return to them, for many nights had been spent on the sands, wondering if they'd be able to find their next meal or if Shoman soldiers would discover where they had been holed up. Still, she missed her family.

The Misfits are your family too.

The thought bit at her mind unbidden, and she reaffirmed it in her head. Despite her aversions at first, they had all made their way into her heart. The thought of leaving their side hurt just as much as being away from the Ghosts, and her chest ached with the conflicting emotions.

"Come. Do not suffer alone in the cold. Linda was asking for you. Something about teaching them and Itale that card game of yours." His eyes flashed, accompanied by a wicked grin. "If you'd like, I could remind you what it's like to lose."

Bumping his shoulder with hers, she scoffed. "You are too cocky for your own good." It was strange looking into Zamir's eyes. It had been so long since she'd seen a hint of her home in someone other than herself that she'd nearly forgotten the warmth of her people.

Tugging his arm, she turned towards the mouth of the alley. Perhaps a few games of Elusive Shahara would pass the time long enough to make it bearable.

TWO
CASSIUS

Cassius sighed happily and sank down in the bath until nothing but his head was settled above the water. He'd joked with Felix when the Misfits had returned from Halvdarc and found out that the dwarves had gifted the Broken Arrow with a pristine bathhouse that he'd never leave it, and he'd almost remained true to his promise. A massive hall, the main bath sat in the middle below a plethora of steam, the floors white marble decorated with golden veins. Cassius had a private bath tucked away in the corner, hidden behind a thick, red curtain, and it was one of many to give those who wanted it a bit of privacy. He hadn't had a bath this nice since his teenage years, when he'd still been in Hestia, enjoying their bath halls.

The warmth of the water chased away any lingering aches and pains from the recent battles, and Cassius shut his eyes, allowing his body to relax. It felt strange, having no more burning brand to occupy his thoughts, no more whispering of Ahma, a woman from the country of Amajin in the far east that had been a thorn in his side since the moment he'd woke in his tome. Since his death and rebirth at the Welker Estate, even his vampiric bloodlust had been less of a burden, a faint scratching at the base of his throat that he easily ignored.

"Cassius-filth."

The vampire opened his eyes to see Rackjack in his dwarf form (his original form that of a large bipedal rat), tugging the curtain aside. A wooden prosthetic had replaced the rakken's right leg below the knee, and Rackjack leaned down to unbuckle it, placing it next to his clothes. Cassius couldn't recall Rackjack having suffered such an injury the last time he'd seen him a few days ago and he was *filthy*, the grime coming off him in small ripples as he waded in after removing his clothes.

"What happened to your leg?"

Rackjack glanced over as he slipped into the bath. "Honor duel. Rakken-rat challenged me. Got my leg-paw, but I got his head, yes-yes." His eyes gleamed as he waded closer.

Annoyance coursed through Cassius, but he did not send Rackjack away. After the initial shock of having learned Rackjack was a rakken, Cassius had shed most of his distrust towards him. Of all the rakken he'd fought and killed, Rackjack seemed different, just as Cassius was different from most vampires. He would be a hypocrite to judge. Plus, he'd killed enough rakken to know where Rackjack's weaknesses lay. One wrong move, and the rakken would seek no mercy from Cassius.

Rackjack glanced nervously behind him. "Close-shut curtain? Turn-shift to rat-rat form?"

Cassius shrugged. "So long as Felix or Patrina don't see you, I do not care."

Rackjack's eyes brightened as he closed the curtain and pried the bead roughly from his beard, shifting from dwarf to rakken. Cassius frowned, eyeing the water as it dirtied around him.

Lovely.

Still, he said nothing as Rackjack sank slowly into the bath. The dwarves had truly outdone themselves in crafting the bathhouse. The runes placed at the bottom of the bath kept the water warm, and Cassius was thankful for it. It chased away the endless cold vampirism caused.

"Have question-concern, mmm, yes-yes," Rackjack said, paddling close.

"Other side," Cassius said darkly, pointing to the other side of the bath. "Just because I have come to accept your true nature does not mean I want your musk all over me."

Rackjack halted, his nose twitching anxiously as he backed away to a respectful distance. Cassius rose to a seated position, pulling himself out of the water enough for his arms to straddle the floor as he relaxed against the side of the bath.

"Does your god speak-talk to you?"

Rackjack's question caught Cassius off guard, and he lulled over it with silent contemplation. Many vampires worshiped the dragon that granted them their undeath, while others gave their allegiance to Drausmírtus, the goddess of death, even though Death viewed vampires with disdain, their immortality a defiance against the eventual Sleep.

Drausmírtus did not turn their back on me, Cassius thought. *No. If anything, they granted me liberation from the shackles of vampirism while allowing me to maintain all its gifts. I owe them my loyalty.*

"I've heard from Death themself just once," Cassius said, tipping a bottle of lavender into the water in a final attempt to rid it of the smell

Rackjack had brought with him. The flowery scent wafted over the water, and Cassius sighed happily as Rackjack's nose twitched. "Why do you ask?"

Cupping his paws, Rackjack poured water over his head, wiping back the fur behind his ears. "Think it connected. Make you special-important. Not everyone can speak-talk to gods."

Rackjack was right, but the notion still made Cassius scoff. "It would be incredibly arrogant to think so." Conflicting emotions tugged at him at the thought. He'd never thought himself to be anyone special, had never taken care to place his faith in the gods. If they were to choose someone to rally for them, he seemed to be the least suited for the task.

Rackjack shook his head. "Not arrogant, no-no. Just face truth-truth."

"Does your god speak to *you*, Rackjack?" Cassius asked, turning the conversation to him.

Rackjack nodded quickly. "Sometimes, yes-yes!"

Cassius' brow furrowed. "What god do you pay homage to?"

Rackjack's nose quivered as he glanced about the bath, the water lapping in small waves as he moved closer. "Rat-King."

The mere mention of the god's name sent a shiver rolling through Cassius, like a horde of small rats were crawling over his skin. He'd never heard of such a god before, but then again, he'd never heard of the rakken prior to his journey through the mountains and his interactions with the dwarves.

"There you are." The curtain was drawn back as Rooster stuck his head in. He quickly pulled it against him once he noticed Rackjack's rakken form. Glancing over his shoulder, he stepped forward, allowing the curtain to sweep shut behind him, and shadowed the edge of the tub.

"I would join you, but..." He trailed off, eyeing the dirty water with ill-concealed disgust. Cassius couldn't blame him. Perhaps it would be time to exit the bath himself. "I'll leave you to it," Rooster continued after a moment. "I just wanted to let you know that Tantien has returned. We leave just before dawn."

Rising to his feet, Cassius sighed. He'd barely gotten to enjoy the very bath hall that had been named after him before they were being thrust back into the heart of battle. He'd thought little of traveling back to his home to rescue one of Helai's Ghosts. Cassius had traveled to Alavae a lot with his mother when he'd been a child. She'd always bribed him with the promise of *chiras*, long strips of bread coated in sugar and honey. He'd enjoyed sweets back then.

"Here you go, mate," Rooster said, offering Cassius a silk robe from the hook near the door. His eyes strayed upwards, as if to give Cassius privacy, and Rooster's awkwardness tugged at Cassius' amusement. Still, he said nothing as he grabbed the robe from Rooster's outstretched hand and slipped it on while stepping out of the bath. The silk was soft against his skin, and he suppressed a shudder as the cold air chased away the warmth from the bath.

"Carter-filth. Must go underground. Must seek-sniff Prelk-rat. Will return when sun rises; we go."

"I do not think you should leave our side. How do we know you are not sneaking off to betray us?" Cassius asked, folding his arms across his chest and frowning. He may have shed a lot of his distrust towards the rakken, but Rackjack sneaking off to speak to other rakken wasn't a good idea.

Rooster seemed to agree. "If you're going anywhere, I'm going with you."

Rackjack shook his head, splashing the water with his paws as he rose up. "No-no. Not good. Not good-wise at all. Will make other rakken-rats question me-me."

"Then make them listen." Rooster folded his arms too. "As your captain, I command it."

Cassius watched on in silence. Rooster didn't call upon his past often, but recently, he'd noticed Rooster had been slipping into the role more and more. It had come as a surprise to the rest of the Misfits when Rackjack and Tantien had revealed the tidbit about Rooster's past. Rackjack called him 'Captain Carter-filth', and curiosity had burned through Cassius ever since. What kind of captain had Rooster been? How had he managed to garner the loyalty of a rakken, a member of a race notorious for their disloyalty?

Rackjack's shoulders sagged as he relented, nodding gently. Slipping his bead back onto his beard, he tucked himself behind the visage of a dwarf and climbed out of the tub. He shook himself, much like a wet dog would do to rid the water from his fur. Then he clipped his prosthetic back on, grabbed the clothes he'd left on the other side of the curtain, and pulled them back on too.

"Yes. Fine-fine. But must do-do as I ask-speak," he uttered in a soft tone. "Rakken only listen to those with strongest musk."

Rakken did not seem to listen to anyone at all, but Cassius didn't say that. He'd spent some time around Rackjack, but his disdain towards rakken hadn't lessened. Rackjack was certainly the exception, and even then, Cassius saw greedy traits in him that were undesirable.

"We will be back before first light," Rooster promised, tugging open the curtain and allowing Rackjack to limp past him.

"Are you sure you want to go alone?" Cassius asked, gazing pointedly at Rackjack's retreating form. The way he moved and twitched... How had it taken so long for any of them to have figured out who he truly was?

Rooster nodded, throwing Cassius an amused grin. "No need for your concern, Cassius. If the rumors are true, I grew up with vampire pirates and captained a ship full of rejects. A sewer full of rats shouldn't be a problem."

Cassius frowned and said nothing else. After a moment, he gave a firm nod, and Rooster left, granting Cassius the alone time he much desired. It was like a sigh of relief, when the world grew silent, when the sound of trickling water was the only thing filling Cassius' ears.

He wanted more wine, so he strolled out into the inn where Felix graciously allowed him to take the whole bottle. "Remind me again, *ami*; why do you even pay for a room when you live in that bath house, hm?" Felix's laughter danced with Cassius' own as the vampire turned without answering and returned to his private bathtub. It really was magnificent—white marble, with a round tube where fresh water came in, washing away Rackjack's grime.

Taking a long draw straight from the wine bottle, Cassius shrugged his robe back off and sighed as he sank back into the bath. He'd go feed soon even though the desperate urges no longer ailed him, but for now? He relished the peace that cradled his heart. It had been so long since he'd been this relaxed.

"Cassius."

Just like that, the soft caress of a familiar voice shattered his peace.

He opened his eyes as Ahma appeared before him, seated on the edge of the bathtub. She was naked with three spectral fox tails darting behind her lower back in a blue luminescence. Now that she'd told him of their family curse, of having been scorned by their fox god, Kisae, it made sense – her illusion magic, the way she walked, talked, the fox devouring the bat. What didn't make sense was her presence. He'd scorned her, told her he was not to be a pawn in her path to bringing back her lost lover by collecting every piece in his armory. He thought he'd seen the last of her.

Apparently not.

Tilting his head back against the lip of the bath, he shut his eyes, ignoring Ahma. Lucky for him, he felt no urge to seek out the next piece of the Ebony Fang. She may have shackled his blood with the desire to seek it out, but he hadn't felt the call to look since he denied her at the Estate. That did not mean she would not tempt him by using the gun and the lance hidden away in his arm. He felt them there now, crawling with power. That power was addicting, although muted to a quiet dull by Drausmírtus' gifts. Had he known they would be tools for her to control him, he would have fought harder against their whispered calls to claim them.

"Cassius…" Ahma's voice was a low purr as he heard her slip into the tub. Her fingers ghosted his chest as she idled up next to him, the slip of her hair brushing his shoulder. He refused to open his eyes, hoping for her sudden absence should he pretend like she wasn't here.

"I'm disappointed, my little knight. You scorned me at the Welker Estate, and now I must send another to go fetch the cuirass."

His curiosity burned. "Why wake me in my tomb? Why choose me for this task?" he asked, his eyes flickering open as she rested a hand on his chest so that her face could hover just above his. Her breath feathered against his lips, and despite knowing this had to be some sort of illusion, Cassius couldn't help but respond to her closeness. An ache settled low in his belly, his own fingers twitching with temptation. It was as if she were a power of her own, one he was desperate to claim.

The gun in his arm warmed, humming with power. It urged him to slip his fingers between her thighs. He stilled that urge by pinning her expression with his own.

Ahma's smile flashed, revealing her fangs. "Because you remind me so much of *him*. My dear, sweet Khoros." The pain in her expression was raw and emotional as she edged closer, her voice growing quiet. "Some would argue you are him reincarnated. That Death himself could not contain his soul. Cassius." Her saying his name sent a shudder through him as her lips danced at the edge of his, as she hovered just above him in the water. His cock twitched, knowing she was near, and he groaned softly before a wordless snarl claimed his lips, and he grabbed the back of her head by her hair, tugging her away.

"You're wrong," he uttered, his eyes darkening as his visage bled away, as his fingers turned to claws and his newly forged wings slipped from his back. His face became sunken, his nose collapsing as his eyes glowed red. "I will never be him."

Ahma's eyes darkened as the torchlight flickered, and the bathtub darkened as well. "It is why I came to tell you that you are liberated from my path. You no longer have to walk its journey. Not since I have found another of the Drakos bloodline."

Cassius' eyes narrowed. "There are no others. Vera turned me, and I haven't turned anyone. The line ends with me." Like most high vampires, Khoros Drakos had been picky with his turns. Only that worthy of his name would be granted his bloodline because with it came certain strengths. Vera never told Cassius why he'd turned her, only that she had been worthy and had seen such worthiness when she'd turned Cassius. He was certain there were others of Khoros' bloodline, but he'd never met them, only knew of their existence due to some old tomes he'd combed through during his time at the Dragon Keep. Thinking of the old castle he'd trained to be a knight at and his old brotherhood sent a pang of sadness through him.

Ahma laughed, her amusement echoing throughout the bath hall. "Your ignorance is pitiful. He will be coming for you, Cassius."

"Why warn me?" he asked, loosening his grip on her hair.

Her eyes narrowed, and she leaned forward again, her fingers dancing beneath the water until one hand wrapped around him. His breath hitched, and her lips met his in a quiet but soft kiss. "Because I still believe you are hungry enough for power to *want* it. Because I chose *you* first. When he comes, cut him down. Take what is yours. He will have the cuirass and the shield by now."

"Who is it?" Cassius asked, snaking one arm around her waist to tug her closer.

Ahma's eyes flashed dangerously. She truly was beautiful, her hair soft as silk, her smile wicked and impossibly red.

"Someone who will test you. Someone from your past," she uttered, and when Cassius blinked in surprise, she was gone.

THREE

ROOSTER

As Rackjack led Rooster through the dark tunnels, he wondered, not for the first time, if he'd made a mistake.

Once they had entered the sewers, Rackjack had shed his dwarven form. He shuffled forward, tiny squeaks fleeing his mouth as he sniffed the air and tried to decide which route to take. It grew too dark for Rooster to see without some sort of light source, so he rubbed his fingers together, urging the magic forward and bringing a small flame to the palm of his hand. He didn't like wielding fire magic—it was too chaotic and difficult to control—but in this instance, he craved sight more.

"We must go-go-go further into the darkness," Rackjack breathed, earning a disgruntled noise from Rooster. He did not like the idea of closing himself off from the outside world when there were an unknown number of rakken in the sewers, but he needed to be able to trust Rackjack. Igraine, his missing lover, did, and in his heart of hearts, he trusted her – even if he didn't quite remember her due to his recent amnesia. Something inside him beckoned him to give Rackjack a chance.

"And you are sure you have the allegiance of whomever we're meeting with? Many battles have been fought, Rackjack. If enemy rakken dwell here, I'm not sure it's a good idea to provoke them." The flame danced in his palm as he drew it out, illuminating the back of Rackjack's fur.

"Bend them to my will-order. Will make them listen-hear," Rackjack said, brimming with confidence. His tail flickered through the water that trailed through the middle of the tunnel, and Rooster paused, his heart thundering in his ears. This reminded him too much of his time in the dwarf tunnels when they'd fought the rakken in their home.

This is all for Igraine, Rooster reminded himself, gritting his teeth together. Ever since Tantien had revealed the truth about Igraine and Rackjack had stumbled into his life, there had been an absence in his throat, a dull ache in his chest.

"Shh," Rackjack hissed suddenly, halting. "Must tread-walk carefully."

Rooster flinched as the flame on his palm burned his hand. It was a flicker of motion, over before it began, but his skin still blistered and smarted due to the slip in his concentration over having to stop abruptly. "A little warning next time," he whispered angrily, noting that Rackjack ignored him save for the twitch of his tail.

Re-centering his concentration, he stared at the flame in his palm until it stopped dancing and settled. Only then did he follow after Rackjack, who was moving again, ignoring the way slime coalesced on the side of the sewer walls. It stank down there too, its unsavory scent wafting into Rooster's nose. His eyes watered as he attempted to breathe through his mouth. This would be his first and last trip through the sewers.

He opened his mouth to tell Rackjack so when a quiet chattering of a rakken sounded through the darkness. Whatever rat was making the noise sat just out of reach of Rooster's light, but Rackjack responded in kind with a quick whispering dialect. The translation was lost on Rooster as Rackjack glanced behind him, meeting Rooster's gaze with his beady red eyes.

"Come-come," he said, lifting a paw to wave him forward. "Somewhere safe to talk-speak."

Rackjack led him into a small room. It was nothing but dirty walls and what looked like trash covering the floors, with a pile of rags shuffled into the corner furthest from the door.

"This place is disgusting." Rooster sighed, finally noticing the other rakken that stood near the rags, their chest rising and falling with quickened breath.

"Stayed here for long time-time," Rackjack said, peering about the room. "Better than most places."

Rooster hummed in disagreement, peering at the room in shock. He couldn't imagine staying in a dark place such as this. It made sense for a rakken. They did not seem the type to care about how dark or smelly a place was.

"Brass rat," the other rakken rasped. He stood a little taller than Rackjack, but where Rackjack was round and broad, the other rakken was tall and thin, his ribs pressing against stretched skin. His nose was curved, and he was a light gray, a sharp contrast to Rackjack's reddish-brown. He hissed at the sight of Rooster, curling in on himself and backing away. "Why do you bring man-filth into the dark-sewers?"

"I do not think I'm very stinky," Rooster protested, raising his arm to give his armpit a whiff. For the first time in a long time he did not reek; he had the new bath hall to thank for that.

The grey rakken's nose twitch. "He speak-speaks freely?"

Rackjack appeared regretful when he met Rooster's gaze. "Will perhaps gnaw off his smallest finger for it. Yes-yes," he said, just as a terrible smell wafted off him. Rooster's eyes burned as he lowered his head, his lips pursed in his silence. Whether he liked it or not, he was at the mercy of Rackjack; he had willingly followed him into his domain. He had no idea how many rakken were down there in the sewers with them. Should Rackjack decide to betray him now, he would not escape with his life.

"How goes the recruitment, mmm, yes-yes?" Rackjack rasped, scuttling forward. The grey rakken did not flinch as Rackjack approached, moving his paws over the rakken's fur.

"Few rats have heard of your whispers-demands. Prelk-rat has made it known. Prelk-rat demands their allegiance. Prelk-rat has had to kill-maim many for their disobedience." The grey rat—Prelk—gnashed his teeth in anger as he spoke. "Have brought you their tails," he said, gesturing to a pile of giant rat tails piled up in the corner. Rooster hadn't noticed them before, but now that he did, uneasy nausea settled in the pit of his stomach. Many of them had not been removed kindly, with some fur still clinging to the end that had once been attached to the body.

"Good-good," Rackjack said, obviously pleased. It tinged his tone, shown through the sparkling glint in his eyes. "Must make them understand-listen. Must make them hear-bow. Only the Brass Rat can lead them along the right path-course." He nuzzled his cheek against Prelk's, humming, and then backed away. "Have to leave-go. Go-go. Skitter-scamper south. Must take charge-lead while I am gone. Beckon the rats. Call them closer. Yes-yes. Keep them close. Tell them Brass Rat will keep them safe."

Rooster's nervousness came from the unsteady way Rackjack bounced on his feet, his quiet exhale, the way his fingers clenched tightly into fists. He did not like the sound of rakken festering beneath the city, much like they had when he'd seen them crawling over each other in the ruins of the dwarf kingdom nearly a year ago. Still, he did not speak as he had before despite the burning questions that pulsed at the edge of his teeth. His gut warred with his head: *do I trust Rackjack?*

Prelk's nose twitched as he sniffed the air. Falling on all fours, he hissed at the door. A small brown rakken appeared, its fur on end as it gnashed its teeth in Rooster's direction. "Man-filth. Gross, tricky man-filth. You are false rat. You will lead us off path. Yes-yes—" Rackjack dashed forward, but it was Prelk who got to him first. The rakken's head rolled into the room as the rusty sword at Prelk's side, now unsheathed, sang through the air. Flecks of blood hit the floor as the body, still quivering, dropped to the ground.

Rooster's mouth parted in shock, but Rackjack seemed pleased with Prelk. "Brass Rat knew he chose right when he found you-you. I know you will not betray me-me." Curling his fingers into Prelk's fur, he pushed him towards the door. "Now go-go. We will be in touch."

As the grey rakken fled the room, Rackjack slowly turned. "Carter-filth, must be quiet when around other rakkens. Do not understand Ratjack-rat being around human-filth."

Rackjack's words might have insulted Rooster had he not gotten so caught up on how Rackjack had just pronounced his name. His head tilting, he asked, "Wait. What did you say your name was?"

Rackjack tugged on his whiskers, his head shaking as a droplet of water from above fell on his head. "Don't know what you mean. It's Ratjack-rat, Carter-filth."

Rooster trailed a hand through his hair and grinned. "Is it *Rat*jack or *Rack*jack?"

Rackjack stared at him for a very long time before answering. "Both sound the same. Think you are being cruel-funny."

Rooster shook his head. "Regardless, I'm going to need you to explain what you are doing. If not now, soon. If you want me to trust you, I'm going to need to know why you're trying to build an army of rakken under Volendam."

Rackjack sniffed, pushing up on two legs. "Keep city safe-safe. More rakken on my side, less enemies. Will be better-good that way." He nodded, stepping closer to Rooster.

Rackjack had a point. They left for Hestia in the morning. It would be a relief to know that Volendam was protected while they were gone. Even if it was by rakken, whom he'd recently thought to be the enemy.

"Do not let your guard down, Carter-filth. Never let your guard down around rakken. Will always try to deceive-trick. Will always try to assert power-command." Rackjack's tone turned serious.

"Why should I trust you then, Rackjack?" Rooster's tone was teasing, but he did not laugh.

"Always trusted me before," Rackjack said. "Saved me from rakken-rats. Owe you life-debt." He looked at Rooster with such honesty and vulnerability that Rooster could not ignore the uncomfortable ache of guilt in his chest.

"Right," he said. "Can we leave these nasty tunnels now? I would love a few hours of sleep before we must leave."

Rackjack nodded repeatedly, then fell onto all fours to scurry back along the path they'd walked, his wooden prosthetic dragging behind him. After a moment, Rooster followed.

FOUR
INTOH

When Intoh woke before dawn the next morning, Khal and Sode, the two greka who had pledged their loyalty to him, were sitting across the room in a seated position, their eyes shut in meditation. Magic rolled off them like smoke, a dusting of the night sky that cast millions of twinkling stars against the ceiling.

Intoh had never seen such magic. He had heard of the priests of Axolli, the goddess of the stars, projecting such magic when they meditated, but Intoh had never been a greka of faith. Ilpoca Tower, the place where all the priests of Axolli went to worship, was further south in Lyvira than Intoh had ever been.

"The prophet has woken," Khal rumbled in Drikotyian, one eye opening to peer at Intoh. "Axolli is silent in these dark days. It must mean we walk the right path."

Intoh frowned as he slithered out of bed but said nothing. Silent gods often spoke volumes of their malice; they did not care for the lives of their disciples. Just because Axolli's will had led Sode and Khal to Intoh did not mean she would intervene should their lives be in danger.

The dusting of stars slowly dissipated as Sode and Khal pulled away from their meditations. The barest hint of light touched the sky outside, and Intoh knew it would be time to leave soon. Linda wasn't in their bed either, which meant they had somehow managed to sneak out of the room without any of the greka knowing. Intoh had never seen a krok'ida so quiet, but Helai had been teaching Linda some tricks to soften their steps and quiet their breathing.

"Should go get something to eat?" Intoh said. "Will likely leave soon."

Khal and Sode nodded silently as they followed him out of the room and down the stairs. Early morning just before dawn was Intoh's favorite time of day. There was just enough light to chase ghosts from the shadows, but the world had not woken from its slumber yet, leaving Intoh to his own company.

The inn was silent. No patrons had trailed through its front doors, and it was only Hilde, the hired barmaid, behind the counter as Intoh appeared.

"Good morning, dear," Hilde said, the corners of her eyes crinkling in delight as she smiled. "Dirk is already hard at work cooking in the back. Do you just want the usual?"

Intoh nodded quickly, tugging himself up into the chair at the counter. "Yes, yes. Perhaps..." He hesitated, his eyes darting with indecision. "I will try the fish with his spices."

Hilde's eyes lit up. "Oh, he'll be so pleased! The same for your two scaly friends as well?" she asked, gesturing to Sode and Khal.

After Intoh nodded, Hilde disappeared into the back kitchen. Sode and Khal stood with their back to Intoh, facing the front door, and Intoh frowned, patting the counter. "Sit, sit. No danger here. Not while we have breakfast."

After a lingering moment, they conceded, the warmth of their presence surrounding him as they took a seat on either side. "Where is Lindrz'kt?" Sode asked in Drikoytian, his voice quiet as Hilde returned from the kitchen. Her braid swung freely, and she smiled brightly at them.

"Dirk said it shouldn't take too long," she said, grabbing a small mug from a shelf. "I expect we'll see the others soon?"

Intoh shrugged. "Haven't seen them. Know where Linda is?"

Hilde nodded and gestured to the door. "They went with Tantien and Itale somewhere. Said they would be back by the time you were down here."

Intoh opened his mouth to reply as Linda ambled in. They had been hiding behind their human illusion less and less lately, and their tail twitched behind them as they brought in a gust of snow-infected air. Tantien and Itale trailed behind them, and Itale trembled, his nose rosy from the cold.

"Gods, I hate winter," Itale said, rubbing his arms. Intoh hummed in agreement; the cold was a greka's worst nightmare. He couldn't use his magic as well in the cold because his joints stiffened and stole his concentration.

"Ah, it's not so bad. It can be welcoming, when one works in a forge a lot of the time," Tantien said, shaking snow from his hair. The red of his locks nearly gleamed in the dim glow of the torchlight of the inn, and the three of them approached as Dirk appeared from the kitchen, carrying a tray with three plates. This was the first time Intoh had seen the cook—a burly, broad-shouldered human with a thick brown beard and kind eyes. A radiant smile graced the man's face as he set the plates down in front of the three greka.

"Hilde told me you were willin' to try the spiced fish. I hope to sway you from your love of raw food." Quiet laughter echoed throughout the inn as Dirk gently squeezed Hilde's shoulder as she scooted around him, then he bowed his head, backing up against the kitchen door. "I'll leave you to it, just wanted to personally deliver the breakfast m'self."

Intoh took a tentative bite and then immediately regretted it. *Too dry.* It seemed his growing love for his human form and his desire to shed his past would not come so easily. His mind warred with itself, desiring both the urge to not disappoint Hilde and Dirk and to not wanting to take another bite. The latter ended up winning, and his eyes flickered to Hilde in apology as he pushed the fish away and shook his head.

Hilde's smile was radiant and understanding as she patted Intoh's hand. "It's okay, dear. It's not suited to everyone's taste. I'll have Dirk prepare a fresh raw one for you."

"Will eat it," Linda said, leaning over Intoh to pluck the fish from the plate before Hilde could take it. "Love spiced fish." The fish was in their hand in one moment, then gone the next as it disappeared down their gullet, and Khal and Sode stared before following suit, their fish eaten before Hilde could set a fresh plate of raw fish in front of Intoh.

"There you go, honey." Hilde's warm smile brightened Intoh's morning, chasing away the lingering worries of what lay ahead, and he ate his new fish with ease as the others chatted around him. He often pretended to tune them out, unable to process his growing care for them, and this time was no different as Itale made Tantien laugh at the end of the counter and Khal swung his feet next to Intoh.

"Prophet." Sode's soft rumbling voice drew Intoh from his shell, and he glanced over, his eyes quickly flickering away as Sode caught his gaze. "Tell us... why do you seek the taboo magics? Seeking a way to live forever scorns the gods." He held up a scaled hand as Intoh opened his mouth to protest, his anger sweeping through him like a storm.

"I mean no offense by it. Axolli *chose* you for a reason. Khal and I are merely curious."

Intoh glanced down at his hands. Tucked behind his ring's illusion, they were naught but human hands. Small, fair, with the same number of fingers as his greka form, but more symmetrical and nearly the same size. "Started out as a friend's dream." He flinched at the thought of speaking about Ekalas to anyone, after not having shared her for so long, but no. He *wanted* to share her story. Even though, in his mind's eye, he saw her begging him not to.

"She was...very passionate greka. Always asked questions and then found the answer to them." He'd met Ekalas at the temples of magic in Lyvira's northern cities. She'd been studying the possibility of wielding and weaving two different types of magic safely together, using a grounding stick like Intoh's staff, and many of the greka had seen potential in her work. It hadn't been long after Intoh had befriended her that they'd scorned her for what they'd thought was unethical.

"Greka do not live very long, as you know," he said, gesturing to both Sode and Khal. "Not long enough to seek more *complicated* answers." He sucked in a deep breath, eyeing Tantien and Itale. He was speaking in Drikotyian and was certain they couldn't understand what he was saying, but Linda looked at Intoh wearily, a great sadness tinging their expression. "She just wanted to find way to live longer, to live forever. Help the universe. Eldrasi live forever, but they do not seek out ways to enhance magic like greka. They are content with asking their gods for strength."

"Nothing wrong with seeking the gods for aid when needed," Khal said, picking a piece of fish off the bone on his plate. "They were the ones that gifted us with magic in the first place. To deny our Long Sleep is to deny our gods and their gifts."

Intoh's brow furrowed. No, no. How foolish he was to think they'd understand. "As you said... I am prophet. Not wise to question me."

Khal blinked slowly as he met Intoh's gaze and then he nodded, lowering his head. "Apologies."

Intoh ignored them both after that, even as the other Misfits trailed in through the front door or down the stairs. There were so many of them now, their numbers having grown much since that time in the slave caravan last year. Intoh could never have guessed he would have ended up here, caring about the wellbeing of anything other than his quest.

But as Tantien rallied them to get ready to leave, Intoh looked up, his chest aching with torn emotions: a war between the desire for his goals and his love for the family he'd found.

FIVE

CASSIUS

They were gifted with the wind as they set sail on the Firebrand later that morning. Cassius had gone out to feed before they'd left even though he wasn't plagued with the curse of bloodlust. He'd lost control before; it was better to be safe before they embarked on a ship with no port call in sight. This time, he fed without killing, his voice soft and laced with compulsion magic as he sent the man on his way. The man had swayed as he stumbled off, and Cassius reflected on his bloodlust on his way to Tantien's ship. He hadn't felt its need since his death by the phoenix dragon and his rebirth by Drausmírtus, the goddess of death, and its lack of demand was strange—not unwelcomed but like a bitter relief had been set upon his shoulders. There was a sense of restlessness that came with its absence, and he found himself pacing the length of the ship as the eldrasi worked around him to sail the Firebrand south.

Cassius glanced up, shielding his eyes from the sun as a headache threatened to set in. It appeared that even though his rebirth had dulled some of his vampiric symptoms, his ailments when it came to the sunlight were still affected.

Rooster stood at the wheel of the ship, speaking to the eldrasi who navigated in Tantien's stead when he was off attending to other matters. He saw no other Misfits. His gifted isolation left a heaviness in his throat, so he found himself at the door to Tantien's forge, his knuckles pressing against the wood as he knocked.

The soft sound of movement echoed inside, and after a moment of silence, the door opened and Cassius was greeted by Tantien. Eldrasi heartbeats were always slow, much like the dwarves, but Tantien's was elevated, beating faster than normal.

"Cassius? Come in." He stepped aside, and Cassius stepped in, his eyes trailing over the walls of the forge. Various weapons lined the walls as usual, and the forge was cold, not having been used in some time. A door to the right was slightly ajar, one that Cassius could not recall having ever noticed before. Sometimes he swore the forge changed and shifted, but the soft patter of a heartbeat beyond the door stole Cassius' attention.

"What can I help you with?" Tantien's voice drew Cassius away from the door, and he studied the eldrasi silently for a moment.

"I just—" Cassius was not a man to be caught off guard, but why had he come to seek Tantien's company? There was nothing he needed to talk to the eldrasi about that hadn't been gone over already. They'd already spoken strategy, and besides, the other Misfits would need to be present for anything concerning the coming battle.

"I was looking for some company," he admitted quietly. He could have sought out any of the other Misfits–any of them would have been glad to pass the time–but something had drawn him into the forge. He blamed his growing interest in the eldrasi.

"Ah." His gaze flickered to the door Cassius couldn't remember being there, and he grinned, tucking a loose strand of hair behind his pointed ear. "Let me grab us some rum. You caught me a little off guard, I will admit."

Oh. Cassius' cheeks threatened to heat in embarrassment, but his composure remained as his own eyes sought out the door. *Right.* "I can leave if you are...busy."

"No, no, nothing like that," Tantien assured. "I was speaking with my boatswain about the plan once we arrive in Alavae's waters." He called out in Eldrasian, and a moment later, a large, curvy eldrasi woman appeared at the door. She was beautiful, as all eldrasi tended to be in an ethereal, natural way. Her skin was an olive tone, slightly lighter than Cassius', and her hair was a mess of swirling brown curls that were pulled back into a ponytail.

Her gaze settled on Cassius as she studied him silently. Her expression hardened, but Cassius couldn't discern what else swam in her gaze as she stepped into the room.

"We'll speak more later," Tantien told her. There was a look that passed between them, an echo of heat that disappeared so quickly, Cassius thought he might have imagined it.

The boatswain lowered her head in acknowledgment and disappeared through the door leading to the deck. It was then that Cassius became acutely aware they were alone.

"Come. My best rum is in my room," Tantien said, gesturing to the door before disappearing through it.

Cassius followed, eager to see what Tantien's private study looked like.

It was small, nothing like the grandeur of his forge. It was apparent where Tantien placed most of his pride, but there was enough room for a large desk made from a deep red-brown wood.

A map sat on the top of it, pinned down by daggers pressed into the wood in each corner, and Cassius noted it was a map of Vilanthris, only there were naval movements, a lot of which Cassius didn't recognize.

The rest of the room was taken up by a large oak bed with a canopy, its pillars etched with trees with faces on them. One of the faces looked familiar, but Cassius was not well versed in eldrasi culture and couldn't recall who it might be.

"Who is that?" he asked, his curiosity refusing to relent until it was sated.

Tantien glanced over from the cabinet he stood in front of, which was filled with various shapes and sizes of bottles with dark liquid in them. Liquors, if Cassius had to guess.

"That's Eirwyn, the lord of Daesthara. Some humans in Rovania revere him as a god of nature and that is why their lands remain so fruitful in harvest, but we eldrasi know him as a caretaker of Daesthara. He's almost as old as the eldrasi goddess, the one who planted the seed of the tree that birthed the first eldrasi kin." Several emotions flickered across his face as he pulled a bottle from the cabinet. Pain. Joy. Sadness. Anger.

Cassius forced his eyes away, not wanting to make Tantien uncomfortable as he studied the rest of the room. A painting hung on the wall, showing a much younger Tantien with a woman who had the same colored hair as him and a radiant smile. His sister, most likely. The one they were going to attempt to free from the eldrasi prison, should they survive the battle in Alavae. She was laughing in the painting, her head tossed back as Tantien had his arm slung across her shoulders. Both looked far happier in the painting than Cassius had ever seen Tantien in real life. Even with his smile and easy-going nature, there was always an air of heaviness that rested on the eldrasi's shoulders.

"You're welcome to sit if you'd like," Tantien said, tugging Cassius' attention away from the painting. Cassius made a mental note to tell Rooster about it in case he wanted to see it, if Tantien was willing. Rooster had been on edge since they'd left Volendam, and Cassius couldn't blame him. Tantien's sister was the key to unlocking Rooster's memories. If Cassius were in that situation, there would be little holding him back from finding her as quickly as possible.

As Cassius sat in the chair, Tantien studied him lightly as he handed over a glass full of rum. He leaned against his desk, to Cassius' left, swirling the rum in his glass thoughtfully. The eldrasi's nearness did the opposite desired effect on Cassius' restlessness, and he busied himself with his rum instead. He wished it was wine.

"Were you from Alavae? Before, that is."

Tantien's question prompted Cassius' head to rise. Their gazes met. Tantien seemed genuinely interested, but the part of Cassius that had had to hide his vampirism for so long threatened to stay his tongue. He shook away his hesitations. Tantien knew he was a vampire.

He gave a slight shake of his head. "Verenzia, closer to the borders of Kythera, but I moved to Wilhaven to live with my uncle when I was eighteen." Memories from a lifetime ago threatened to well up, but he kept his expression blank as he raised his glass to his lips.

He felt Tantien's unspoken question burning between them, but the eldrasi was kind and did not ask. Still, it hung there, suspended, beckoning to be answered.

"I was twenty-eight when my sire turned me." He didn't think about that night, not anymore. Vera had saved him. That's what he'd always told himself. Some days he believed it. Some days he was sure she'd damned him.

"I didn't mean to—" Tantien started, but Cassius interrupted him.

"No, it's okay." He swallowed as power thrummed through him, settling in his bones but making him dizzy.

He gulped down more rum, but it did little to chase away the feeling that burrowed within him. Sitting still was making him just as anxious as pacing had. The looming battle would be almost welcomed. His father had carved him into the likes of a soldier; it seemed bittersweet that fighting seemed to cure his anxieties while simultaneously forcing more upon him.

He suddenly couldn't sit any longer.

He pushed his chair back and rose, much to Tantien's surprise.

"I apologize." Cassius set his glass down on the desk and backed away towards the door. "The threat of the coming battle is making me restless. I think I shall go and aid some of your men with boat duties."

Tantien's gaze darkened. A slow smile creeping across his lips, he set his glass down beside Cassius' abandoned one. "Or," he said, his gaze flickering towards the bed, "I have quite the talent of helping with nervous energy before battle."

Cassius felt his words travel all the way to his groin, spreading warmth as it traveled down. His gaze found the bed, and when he met Tantien's eyes, they were hungry and dark. Cassius' desire was the hottest it'd burned since his rebirth.

Tantien didn't waste any time, pushing Cassius against the back of the door and threading his fingers through the vampire's hair. When his lips brushed against Cassius', a low, primal growl cradled the base of the vampire's throat, and Cassius reached out to tug Tantien's hips against his.

Tantien kissed with reckless passion as he pressed Cassius into the wood, one hand flat against the wall beside Cassius' head, the other tangled in his hair. Kissing Tantien was different to kissing humans. His heart rate, even elevated, was a slow beat against his throat, a quiet temptation to feed even without the desperation of the bloodlust. He recalled the sweetness of Tantien's blood, and his bloodlust beckoned him to indulge again.

Tantien pulled away, peppering kisses over Cassius' jaw and down his neck. His hand moved to chase his shirt away from his shoulder. He kissed along his clavicle, and his pupils were blown so wide that the blue of his eyes was almost gone when he met the lust in Cassius' expression.

Tantien's knees kissed the floor, and Cassius' nostrils flared as he thanked whatever god might be listening that Rooster had convinced him to take some time out of his armor. He was only dressed in his simple trousers and a loose shirt, and Tantien had little trouble tugging his trousers down to his ankles.

Cassius hadn't been intimate with anyone since Gabrielle had visited him at the dwarf outpost just after they'd aided the dwarves against the rakken, and the stress and restlessness he'd felt since had sat coiled in his belly, fuel for his desire. As Tantien took him into his mouth, he moaned, unable to do anything but lean against the door and weave his fingers roughly through Tantien's hair. The strands of his hair were like liquid fire, and Cassius pressed his head to the door and shut his eyes, allowing himself to be taken away by the feeling simmering low in his belly.

Tantien dragged him over the edge quicker than he'd anticipated. His hips thrust forward sharply as he came, and Tantien pulled away, his expression bright and full of mirth as Cassius panted, his mind clear of pain and worry for the first time since he'd been in that bath with Gabrielle.

A rapt knock on the door startled Cassius, sounding just behind his ear. It was enough to make Cassius' illusion bleed away, only just, his face decaying as his fangs stretched out over bared lips. His wings thumped against the door as he jerked forward, and a shuffling could be heard from Tantien's forge.

Tantien looked at him gently as he rose, wiping the corner of his mouth. "Yes?" His voice was surprisingly level despite what had just transpired.

Cassius shuffled out of the way, reaching down to pull his trousers back up. He tucked the monstrosity of his visage back behind his human face. He didn't know what to do with himself, so he slipped behind Tantien to reclaim his rum. He downed it, grimacing as it burned his throat.

"We are hitting rougher seas, Captain. Ely would feel better with you at the wheel if you're not busy." A woman's voice carried through the closed door, muffled by the wood, and Tantien turned to give Cassius a guarded stare before he nodded firmly to himself.

"Tell her I'll be up in a moment."

As the heartbeat of the eldrasi woman faded, the silence grew between them. Cassius leaned against the desk, nursing his empty cup. He was only just beginning to come down from the high of his orgasm. His gaze lingered loosely on Tantien's form as he trailed his fingers through his hair and smiled.

"I'm needed elsewhere I'm afraid," he said, his voice rumbling and low as he stepped forward into Cassius' space. Cassius was acutely aware of how Tantien's gaze darkened, at the way he sauntered forward as if he knew the effect he had.

"Go," Cassius said softly, his desire rising once more like a sleeping dragon finally waking. If Tantien didn't leave, Cassius wasn't sure he'd let him. "Before I return the favor."

Tantien stayed for one moment more before lowering his head and backing away. He paused at the door, hesitation a home in his expression as his mouth parted. "Cassius," he said softly. "I hope you don't misinterpret my interest with something...more than what it is. You understand?"

Cassius was familiar with the art of casual intimacy. He'd been a master of the craft himself for as long as he could remember. Why did Tantien's words hurt so much then, like a blow to the chest? His desire died with them, and his throat grew dry as he blinked, struggling to keep his face free from expression. "Of course."

Tantien's gaze softened, and he moved closer, his fingers coming to trail along Cassius' arm. His fingers were warm, like forged fire, and he raised one of Cassius' hands to his mouth, pressing a gentle kiss to the heel of his palm. "My world is dark right now. The path I'm on distracts from the very thing you desire. You deserve someone to grant you full attention, Cassius, and I cannot give that to you."

No, Cassius wanted to say, *that's not what I want.* But the words caught at the edge of his tongue as if beckoning a different response. He was right. The ache for companionship had grown beyond the occasional moment of intimacy. He wanted something more than that. He *deserved* more than that.

"In another life, perhaps," Cassius said, a bit breathless as he tugged his hand away.

Tantien straightened, and there was a sadness in his eyes as he turned away. "Yes, in another life. I understand if I do not find you seeking me out for company after today."

Cassius understood the obligation of duty and did not try to stop him as he left the room without saying anything else, granting Cassius a bit of privacy as his head warred with emotion. He and Tantien had been dancing around each other for so long that he wasn't sure what to do now that they'd finally done something about it. The thought of the eldrasi sinking to his knees in front of him still unlocked traces of desire, but they could no longer entertained. Tantien's small rejection stung more than Cassius cared to admit.

He sighed, setting his empty glass on Tantien's desk. Loneliness began to take hold once more, souring his thoughts, and he fled Tantien's private quarters before it could poison the moment he'd just had, however bittersweet it'd been.

SIX

LINDA

"Okay... stab me."

Itale's eyes widened as the dagger shook in his palm. "What?" He protested, his gaze darting about. They'd been traveling for three days before Linda had found out that Itale had never fought with a blade once in his short life, so they'd decided it was time to teach him.

Linda followed his gaze as it darted to Cassius leaning against the rail of the ship and Rooster, who watched on with a mug of rum in his grasp.

"Will be okay," Linda said, nodding with encouragement as Helai kicked off the mast and moved up next to Itale, holding up her hands when he flinched in surprise.

"You're too stiff. If you come at someone like that, they'll be able to break your defenses with ease. Like with any weapon, you must find balance. Loosen your grip but don't be so loose that your enemy can just wrangle the blade from your grasp." Unsheathing a dagger, she held it in her hand expertly, twirling it between her fingers before tightening her grip around the hilt and stabbing it outwards a few times. She watched Itale flex his fingers around the blade she'd let him borrow and shook her head. Re-sheathing her dagger, she reached forward, helping Itale curl his hand more securely.

"Now stab me," Linda said, shifting their weight as they held up their hands, palm out. They were unarmed, but with Itale's size and lack of skill, they weren't too worried about Itale causing any real harm.

Furrowing his brow, Itale lunged forward. *Too predictable.* Linda dodged with ease, reaching out to grab Itale's arm. They had to take care not to grasp too tightly and break his bones, but it mattered little. Itale was far quicker than Linda had given him credit for, and soon enough, a pinprick of pain blossomed at Linda's back. It was faint, nothing more than an annoying poke, but as they turned, the blade of Itale's dagger was lined with their blood. Itale's satisfaction was an ample enough distraction for Linda to lash out, pushing Itale onto his back and pinning him underneath their massive claws.

Itale trembled as all his glee was wiped from his face. It was replaced with cold terror, and after a moment, Linda gently raised their hand, their expression sheepish. "Don't know strength," they said with a shrug, offering Itale a claw to grab on to. "Will be better." The words echoed with Linda's lingering guilt. They didn't want to hurt their friends. They would never do so out of intention, only by mere accident. Itale hadn't been with the Misfits long enough to know that. At least, Linda didn't think so.

Still, after a moment, Itale wrapped his fingers around Linda's claw, allowing them to pull him to his feet, where he handed the dagger back to Helai.

"My skill lies in necromancy, I think..." He hesitated, his gaze flickering from Linda and Helai over to Cassius, who leaned against the railing of the ship with his arms folded across his chest as he watched on. "You promised you'd teach me."

Cassius nodded firmly, pushing off the railing. "My own necromancy is minimal at best. I prefer to fight with a sword and shield, not wield magic from a distance. Still, I can show you how to wield the very basics before we land in Alavae."

Itale's eyes lit up, and he turned his shining gaze to Linda, nodding his head eagerly. "Thank you for sparring with me, Linda. I think I learned something valuable today."

Linda lowered their head and rested the bottom of their jaw atop Itale's head in a silent fondness. They had only been traveling with Itale for a short time, but his gentle kindness had begun to grow on Linda. They had even taken to drinking his tea to spend time with him even though they could never seem to get over how utterly bitter the drink was.

Itale's hand reached up to brush the side of Linda's face, and then he turned away to speak with Cassius.

"Linda, may I have a word?" Tantien's voice carried down from the wheel of the ship, and Linda looked up to the eldrasi smiling down at them, his fingers curled over the railing behind the wheel. "I have something for you if you'd like it."

Burning curiosity coursed through Linda as they hurried up the stairs. "Have for me?" they asked. Even with Tantien's tall stature, Linda loomed over him, and he stared up at them with an eager smile on his face as he reached out and placed a hand on their forearm. For an eldrasi, his touch was surprisingly warm.

"I thought, as a manner of sharing a continued good faith between us, I'd have this amulet forged for you. I was able to keep a bit of that sapphire you got for me all that time ago at the *Silver Moon Club*, and you can even attach it on the string you have your, ah, tooth necklace."

Linda recalled the time when the Misfits had first arrived in Volendam, and Tantien—who they thought was called Velius—had tasked them with stealing gems from the exclusive club in the Sails District. Linda's war hammer, *Volroth*, had a piece of those sapphires forged into its hilt.

"It can attach to your necklace. See, I've put a clasp on it." He offered his hand out to Linda, and when he dropped it into their open palm, they drew it close to study it. The sapphire was shiny and gleaming, embellished with a clasp made from some kind of tooth.

"What it do?" Linda knew Tantien enough by now to know this wasn't any ordinary pendant.

"It's been imbued magically with different languages. I'm afraid I'm not well versed in all of them, but you'll be able to understand and speak Vilris, Eldrasian, and I've even been able to convince Rackjack to speak a few common phrases of Squeakspeak into the sapphire." Tantien laughed, resting his hand on the wheel of the ship as Linda stared down at him in shock. "I know, I've not quite mastered the accent, but knowing the language of the rakken might come in handy. You could ask the other Misfits to speak to it in their tongues as well. Eventually, it'll learn."

Linda didn't say anything as they handed the pendant back to Tantien and bent, offering their neck to him. It was strange, the magic that flowed over them as Tantien clasped it to their tooth necklace. It was as if something had been unlocked inside them, another shackle on their chains broken.

"Words are still hard to find, but easier to speak," Linda said, an unfamiliar emotion budding in their chest. Krok'ida couldn't cry—Linda didn't know how—but the swell of emotion was nearly too much as Tantien beamed up at them.

"If any deserves the ability to speak freely about what they think, it's you, Linda," Tantien said. His words were clearer, spoken in a way Linda could now understand with ease. It was as if the language barrier between them had been shattered.

"Can't ever repay you," Linda said, reaching down to rest a massive hand atop Tantien's head. "Good sir, good. Will always remember the kindness you show me."

Tantien's laughter rang out across the ship as Linda stepped away. His hair was in disarray, but he didn't seem to mind as he waved his free hand at them. "Help me free my sister, and consider the debt repaid." His face grew somber, his expression haunted. "No one deserves the horrors faced in that prison, but my sister deserves it least of all."

"What is she like?" Linda asked, watching Rooster ascend the stairs in approach.

"Igraine?" Tantien eyed Rooster, his smile grim. "She's fire incarnate. Passionate, strong, reckless—" He sighed, his hand moving to the nape of his neck. Smoke unfurled in the distance; Linda wondered if that was Alavae. The closer they got to the war-ravaged city, the more their blood sang for combat.

"She's the one that convinced me we were not meant to be guards for a city that had scorned us."

"Scorned you? Why?" Rooster asked, leaning against the railing to Tantien's right.

Tantien was silent for some time. "Our grandfather stole a seed from our god's tree in Daesthara; it's the reason the eldrasi of Míradan look more like humans. Our god scorned us and cursed us for our thievery."

Rooster scoffed. "The gods are ever cruel, aren't they?"

The laughter that slipped from Tantien's lips turned sour. "Indeed. Our grandfather led a revolution. We were tired of living the Old Ways. We were curious, eager to learn about the world outside the forest, and we were cast out because of it. Many haven't forgiven my grandfather for the curse he placed on the eldrasi of Míradan." His face lightened. "But no matter; it has been quite some time since I liberated myself from my past."

Linda nodded, the ghosts of their own past threatening to kick up dust that had long since settled. "Sometimes it's better than clinging to it. Clinging to past can sometimes hurt." They could remember a time when the hurt had ached in their chest so badly, they'd been unable to stand it, unable to cope with it just *sitting* there. They'd ripped a whole grove apart with their bare hands.

Rooster cocked his head to the side. "Linda, you're speaking more than three words at a time."

Linda's chest swelled with pride, tucking those painful memories away once more. No use in remembering. Not when there was so much at stake in the present. Not when they had found their family in the Misfits. "Tantien gave me amulet. Let me speak and understand."

Rooster's face split into a wide grin as he kicked off the railing. "That's great."

It was. Linda couldn't remember the last time someone had given them such a thoughtful gift. They patted Tantien on the head again, their stomach twisting in emotion.

"We are maybe a day or two out," Tantien said, his smile fading as he looked up from beneath Linda's hand. "Once we arrive, I urge you to seek safety within the city as soon as possible. I am not sure what state we'll find it in." He gestured to the front of his ship, where cannons rested in rows on either side. Vines curled around the barrel of each cannon and wrapped around the railing of the Firebrand, securing them in place.

"The Firebrand is prepared to engage in combat at sea, should we arrive to a fleet of Shoman ships." He placed his hands on the wheel of the ship as Linda stepped away and peered out at the rolling waves. There was no sign of warfare they could detect yet, but Linda knew it was only a matter of time. They could almost smell it in the air; the anticipation of combat curled around them like a snake waiting to strike.

"Will stay on ship with you. Provide aid in what magic I can," Intoh said, climbing the stairs up to them. He'd spent the better part of the week up in the crow's nest, aiding the lookout and urging the wind to their favor with magic. Exhaustion grayed the skin under his eyes, and his mouth pressed into a thin line. "Will rest until we arrive. Be in top shape for coming storm."

Tantien nodded. "I will not deny that your help would be most welcome, Intoh. Greka magic is not to be underestimated, and if there are jinn aboard those other ships, we'll need all the mages we can get."

"The only ships that will have jinn aboard are the generals'," Helai said, leaning against the railing of the other stairs. Linda hadn't seen nor heard Helai approach, and her sudden appearance was rather jarring. Helai had been teaching Linda the art of sneaking since they'd expressed interest in it some time ago, and though they'd gotten better at remaining quiet, nothing compared to the silent step of Helai or Zamir.

"Then that is who I'll focus on first," Tantien said slowly, his gaze unfocused in thought. "Shoma's naval fleet pales in comparison to Hestia's capital, and I have hope that we won't be alone in our fight when we arrive."

"Give me enemy to hit with hammer, I happy," Linda said. They did not care to strategize; their fellow Misfits were far better at it than them, who'd always been on the receiving end of command. They would do what was asked of them, would fight the enemy that Rooster or Cassius pointed at, and would do so gladly.

As the others continued to speak about the coming battle, Linda contented themself with sitting on the top deck, the sun bathing their scales in a brilliant glow. Smoke thickened over the horizon, rolling out to sea from land, and Linda knew it in their heart:

It would not be long before they went to battle.

SEVEN
HELAI

Smoke unfurled from the ruinous city, making Helai's eyes water. It had been a beautiful city, once, its marbled walls tainted grey with ash. The hair on Helai's arms stood up as the electrical current of magic soaked the air, and she reached out to hold on to the railing of the ship as it dipped with the movement of the waves. Off in the distance were the ships of her people. Her heart squeezed, and a rush of anger threatened to fill her lungs at the sight.

"I did not want to believe it at first either," Zamir said, speaking beside her in Shoman. His hair was tugged back into a tight ponytail, his fingers grazing the hilt of the sword at his hip. "The monstrosity of man...it takes my breath away at times. We scorn those in the desert who allowed their greed and anger to fester so much that they turned themselves into monsters." His gaze slid over and greeted hers, and her mouth dried at how much pain was settled in his expression. "I fear Mohalis may have doomed our country."

Helai swallowed the lump of grief and fear in her throat as she pushed away tears that settled at the corner of her eyes. She didn't want to believe Zamir's words. She'd fought so hard her entire life to see the sands of Shoma liberated from the shackles of the wealthy and powerful. Mohalis had taken the seat of power by force. Helai knew the rumors like the back of her hand now, as it had happened before she was born. Mohalis had been subjected to the same life Helai had suffered, nothing but a street rat who sold his soul to garner riches and power. Some thought it was a jinn he'd shackled himself to, others whispered it was Qevayla, the dragon of dreams. Helai didn't know which it was; she didn't care. It didn't change the fact that Mohalis' ruinous rule had stripped her people of their beauty and had all but silenced their culture. It was all about skaels, land, and power, and someone had to continue fighting and hoping for the beauty of her people again.

"You and I will see the day when the sun shines freedom upon our home," she said softly, reaching out to take Zamir's hand. It was warm, an anchor against the maelstrom of fear for the upcoming battle, and Helai gripped it tightly as faithful determination paved pathways over her face. "Faith is the only thing our enemies cannot take from us."

"Your faith has always been so...unwavering," Zamir said bitterly, tugging his hands away. "Don't you get tired of it?" His anger swept through Helai like poison, and she pulled away as if he'd slapped her. Zamir had always been the biggest questioner of faith; this should not have come as a surprise to Helai.

"Never," Helai breathed, her brow furrowing in shock. Once, when she'd been a little girl, she'd recalled standing in the shadow of an alleyway, shielded by Massoud's protective nature as he'd tried to figure out where they were going to sleep that night.

"Stay here, abib," he'd said, stepping out into the bustling street and disappearing among the people. Everyone had been off to the markets, and much of the poor had roamed the street, desperate for food or coin.

To this day, she felt the soft caress of fingers against the nape of her small neck, she heard the whispered words of a man uttering against the cusp of her ear: *"Dalnor takes care of his own."* When she'd turned around, there had been no one in sight, but a warm loaf of bread had been left on the ground behind her.

She'd been starving, and Dalnor had sent one of his disciples to help her when she'd needed it the most. Dalnor had never been a cruel god to those devoted to serving him, and Helai had been the most devoted of all.

Her gut twisted mercilessly as Zamir shook his head before peering out at the rolling waves of the sea. "Not all of us share that dream, Helai. Some of us are just... so *tired.*"

Helai opened her mouth to retort, but Tantien's voice rang out over the ship. "We will make it to Alavae soon. Prepare for battle!"

Zamir turned, slipping away into the shadows before Helai could say anything. Her fingers curled into a fist as she sighed, trying to soothe the knot in her throat. If they all gave up on Shoma, who would free its people? Who would stand up for the children starving on the streets, like someone had done for her when she'd been a little girl? Who would challenge Mohalis and those that were loyal to him over their wicked ways?

"Helai!" Rooster's voice carried over to her, and she turned, locking eyes with him as he approached. He looked at ease, but Rooster had always found peace at sea. "Cassius wants to speak with all of us." He halted, staring at her with concern. "What happened?"

"Nothing." The word cleaved Rooster in her misdirected anger, and his gaze hardened. Before she could apologize, he turned, gesturing with his thumb over to where the other Misfits stood. Cassius appeared on edge, his back rigid as he stared out at the desolate kingdom they were approaching. Smoke curled out from the beach where soldiers were fighting, and Helai's courage faltered, as it had when the dyrvak had laid siege to Volendam.

"Come quickly," Rooster said softly.

Helai followed him without another word. Massoud was somewhere out there, and the quicker they pushed through the fighting on the beach and made it into the city, the quicker they'd be able to figure out where he might be.

"Hestia is known for their fortified cities," Cassius was saying as they approached. Helai wasn't surprised to see him in his full set of armor; he'd only recently started taking it off. "It won't be like Volendam. The Hestian soldiers should have the upper hand."

"Then why fight at beach? Makes little sense," Intoh said, pacing as he thumbed his chin. Khal and Sode stood near him, the tips of their spears gleaming in the sun.

"Mohalis has a steady source of jinn magic," Helai said. "It's possible he drew them out that way. I'm surprised the battle hasn't already been lost." Jinn were fickle but a more powerful entity than the raw nature of the magic that encompassed Vilanthris. They were often outwitted and forced into lamps or jars, where their magic was shackled, confined to the space they had been forced into. While the lamps kept them from harming whoever held it, they also kept the wielder from doing anything too powerful. It was the only thing keeping Mohalis from claiming the entirety of the world.

"We must keep that in mind when we're fighting his men," Cassius said. "We don't know who could be wielding one."

Helai shook her head. "Jinn aren't granted to foot soldiers. If anyone has a jinn, it'll be the generals, the people of power. My culture believes only the powerful and worthy have the right to handle dealings with jinn." Her words made the lamp at her hip feel heavier in the reminder of what she'd done to claim it. The man she'd stolen it from hadn't struggled. *He would have used it for some evil*, Helai told herself often, a reminder that using her shadow magic to drown him in the sea had been justified.

"It's likely the generals are focused on taking the city. My guess is the soldiers on the beach are from their coastal units. Regardless, we need to make it to the city and find whoever is in charge."

"Angelika is one of the Hestian generals. If we can find her, she'll know the state of things," Zamir said, reappearing as he adjusted a bracer, tightening the straps on his arm. He refused to look at Helai, his face grim. Guilt swam through Helai, but it was quickly stifled by her bitter determination that she was *right*.

Cassius nodded firmly. "Then we fight our way to the city."

Linda hissed, raising their jaw in the air as they gripped their war hammer. Their scales shimmered brightly in the sun, and Helai's stomach rolled as the Firebrand slowed, and the eldrasi around them prepared the rowboats. The clashing of metal and the shouts of battle could be heard from where they stood, and Helai steeled herself in preparation. Her daggers were a comfort at her waist, and she palmed one of the hilts absentmindedly as Intoh turned to the other greka, speaking quietly to them in Drikotyian.

"We will offer aid from the Firebrand, but we cannot leave this ship unattended. If the enemy were to find my doorway aboard..." Tantien trailed off as he turned the wheel, urging the Firebrand as close as he could get. With his words, the severity of the situation took hold. Cassius spoke softly to Itale, who had gone pale at the sight of the fighting.

"Helai," Zamir said softly, reaching out to brush her arm. She shrugged him away, moving past him towards one of the rowboats. Her anger still simmered in her chest; she didn't want to talk about the state of Shoma with him when they were clearly on different sides. Not when they were about to go and slaughter their own people, even if they were the enemy.

Zamir let her go, and she climbed down the ladder on the side of the ship and into the rowboat, followed quickly by Linda. Water slashed into the boat as Linda lowered themself in. Helai frowned, pulling her legs up on the seat to save her boots from the water.

"Sorry," Linda said sheepishly as they took up the oars, their muscles flexing as they moved them away from the Firebrand.

The air shuddered, and the hair on Helai's arms rose as shadows caressed her back. Then Zamir appeared at her side, the echoing of crows cawing disappearing into the wind as his magic departed.

"Helai." His voice was quiet, his expression mournful as he stared at his hands. "I apologize. I do not want to discredit your faith."

The words were painful, and Helai struggled to speak as she gripped the seat of the rowboat with her hands. "When did you abandon the cause?" The revelation came suddenly and with it, the fear that the other Ghosts had followed Zamir into forsaking their dream of ridding Shoma of its corrupt sultan.

Zamir shook his head. "I always hope for Shoma's betterment. I want my home to see a return to its former glory, to see streets where our people are not suffering. I do not want to sacrifice my life for it." The water lapped against the side of the boat as Linda rowed them into a wave, and Helai stared at the side of Zamir's head as she lowered her feet to the floor.

"We just need to—"

"No, Helai. Even if we manage to kill Mohalis, the corruption does not stop there. Cut the head off one snake, there is still more evil to purge. Our lives have been dedicated to the cause, but I've found my life has flourished elsewhere. I deserve to be selfish for once." His smile was soft as he raised his head to meet her gaze. "I am going to be a father."

The air left Helai's lungs. His news sank into her slowly, like she'd fallen in quicksand. She warred with herself, a state of elation and excitement mixed with bitter horror. The excitement made it to her face, and she threw her arms around Zamir, shoving her face into the crook of his neck. He smelled of sweat and some spice from home.

"I am so excited for you, Zamir. You're going to be a great father."

Zamir's eyes shone as she pulled away. "The world is scary, Helai. I hope—well, it is why I need to set the ideas of revolution aside and create a safe life for my family."

Helai's heart sank. She knew he was right, but the idea of overthrowing Mohalis had been ingrained in her for so long...she didn't know who she was without it. Her heart pounded fearfully in her ears at the thought of the others abandoning the cause.

Massoud would know what to do. He always did.

They neared the beaches, which were stained red with the blood of Shoma and Hestia alike. A Shoman soldier tackled a Hestian knight into the water in front of their boat, and neither resurfaced. Linda roared, stood, and dove into the ocean, only to reappear on the shores, their war hammer glittering as the sun hit the droplets of water clinging to the hilt. Helai glanced beside her and met Zamir's gaze, who nodded grimly. It was time.

As soon as the ship hit the sands, Helai found her courage, took a deep breath, and unsheathed her daggers.

EIGHT

HELAI

She'd spent so much time in the recent months fighting dyrvak and rakken, she'd nearly forgotten what it was like to fight fellow humans. They fought with more calculation than the rakken but less care than the dyrvak. A khopesh swung at her, narrowly missing her left shoulder, and she rolled, slipping her dagger over the Shoman's leg. Cassius finished him off as she shot forward. Zamir slipped into the shadows and reappeared behind another soldier.

It was a bloodbath. The sand was stained red as soldiers died around them. Helai swung away from the sword of a Hestian guard, her brow furrowed in panic. "I'm not the enemy," she shouted, but the Hestian was relentless, snarling and charging her with thoughtless regard.

It was Cassius who came to her rescue, catching the guard's sword with the edge of his own. Cassius spoke quickly to the guard in Hestian, gesturing to Helai as she sank her dagger into an approaching Shoman. His blood splattered across her chest as she pried the dagger out of his body, his eyes flickering with rage as he died. Zamir appeared behind another soldier a few feet away, his armor slick with blood, his eyes shining brightly from the adrenaline of battle. He slipped his hand over the soldier's mouth and pulled him flush against him. The air grew cold as he called upon the shadows and directed them into every opening on the man's face. His screams were drowned out by the clashing of metal, but Helai watched him thrash for several moments before Zamir dropped him to the ground. He died choking on the shadows that had consumed his mouth and eyes.

A part of the sight sickened Helai to her core. It warred with the side of her that was filled with bitter satisfaction. War was bloody and merciless.

"Helai!" Zamir shouted. "Fight near me. The Hestian soldiers know me."

Dalnor, grant my steps the power to move swiftly through the fighting, Helai thought, fighting her way over to Zamir. Helai wasn't sure who was winning. Several Shoman rowboats were docked against the beach, the rest of their fleet some distance from shore, but the Hestian soldiers were holding their ground, the red and gold of their metal armor a sharp contrast against the dark leathers of the Shoman army.

She fought her way to Zamir with ease, and it was like they were back in the sands all over again, fleeing Dalasae after having failed to assassinate the sultan. They covered each other's weaknesses, forcing the Shoman soldiers to come at them with full force, but no one could break their defenses. Zamir was the weaker fighter, but he made up for it with his exceptional movement, dodging every attack and allowing Helai to strike out with her blades.

Off in the distance, Linda's roar curled out over the fighting. It demanded attention, and Helai was given a moment's reprieve from the fighting as nearly everyone turned to watch as Linda lashed out and bit down on a soldier. Flames burst out from between their jaws, accompanied by the soldier's blood, and the soldier screamed as he was burned alive.

"Never heard of a krok'ida wielding that sort of magic," Zamir said, breathing heavily beside her. "It's sort of beau—" A strangled exhale of air escaped Zamir. Helai looked over to see a khopesh sticking out of his chest, gleaming with his blood. He looked down, shocked, and then locked eyes with Helai as all the breath left her lungs, and rage in its purest form blinded her.

The Shoman that had stabbed Zamir didn't stand a chance. Her dagger lashed out so quickly it blurred before sinking into his eye. The man screamed, but it was quiet and warped, consumed by Helai's anger as she pulled the dagger out and stabbed him again, forcing him to stumble back and collapse. He pried his khopesh loose as he did, and Zamir fell forward. Helai attempted to catch him, but he was heavier than she'd thought and she fell with him, hitting the sand hard.

Her breath rattled in her lungs as she tugged Zamir onto her lap. "Intoh!" she cried out, forgetting Intoh had remained on the Firebrand. She was unable to tear her eyes away from the wound on Zamir's chest. It wept red, blossoming over Zamir's clothes and dripping to the sand. Helai refused to weep, even as her hysteria built and threatened to pry itself from her lungs. "Intoh!" she screamed again, pressing her hands to the wound. If she could just get Intoh to heal him. "No, no, Zamir. Please don't go. Please don't—"

"Helai." His voice was a ghost, a whispered echo of the vibrancy it once was. His eyes were glossing over quickly. "My locket... Angelika..." Blood gurgled from his lips as his gaze sought hers. They were full of fear as he attempted to reach up to his neck where a small locket lay against his throat. His hand never made it that far, dropping as he shuddered and died.

Helai could not understand why no one was coming to take advantage of her distracted state nor why she wasn't making any noise. The world went silent. Silent, still, and ugly. Her hands shook, the red of them *too* red as the grief welled up inside her, as the sickness of rage festered in her belly. She wanted to wail, but it was lodged in her throat as she trailed her fingers over Zamir's face, his eyes unseeing as he stared up at the sky. A single tear had trailed a small pathway down his cheek...

Something pressed against her shoulder—a hand.

The world hadn't stopped, after all. No, no. The roar of battle came back to her all at once. The blood, the clashing of metal, the screams of soldiers. They pierced her ears, made her head spin. She lashed away from whoever had grabbed her, curling down onto Zamir's body as the dam broke inside her, and she wailed. She did not care if a soldier struck her down in this moment. She did not care about anything at all as she wrapped her arms around Zamir and shook, crying until she could not see, until she could not breathe. Wait... the lamp. She could use the lamp to bring him back.

"Helai." Rooster reached out a hand, tugging her from the numbing bubble of grief she'd forced herself into. "He is gone, Helai. Please—think of Massoud. Think of those who still might yet live."

Helai glanced up at him, the pain in her eyes meeting Rooster's sympathy. The thought of Massoud stilled her hand as it sought out the lamp. What if the Shoman soldiers were torturing him? What if he was dead and she no longer had a way to save him? Oh, her chest ached so badly she could scarcely breathe. Cassius fought beside Rooster, keeping the enemy at bay, and Rooster knelt, offering Helai his hand. "Once this battle has been won, I promise he will get the burial he deserves. Do not make us bury you too."

"The ugliness of war," Cassius called out after decapitating a Shoman soldier. "Only may we mourn them when our lives aren't in danger."

It felt like Zahra's death all over again, only Zamir had a family and a baby on the way. But Massoud...he was the only family she'd ever had, a brother in all but blood. She'd never forgive herself if she got to him too late with no way to save him.

Sobs shook Helai's shoulders as she reached out and broke the chain of Zamir's locket. Pocketing it, she took Rooster's hand. The others were right; she could not sit and mourn him when there was still fighting to be done.

She forced her grief down into her chest until it was locked away, until a numbness took hold. All that was left was cold, calculated anger. She looked at the enemies before her. They were no match for her blades, and they fell beneath the merciless darkness of her magic. The blades sang through skin like butter as she fought forward with Cassius and Rooster. The sand was stained red with the evidence of battle, but it seemed the Hestian soldiers were pushing the Shoman back. Soon all the Misfits were reunited, minus Intoh, and they fought alongside one another until they were close to the city's gate.

By some miracle, the gate still stood, barred by a wooden door that Hestian soldiers had been fighting in front of. The stench of smoke clogged Helai's throat and made her eyes water. Many Shoman that came at them from their left were no match for *Volroth* nor the krok'ida who wielded it. Linda's roars carried out through the battlefield as Cassius pushed towards the gate, shouting at the soldiers in Hestian.

"Tell them we're looking for Angelika," Helai shouted, her voice hoarse from grief.

Cassius said something else, and one of the soldiers looked at Helai and the others before waving them through the line. The world was a daze as Helai swam through her grief and pushed through with the other Misfits. The gate was opened *just* enough to allow them passage, then quickly shut the moment Linda stepped inside, bringing up the rear. The city, even in its war-torn state, was breathtaking, with white and gold walls embellished with red fabrics and golden flowers. The streets were cobbled, so unlike the sandy streets of Shoma or the muddy dirt roads of Volendam, and Helai's eyes glazed over as a woman in full armor approached, her cheeks dirty with grime and blood.

"Come. I'll take you to the general."

NINE

ROOSTER

War continued around them. Alavae's soldiers shouted in a language that tugged on the edges of Rooster's mind, like a song he *almost* knew the words to. The only one who seemed to understand was Cassius, who spoke quick and low to the soldier leading them to the general. Helai was silent beside him, the wave of her grief threatening to drown him too. He hadn't known Zamir for very long, but the suddenness of his death tugged at his heartstrings, and he couldn't possibly imagine the turmoil Helai was going through. She was no longer crying, her eyes vacant as they stared ahead of them. Zamir's crow rested on her shoulder, still as stone, and Rooster wished desperately there was some drink in his flask to save him from the heavy weight in the air.

As they traveled further into the city, it grew quiet, the sounds of metal clashing and soldiers shouting becoming little more than a muted noise. The city had been beautiful once before war had stripped it away. Some of the buildings remained intact despite their neighbors being nothing but ruined rubble, and Rooster was saddened by the destruction.

"I remember these streets," Cassius muttered beside him. "This city was beautiful once." There was a strange look in his eye, the eye of remembering old ghosts, and Rooster hummed in acknowledgment. He didn't want to push Cassius to talk if he didn't want to, but he could see the potential of beauty. If he squinted his eyes.

"Alavae was known for its flowers. Large, red, beautiful flowers. It would cover the windowsills and boxes in a brilliant color, and summertime would be hot, but it would be worth it because the flowers would be in bloom." Cassius muttered something in Hestian, his hand raising to press against the back of his head as a dog lunged out of an alleyway and shot down the street. Ribs etched its starving belly, and Rooster watched it go before reaching over to press a hand to Cassius' shoulder and offer some words of comfort.

"Come, she is through this building," the soldier said before he could. Her Hestian accent was thick, and she glanced at the Misfits before slipping through the door of a small building.

Stone and marble were decorated with mosaic flowers as the building opened to a courtyard in the middle, where a war table had been set up.

A tall woman with dark skin stood at the end of the long table, pouring over what appeared to be the warring armies. She was young, perhaps a little older than thirty winters, and lines worried her face as she brushed her hair back. Her helmet lay discarded on the table beside her, and she glanced up when the Misfits entered the room.

"Sadiki?"

The crow cried out as she took off from Helai's shoulder. Sadiki landed on the table beside Angelika. The soft taps of the crow's feet echoed through the room as everyone went silent.

Angelika looked from Sadiki to Helai. "What is Zamir's bird doing with you? Where is he?"

Thickness tinged the room as Rooster's resolve hardened. He stepped forward to speak, not wanting to force Helai to say the words, but she spoke them regardless.

"Zamir's dead."

The words cut through the air as if they were a blade, and Angelika's face crumpled in despair as they sliced her, but she did not cry, save for a single tear that rolled down her cheek. Her fingers clenched into fists as she pressed them against the table, and the magical lights that danced about the room brightened before exploding as Angelika's eyes shined a yellow-white.

Rooster flinched as the heat from the orbs cascaded about the courtyard. Then Angelika composed herself, whispering into her palm as light balls formed and fluttered away to light the courtyard again.

"No time to mourn," she said sadly. "No time to honor our lost until our beloved home has been liberated from the enemy." She pressed a hand to her belly, and Rooster's stomach lurched from the implications. His gaze flickered to Helai as she stared at Angelika's belly, but no one said anything. No one said anything at all.

Each side of the table was lined with men and women, all dressed in armor with swords in sheaths at their sides. Many of them stared at the

Misfits with either curiosity or suspicion, particularly when their eyes grazed over Helai.

"We have come to offer our aid to the city. Has Shoma given reason to their attacks?" Cassius asked, stepping closer to the table. He uttered a whisper in Hestian as he stared at the battlefield, and Rooster stepped up beside him, his gaze turning back to Angelika.

Her grief was still present on her face, but it was muted like she had shoved it away to deal with later.

Shaking her head, she pressed her hands to the table. "Who are you, exactly?"

"Massoud Al'Bassar. Do you know him?" Helai stepped up next to a man twice her size, her brows furrowed in a way Rooster had grown familiar with: Helai would not stop pushing until she got the answers she sought.

Angelika's eyes flickered in recognition. "Zamir's friend. Yes, he was feeding us intel straight from the Shoma camp some miles out. We haven't heard from him in three days."

Rooster watched one of Helai's eyes twitch. "Why wasn't he aiding from this side?"

Angelika sighed, rubbing a hand over her face. "He managed to convince them he wanted to be a soldier. One of their generals, General Sarem, caught him on one of their ships. I don't know how he did it as the general has a jinn, but he convinced him that he was there to fight for their cause."

"Does this sound like the Massoud you know?" Rooster asked.

Helai's lips suppressed a smile. "Yes, the fool." She cursed in Shoman, reaching up to cling to her eye necklace. "It's not like him to fall silent. His survival is of uttermost importance."

One of the others, a woman with light hair pulled back into a tight bun, gestured to the Misfits. "You never answered the general's question. Who are you?"

Rooster's smile turned devious. He knew it wasn't the time nor the place, but the fear of battle and the adrenaline of war made him antsy. "We're the fuckin' Misfits, but *I'm* Rooster, gorgeous." He winked at the woman as Cassius grabbed his arm, his fingers tightening against Rooster's forearm in warning.

But no one seemed to pay his flirtations any mind. Not when grief still floated heavily in the air. Not when the sounds of war still echoed in the distance.

"What he means to say is that we're a small mercenary group. Our comrade, Helai," Cassius said, pointing to Helai, "has been searching for her friend for quite a while. Once we learned Massoud was here, we came to find him and offer our aid."

Angelika's expression was carefully guarded as it landed on Cassius. "You are Hestian, no?"

Cassius nodded slowly. "My family is from Verenzia. Holding this city is very important to me."

Angelika nodded firmly, gesturing to the table. "Their main forces are on land, but I've just received reports of naval ships entering Hestian waters, ships bearing the flag of Mohalis."

Helai sucked in a breath at the mention of the sultan, her eyes blazing. "My people weren't always this cruel," she said, her voice deceptively soft for the anger bleeding through each word. "Many still aren't. Those loyal to Mohalis have spent many years painting an ugly picture of my home." A single tear rolled down her cheek. "Mohalis came from the north with his men, came into our cities, and told us to bow or die. I beg you all..." Her brow furrowed as she went silent, staring at each person standing at the table. "Do not blame Shoma for the actions of one man. Do not let him poison your hearts with the idea of revenge. Believe me; I know all about wanting revenge." Her laughter was hollow. "But Mohalis is the snake whose head you need to cut off, not Shoma."

Angelika's mouth was thin as she pressed her lips together and stared at Helai for so long, Rooster wondered if she were ever going to speak. No one else dared to, their eyes flickering from Helai to Angelika. Some looked uncertain; one person on Angelika's left shook with rage.

"It does not take care of the army that stands on our doorstep," Angelika said, tearing her gaze away from Helai to stare at the table. "We must survive this siege first if we are to worry about what is to come next."

Tension bled into the air, thick as smoke, and Angelika pressed two fingers to the bridge of her nose, sighing roughly. "Helai is right about one thing, at least; we need to cut off the head of the snake. For this siege, it's their generals. If we do not kill their generals, they will continue to have full use of their jinn." She gestured to the table and three different spots. One was in the northern part of the city, the other on a ship near where they'd rowed to shore. The final general sculpture was at a series of camps beyond a small, open field outside the city. "To our knowledge there are three generals: two on the battlefield and one that remains tucked away in their camp, which is here," she said, pointing to a cluster near a cliff by the sea. It sat beyond the field, and Helai took great interest in the camp, looking up at Angelika.

"Is that where they hold prisoners?" she asked.

Angelika nodded. "Massoud is most likely there. We cannot break past their defenses to infiltrate their camp; otherwise, we would have done so by now. We also cannot spare any men for a stealth mission." Angelika's shoulders slumped, and the grief in her expression was palpable. "We're losing this battle. Our soldiers are better trained, but Shoma has the power of jinn to keep their fighters from tiring."

Concern sank against Rooster at the thought. The longer the battle went on, the worse off the Hestian soldiers would be. As they tired, they'd suffer more casualties. They needed to find a way to win the battle quickly.

"We have been sending small units of men to the crypts in the northern part of the city, but they've never come back." She gestured to one of the pieces on the map in the north. "One of the generals is holed up there and has some kind of aid. Our scouts have reported giant rats, but we're not sure what to make of that. Retrieving a jinn lamp could change the tides of this battle."

Rooster locked eyes with Rackjack as he nervously pulled at his beard, then Helai, who pressed her hand anxiously to her waist, hiding her own jinn lamp from view. It made Rooster wonder; why hadn't she used it to win the battle?

"There are enemies in the city?" he asked. Helai was smart. If she was hiding her lamp, it was for a specific reason. He made a mental note to ask her once they were alone.

Angelika nodded. "We believe it is only a small unit with the general. We have managed to set up barricades that block off the northern districts. We still aren't certain how they got in. Jinn work, probably, but we haven't the slightest idea why they would target the crypts."

"Send the two of us," Cassius said, gesturing to Rackjack and himself. He eyed the area Angelika had pointed to with vague interest. "If we do not survive, it will hardly be a loss, and if we succeed, we'll bring the jinn lamp back to you."

"We should go together," Rooster said sharply. The idea of them splitting up so significantly felt like a bad idea.

"I cannot wait to rescue Massoud," Helai said sharply. "Besides, we need him alive."

She was right, but this battle seemed bigger than the siege at Volendam.

"Go with her," Linda said. "Keep her safe."

"That isn't a bad idea," Angelika said thoughtfully. "It could turn the tides of battle if two generals were apprehended. Sarem, the general at their camp, he's one of Mohalis' head generals. Killing him would be very good for us."

Rooster saw the revenge in Helai's eyes and knew she would not be dissuaded from going. There were multiple reasons for her wanting Sarem dead, and Rooster was not one to try to convince her otherwise. Helai was right; they needed Massoud. The longer it took for them to free Igraine, the longer she would be tortured at that prison. The very thought made his heart ache.

I'm coming, Igraine.

A promise he told himself in the darkness of night, when the anxiety threatened to take hold. That promise and Tantien's copious amount of rum stock had been the only thing holding him together so far.

"Then I'm coming with you," Rooster said to Cassius and Rackjack. "I will do more help aiding you there than I will here."

Cassius nodded, turning to Angelika. "Does this sound agreeable? We have come to aid the city in whatever way we can. Tell us where our help would be best given."

"You carry our accent," a woman to Angelika's right spoke. She was young, almost too young to be carrying such weight on her shoulders, but Rooster knew the cost of war. It did not care who suffered its wrath. "And your armor speaks of the White Dawn. Do we have their support in the war efforts?"

Cassius stiffened beside him. "I'm afraid I haven't had contact with the Order in quite some time. I can send word if you believe this to be a matter of great importance, but I would not hold out hope. The Order of the White Dawn has never set foot in Hestia. I believe it has to do with the desolation of Ji'noa and the demonic presence that soaks the earth."

"No matter, Octavia. By the time they receive word and respond, it'll be too late," Angelika said, pressing a hand to Octavia's shoulder. "Our priority is the generals and their lamps." Gesturing to the soldiers beyond the wall, she looked around the table. "We'll pull our men back. Order a retreat and barricade the walls. Then we'll give you two days." Her gaze darkened. "Two days before we ride out and meet them for one last push."

Rooster felt the exhaustion of the soldiers in the room, a heavy blanket of hopelessness that curdled around their shoulders. Rackjack remained ever silent beside him, twitching slightly, and Rooster laid a hand on his shoulder to steady him as he nodded.

"Right. We'll leave right away."

A soldier burst through the door, his chest heaving. His face was dirtied with the grime of war, and he clutched his chest, his sword hanging limply at his side. "I have... I have confirmation of jinn magic in the bay. Our ships are struggling to bring down the enemy fleet."

Linda let loose a roar that sent the room into a flurry of panic. Many of them grabbed their weapons before realizing Linda wasn't going to murder them all, and Rooster locked eyes with Cassius.

His worry was mirrored in the vampire's expression.

He hoped Intoh was okay.

TEN

INTOH

Intoh's belly had filled with guilt the moment the other Misfits left. Perhaps he should have gone with them. Perhaps he would have been more helpful to them on the beach. The trails of magic in the air felt wrong, and a sour taste peppered the air as he leaned against the railing and watched his friends row to shore. Linda had barreled through the enemy with ease, and he gripped the railing so tightly his fingers ached when Rooster narrowly avoided a blow to the head.

Panic flourished through him when Zamir died.

Helai had collapsed with him, and though Intoh couldn't hear her cries, he watched the way her shoulders shook, the way she rocked back and forth as she looked around frantically. Who was she looking for?

Fool, Intoh thought fearfully, *they're going to kill you!*

He worried he was too far away as he lashed out with his magic anyway as the wind howled unnaturally, and it shoved back any Shoman soldier that got too close. The air was squeezed from Intoh's lungs, a punishment for sending his magic out so far away, and he saw stars before he released his magic and gasped, clawing at his throat. Rooster and Cassius had reached Helai's side; he had to trust that they would protect her now.

"Are you okay?" Itale whispered, drawing forward to steady Intoh as he swayed.

"Fine, fine," Intoh muttered, pulling away. He trusted the other Misfits, but Itale was still a stranger to him. His trust ended with Cassius, Rooster, Linda, and Helai.

Tantien shouted something in Eldrasian and Itale and Intoh both raised their heads towards the wheel of the ship as they approached the enemy's fleet. The Hestian ships came in various sizes. Smoke curled in the air as canon fire sounded off in the distance. The Shoman ships were smaller, but they moved with ease through the water, dodging the Firebrand's canon fire with little issue.

"Intoh, can you gift our sails with some wind?" Tantien called down, and Intoh turned and raised his cold hands towards the sails while taking a calm, deep breath. Magic that manipulated the air and wind was by far one of the easiest magics to wield, but it was also one that required a lot of concentration. Air wasn't tangible like water or fire, but coaxing it was as simple as exhaling in the right direction.

He urged the wind to press against the fabric of the sails, causing them to shoot forward, quicker than a ship as big as the Firebrand should be able to move. He was unprepared for such quickness and lurched forward. He was thankful for Khal's hands as he reached out to steady him.

They quickly approached a small cluster of Shoman ships, and the enemy's khopeshs gleamed in the sun as their wielders sneered at them from the decks of their ships.

Tantien shouted in Eldrasian, and more cannons went off, jolting the ship back as the cannon balls slammed into the side of a ship opposite of them. The cannons tore through wood, and Itale cowered beside Intoh, his face drawn in terror.

"I don't think I'm cut out for this," he cried, and Intoh looked at him sharply.

"Don't have a choice. Have to fight or die. No other option. Others take time to teach you to fight... so fight."

Itale's chin trembled, but he nodded, clutching the small dagger Tantien had let him take from his forge. His hand shook.

"Stay close to me. Keep you safe. Remember what others taught you." He tapped the back of Itale's hand. "Loosen slightly, and don't depend on it. Depend on magic. Part of you — more dependable."

Itale dipped his head as he visibly loosened his grip on the dagger. "Thanks, Intoh."

Intoh scowled at the uncomfortable feelings rising in his belly at Itale's gratitude and shook his head. He hated the feeling of vulnerability that it wrought, but a warmth accompanied it, a simple joy that he hadn't felt before meeting the Misfits. "No thank," he told him. "Just survive."

Itale nodded as the air tensed around him. Death clung to the boy like a second skin, and Intoh's magic flinched away, like it feared death could touch it too. It was utterly fascinating, something Intoh hadn't taken the time to properly study since having learned of Itale's necromancy, but the desire fled from him the moment the ship jerked sharply to one side and an unnatural howl pierced the air.

"They have a jinn," Tantien shouted from the wheel, the red of his hair a beacon of vibrant color as the sky dimmed, and angry clouds formed overhead. Intoh's fingers tingled from the lightning in the air, and he turned to Khal, switching quickly to Drikotyian, the language of his people.

"I need my staff. The jinn's magic is too chaotic for me to wield wild magic without something to channel through. Should be leaning near my hammock. Go and grab it."

Khal nodded and disappeared down into the lower decks of the ship as Intoh pushed his damp hair out of his face. Sode remained, ever vigilant next to him. He rarely spoke, unlike Khal, who seemed more compelled to loosen up when the other Misfits were around. Greka culture demanded order and precision when it came to all things. It was a difficult way of life to unlearn, and Intoh was only now beginning to feel its shackles loosen on him.

"Get down," Sode growled, his hand darting out to shove Intoh away as a khopesh sliced through the air where he just was. Intoh looked up as a Shoman woman snarled in frustration, her dark hair whipping wildly around her face as she raised the khopesh again.

Magic radiated off her, a seductive energy that made Intoh shiver in want for the first time in his life. It caressed him unlike any other magic had caressed him, beckoning him to lay down his staff and kneel before the soldier. The magic that trailed off her was unlike anything Intoh had ever felt, except, perhaps...

At the Welker Estate... or in the brand he'd just been liberated from.

He ripped away from the magic as if it had burned him.

"The One has her eye fixed on you, Intoh'gask," she uttered, her smile almost unnatural as she darted close, her accent thick like Helai's. "Keep on this path of yours, Chosen, and the One will be eager to devour you." She raised her khopesh, but Sode struck her down before Intoh could process what she'd said.

Who was the One? How did this random soldier know his name?

The shock nearly got him killed as another soldier rushed his left, only to be pierced in the belly by Itale, who'd lashed out with his dagger. He trembled, but his face was forged in determination as he pulled the blade out. Intoh cast lightning from his fingers, shoving the soldier away.

Where were they all coming from? Intoh hadn't seen a ship pull close enough for them to get over to the Firebrand, but the decks of their ship were now crawling with Shoman soldiers.

"The jinn must have transported them here," Tantien snarled, answering Intoh's unspoken question from the stairs behind him. He gripped his hammer and shield in his hands. Up top, another eldrasi had taken the helm, their hands deftly carrying the Firebrand through the water. Above, Tantien's gryphon sailed through the dark clouds, diving occasionally to grab an ignorant enemy soldier.

A soft moan echoed from behind Intoh as Khal returned with his staff. Intoh dodged to the side as a small dagger sailed through the air and embedded itself into the wood behind him. As he looked back, he saw Itale kneeling over the body of a fallen Shoman soldier. Dark tendrils poured from the boy's mouth and eyes, his cheeks growing gaunt as the magic siphoned energy from his body and poured it into the corpse.

Necromancy.

Intoh flinched away from it immediately. Despite his interest in Cassius' ability to live forever, his magic vehemently abhorred death magic, and it bled off Itale in a wild power that even Cassius did not reek of.

The corpse that Itale was bent over writhed against the deck. Cassius was not prone to use necromancy, not unless he was teaching Itale how to harness it safely, and Intoh watched on with a mixture of disgust and fascination as the animated corpse rose up and grabbed its khopesh from the ground.

"By the Forest Father's wrath, Itale," Tantien said. "Consider me impressed. You couldn't do something like that a week ago."

Color brushed Itale's cheeks as he sent the corpse across the deck of the ship, towards a Shoman soldier that was pressing an eldrasi sailor into the railing. The soldier was brought down with a cry of surprise as Itale had the corpse push its sword into the soldier's back.

Intoh was more impressed as time went on and Itale kept a grip on his magic. The corpse cut down two more soldiers before Intoh was forced to turn away from watching and focus on keeping himself alive, even though Khal and Sode had been doing a great job of that already.

"Once we fight off these soldiers," Tantien said, stepping up beside Intoh and bashing his shield into the face of a soldier. The soldier's head whipped back, and Tantien brought his hammer down atop the soldier's head, forcing him to crumple to the ground. "We'll need to sail our way over there." He gestured out at sea, where the majority of the Hestian ships were moving closer together. Intoh couldn't see the intelligence in such a movement, not with all of them bunched together to be attacked at once.

The hair on the back of his neck stood on end as a high-pitched wail pierced the air. It was an uncomfortable feeling, and he shuddered away from the noise before it could paralyze him in fear. At first, he thought it might be coming from Itale, with his fingers black and rotting from the necromancy, but no. Itale stood behind a barrel near the door to Tantien's forge, his eyes trained on the now two corpses he'd reanimated.

Something stretched over the sea, a pocket of air that formed some semblance of a man. It yowled, and a Hestian ship was struck by its wind so severely, it splintered in half.

Intoh stared at the entity at sea in horror. It was the jinn.

"How are we supposed to fight that?" he asked Tantien, who stared out at the jinn with ill-concealed concern.

"I don't know."

A high-pitched scream washed out over the water. Intoh clasped his hands over his ears as the jinn solidified and formed into the visage of a giant sea dragon. Its scales were dark; its face was long and thin, with trailing whiskers jutting out of its nose. It hit the water and sank beneath the waves. Everything seemed to go still.

"That...is not good." Tantien's words barely left his lips before the serpent burst from the water and using its lanky body to tear a nearby ship apart. The destruction would have been beautiful had Intoh not feared for their lives. He didn't know what to do; his magic was useless against a serpent of the sea.

Tantien shouted to his crew in Eldrasian, but his words were panicked as he fought the Shoman soldiers still on the ship. The Shoma forces were beginning to overwhelm them, and Intoh despaired, clinging to the railing as it began to rain.

"Vampires," Sode grunted, pointing.

Intoh wiped his hair from his eyes and looked. His heart flickered wildly between fear and hope as a hydra breached the water, her many heads roaring at the same time. One head snapped at another as she raced towards the jinn, followed closely by Delroy's small fleet. They'd met the vampire pirate and his hydra on their way to Halvdarc, when it was revealed what Rooster's real name was and that he had been a pirate himself before he lost his memories. Intoh didn't have the slightest idea why Delroy was here, but it didn't matter. As one of the hydra's heads bared her many teeth and shot a torrent of water at one of the Shoman ships, he decided he had never been so glad to see the hydra in his life, even if Delroy's appearance could mean nothing good.

ELEVEN
HELAI

Helai exhaled slowly while pressed up against a tree near the Shoma camp. Linda's bulk was too big to hide easily behind a tree, so they hovered low to the ground, taking care to keep out of sight of the flickering flames of the bonfires. It had taken them all day and into the night to sneak over to the camp. If Massoud had been discovered, then they were likely holding him in the center of camp. That was if he wasn't...

No. She wouldn't even entertain the idea. He was alive. She could feel it.

Glancing at Linda, she nodded once, then gestured to the tents lining the cliff. Perhaps they could sneak through or around them. It was going to be easy; most of the Shoman forces were sieging at Alavae's walls, which only left guards to patrol the camp while the soldiers were away, but Helai wasn't foolish and did not let her guard down. She was told that the general here had a jinn.

"Helai," Linda rumbled, pointing to one of the tents. "Sneak through?"

Helai hesitated. Without knowing who or what was inside the tents, it would be risky moving from one to the other. It would provide them with ample cover, however, given there were flaps at both ends, should they wish to remain stealthy. So even though her daggers sang for blood, she kept them sheathed, giving Linda the briefest of nods.

"Let me check," she whispered, edging forward. The moon was absent in the sky, and Helai was grateful for it. The only light was that of the bonfire, and Helai was able to sneak to the flap of the tent without coming across another soul. Smoke soaked the air, filling Helai's nose, and every breeze felt like the enemy. Mohalis was known for abusing the will of jinn, of bending them to his will. Every caress of the wind could be their watchful gaze; a shiver ran up Helai's spine. The quicker they found Massoud, the quicker they could make it out of the camp, the better. She couldn't hope to remain unnoticed for long, but she was relieved to find the tent empty.

Looking over her shoulder, she gestured to Linda.

The krok'ida had learned to be quiet in the time Helai had known them. It was eerie, watching something so large move so silently. They didn't even make a sound as they walked, their crocodilian head appearing out of the darkness as they drew closer.

"It's clear," Helai uttered, disappearing into the tent.

Linda followed, pulling the tent flap shut behind them. The darkness was almost overwhelming with no light inside the tent, but Helai was a master of the shadows and moved with ease, dodging the cots laid out inside. She tossed her gaze over her shoulder. "You can hold on to me if you need to," she whispered to Linda.

The silhouette of Linda's form shifted. "I can see. Even in dark."

That's right. Helai recalled Linda having moved with ease when she'd taken them with her into the sewers back in Volendam. Linda had the potential to be just as formidable in the shadows as they did on the front line if Helai could find the time to offer them more of her teachings.

"If he's here, he'll be in the center of the camp," Helai said, padding to the other side of the tent. A quiet echo of voices sounded off in the distance, the laughter of her people carried through the wind. It filled her with dread and rage, knowing that Massoud was out there, likely being tortured while the Shoman soldiers smoked and laughed about trivial things. Helai stilled as voices sounded far closer, speaking in Shoman.

"I know better than to question Sarem, but the traitor won't talk. Any more and the street rat will die."

"With that mouth on him, I'm surprised they haven't killed him yet."

"He's..."

The rest of the conversation was whisked away as the soldiers moved away, and Helai nearly collapsed in relief, her heartbeat roaring in her ears. *Massoud is alive.* They had been talking about Massoud; they had to have been.

"We have to hurry." Helai swallowed past the panic as she shoved her way through the tent, risking discretion for haste. She quickly waved her hands towards the lit torches nestled next to the flap of the tent. Her skin crawled as the shadow magic whispered over her skin and left a trail of goosebumps in its wake. She moved as the fire dimmed, feeling the intimidating presence of Linda behind her.

They came upon another tent. The quiet voices of Shoman soldiers trailed from inside. She stilled to listen, attempting to discern how many voices she was hearing. They spoke too low for her to hear the conversation, but she thought she could make out three individual voices, which was a relief. She was confident she and Linda could work together to take out three guards without alerting anyone if they were quick and quiet.

"The Hestians stand no chance. Mohalis was not able to spare many jinn, but no matter. Our forces will overwhelm the city."

"What does the sultan want with Hestia anyway?"

"It is not our will to know."

Helai realized with horror that two other guards were approaching, coming from the center of camp. Linda's bulky stature forced them to move quickly before they were seen. Bounding around the side of the tent, they slipped through the open flap and went inside.

Helai had been right. Three guards stood in the center of the tent, seated and drinking. A table with an open scroll sat at the other end, and the room was filled with prisoners, their wrists and ankles bound with rope. Many of them were severely malnourished, their cheeks dirty. It wasn't uncommon for Shoma to take prisoners, but the number of them took Helai's breath away. What could Mohalis possibly want with so many of them?

She didn't have time to think about it, not when all three soldiers raised their heads at the same time and jumped to their feet, knocking over their chairs as they did so. One shouted, but Helai threw her right hand out as dark smoke curled over her fingertips. She sent it through the tent, masking the place in silence from the outside.

"Go, Linda," Helai uttered. The krok'ida slunk around her, opening their jaw and disappearing into the smoke as the prisoners screamed in terror, and the soldiers shouted in Shoman. The sound of bones cracking and a squelching sound echoed throughout the tent and then a line of blood hit Helai's boot. Helai kept her hand out to control her magic; a bead of sweat rolled down the side of her face. She reached down with her free hand to unsheathe one of the daggers at her waist, raising it to deflect the blow of a soldier that had materialized from the smoke.

"Traitorous bitch," he seethed upon seeing Helai, his eyes lit up with fury. He favored his left side as blood seeped from a wound at his waist, and his face was splattered with blood. Behind him, Helai heard the panicked cries of the prisoners as they pressed themselves into the corners of the tent, as well as Linda's merciless attacks against the other two guards.

Traitorous bitch. Street rat. Scum of the sand. Helai had been called many names in her life. They'd stopped stinging long ago in the sands of her home. If anything, they'd fueled the fire in her belly for change. Shoma was a beautiful country; Helai had always loved her home fiercely, but something had to *change.* Too long had her people suffered at the boots of their oppressors. Too long had the wealthy sneered down at the poor upon their silk chairs. Too long had they hidden behind the Shoman soldiers, like the one that stood before Helai now.

No longer.

The fire burned in her now as she stared into the eyes of a man who'd likely killed countless street rats like her, who fought for a sultan so consumed by temptation and power, he'd see the end of his people. Redirecting the soldier's blade, Helai flinched away, then ducked beneath his next attack. She stabbed forward, satisfied when the blade contacted skin. He gasped in surprise, and her magic shuddered from her slip in concentration. Her right fingers cramped up in retaliation. Pulling the blade free as the smoke around her dissipated, she stabbed him again, reaching forward to cover his mouth with her other hand. The residual smoke from her magic poured into his mouth as he died, and she maintained eye contact with him as she lowered him to the floor and watched the light fade from his eyes.

Something shuddered through her as a gaze struck the nape of her neck, causing the hair there to rise on its end. A familiar touch grazed her shoulder as if beckoning approval, but when she turned to look, no one was there. The feeling faded as Linda appeared once more. The prisoners all sat huddled together in the corners. The soldiers were all dead. Linda had massacred the other two, ripping them apart with their teeth. The soldiers' blood trailed over the ground; their lifeless eyes were twisted with wordless cries.

Helai shushed the crying prisoners. She was horrified to see two children among them—two young girls with tear stains along both their cheeks. "We're here to help you."

Many of them looked at Linda as if they didn't believe Helai, their eyes wide with fear.

Linda glanced at Helai, then lowered their war hammer. "Good sir, good," they said, pressing a hand to their chest. "Will not harm."

"The center of camp—do they have a prisoner there?" Helai asked.

One of the prisoners nodded slowly, pointing. "A Shoman man. Didn't look good," they said in broken Vilris, their Hestian accent thick on their tongue.

"When I cut you free, head back that way," Helai said, gesturing back the way they had come. Sweat coated her palms as she raised her dagger again, using it to cut the ropes from the prisoners. Darkness consumed her. *Leave them*, it begged. *You're running out of time.*

The prisoners bolted the moment they were free, not even sparing a glance Helai's way. She couldn't say she blamed them and hoped they would make it to safety. Clinging to the last bit of hope, she sheathed her dagger and twirled on her heel, looking at Linda.

"I don't know if this will work, but what if we pretend that I've taken you prisoner?"

Linda cocked their head to the side. "Pretend?"

Helai nodded. "I'll tie your wrists loosely. Loose enough for you to break free if you need to. We don't know what we're walking into." The rage in her belly burned ever brighter as her expression darkened. "Once we have eyes on Massoud, I need you to get him out of here."

Linda nodded, hid themself behind their human illusion, and then held out their wrists. As Helai tied the rope around them, she couldn't help the flame of hope from igniting in her chest.

TWELVE
LINDA

L inda walked willingly behind Helai, their hands tied in front of them. They'd left their hammer behind in the tent at Helai's suggestion, and the absence of *Volroth's* weight left them restless. They also didn't like the feeling of rope around their wrists, having spent much of their early life chained up this way when the greka had wanted to send them to different cities. *To help Helai,* they kept telling themself.

Helai walked with purpose, as if she belonged in the camp, and no one paid her any mind. Torch-light flickered off the tents as they walked by, and they were only stopped when they neared the center of the camp.

"*Wahquf!*" one of the Shoman guards said as they approached a series of small fires, very much like how the dwarves had set up camp in the Spine Mountains all that time ago, only this camp also had a massive fire in the middle of the smaller ones, burning high and bright. Something about that fire was making Linda's skin crawl, like it was magical in nature. A man stood before it, right on the edge, on some sort of contraption. At first glance, it looked to be made of wood, but the fire wasn't burning it away. With the amount of magic that thickened the air though, Linda didn't have much cause to question it.

The man's hands were spread wide and bound. He had his back to the flames. The smell of his burning flesh sat with such thickness in the air that Linda could almost taste it; it was making them hungry. They wondered if Helai would let them eat just a few of these soldiers... If this was Massoud, then she probably would.

It didn't appear as if he had bathed in some time, his long hair falling around his face in dirty clumps. His naked chest was covered in bruises; they had beaten him badly, and the hair on his chest was stained with blood. His wrists had been rubbed raw where the rope binding them still cut into his skin, and blood had traveled down his arms and dried there too. His head hung forward as if he were dead, but his chest rose and fell unsteadily.

Helai spoke to the guard quickly and at low volume, her eyes darting to the man at the large fire. It was obvious he was who Helai had been searching for. He was the only Shoman man that was tied up, and he didn't look too good.

The guard held up his hand and gestured to Linda.

Linda's gaze tore away from the man at the fire as they realized that Helai was speaking in her native tongue and Linda understood what she was saying. A whisper echoed out from the pendant in the center of Linda's tooth necklace, and Linda watched Helai and the guard argue, unable to comprehend what they were saying as they were too busy marveling at just being able to *understand*. It felt liberating in a way, and Linda hummed as warmth flooded through them once more over Tantien's gift.

"Caught them trying to sneak in at the edge of camp," Helai said. "I think they came from the city." Helai spat at the ground at Linda's feet, and the look of disgust Helai gave them sent a chill coursing through Linda. The krok'ida knew it was all for show, that she had to convince the guards she was not the enemy, but the look still cut through them without mercy. Anger swept through them like a maelstrom. Who would stop them from slaughtering this entire camp?

"Bring them. Our general has just returned from the front lines. He will decide their fate."

Helai tugged Linda forward as they followed the guard towards the fire. Many of the soldiers sitting around the smaller fires looked up as Helai and Linda trailed past. Luckily for Linda, they had switched into their human form before they and Helai had revealed themselves to the guards, so no one knew Linda was a krok'ida. That was one of the only reasons Linda enjoyed being tucked behind the ring. The look on an enemy's face when Linda shifted and they realized they'd been deceived was almost *intoxicating*.

The camp was relatively bare, with the majority of the soldiers still fighting against Alavae's walls. It would make saving Massoud all the easier, and Linda turned as they halted in front of what appeared to be the general the guard had spoken of. He radiated power, his eyebrows thick as he regarded them in silence. There was no emotion in his eyes, save for the cold calculation of rage. The sheath of a curved blade hung on one hip, a lamp on the other. It shone in the light of the fire and looked almost identical to the one Helai carried, only Helai always tucked hers away. The general wore his with pride.

"Who are they?" The general turned to the guard. Now that they were close, Linda could see the man near the fire had terrible burns all along his back. Pathways of wounds covered old ones; they looked like whip lacerations.

Helai stood in front of Linda, and for a moment, the krok'ida thought she was going to break their cover. The pain in her eyes was so extreme, so real, Linda thought they could feel it as a tangible thing that was wrapping around them and filling them with their own sense of rage. The man had to be Massoud.

"You." The general looked down at Helai, his gaze imploring. "I do not recognize you. What is your name?"

Helai's face fell back behind a stone mask of indifference as she met the general's eyes. "A lost street rat who has found her way back to the One." Helai dropped to her knees in front of the general, and Linda growled at the obvious display of submission.

Helai ignored them as her head kissed the ground right in front of the general's boots. "I found this one setting your prisoners free. I thought you might want to deal with them yourself."

The general's gaze turned to Linda, his eyes blazing with fury. His mouth hid behind a thick dark beard, revealed only by the gleam of his sneer. "This one is about to return to the will of the One," he said, gesturing to Massoud. "This prisoner will take his place."

He snapped his fingers at the guards, then gestured to Massoud as he turned back to Helai. "Rise. What is your name?" He offered his hand to her. "I am General Sarem, head general of Mohalis' army."

The guards moved past Linda, towards Massoud, and it was then that Linda realized that if they didn't act soon, Massoud would be taken away and Helai would be too close to the general to stop them. The urge to act burned inside Linda brighter than any fire.

A guard reached up and cut Massoud's wrists free from the stakes. Massoud slumped to the ground. If his chest wasn't rising and falling, no matter how slight, Linda might have been certain that he was already dead.

Threading their fingers together, Linda twisted the ring on their finger.

The ropes that bound their hands broke easily as Linda grew. Their bones broke and reshaped; their jaw extended into its crocodile-like shape. It felt good, being so much bigger than everyone else in camp, to feel their shock and fear sink into the air. It was nearly solid enough to taste, and Linda roared as many of the Shoman soldiers rose to their feet, their hands reaching for the khopeshs they had abandoned for warmth and drink.

"What—" General Sarem said, but he was immediately preoccupied by Helai, who ducked low as a swirl of black shadows trailed from her fingers. It hid her and Sarem away as it rolled out over the campgrounds.

Linda lashed out with their mouth at the guard nearest them and found his shoulder with ease. His scream was quickly cut short as they bit down into their neck, crushing the guard's windpipe. His blood was sweet, sickeningly so, and Linda threw him away as more soldiers approached. Reaching down, they scooped Massoud from the ground and cradled him against their side. If they could just get to their war hammer, they'd be way better off dealing with the soldiers, but they didn't want to leave Helai.

A soldier appeared through the fog, screaming. His khopesh was raised to strike, and Linda reached out with their free hand. Cupping his head, they flung him as hard as they could across the campgrounds. His screams faded as he was replaced with more soldiers, their eyes wild with anger.

"This one defiles Qevayla's vision. This one must be purged," one said, and another one spat at the ground as his comrade spoke. Linda's heart thumped with the excitement of combat. Tightening their grasp on Massoud, they planted their feet and roared again; the tendrils of satisfaction curled against their chest when a few of the soldiers flinched away in fear.

What soldiers kept their courage charged forward, and Linda fell into a familiar pattern as they fought. Dodging the swings of their khopeshs, they lashed out when there was a weak spot Linda could reach. They missed their hammer, and fighting with only one hand would only be successful for a short time.

They needed to flee.

"Helai," they shouted, swiping out with their tail to trip up two soldiers that had approached as they'd turned, searching for any part of Helai in the fog. *There.* They could see the twirl of her braid and the flickering blue of her eye necklace as she danced away from someone she fought; Linda could only assume it was Sarem by the way he carried himself more elegantly than the others. Helai moved quickly and expertly, but Sarem moved with the strength of a seasoned soldier. His khopesh caught Helai's blade before she could drive it into his side.

Pain flourished against Linda's own side, and they growled as they peered down and saw a khopesh glancing off their body. The soldier attacking them hadn't managed to get past Linda's scales, but they had still left a shallow cut.

Reaching out, Linda grabbed the soldier's head just like they had the other one, only this time, instead of throwing him, they squeezed until his screams stopped and his skull collapsed between their fingers, coating their hand in gore and blood. They barely registered dropping his body before they moved forward to aid Helai.

Only Helai didn't need aid. A shadowy hand burst from the ground and grabbed Sarem's wrist as he reached for the lamp at his hip. Soon after, another grabbed his other wrist, forcing him to his knees as Helai stood before him. She looked like a goddess among men, the rising sun bathing her in an ethereal glow as the shadows faded around her.

She didn't say anything, didn't spit in his face, didn't yell. Silence steadied her hand as she reached down and grabbed a fallen soldier's khopesh. Sarem didn't beg either as Linda stood watch to make sure no one intervened.

With one swift, fluid movement, Helai reared back and thrust the khopesh into Sarem's chest, shoving it all the way through until it slipped out through his back, the metal stained with his blood. The silence was overwhelming. Sarem gritted his teeth. Blood spurt from his lips as he keeled over. He opened his mouth to speak, his teeth a bloodstained snarl, but Helai didn't let him. She beckoned the shadowy hands to claw their way over his arms and consume his face. His eyes, dark and full of rage, were the last to disappear behind wisps of shadow. Within moments, every part of him was covered but the small golden lamp.

Helai bent over to take it off him. Silence encompassed the camp now that everyone nearby was dead. Linda loosened their hold on Massoud and glanced down to see that he was still breathing. His heartbeat felt like a trapped bird against the palm of their hand, and Linda growled quietly as Helai stood frozen in place, her chest heaving.

"Have to go," they said. "Reinforcements coming, and Massoud need help. Badly hurt." His blood coated their fingers, and Helai's chin trembled as she pulled herself out of the trance she was in. Her magic disappeared, leaving behind the corpse of the general, and Helai reached down to cut his pinky off.

"To show the council that we killed him," Helai explained, seeing Linda's questioning glance. She did not look at Massoud as she strolled past Linda. "Come on. I think there were horses nearby."

"Can't ride horse," Linda said, following behind as they cradled Massoud against their shoulder. "You take Massoud. I fight back."

Helai nodded, and they trailed through the camp silently until they found the horses Helai had spoken about. Many of them cried and rolled their eyes in fright as Linda approached, tugging at the ropes that tied them to wooden posts in an attempt to get away.

Helai was able to soothe one, her soft coos and soft touches coaxing it to stop tossing its head back. It stared at Linda with fearful but intelligent eyes, but Helai managed to pull its attention to her.

Linda stilled as their friend untied the horse and swung her leg up, settling into the soft saddle the horse had on its back.

"Helai," Linda said quietly, pulling Massoud away from their shoulder to stare down at him. His chest was no longer rising and falling. "Helai...think he—"

"Don't," Helai snarled, her eyes wide with a determined coldness. "Put him in front of me and quickly. We need to get out of here before anyone notices what's happened."

The sting of Helai's harsh tone traveled all the way down to their bones, and they silently transported Massoud over to the horse, setting him as gently as they could in front of Helai. She wrapped one arm securely around his waist.

"I'm sorry, Linda," Helai whispered, her voice breaking. "I just—I can't lose him. I have an idea, and I – I have to go."

Linda nodded. "Would be the same if you. Go. Will find way back to city."

Helai nodded, her eyes swimming with tears. Then she clicked her tongue and ushered the horse forward. As Helai disappeared into the darkness, the krok'ida freed the rest of the horses. They went back to the tent to retrieve *Volroth* before moving through the campgrounds, cutting down anyone who tried to stop them.

Despite all odds, they hoped Massoud would pull through.

THIRTEEN
HELAI

Helai urged the horse away from the camp, further and further until they reached a small etching of trees away from the siege of Alavae and any danger. Tears clung stubbornly to her cheeks, and she violently wiped them away as she dismounted the horse and led him slowly to the wood's edge. Massoud was too heavy for her to carry, so she led the horse as far as they could go into the trees before tugging Massoud down. He hit the ground hard, and Helai flinched from the guilt of it before she laid him on his back and brushed his hair from his face.

A sob threatened her lungs, but she choked it down. He was dead, but only for the moment.

"Don't worry, big brother," she whispered, plucking her lamp from her hip. "The shadows have no right to you yet." She studied her lamp, the one she'd plucked off a noble over a year ago in the sands of Dalasae. Many jinn were not strong enough to ferry the dead back to the world of the living, but she had to try.

Hesitation was absent from Helai as she knelt on the ground next to Massoud and rubbed her hand across the lamp. Her heart thundered in her chest. Jinn were wayward spirits, a being to be treated with the uttermost respect. Their enslavement to the whims of humans was rooted in greed and the desire for power, but Helai couldn't think of her guilt in forcing this jinn to do what she wanted as the wind wailed through the trees and whipped her hair around her face. She had no time to fear the jinn either as a soft sigh echoed to her right. A form collected in front of her, a translucent being that the wind threatened to carry away if it weren't for its immense power. It vaguely resembled a man but not really. Jinn were not made the same as men. It bore no face to speak of, nothing but claws and teeth and the vague sense of a form. The dashing of stars echoed along what appeared as its skin.

Helai scooted back and bent over her knees, pressing her forehead to the ground just as she had before General Sarem. Only this time, she meant her respect. Her eye necklace dangled precariously from her neck as a reminder that she was safe from the wrath of the jinn should it deem her unworthy of its aid.

"Speak." The jinn's command sailed through the air, a quiet whisper that etched against Helai's skin and beckoned her to shiver. She refrained. A test, she deemed. She would force her will to stand unyielding against whatever magic the jinn tested against her.

For Massoud.

"I wish for you to resurrect Massoud Al'Bassar as he was, with sound mind and body." The words flowed from her lips shakily. One wrong word, and the jinn could twist her wish with malicious intent, could give him back to her as a husk or just as he'd been right before he'd died or with a broken mind.

"Rise," the jinn uttered, the trees shuttering against the weight of its magic. Helai rose obediently. "Your wish bears a heavy burden. Are you willing to shoulder its weight?" The jinn sounded almost gleeful as wind pulled at Helai's hair like little fingers caressing strands of her locks.

Helai resisted the urge to reach up and clasp her eye necklace, knowing doing so would offend the jinn. Her gaze trailed down to Massoud's body, which was covered in blood, his eyes devoid of life. They'd whipped him and then burned him slowly over the fire, and that alone made Helai sick with rage.

She would fight to the ends of Vilanthris for the ones she loved.

"If that's what is required of me, I will. Whatever weight the wish instills, I will bear it if I must." She tossed her head up high and jutted her chin out. The jinn seemed pleased as vibrant colors danced across the dashing of stars that made up its body.

"Freedom, at last," it sighed just as Massoud gasped and the jinn started to disappear, its tail snapping free of its shackle at the lip of the lamp. Something inside Helai grew heavier as the jinn vanished entirely, a weight on her shoulders that cracked at her faith, but she ignored it as she sobbed and threw herself down against Massoud, ignoring his yelp of surprise as she wrapped her arms so tightly around him, she feared she would never let go.

"I never stopped looking for you, big brother," she cried as great big tears rolled down her cheeks. Massoud was warm, his body brimming with life, and her hands grazed his ruined back. The jinn had brought him back and healed him, but he'd bear the scars of his torture for the rest of his life.

"Ah, I always knew you had a soft spot for me, little sister," Massoud mused, his weak laughter smothered against her hair. "Brought me back from the dead and wasn't even kind enough to have a drink waiting for me. I see where your true allegiances lie."

Helai choked on her own laughter as Massoud's hazy form swam through her tears when she pulled away. So long. She had been searching for Massoud for so long. She pinched herself to make sure she wasn't dreaming and then hissed when it hurt.

"I'm really here, Helai," he said softly, pushing himself into a seated position as he reached out to trail his fingers along her arms.

She stared down at the contact. He used to do that when she was little and sick or scared. Massoud had been a child on the streets, just like her and Aryan. He'd never been obligated to take up the mantle of raising them, and yet, he had. He'd done everything to ensure they'd seen their eighteenth birthday.

"You should have seen me," she whispered, falling back on her legs to sit on her heels. "My rage was so ugly, but I saw you on that pyre and—" Her throat constricted, and fresh tears rolled down her cheeks. "I should have looked harder, come sooner." Guilt made a home in her, forged stronger each time Massoud moved, then winced due to his newly healed back. Shadows darkened the underside of his eyes, but his smile, ever present, was radiant on his face.

"I'm sure you had your reasons."

Helai shook her head, cursing the situation she'd gotten herself into a year ago, when the shoma'kah had snatched her, and the rakken had put a brand on her back. If she'd just pushed harder, she might have saved Massoud from his gruesome fate in the first place.

"Helai." He said her name like he'd used to whenever she'd disappointed him or hadn't listened to what he'd said and had nearly got them caught by guards. Exasperation tinged with adoration mingled on his tongue. He leaned forward, brushing the tears from her cheeks. "*Abibi*. Those tears better not be for me. You are made of fire, and I know nothing would've kept you from finding me unless there was good reason for it. Please just tell me that you weren't all alone out there."

Helai cracked a weak smile, refusing to shut her eyes for fear that he would disappear from right in front of her. She'd never used a jinn wish before, didn't know how reliable their words were once they were free from the lamp, but Massoud seemed solid enough. "Of course not. You know better than anyone that I find a home in people. It took me a while to warm up to them, but..." Her smile strengthened. "I think you'll like the Misfits."

"Misfits, hm?" Massoud mused, pushing himself to his feet. "I can't wait to meet them. Were you able to find Zamir? He said he was going to try to find you. He was more worried than I was; I knew that you were perfectly capable of taking care of yourself."

Helai stilled, all the joy from Massoud's resurrection draining from her face as the grief of losing Zamir washed over her all over again. This life was cruel, but Helai still couldn't find it in her to regret not having used the wish to save Zamir. Not with Massoud staring at her, concerned but alive. Although she had the other jinn from the general now, she hadn't *then*. She couldn't have known she could have saved them both. She couldn't have known. She couldn't have *known*. She repeated it like a mantra in her head, but it didn't chase the bile of guilt that rose in his throat.

"He's dead." The words left her, and it almost didn't sound like her voice that had spoken and willed them into existence. She'd been forced to shove his loss away, to deal with it later. Massoud had been the priority, but now that he was safe, Zamir's death crashed down upon her all over again. It hurt to breathe, just like it had when Zahra, the youngest ghost of her group of thieves, had died. Massoud had been there to pick up the pieces then too.

"Helai." Massoud pressed his hands to her shoulders, and she met his expression. "Clear mind, clear soul. *Breathe.*" He inhaled slowly, held his breath, and exhaled, doing it several more times as Helai mirrored him. Slowly, the world centered itself, and the grief faded to her chest, where it sat, prickly as a rose bush.

"War does not care for the innocent and guilty. War is bloodshed, and Zamir knew the risks when he joined Hestia's ranks, just as I did. His memory will live on in us." Massoud hid his grief well, as he always had, but Helai saw it etched in his eyes. Painful. Soul-crushing. Ragged.

"From the mountains to the sea," she said fiercely, her grief turning to anger. How many Ghosts were doomed to die for the greed of their leaders?

"From the mountains to the sea," Massoud repeated, brushing her hair back and fussing over her necklace, making sure the clasp was on the back. "Your love for our country is admirable, Helai. Hope will shine upon our home again."

Helai wanted that reality so desperately it hurt. She'd been dreaming of the liberation of her home from their oppressors since she'd been a child, able to comprehend the corruption etched into the sands.

She nodded, gesturing to the treeline behind her. "There's a battle to be won first. I'm not sure which side the gods favor, but it was looking pretty bleak when I left to save you."

Massoud's eyebrow quirked. "I meant to ask you, little sister, did you save me all on your lonesome?"

As they headed out of the trees, Helai was pleased to find the horse she'd stolen had remained close, grazing on patches of grass nearby. She grinned as she mounted the horse behind Massoud.

"No, I had Linda with me. You're going to love them."

FOURTEEN
CASSIUS

Two hours ago

As the door shut behind them, the crypt silenced any outside noise, and Cassius couldn't help feeling like they were walking into some sort of trap. The tombs of Hestia were grand, built to honor their dead, and it remained pure in its grandeur even now. Marble encompassed the floor and walls, having been decorated by Hestian Inquisitors that rested next to their tombs, which had been sculpted in their likeness.

"Hestians value not only their soldiers, but the blacksmiths that forge their swords, the farmers that feed their troops, the women that sacrifice their lives just as often as their men." Cassius spoke as he approached the nearest sculpture, his fingers coming to gently rest against its marble cheek. "They are buried here, deemed the glorious dead." Shadows of memories were being called back, fabricated by the beckoning whispers of the catacombs beneath the bell tower. He had not thought about his human life for a very long time, but standing in these halls reminded him of when he'd been a young soldier, when his father's troops had returned with the news that Cassius would never see his father again. With no corpse to bury, Cassius had never been able to say goodbye. He spit on the ground. The dead did not deserve grief long laid to rest. His father deserved it even less so.

"Seems very creepy to me. Why not just burn your dead and be done with it?" Rooster said, trailing his fingers across the tomb of a blacksmith.

Cassius shook his head, his face pulled by disgust. "It's dishonorable to burn your dead."

Rooster scoffed, running a hand through his hair. "They're *dead*. They don't give a fuck whether you're honoring them or not. Besides," he said, staring into the eyes of a statue. "There are better ways to honor them than by building cold, dark crypts."

Rackjack had twisted his ring upon entry, and he now stood in his rakken form. He tugged on Cassius' arm before he could reply. "I smell something dead-bad."

A stench so harrowing built up to invade his senses until he was forced to flinch away in repulsion.

"You speak too plainly Rackjack. That smell is much *fouler*." It seemed to be coming from their right, and as they took a step forward, a grotesque sight met them. A pile of flesh and bone festered, half-eaten, within a pocket of space in the wall, large enough for them to stand in and investigate.

"I guess we know what happened to the first people the general sent to do this task. Let us hope there are some that yet live," Rooster said.

Cassius' nose crinkled up in horror as he approached the pile, noting the Hestian armor that sat among the bones. "Does this look like something's been eating them to you? Perhaps the rakken Angelika spoke of?"

Rackjack pushed past towards the wall beyond the corpses. He tapped at the stone and marble, his nose twitching as he sniffed the air. He did not answer; instead, he studied the wall with much interest. Something had been carved into it, similar to the mark of Gorvayne, one of the dead dragons, but different. Instead of three diagonal lines having been carved, there was a vertical line with a hook at the top and two diagonal lines running across its bottom. It glowed vaguely in a purple light.

Cassius had never seen it before, but Rackjack looked at it with familiarity, his fingers moving deftly as he touched it in certain spots.

"This is scratch-mark of dragon in Shoma land-sand," he said, sparing Cassius a quick glance. "Name Qevayla. Dragon of dreams, dragon of magic. Soak their earth-ground with magic and create jinn-things." His fingers expertly darted along the glowing stone, and Cassius frowned. Another dragon? That could not be the bringer of any good news.

Cassius sidled up next to the rotting pile, pushing through the bones and gore with the tip of his sword. A glint of metal drew his eye and then Cassius saw Hestia's sigil: The vague visage of a woman in silver armor, with the country's red flower surrounding her. Her sword was clasped in both hands, the tip of her blade poised against where the ground would be.

"One day we'll be free of going places where it's smelly and dark," Rooster complained, waving his hand as if it would liberate the air of its stench. "Which way do we need to go?"

"Rakken-rats," Rackjack warned, his nose twitching as he sniffed the air. "Can hear them scurrying-scampering. Must tread carefully," he said in hushed whispers. "Must hurry away-way when we find captain-general and take his magic-lamp. Come. Come-come. Into the shadows. We must hide, and I can musk-mask our scent-smell."

Cassius and Rooster locked eyes in a despairing sense of brotherhood: Cassius could see the same exhaustion in Rooster's eyes that mirrored his own. They were both tired of dealing with giant rats.

But they both complied, following Rackjack to a small dark corner behind one of the marble statues. Spiders scuttled from their homes as they were disturbed, and long-settled dust was kicked up as they knelt behind the statue. Rooster wrinkled his nose and sneezed.

A foul stench wafted over them, and Cassius stopped breathing as Rooster frowned in disgust beside him. "These are one of the few times I envy you, Cassius. Choosing whether or not to breathe is a gift."

Cassius didn't answer as the sound of approaching rakken drew closer, the scuttle of their claws clicking across the marble floors. The first rakken that appeared was smaller than the ones Cassius had seen before and with darker fur. It moved on all fours, sniffing first the air, then the floor as it came upon the corpse pile they'd been investigating.

Another joined it and then another. They didn't seem dangerous enough that the three of them wouldn't be able to handle them, but Rackjack shook his head, fear splattered across his beady red eyes. The marble was cool against Cassius' back, and he watched as the rakken on the other side of the room tore into the flesh of some of the corpses, content that no one else was in the room.

"Ah, I see you-you," a voice whispered in the dark, and Cassius sensed the quick heartbeat a moment too late as pain pierced his lower back on the left side. A rakken slipped from the shadows, bearing two small daggers, and it was *quick* as it scampered across the floor and disappeared into a trail of shadows.

"They sneak-scamper," Rackjack hissed as the other rakken raised their heads from the corpse pile and bared their teeth in their direction. "Very good with shadow. Blade was likely poisoned. Yes-yes."

Pain radiated from the wound on Cassius' back, but it healed quickly as his body purged the poison from the injury, forcing it to drip down to the floor. Cassius leaned heavily against the wall, his sword and shield at the ready as the rakken ahead all slipped into the shadows and disappeared.

"Don't like that," Rooster muttered, his own sword unsheathed.

"Rakken of south like to sneak-sneak in the shadows," Rackjack said nervously, edging closer to Rooster while holding his arm out. The fire weapon attached to his forearm had been surprisingly handy over the time Rackjack had spent with them.

"Can you smell them?" Cassius asked.

Rackjack nodded. "Can smell magic one too, yes-yes. Deeper in tomb. Must go down, but that's where they scamper-sneak most. Can also sense big one. War beast-rat. Will have to be careful, yes-yes." Cassius could sense it too: the smell of bloated corpses and the chattering of teeth in the darkness. It cloaked them, tucking the enemy away behind the mask of shadows, but it did not hide them completely.

A wail rattled down the halls of the tomb, waking the creaky bones that had long laid at rest inside their wombs of stone. Long pale, translucent fingers ghosted Cassius' arms, and he brushed the spectral aside as a ghostly figure pried itself from the floor. It yawned, its mouth long and gaping, and Cassius frowned. He couldn't recall having used his necromancy to beckon the dead. And yet, they came regardless, peeling themselves from the shadows as more clawed out of the floor. They were all Hestians lost to time, and they whispered through the tomb towards Cassius as if he were a beacon.

"How long have you been able to do *that?*" Rooster asked behind him, his voice hushed by mingled uncertainty and awe.

"Comes with vampirism," Cassius replied sharply, his eyes trained on the ghosts as they approached. "Necromancy usually flourishes in two forms: the flesh or the spirit. As you can see" –he gestured to the approaching apparitions– "mine forms the latter."

A chill coursed through the tomb as the spirits drew closer, as they ghosted Cassius' skin with their spectral fingers. They whispered gentle words into the dark, too softly for Cassius to pick up what they were saying, but one pointed down a desecrated hall that led further into the tomb, his eyes solemn and terrified.

"Our general is down that way," Cassius said, gesturing. "The spirits are restless. I imagine the presence of the jinn is doing little to comfort them." In turn, his own restlessness clung to his limbs. He felt his wings shift beneath his illusion as his cloak billowed gently from a faint breeze, and Rooster frowned.

"Don't like that. If the ghosts are scared, I am hesitant to chase down the source of their fear."

"Can smell the magic down-down-down," Rackjack stuttered, his nose trembling as he scuttled forward and stared at a stairwell that led deeper into the tomb.

The void of darkness that reached out from the bowels of the tomb reached up to Cassius and swallowed him up, forcing him to remember the last time he'd been inside a tomb.

"Cassius, I'm sorry." Vera's eyes were pain stricken as she stood before the opening to his imprisonment.

Cassius stared straight ahead. They were alone, a kindness he knew they didn't think he deserved. He'd betrayed the Order, had told Dmitri to go fuck himself when he'd demanded the blood of a child.

"Do not spare me your pity," Cassius growled low. "I do not regret sparing Rembrandt's life. How long has Dmitri condemned me to my tomb?"

Vera's gaze hardened. "Five years."

A shudder threatened Cassius' shoulders. Five years to starve in a tomb, and still, the lack of regret or guilt was liberating. The child still lived, and he'd happily pay the price for having spared him.

Courage, Cassius.

And yet, the courage fled him when Vera stepped aside and said nothing else. The darkness of the tomb swallowed him whole as he steeled himself against it.

"You alright, mate?"

Rooster pried Cassius from the darkness, liberating him from the shackles of fear that had sent him into a dizzying panic. It still clung to him now, even as he returned to the Hestian tomb, even as Rackjack's and Rooster's faces swam before him, etched with concerned. He didn't want their concern nor their pity. They looked at him as Vera had, and it sickened him.

He pursed his lips and brushed past them, forcing himself down the stairs despite the hands of fear threatening to strangle him. *It's just the dark. Since when are monsters afraid of the dark?*

Somewhere off to their right, a low hiss echoed from the shadows. Whatever it was, it was quick, but Rackjack was quicker, lashing out before Cassius could get stabbed again. A glint of metal pierced what light was granted inside the tomb, and Rackjack's teeth chattered as he threw himself against another rakken and pried the small dagger from its grasp.

"You will wield-surrender," Rackjack hissed, pressing the rakken into the ground as the air fouled with his musk. "Scream-yell, and I will rip your tongue out." The warning seemed to resonate with the rakken for he stilled, his breath rapid on his tongue as he stared up at Rackjack with a hateful expression. He began to speak in quick, rapid chattering squeaks, and for a moment, Cassius thought he was mad until Rackjack responded to him in kind.

"Is it strange that I can understand a word or two of that?" Rooster was scratching his head when Cassius glanced over, and he nodded. Very strange indeed.

"This is Hiss-rat-rat. Going to lead us to magic man-filth," Rackjack rasped, slowly releasing his hold on Hiss, who stood slowly. He was much smaller than Rackjack, his hair a darker brown, and he exhaled sharply as he threw himself into the darkness of the stairs. Rackjack lashed out, grabbing the other rakken's arm and ignoring his howls of protests. He seemed to study something intently on his arm before letting go and turning quickly to Cassius and Rooster.

"Cannot speak man-filth tongue," Rackjack said as he started after him. "Will have to trust me-me."

Cassius nearly laughed at the notion of trusting a rakken, even if that rakken was Rackjack, but Rooster nodded and followed, leaving Cassius with the spirits that still clung to his armor.So he took a step forward and followed Rackjack and Rooster into the dark.

The tomb was a plethora of soft noises echoing in the shadows. Despite Cassius' anxiety, his knightly training kept his fear from paralyzing him. Still, he couldn't help but wonder, *Where have those other rakken assassins gone?*

FIFTEEN

ROOSTER

"Are you sure he's taking us the right way?" Rooster squinted along the dim path. He cursed silently as another questionable liquid dripped onto his head. He glanced behind him at Cassius, who was silent as he stared through the darkness with glowing red eyes. The air was stale, and Rackjack scurried around the corner as Hiss faded into the shadows. His disappearance sent a shiver down Rooster's spine. Every shadow felt like an enemy, like the chattering of teeth or the whisper of one of those rakkens blades.

"Yes-yes. Does not like the presence of magical man-filth." Rackjack pushed up on two feet, his nose twitching as he sniffed the air. "Plus, musked him good-well. Will not deceive."

"What is a general doing down here anyway, I wonder?" Cassius' words carried a question Rooster had been thinking since they'd been sent on this mission. The tombs hardly seemed a place of interest for a Shoman general.

"Maybe he'll tell us when we find him," Rooster said sarcastically. "I'm sure he'll be overjoyed that we've come all this way to ruin his plans."

"Your sarcasm is unwarranted, Rooster," Cassius said from behind him.

"How ever will we get through this dark place without a little humor?" Rooster whispered. "Tell us, Rackjack, how far down is this Hiss intending to take us?"

Rackjack squeaked, and out of the darkness came a reply.

"Not much further, but we must hurry-scamper. General using jinn for dark magic-summoning. Says he is trying to create portal-door."

Rooster's concern was mirrored on Cassius' face when he glanced back, and they hurried down the hall after Rackjack until they were deep within the tomb. The further they went in, the more Rooster felt it; it was like the air was being pulled towards something. The taste of magic was so strong it sat tangibly on Rooster's tongue, and they approached a room that seemed to be full of chattering rats and someone speaking low in tongues.

The hair on the back of Rooster's neck stood up. He thought it might be more of Cassius' spirits, but none of them presented themselves. He would have preferred their company to whatever they were about to walk into.

"Shhh. Quiet-silence," Rackjack whispered, pressing a paw to his mouth. Rooster longed to retort, as he often did when one of the Misfits demanded things that only made sense, but he stayed his tongue. Something dark stitched itself in the air, something wicked. If the spirits were terrified, Rooster had no right to his courage.

Cold seeped into his palm as he pressed it to the wall, drawing further into the shadows as if they would shield him from detection. He heard Cassius draw close behind him. When a small rock went scuttling across the floor, Rooster glanced back with a scowl.

"Linda's quieter than you are."

Cassius frowned. "My armor is not exactly the easiest to sneak around in. Nothing like the leather you wear." It was true. Rooster's leathers were light and easy to maneuver in, nothing like the metal that Cassius wore to keep him safe on the front lines.

A soft exhale sounded in front of them, ending their quiet argument before it could truly begin. Hiss re-materialized from the shadows, his dark eyes glittering in the torchlight. He gestured to the room down the hall with his dark paw, squeaking quietly at Rackjack.

"Magic man-filth in there," Rackjack whispered. "Surrounded by rakken-rats. Hiss-rat does not think we can go in there. Will be eaten-ripped apart."

"Ask him how the rakken got here," Rooster said.

Rackjack turned back to Hiss, and the hallway of the tomb became a mantra of hushed chittering. The fur on the back of Rackjack's neck between his armor stood on end, and he hissed, scampering backwards away from the door.

"Magic man-filth has opened door-door to Shoma. Rakken-rats come through there. Going to use them to flood city-streets."

"Then we must stop them," Cassius said sharply. "If we allow them to bleed into the city, the war will be lost."

"What will the three—er, four, if this one doesn't stab us in the back the moment we turn it to him," Rooster said, gazing sidelong at Hiss with a sense of uncertainty, "be able to do against a room full of rakken, a Shoman general, and his jinn?" Rooster shook his head, his stomach twisting in knots. "No, I think we are in way over our heads. Our best bet is to retreat, come up with a plan, and then come back."

"I am not certain we have the time." Cassius' concern stood on valid grounds, and Rooster raised a hand to tug at his hair in indecision and anxiety. Rackjack looked to him for guidance, and the other rakken, Hiss, eyed them with disgust and suspicion.

A foul smell washed over them, fouler still than the tomb's already unpleasant stench, and Rooster wrinkled his nose. "Rackjack, did you musk again?"

Rackjack nodded repeatedly. "Must-must. Will keep us safe-hidden from harm, yes-yes. Assassin rakken-rats will find us if they haven't already." Hiss spoke quickly and quietly in their language, and Rackjack nodded.

"Too many smell-musks down here. Assassin rakken-rats won't see us now."

"Let me go and take a look then," Rooster uttered, signaling for everyone else to stay behind while he scooted along the wall towards the entrance, where a purple light drenched the room in a soft glow. The low chanting continued, and Rooster took a deep breath before peeking around the corner.

He was met with a horrifying sight.

Just as they had in the dwarf cavern, the rakken crawled over each other in a disgusting rat pile as a Shoman man stood before a large round portal. Next to him was a different kind of rat – bulky, broad, and *massive* as it stood guard. Drool dripped from its teeth. A small lamp sat in the man's left hand, outstretched towards the ceiling. This lamp was unlike Helai's; rather, it was circular in appearance and swirling with vibrant, colorful magic. The lid had been unclasped, and *something was* unfurling from inside and towards the ceiling, where the weight of its presence bore down on Rooster. The chattering of rats rattled around in Rooster's head as rakken poured through the portal, adding to the horrifying pile of rats already making up the room.

If they didn't act fast, they were going to be too late. Cassius was right; they didn't have time.

Sliding away from the door, he looked back at the others. Statues of the dead stood tall against the opposite walls, next to their body's resting place, their eyes unseeing as they stared out, and Rooster studied them quietly for a moment before he turned to Cassius.

"Can the spirits of this place help?"

Cassius blinked, his mouth twisting in hesitation. "I do not like to bend them to my will, but perhaps if they know it is to defend their final resting place..." He trailed off, giving a firm nod as he turned away. "I will return."

As he disappeared back up the stairs, Rooster turned to Rackjack. "We should attack immediately. I'm not sure what that jinn is capable of, but we must hope its magic is being funneled into the portal, which gives you time to deal with the rakken in the room using that," he said, pointing to the metal on Rackjack's arm. "They'll go up in flames before they realize what's going on." His own hand itched for the hilt of his blade, for the feeling of safety it brought when it was unsheathed.

Rackjack nodded quickly while raising his arm in readiness. "Yes-yes," he whispered hoarsely.

Rooster nodded towards Hiss as he sniffed the air, his ears twitching erratically. "Can we trust him?"

Rackjack shook his head. "Never trust rakken-rats. Remember, I told you."

"Then we'll need to do something about him so he can't stab us in the back while we're fighting."

Rackjack's fur bristled as his foul stench wafted over the air once more, and Hiss ducked low to the ground and hissed, his teeth clacking together in rapid succession. He responded quickly to whatever Rackjack told him, then stepped back until he disappeared into the shadows of the tomb.

"Told him to hunt-find the other assassin rats," Rackjack said, turning back towards the door. "Will kill-maim if he comes back."

Rooster nodded, looking into the room once more. It was filling quickly with grotesque, wiggling bodies, and they had no more time. If they were going to act, it needed to be now. Cassius still hadn't returned, but he gave Rackjack a firm nod.

"Now, Rackjack!"

Rackjack rounded the corner as the metal on his arm glowed purple, and flames shot out over the room. Burning flesh and fur burned Rooster's nose, but Rackjack didn't stop, not even when the metal contraption on his arm began to turn white with heat.

The rakken in the room were a maelstrom of surprised bodies, the wails of their anger and despair as they burned alive a chorus that rang throughout the tomb.

"Have to stop," Rackjack yelled, jerking his arm away as the metal tube stopped its steady stream of fire. "Getting too hot."

The loss of his fire was felt the moment it stopped. A wail, so high-pitched in nature Rooster nearly didn't hear it, echoed throughout the tomb. The smell of burning flesh assaulted Rooster, and he gagged, his fingers pressed against the wall. Surely, they were all dead. Surely...

The portal crumbled and collapsed, and a shadow peeled itself from where it had been protecting the general. None of the flames had touched him, or the massive rat that guarded him, and Rooster's gut plummeted in fear as the Shoman general's gaze affixed upon them.

Rooster's sword felt useless in his hand. Several of the rakken nearest the door had died instantly to Rackjack's flames, but many of them were either still on fire or fairly uninjured. Those not on fire flinched away and hissed at those who were, and many fled into a deeper room on the opposite side of Rooster and Rackjack, swallowed by darkness.

"Deplorable," the general hissed, his eyes widening with anger. "This land now belongs to the One."

"Oh, do, uh," Rooster said, steeling himself against his fear and gesturing a thumb behind him, "do the Hestians know that?"

The general growled in rage. "I hope you have grown accustomed to this tomb, for it will be your final resting place." When he gestured, the giant rat shot forward, following his command. A sharp whistle pierced the air, and whatever rakken had survived Rackjack's fire fell into line behind him. Rooster flinched away with Rackjack close behind. They needed to deal with these rakken and then get to the jinn before the general re-opened the portal and called more rakken through.

"Cassius, where are you?" Rooster grunted, ducking beneath a sarcophagus as the giant rat hissed and dragged its elongated claws across the stone. The sound of its nails screeching against it sent a shiver down Rooster's spine, and he lost sight of Rackjack as he struggled to keep clear of the rakken's attacks. Drool fell from the giant rakken's parted jaw as it stared down at Rooster, only for a rock to hit the side of its head as it started towards him. It howled in rage and turned towards the source of where the rock had been thrown, where Rackjack stood tall in defiance.

Several rakken were shoved aside as the giant rat barreled away, leaving Rooster to deal with a sea of rakken soldiers as they separated him from the general, who had turned with the jinn towards the wall where the portal had been. Rooster lashed out with his sword, cutting down a rakken only to have more replace it, and he despaired. There were too many of them, and if the general managed to open that portal again, there would be no hope of killing them all.

As if by some miracle, Cassius materialized from the darkness as if they had been forged for him. He was uncloaked, his fangs bared, and his eyes a mixture of red and black. Two monstrous, black draconic wings stood tall behind him. His cheekbones were peppered with decay.

"The heroes of this hall demand you to leave." Out of the shadows, the spirits of the tomb followed Cassius as if he were their general, leading them into a charge. There was more than there had been at the front of the tomb, and fear no longer stained their expressions, which were now replaced with the hard lines of rage. "You have desecrated their halls with your dark magic and dishonored their memory."

A few spirits passed through Rooster, and he shuddered. It was as if a cold bucket of water had been dumped over his head. They were barely corporeal, but where they left him unharmed, the rakken were slaughtered in droves, pulled apart by wispy fingers. Eyeballs were plucked from skulls, bellies were peeled open, and intestines were pulled out. The spirits did not hold back, and Rooster pressed against the wall, heaving as they slipped by. Rakken blood splattered his skin, his tongue darting out instinctively as a droplet fell on his lower lip.

Rattling laughter echoed from inside the room, bouncing off the walls as it shuddered.

"Foolish." The word was uttered, screamed, whispered, all at once.

With the rakken in front of him dead, Rooster kicked off the wall, reaffirming his grip on his sword as he peered into the room where the general was. The room was splattered with rakken blood and burnt corpses, but all the flames had extinguished, with only a haze of smoke that clung to the air. The jinn remained tucked above the general's shoulder, and Rooster blinked as the spirits rushed him all at once, only for a flare of magic to burst from the jinn and send the spirits sailing back. They slammed into the walls and dissipated, leaving behind a vague outline of human visages where they had struck the wall.

So much for their aid.

The general glowered at them in rage as the jinn lowered itself to the ground. Two shadowy feet materialized as they touched the bloody floor, and its form went from translucent to something semi-solid even though Rooster's mind couldn't make sense of it. Its skin was slick, its shape almost humanoid, but it kept shifting through forms as if it couldn't decide how to present itself. Smoke that unfurled from its neck tethered it to the lamp still in the general's hand. It flickered between two stone statues carved in the likeness of a man and a woman. "You cannot banish me, not after I have been called forth to this plane," the jinn whispered, its sharp teeth etching into the smoke of its skin. Pain pricked the corners of Rooster's face as if he were being pinched. "One more wish, and I could've been free," the jinn cried angrily, its voice hoarse and echoing as it lashed out, grabbed Rooster by the throat, and threw him against the wall.

He hit the wall hard, his head ringing as he moaned in pain. His breathing became ragged. Had he broken a rib? *No*, he thought as he pressed a hand to his rib cage and winced, *just bruised*. Still, the force with which he'd been thrown left him dazed and confused, a muddle of disjointed thoughts as he stared up at the shadowy form in front of him.

The jinn melted away until it was naught but tooth and claw. The air whooshed in a flurry of activity as the jinn pushed Rooster forcibly against the wall and lifted him towards the ceiling.

"Ah, fuck. You got me," Rooster said, grimacing as the movement caused his ribs to scream in protest. He tasted something sharp and metallic on his tongue; his lips were damp. His mind fought against defeat, Igraine's face at the forefront of his mind.

I have to survive. I have to survive for her.

But the world went dark anyway.

SIXTEEN
RACKJACK

Rackjack slipped into an empty room just as the rat ogre came crashing past the door, enraged by the rock Rackjack had struck him with. It forced itself through the doorway, its fingers peeling away crumbling rock as it crashed into the room and halted to a stop just before Rackjack, where it roared.

Spittle flew into his face as he raised his head to greet the expression of the giant rat ogre. Rat ogres were rare, so much so even Rackjack had been uncertain of their existence up until now. He barely even noticed the pain that coursed through him, not when the thought of bending a rat ogre to his will was too tempting to ignore.

"Honor duel," he rasped, but the rat ogre did not seem to hear him as he swiped at Rackjack's head. Rackjack ducked just in time, and the rat ogre's claws scraped against the wall. He pushed away from the wall, rolling to his feet, but he stumbled when his wooden leg refused to cooperate. He musked, his stench ripening in the air, but that only seemed to enrage the beast as he rose on two legs and roared. Outside of the room, spirits piled up in the halls, and Rackjack's heart screamed at him to leave and check to make sure Carter-filth was okay. The rat ogre was blocking the way, though, and Rackjack, tried as he might, could not get past.

He would need to figure out a way to either kill the rat ogre or get him to submit.

The rat ogre charged, and Rackjack was only barely able to launch himself out of the way as the rat ogre crashed into the wall behind him before howling in pain.

"Keep. Still," the rat ogre shouted. He managed to grab Rackjack's wooden leg before he could scurry away. A crunching sound crashed around the room as the rat ogre bit into Rackjack's prosthesis and chewed it clean off, the wood splintering in the rat ogre's mouth. It didn't hurt Rackjack, but the movement was jarring enough to send him into a flurry of panic. Tugging himself away, he wrangled the last piece of draugmin he had and shoved it into his mouth.

He shuddered as the magic of the draugmin took hold of him. It sank into his skin and unlocked the barriers that kept his body safe from magical harm. He was stronger and faster but knew that if he went too far, his body would be damaged beyond repair. He had to be careful, but as the magic flowed through him, a dark thought tempted him: *Let go.*

The rat ogre was no match as Rackjack's magic danced at the edges of his fingers, a flourish of purple energy that lit his eyes up. Despite his inability to stand, he found that he didn't need to as magic swelled in the air, as he felt the breath of Rat-King at his neck. He had his god's blessing, so he did what the magic wanted. He let go.

The rat ogre howled as the magic forced him down. It held him there until he submitted, his howls soothing until they were naught but soft whimpers. Rackjack's chest heaved as he dragged himself forward, his broken prosthesis useless. He'd have to seek Tantien's aid in forging a new, better one, one that would not easily be taken from him.

"Shh, quiet, rakken-rat," he cooed as his hand reached out to rest on the rat ogre's head. "Rackjack-rat will take care of you now, yes-yes." The beast breathed shallowly with quick breaths, its eyes looking up at Rackjack fearfully. Perhaps the Shoman general had not treated this war beast correctly. Rackjack hoped to be better.

"Fight for me, will promise to give you food to eat-feast." As the magic sang through him, Rackjack pressed his paw into the war beast's head. The rat ogre quickly disappeared behind a flash of purple light, then reappeared as an illusion of a small rat, one of many commonly seen scurrying through a city.

"I shall call you Kratch-rat," Rackjack rasped, beckoning for the rat. Kratch scampered forward obediently, and Rackjack pulled a small piece of flesh from one of the nearby rakken corpses, offering it to Kratch as he nestled into Rackjack's fur.

Kratch lashed out to snatch the piece of flesh, and as he nibbled it down, Rackjack turned back towards the door, hopeful in his magic-induced state that it wasn't too late for him to help Cassius and Carter-filth.

SEVENTEEN
INTOH

The hydra was as terrifying as it had been the first time Intoh had seen her from the crow's nest of that travel ship they'd chartered to Halvdarc.

"Ah, it looks like you be needin' some assistance, Tantien!" Delroy shouted from the deck of his ship. The Crimson Nightshade was about as large as the Firebrand only ten times more terrifying in appearance, with torn black sails and deep-red cherry wood, with what looked like a white skeletal structure that hugged the front where the figurehead should be. The flag, a skull with vampire fangs, fluttered wildly in the wind, and

Delroy's sailors were silent as they disappeared into a cluster of bats or waited for the ship to be close enough to board an enemy ship.

"Know him?" Intoh asked, his tone tinged with suspicion. Delroy had called Tantien by name, and the eldrasi was known for keeping secrets. He still didn't trust Delroy, not like he trusted the Misfits, and Tantien knowing him, even if he was aiding in their battles, made him wary.

Tantien laughed as he cut down a soldier who attempted to veer away from his wrath. "One day you'll trust me, Intoh! I'm on your side." Intoh called water up from the side of the ship and forced it down another soldier's throat, drowning him before he could strike down one of the eldrasi sailors. Tantien nodded wordlessly in thanks, and Intoh frowned.

"Not that I don't trust you," he said. "Just curious."

Khal and Sode stabbed at soldiers attempting to swing across from their ships, and Tantien sighed, his smile turning grim as the laughter died on his tongue.

"Everyone knows of Delroy Greaves, the captain of the sea vampires."

"Dat's no way ta treat an old friend, yeah?" Delroy materialized beside Tantien, his grin wicked and sharp. Fangs hung from parted lips as his eyes glowed in the faint light of the threatening storm. His sunken cheeks, decaying skin, and lack of nose reminded Intoh just how much Cassius tucked his vampirism away behind his illusion. The vampire stood tall in his dark coat, thick locs tucked neatly under his black hat. He radiated so much dark, dead energy that Intoh's skin crawled, his magic desperate to flinch away from Delroy's aura. Another dark part of him craved to learn more. Perhaps necromancy *was* the key he'd been looking for.

"To what do I owe the pleasure?" Tantien asked. "Have you offered your allegiance against our common enemy?"

Delroy sidestepped an approaching soldier, his fangs bared as he plucked the soldier by the back of the head and bit down on his neck. The soldier thrashed as blood cascaded between Delroy's lips. He drank deeply until the soldier's eyes rolled in the back of his head, and he went limp. "I hear yer planning a rescue mission. You know my sister is Cap'n Carta Wingmon's rum runna." Delroy's eyes glowed darkly as the air thinned around him. Intoh's lungs became harder to fill, and he gulped as the ship lurched. The hydra known as Sollatso swam past, two of her heads breaching the surface as she assaulted a few nearby ships. Their screams of terror cast out amidst the chaos of battle. Intoh wondered if she had taken care of the jinn, or if it had disappeared after its master's wish had been granted. Either way, it was nowhere to be seen, and Intoh's unease grew.

A Shoman soldier stabbed one of the vampires through the stomach, and the vampire grinned, her smile bloody and fanged as she reached out and grabbed the Shoman soldier by the throat and lifted him up into the air. The soldier scrambled in a panic as his khopesh clamored to the ground, and the vampire slammed the soldier to the ground and began feasting on his neck. He stopped thrashing within a few seconds, his leg twitching as the vampire drank his blood.

It was much of the same everywhere Intoh turned. Delroy's vampires did not fight like Cassius, who fought deliberately and with calculation. These vampires fought with reckless abandon, like they did not fear their own mortality, and while the soldiers of Shoma fought valiantly, they stood no chance. Intoh watched several vampires disappear into a flurry of bats that shot towards another ship, where they materialized on the deck and cut down soldiers.

Stop. It was naught more than a whisper that shuddered across the back of Intoh's neck, and he curled his fingers around the railing of the Firebrand as a shadow passed overhead.

"Are we to hope to do anything about that?" Itale uttered in horror beside him. Intoh didn't know when the necromancer had approached, the air frigid surrounding him, and Intoh looked over and followed his gaze upwards.

A dragon-jinn sailed overhead. It bore no wings to speak of and it was translucent, like it was more spirit than beast, its long, wiggling body trailing through the air as it roared, its cry loud and quiet all at once. Fire peeled from its open jaw, a flame of brilliant colors, and a line of Hestian ships burst into flames where it had struck.

Heat brushed against Intoh's face as Tantien's shouting echoed in the background, dulled by a ringing in Intoh's ears. His heart in his throat, he grew dizzy as he was tugged around and Tantien's face swam into view.

"Intoh!" Tantien shook his shoulders, his gaze panicked. "We need you." The ship lurched violently as the hydra swam by, and Intoh grabbed the railing again for support as the world returned to him all at once.

"Think hydra can kill jinn?" He asked, turning to Delroy.

The vampire eyed him silently for a moment before nodding. "I do, but da scaly beast knows ta stay away from dem waters lest it get snared by Sollatso's heads."

"Can Sollatso breathe fire?" Intoh asked.

Delroy shook his head. "She is a scaly beast of da sea, boy. If she is able ta breathe fire, she has never done it before."

An idea began forming in Intoh's mind. It was a foolish idea, one that wouldn't work if the jinn was able to deny his magic, but it was all they had.

"Keep Firebrand from sinking," Intoh said, hurrying towards the mast. "Don't let us drown."

"What have you got planned, Intoh? A little insight would be nice," Tantien called out, but Intoh ignored him, as he ignored everyone. He didn't need Tantien to know the plan. He just needed Tantien to keep the ship from sinking while he dealt with the jinn.

"Also, make sure hydra stays close. Tell her to be ready," Intoh called over his shoulder as he slipped his hands through the loops of the ladder and began to ascend towards the crow's nest. The wind howled, whipping Intoh's hair around his face as he clung to the ladder and dragged himself into the nest. The jinn flew overhead, and below, Sollatso waited, several of her heads snapping at each other in frustration.

Intoh exhaled slowly, dragging himself to his feet and taking care not to let the wind topple over the side of the crow's nest. The Shoma ships were overwhelming what Hestian ships had survived the jinn's attacks, and even with the vampires' aid, they were losing.

An ache settled low in Intoh's belly, and he shivered as he called to his magic and he lashed out, attempting to cling to any part of the jinn that would catch. From what he gathered from Helai's explanations and his readings, jinn were of a different plane, a manifestation of magic in its purest form. If he could latch onto it...

The jinn howled in rage, sensing Intoh's presence immediately. The jinn's presence washed over Intoh, pressing against him, forcing a headache to immediately form in Intoh's temples. But Intoh didn't relent, reaching out with his mind to dig into the jinn's dragon-like belly and tug as hard as he could towards the sea.

The jinn was vastly stronger than anything Intoh had ever encountered, save for perhaps Rhavna. It barely budged from where Intoh pulled, and it turned to fix its gaze on him as Tantien and the others shouted below. Intoh panted, his heart in his throat as the jinn sailed towards him, its jaw open as vibrant fire licked the back of its throat.

Intoh despaired. He wasn't strong enough.

Let go.

It was softly spoken, no louder than a whisper that caressed the cusp of his ear as he was flooded with magic, as wind collected in his palm and shot outwards. The jinn jerked and was pushed towards the sea, where Sollatso reached up with three heads and pierced the jinn's belly with her teeth. She dragged it, screaming, beneath the waves as she ripped it apart.

All the wind in the area died as the jinn did. The tides were beginning to change; Hestia was regaining control of the sea as the Shoma fleet had no jinn to aid their attacks. It was a welcomed sight, and a sight Intoh wasn't sure they would have seen had Delroy's hydra not killed the jinn. Intoh slumped against the mast, his ears ringing as exhaustion stole his breath away. He would need to sleep off the overuse of magic for some time, his hands shaking violently as he retreated down to the deck of the ship.

Tantien's hand gripped the railing of his ship as his gryphon sailed overhead, his calls echoing throughout the battlefield as Tantien's crew cut down the last of the Shoman soldiers that had made their way aboard the Firebrand.

Khal and Sode approached, covered in blood and water. They were both silent and free of injury, and Intoh was glad for it. Even Itale, his eyes normal and his magic absent, was uninjured as he grasped his chest, heaving. Dark circles etched the skin under his eyes, but he was triumphant as the corpses he'd reanimated fell dead against the deck of the ship.

"I wish Cassius had been here to see that," he whispered, his voice tinged with exhaustion. The tips of his fingers were stained black, and darkness slithered through the veins in his cheeks, but the color quickly disappeared as Intoh smiled and patted Itale on the back.

"Would have been very proud. Certain of it," he said. Cassius had been working with Itale since they'd returned to Volendam, teaching him how to control his necromancy. Intoh had taken an interest, and Cassius had explained that necromancy was a chaotic magic that often tried to consume its wielder before they could reach a certain age. If left unchecked, the mortality rate was high.

Itale beamed. "You think?"

"You hide behind dem illusions, boy." Intoh wasn't sure when Delroy had approached them, but his words forced him to flinch. Khal and Sode raised their spears. Khal's frills shot out as he hissed in warning, and Sode grunted, pointing his spear in Delroy's direction.

"Step no closer, Dead Walker." The words came out of Khal's and Sode's mouths simultaneously, and Delroy's grin was anything but kind as he bared his teeth and held up his hands. The stench of decay and death wafted over, and Intoh crinkled his nose.

"I mean da scaly one no 'arm," he said, his eyes flashing dangerously. "But if you don't remove your spears from my vicinity, I will not hesitate to make you *bleed*."

Tension infected the air, and Tantien moved forward, clasping a hand on Delroy's shoulder and smiling nervously. "I won't tolerate such violence onboard my ship, and I can assure both parties involved that there is no need. Delroy's mercy is nonexistent, but he has no quarrels with anyone here."

"It's okay, Sode. Khal." Intoh reached out to assure both of them that he faced no dangers with Delroy, and they slowly lowered their weapons. The state of their distrust did not change, and they guarded Intoh with unyielding loyalty.

"What do you call yourself, hm?" Delroy stepped back to show good faith, and Tantien's hand fell to his side. "Da Misfits, is dat it? Where are da others? I have some information I'd like ta share with da Misfits and der crew."

Intoh's heart thundered in his throat. The last time Delroy had spoken to them, he'd come with a warning: a dead dragon was waking in the heart of Lyvira. The news had been unsettling, especially after all of the cult activity and the resurrection of Rhavna in the heart of the Welker Estate.

"Out fighting," Intoh said, gesturing to the smoking city. "Can't talk until it is done."

"I can take my friend out over the city and see how the war is faring on the land front," Tantien said, gesturing to the passing gryphon.

"What about fight here?" Intoh said, his heart plummeting into his stomach.

"Look around," Delroy said, his hand moving about the battlefield. "It has already been won, ya?"

Delroy was right. What enemy remained stood upon ruined ships or had turned to retreat, only to be assailed by the pursuit of Hestian ships. The water was a graveyard of desecrated ships as Sollatso pushed through to settle near the Firebrand. Two of her heads fought each other, the gleam of their scales shining brightly in the daylight as a third came to rest near Delroy, who pressed a decaying hand to her snout. Each head had four eyes, two large ones with two smaller ones behind, and they all eyed Intoh with a fierce intelligence as she opened her mouth wide and revealed several rows of sharp teeth. The jinn was nowhere to be seen. Intoh wasn't sure if that meant Sollatso had taken care of it or if it had returned to the general's lamp.

Sode and Khal did not flinch from the hydra, and Intoh's chest swelled at the lengths they would go to for their loyalty. Would they truly die for him? Perhaps, but his growing fondness of their company made him disinclined to find out.

"Will keep watchful eye over ship." Intoh stilled, his heart swimming with conflicting emotions. "You make sure my friends are okay. Worry about Linda; they get too excited about combat."

Tantien gave a firm but silent nod as he looked up to the sky. A gentle, haunting melody passed his lips, the sound digging at a deep, innate part of Intoh that compelled him to draw closer.

The gryphon responded immediately, banking left around the mast of a nearby ship and landing gracefully upon the front of the Firebrand. He eyed Sollatso with contempt, his wings flapping in distress, but Tantien's soft words were soothing enough for him to settle. Intoh hadn't noticed it from far away, but the gryphon had a saddle, one that seated Tantien comfortably as he sheathed his hammer to a loop on the saddle and swung his leg up.

Calling down to several of the eldrasi sailors, he gave an arrogant smile to Intoh and Delroy. "I will report back as soon as I am able." As his gryphon pushed off the ship, Intoh raised a hand to quiet the air that buffeted against them, noticing Itale watching Tantien fly away with a look of awe stitched across his face.

"Incredible," Itale murmured, turning back to face Delroy. "You are a vampire."

Delroy grinned, revealing the full extent of his fangs. "Good observation, boy." He turned back to Intoh, his fingers stroking the edge of Sollatso's nose as he pondered, his eyes glazed in thought.

"When da Misfits are freed, tell dem I will be waiting aboard my ship ta speak ta dem. It be very urgent, so make sure dey don't delay." His words were mingled with a threatening tone, and Intoh scowled, thinking of defying him. They shouldn't be working with the likes of him. Vampire pirates were a common problem for his people, craving the trade the drikoty often ferried from their homeland to the eldrasi island of Míradan. How were they going to trust the word of a pirate, especially a pirate captain?

But still, he nodded.

What choice did they have?

EIGHTEEN

LINDA

The sun had officially risen as dawn broke, shattering the cover of darkness that Linda had been relying on as they made their way through the trees back towards the city. War was rampant in the distance, and Linda clung to *Volroth* with tight hands, their heart begging for combat.

Soon, they promised it. Their blood sang for it. Linda quivered with their promise.

They'd been walking for quite some time and could only hope that Helai was alright. *Should have figured out a way to go with her*, Linda thought sullenly. They didn't like the thought of Helai somewhere out there all alone, especially when Helai had seemed so distraught over Massoud.

They hoped Massoud was alright too. If anyone knew how to ensure his survival, it was Helai. Linda had never met anyone more committed to fulfilling their wishes than her.

The tree line parted, and Linda veered off to the right, deciding to stay near the edges of the battle. They were confident in their combat abilities but did not want to test its limits.

Peering out at the fields before the walls of Alavae, Linda hummed quietly. They were likely still hours out from the city, and a small sea of enemies fought between them. They were going to have to be crafty and quiet if they were going to make it back unscathed.

"Linda?"

Linda lifted their head, overjoyed as a lone dwarf materialized from the wood, only it wasn't just any dwarf.

"Drithan?" Linda pondered. "What doing here? Where are others?"

Drithan *hmphed*, pressing his hand to the back of his head as he twirled an axe in his right hand. He was drenched in mud and gore, like he had been fighting for some time, but Linda was happy to see him uninjured. He drew close enough for Linda to see his sheepish expression, and his cheeks blossomed red beneath his beard. "I was... well, you see..." He coughed. "Have you seen Helai? The other dwarves, they fight at the gate."

"She went away on horse," Linda explained. "Must get back to the city. Said she would meet me back there."

"Linda," Drithan said, surprised. "You're speaking in fuller sentences."

Linda's chest swelled with pride as a hand reached up to brush against the gold amulet in the middle of their tooth necklace, but nearby shouting forced them both to fall into battle-ready stances.

A small unit of Shoman soldiers approached them on foot. One of them suffered from shallow wounds, but they all approached with enough vigor to sneer and wield their khopeshes as they flung themselves forward with reckless abandon.

Linda and Drithan met them straight on, standing side by side. It was obvious that Drithan did better with ranged weapons, but his hesitation was lost on Linda as they shot forward, meeting three enemies at once.

"What's a krok'ida doing in Alavae?" one said. He spoke in Shoman, but the undercurrent of the words were spoken in Drikoytian.

"It matters little! General Sarem will surely reward the person that brings back this beast's head," another cried, looking Linda up and down. "Their scales would make for good armor."

Linda's heart was a wild animal in their chest as they raised their hammer over their head, but a low cry forced them to pause. They turned to see Drithan on the ground, his axe just out of reach as a Shoman soldier pressed his foot into the crook of Drithan's elbow and pinned it to the ground. No matter how much he squirmed, he could not free himself from the soldier as he raised his khopesh to bring it down.

"No!" Linda howled, fear coursing through them so quickly they grew dizzy, then blind. White, they were surrounded by so much white. The soldier was going to kill Drithan. They couldn't let that happen.

They ambled forward without seeing, struggling against a weight that pressed in around them until they had fallen to their knees, their cries echoing out to the vast void of endless white.

It was so bright, the second membrane on their eye blinked, trying to shield their eyes from the vibrancy of it all.

Lindrz'kt.

The voice washed over Linda like a warm summer's day, like the slow crawl of heat over a water's edge. It sank into their skin like they often sank into water, beckoning sleep. What were they doing? They couldn't seem to remember…

The white fog cleared like the sun's rays had finally chased away the threat of rain. Before Linda stood a dragon, one so large that they struggled to comprehend where the dragon ended. It was crocodilian in nature, with a long, thin snout and several jagged teeth that clung to the sides of its maw. Its scales were a dusting of orange and brilliant gold, and atop its head sat a sunbeam of horns that crested between two massive eyes that stared down at Linda through amber hues. Wings jutted out of its back, almost translucent in nature, as if they carried the sun within them. They were painful to look at, so Linda refocused on the dragon's face, their mouth parting in awe.

Somehow, they knew they stood in the presence of a god.

The dragon did not say anything else, and Linda could not move from where they stood no matter how hard they tried, not even when the memories slowly returned. That was right. They were saving Drithan. They had to save Drithan!

"Let me go," they growled, tilting their face up towards the great maw of the dragon. "Must save my friend."

You dare speak in the presence of Ikotia, Chosen?

His words rattled against Linda's brain, pressing against their mind as if testing Linda's sheer will. Linda was stronger. Linda had always been stronger. One day, long ago, they'd promised themself that they'd grow so big they'd swallow the sun and use its fire to burn down their enemies.

Linda pushed back, parting their maw to unleash a roar. The sound echoed throughout the endless white, and Ikotia cocked his head as a rush of amusement washed over Linda.

Good, Ikotia said, his mind melding with Linda's as he lowered his head, pressing the bottom of his chin to the top of Linda's head. *You are ready.*

As the dragon touched Linda, fire washed through their veins and licked the underside of their scales. They were unmade and reforged, torn apart, and put back together again. Linda couldn't remember crying out or the tears that fell from their face, but both happened simultaneously as they were tugged away, Ikotia watching with knowing eyes.

Soon, you will return to your homeland, and you will be tested.

Linda wanted to call out, *What do you mean?* but then they were back in the field, the soldier still over Drithan, with his khopesh poised and ready to pierce through Drithan's throat.

Linda lashed out like a snake, their teeth clamping down on the soldier's shoulder. The moment their teeth sank in, the soldier became aflame as golden fire flourished through Linda's throat and trailed out the sides of their mouth. The soldier screamed, but Linda's ears echoed with a subtle hum as the fire peeled away at the soldier's skin, and he attempted to pry away from Linda's attacks.

Linda was stronger.

Prying the soldier away from Drithan, Linda flung the soldier to the side and slammed him into the ground, releasing him only because the fire burned their eyes. His screams died as he did, his body curdling until he was naught but bone and ash. Something swam through Linda, an unfamiliar feeling, like they had swallowed a colony of angry bees. It slipped through their blood, igniting it, and Linda pushed themself to their feet, raised their head to the sky, and let out a roar that teared at their throat. Something begged them to let go, so they did, and fire peeled from their mouth and shot into the air. All at once, the feeling left them, and they heaved as they looked down to see Drithan gazing at them with a marveled expression.

"Did you just breathe fire?" he asked, astonished. The rest of the soldiers were dead, and they were granted a momentary reprieve from the fighting.

Linda reached out a hand and held very still as Drithan pulled himself to his feet.

"Think so," Linda said uncertainly. "Don't know how. Think…" They hesitated. Would Drithan even believe they had seen a god? No, better keep that to themself until they could speak with Intoh.

They shook their head. "Never mind."

Drithan patted Linda on the arm, his fingers rough against their scales. "Thank you." His words were injected with gratitude, and it made warmth seep through Linda, the same warmth they felt when they got to be around the Misfits.

They reached up and placed their hand gently atop Drithan's head. "Good, sir, good."

Drithan leaned down to pick up his axe, and Linda did the same with *Volroth*, uncertain when they had dropped it. Their blood still sang, like lightning was coursing through it. Was this how Intoh felt all the time? How did he focus on anything else?

"Alone?" Linda asked. "Said there are other dwarves?"

Drithan nodded, gesturing towards the city. "It took some time for us to arrive, but King Stoneheart sent a small unit of dwarves to aid."

"Kind of him."

Drithan smiled through his beard, bringing his axe down on the neck of a soldier still choking on his own blood. The soldier stilled, and Drithan pried his axe away. "Our king still hasn't forgotten your aid. Plus, Hestia's downfall to Shoma would not be good for the dwarven kingdoms."

Linda didn't understand the intricacies of human politics – or dwarven ones, for that matter, so they just nodded.

"Linda, *Drithan*?" Helai's voice called out from the tree line as she approached on horseback, Massoud at her back. It was as if some sort of miracle had struck him. Linda was certain he had not been breathing when they had handed him off to Helai, but here he was now, and he was conscious even. Linda burned with curiosity as the horse snorted and pawed at the ground at their approach.

"He not dead!" Linda shouted as the horse wove in circles. Try as she might, Helai couldn't get the horse to settle, so she and Massoud dismounted, and the horse bolted. Helai's eyes kept darting between Linda and Drithan, who seemed at a sudden loss for words.

"Alas, it takes a lot more than that to kill the infamous Massoud Al'Bassar," Massoud exclaimed, tossing his arms out in dramatics. Other than the exhausted look in his eye and his desperate need for a bath, he looked entirely uninjured.

"Yes, I, ah, will explain later," Helai said simply, her gaze flickering to Massoud quickly before she gestured between them. "Linda, Drithan, this is my brother, Massoud. Well, not really my brother but close enough to call him one."

"Linda, eh? Helai, when you mentioned Linda, a krok'ida wasn't what I expected."

Massoud coughed and swayed, and Helai caught him, her eyes darting towards Drithan and Linda. Perhaps he wasn't as uninjured as Linda thought.

"Let's head towards the northern city gate; it is where the other rangers are," Drithan replied gruffly, turning on his heel and gesturing to the city. "We'll find Obrand there. He'll be happy to see you both alive."

Linda twirled *Volroth* in their hands, their belly humming with anticipation as they all started towards the city. Surely there was more fighting to be had.

Linda was ready for it.

NINETEEN
CASSIUS

The moment Rooster had slammed against the wall, Cassius had a sudden thought. Rackjack had been dragged away, and Cassius had no time to seek out his wellbeing. He had to hope Rackjack knew how to take care of himself until Rooster was safe.

"Jinn, if I wish for you, your shackles will then be broken, yes?" Cassius called out.

The jinn turned, the shadowy form of its hand still pressed against Rooster, holding him in place. "Yes," it uttered, a whisper that trailed through the hall, etching into the curve of Cassius' ear. "So long as you are willing to bear the weight of it." Long, sharp teeth appeared where its mouth should be, and Cassius' mind rebelled as if it couldn't comprehend the jinn's appearance. It was strange to think they'd been traveling with one all this time, strapped to Helai's belt.

"You must hold my lamp," it instructed, and Cassius followed its shadowy hand as it released Rooster. He slumped to the floor, his head falling to the side, and Rackjack darted back out of the room he'd been dragged into. He folded his body around Rooster's unconscious one.

Cassius moved over to the lamp, studying it with mild interest. It was prettier than Helai's, and Cassius knelt and picked it up, ignoring the spike of pain that shot through his arm where the gun and lance resided. *Strange*, he thought. Perhaps the jinn's magic did not like the magic of Khoros' weapons. He tightened his hold on it regardless and shuddered as the jinn's magic washed over him.

A dark thought came to him: he could wish for his humanity back. A part of him had always longed to be freed of the burden of vampirism, but no. The jinn would simply give it back to him, and old age would catch up and turn him to ash and bone. *Wish for the battle to be won, for the generals to die.* It came to him, the wish humming at the back of his throat, but then his eyes locked onto Rooster.

"I want you to heal him."

The jinn gasped, a sharp inhale that whistled through the air. Its shadowy hand rose and pointed. "You must *wish* it."

"I wish for you to heal him."

The air became heavy and light all at once, and the jinn's essence was liberated from the lamp as it sighed, grew, and then flung itself from the tomb's halls, leaving behind nothing but the echoes of a whistle that hurt Cassius' ears as it rattled the metal cages that surrounded the torches on the walls.

Cassius dropped the lamp, which was now black and empty of the earlier vibrant colors that had swirled at its center, and sheathed his sword. One or two spirits still haunted the halls, their distress clearly not sated. But Cassius didn't know how to help them, so he left them alone.

Cassius turned his attention to Rackjack, who was still curled over Rooster, and Cassius' nostrils flared as his gaze fell on the rakken's maimed leg. His wooden prosthesis was gone, chewed down to the nub at his hip.

"Rackjack, are you hurt? What happened?"

"Fought war beast. Won, but he took my leg-paw," Rackjack protested. His heart, usually extremely fast, had slowed. "Must see Tantien-filth as soon as possible. Need bell at top of tower. Will have him make me new leg-paw."

Exasperation tinged Cassius' expression. "You are not fit to climb all that way. Wait here with Rooster." After inspecting Rooster and being convinced he had not been seriously injured by the jinn, Cassius left the bottom of the crypts, where he noted the general had died, ravaged by weeping wounds as his lifeless body sat slumped against a wall. When he reached the top of the stairs, he was greeted with a massacre of rakken bodies that were spilled out across the marble. Entrails strung throughout the room, and it looked as if some of the corpses had been fed upon, much like the corpses when they'd entered. The stench made Cassius' eyes water, and he hurried on.

It did not take him long to climb up to the bell Rackjack had wanted to seek out in the first place, but it was entirely too large and heavy for Cassius to bring with him.

"We will have to come back for it if there is time," Cassius said upon his return. Rackjack had pressed himself protectively against Rooster, and his eyes were shut. Had it not been the steady rise and fall of his chest or Cassius' vampiric hearing, he might have thought the rakken was dead.

"Very important to me-me," he said as he opened his eyes.

"For now, we need to get out of here. We'll come back with help. Are you able to walk? I will have to carry Rooster."

After a moment, Rackjack nodded. "Can walk-crawl on all fours."

Cassius pulled Rooster into his arms and turned. *Khoros guide me should any enemies present themselves at the stairs.*

The tomb was silent, thankfully so, but every shuffle of movement detected by Cassius' heightened sense of hearing set him on edge.

They hurried out of the tomb and were met with the glare of the sun. Cassius squinted in irritation as a headache pierced his skull, and he groaned, hugging Rooster close as they strode forward into the ruined street. Dust and stone collected over the cobbled road, and a loud melodic note sounded overhead as Tantien's gryphon flew by, her wings outstretched.

"Rackjack," Cassius hissed, turning back to see Rackjack still in his rakken form. "Your ring before someone sees you and mistakes you for the enemy."

Rackjack plucked it from his pocket and threaded it through the hair at his chin. He was a dwarf once more by the time Tantien drew close enough to see his face. They landed before them, the sharp expression of the captain's gryphon begging for someone to intimidate. Rackjack leaned heavily against the crypt for support, his mouth drawn into a thin line beneath his beard.

"The general of this city told me I would be able to find you here and that Linda and Helai went to infiltrate a—" He paused, his face paling when he saw Rooster. "Is he okay?" His gaze trailed to Rackjack and his missing leg. "What happened here?"

Cassius nodded. "Rooster thought he could taunt a jinn. Rackjack will be in dire need of a new prosthesis the moment we are safe from this battle."

"Killed a war beast," Rackjack explained, rubbing the back of his neck nervously. It was only then that Cassius noted a small rat wiggling in Rackjack's beard near his neck, and he scowled in disgust. "Look worse than is."

"Do you have room for them?" Cassius asked, drawing Tantien's attention back to him.

Tantien nodded. "Of course, though... I do not think he will be able to carry all of you."

"I don't need a ride," Cassius said. Tantien looked at Rackjack.

"Take Carter-filth. Will stay with Cassius-filth," Rackjack said. "Carter-filth more important, yes-yes."

"Right, then. Careful not to spook my friend here. He will peck an eye out if you offend her." As Tantien gestured him over, a loud explosion sounded from the other side of the wall before an unholy, high-pitched shriek echoed throughout the city.

"Hurry now!" Cassius lifted Rooster to Tantien.

He turned his gryphon back towards the way he'd come. "You sure the two of you will be okay?" he asked, only patting the gryphon's side to urge him forward when Cassius nodded.

"Just take Rooster to safety. We're going to go help at the wall."

Rackjack shuddered violently as Tantien and his gryphon took off, sailing towards the inner city where it was safest. Cassius wasted little time, flinging his hand out and urging the will of his pegasus.

Fírnster rose from the ground like a horse carved from darkness. Under the guise of his illusion, he was beautiful, large enough to carry Cassius and

Rackjack with ease, his wings feathered and full. He pawed at the ground and tossed his mane back.

"Hurry now, Rackjack," Cassius said, helping him mount before he strapped his shield to Fírnster's side and tugged himself up in front of Rackjack. Fírnster breathed slowly beneath him, and he offered the pegasus a firm pat of affection before clicking his tongue and urging him forward.

Rackjack's arm slipped around Cassius' middle as they took off, and Fírnster gained enough speed to take off, buffeting the ground with the flap of his wings. The city, even in its ruined state, was gorgeous as they flew above it. The fighting continued, but it finally seemed as if the Hestians were gaining ground. With at least one of their generals dead, Cassius could only hope Linda and Helai were successful as well, and then the army would collapse.

Off in the distance, Tantien's gryphon soared out towards the sea, where a plethora of ships lay in ruin. Hestia's colors sailed victorious, and Cassius' stomach rolled at the sight of Delroy's flags. His visit could never bring good news.

It was liberating, being so high up that the world could not touch him. His own wings begged to be released from the prison of his back, and he couldn't chase the smile from forging on his lips as Fírnster pushed forward, banking over the two warring armies.

With no generals to lead them, the Shoman soldiers were attempting to retreat, scrambling to defend themselves as the Hestian knights pushed forward, slaughtering without mercy. The plains set before Alavae were awash with red, so much blood that Cassius could smell the barest hint of it calling to his vampirism even from where they flew.

"Rackjack, I—" His words were cut off as something hard struck him in the side of the head, flinging him from Fírnster. The pain that flourished across his skull was excruciating, and the wind curled around him as he plummeted, falling towards the earth.

Don't panic. Think. Look around. Find Fírnster and Rackjack.

His thoughts were jumbled as he blinked away the pain and looked around, noting Rackjack was also free falling, and Fírnster was nowhere to be found. He must have disappeared the moment Cassius had left his back. The vampire shivered as he tried to call out for Fírnster, but his head was muddled, and his concentration slipped. The edges of his mind threatened unconsciousness, but he managed to fight it off enough to reach out and snag Rackjack's arm, tugging him close. The rakken's fear was palpable, and Cassius groaned as he forced his wings to spread out. His body jerked violently against the wind as their descent slowed.

But it was too late. They were too close to the ground.

Cassius twisted his body around. If he hit the ground first, there may be a chance for both of them. Rackjack fought him, but Cassius' grip was made of steel as he slammed into the blood-soaked ground that dead soldiers surrounded.

The pain was instantaneous. How he remained conscious was a gift from the gods, but in his dim awareness that shuttered in and out of clarity, movement was not an option. It felt like every bone in his body was broken, and he was a vampire just waking from his tomb once more, a prisoner in his own body. He tried to cry out. His eyes were unfocused as blood spurt from his mouth and Rackjack rolled off him, his fingers coming to grab his battered arm.

"Must leave-go. Where enemies are. Can't stay here-here!" He heard Rackjack cry, but he couldn't respond, nor could he move. The world was naught but a maelstrom of pain.

TWENTY
RACKJACK

The pain that coursed through him was but an afterthought as he was immediately met with the rage of a retreating soldier, his khopesh freshly used as it dripped with blood.

The soldier screamed something, and Rackjack hissed, forgetting he was in his dwarf form before raising his arm and calling forth the fire that shot out of the metal weapon strapped there. The soldier went up in flames, and Rackjack ignored his screams as he turned back to Cassius and shook his shoulders.

"Rackjack, we have to leave," Cassius said, blood splattering against his lips as he cried out. "Rackjack, we need to—" He passed out, his head lolling to the side as Rackjack cursed. His language did not have sufficient verbiage to display his frustration as he grabbed Cassius' pauldrons and attempted to tug him across the battlefield, cursing the loss of his leg as he half-dragged himself along too.

The vampire was heavy, and they moved slowly. Despite the battle concluding, the enemies still came at Rackjack with their last attempts, and Rackjack cried out to his god as he struck down the next enemy to approach.

Will owe you favor. Cassius will owe you favor. Need help-aid, please-please.

In his mind's eye, he saw him: Rat-King, his visage a wiggling mass of rats tied together at the tail as they crawled over the rotting form of a dwarf. The god of rakken sat on a brass throne, and the vibrancy of it burned Rackjack's eyes.

One favor, Rat-King rasped, reaching a paw formed from several wiggling bodies out towards Rackjack. *The dead-walker owes me one.*

Rackjack blinked, and he and Cassius were suddenly on the outskirts of the battle, where Linda charged across the battlefield, their war hammer swinging in calculation as they slammed into fleeing soldiers, flinging them several feet away. Helai fought alongside Drithan and another Shoman man. Rackjack thought him to be the enemy until he noted the tattered distress of his clothes and the way Helai slunk around him protectively, pushing back anyone that came too close.

"Linda-filth," Rackjack cried out, his body suddenly riddled with exhaustion. The toll of the war was finally setting in, and Rackjack didn't know how much longer he could go without food and rest.

Linda's head turned, and as they saw him and Cassius, so did the others; they fought their way over. Hestian knights rode around them on horseback, picking off the rest of the Shoman enemy as clouds blotted out the sun, and a steady rain set in, mingling the ground with mud and blood. Cries of the dying rang out over the battlefield, and Rackjack's instincts urged him to feast. His blood called-sang for it, but no. Not until Cassius-filth was safe. Not until the cover of night-dark.

"We have to get to the walls," Helai said. She stank of blood and grime, but Rackjack smelled the faint dusting of ancient magic in her blood, and a white streak of hair now ran down the side of her head, like it had been bleached of all color. The Shoman man with her looked at Rackjack with a sense of curiosity, his eyes tinged with exhaustion.

"Is that a vampire?" the Shoman man asked, gesturing to Cassius' unconscious body. Rackjack had been so focused on saving Cassius' life that he hadn't noticed his illusion had bled away to reveal decayed cheekbones and wings that lay tattered and broken at his back. "Helai, you *loathe* vampires. You have a lot of explaining to do, little sister."

So this was Massoud-filth. The one Linda and Helai had gone to rescue. It made sense, and Rackjack bent low against Cassius, his mouth pulling down into a scowl.

"You will stay away-way." Helai had never given Rackjack her trust. A part of him knew he didn't deserve it, with his kind being the way they were, but her distrust in him made him feel similar to her in kind, so he turned to Linda. "Carry him?"

Linda ambled over, hesitating for a moment before setting their hammer down next to Rackjack. "Keep it safe, and I carry him."

"Is he okay?" Helai asked, her face pinched in concern. "The amount of times we find him in this state..."

"We fell from up there," Rackjack said, pointing towards the sky. Rain cascaded down his face, washing away the blood and mud coating his face, and Helai's expression turned from concern to horror. She pressed her fingers to her mouth, murmuring something in her native tongue, and then met Rackjack's gaze.

"How did you survive?"

Rackjack pointed to Cassius as Linda knelt to pick him up. "Didn't see-spot what hit us. Landed-fell on him. He used his wings to slow." He moved to pick up *Volroth*, hissing softly as if he'd forgotten how heavy the war hammer was, and his own injuries screamed in protest. Cassius' wings had buffeted their fall *just* enough to keep Rackjack from serious harm, but his body still ached everywhere. "Think his vampire curse will heal him."

Helai nodded. "Just like after the siege in Volendam. Where is Rooster?"

So many questions. Rackjack's nose twitched in irritation. "Tried to escape jinn. Long story-tale. Tantien took him behind walls."

Relief flourished against Helai's expression, and Rackjack settled with dragging *Volroth* behind him, fighting against his instinct to drop it and consume the closest corpse that bloated and festered and beckoned for him to soothe his hunger. It was almost excruciating, ignoring its demands as they turned back towards the city.

TWENTY-ONE
HELAI

Drithan's eyes burned into her the entire way back to the wall, where Alavae's knights were securing the gates. The battle had been won, but there was always much to be done in the aftermath of war. They were lucky enough that the soldiers of the city were too preoccupied with other tasks to take note of Helai's and Massoud's heritage as they made their way through the city, where bells were ringing, and soldiers were screaming in victorious cheer.

Helai's heart warred with bitter relief and numb sadness. Her people had been slaughtered, some of them so twisted by the seductive preach of their sultan that they'd known not what they'd fought for. On the other hand, so many innocent Hestian people died today defending their homes.

They found Obrand and the other rangers at the northern gates.

Though a bit battle-weary, they all seemed unharmed, and Drithan strode forward to clasp Obrand's forearm as they spoke softly to each other in Alkazed.

"Met many interesting folks on my way to Volendam to meet you," Helai said to Massoud in Shoman. "Our world was so small in Shoma, and now I've met dwarves, eldrasi, vampires, drikoty…" She paused, trailing off. So many cultures, so many new friends. She loved the Misfits, but she couldn't deny the sense of calm she felt being around Massoud, like a piece of home had been returned to her. Now that the battle was over and they had won, the weight of losing Zamir crashed against her. She wasn't one to turn to a bottle to soothe her unrest, but she craved one now. Perhaps she could convince Drithan to share one with her if they weren't set to sail immediately.

"Helai, Linda, it's good ta see you," Obrand said, approaching. "What aid we could offer, we did, but I fear we must make haste back north. Our king has sent word that the rakken activity has begun to fester again. We have been away from our home for too long."

"I understand," Helai said. "The city is grateful for your aid, I'm certain. We'd stay and chat longer, but I think we all have places to be. Cassius would do well in a bed instead of out here in the rain and mud." She pointed to Linda, who had set Cassius down on the road where the rain had washed away the blood. "We need to find a way to transport them back to the Firebrand."

"Stay safe out there, Misfits. The world is growing dark. Things that once stayed in the dark recesses of the world are crawling their way out." Obrand's warning tugged Helai back to the Welker Estate and the phoenix dragon that had been brought back from the dust of her old bones. Rhavna was out there somewhere, regaining strength. Delroy had spoken of a dragon in Lyvira attempting the same. Who was to say there wouldn't be more?

She pressed a hand to Obrand's shoulder. "You too." Her heart squeezed painfully as she turned and met Drithan's gaze. If the dwarves were leaving, it seemed she wouldn't be able to share some ale with Drithan after all.

"Will find someone to help," Linda said, pointing to some soldiers being carried into the city on slabs of cloth.

"Helai, talk a moment?" Drithan asked as the other dwarves began to move in unison through the gate.

"Go with Linda. I'll catch up in a minute," Helai told Massoud. "There's something we'll need to talk about when we're all together, but I just need to speak with Drithan before he leaves."

Massoud lowered his head, staring at Drithan with a knowing expression before he turned and caught up to Linda as they ambled down the street. Smoke curled over the buildings, and the rain had reduced itself to a light sprinkling. Helai steeled herself against the disappointment of Drithan's departure as she forced her gaze to meet his.

"I'm coming with you."

His words were not at all what she'd expected, and her heart flipped over in her chest as her mouth dropped open. "What?" She shook her head, glancing over to Obrand and the other rangers still here. "I thought you were studying to be a rhun priest?"

Warring emotions waged through Drithan's expression as his eyes darted over the ruinous city. "Can we find somewhere...eh, private, to talk?"

Helai nodded. "I'm sure there's a private courtyard where we can tuck ourselves away in." There was a heated expression in Drithan's gaze as she turned and led them through the streets. The main ones were bustling with soldiers, but Helai turned down one of the side streets and was able to find a courtyard that had been untouched by the battle and seemingly abandoned for the moment.

"Will this—" she asked, only for Drithan to press her up against a wall between two massive pots of red flowers. The movement was so sudden it took Helai's breath away, but the grief and adrenaline from fighting came crashing through her all at once as she tugged Drithan closer. She wanted to crawl into him, to flee her turmoil. She settled instead with kissing him, with pressing against him so fiercely she ached. She wanted him. She wanted him to worship her. She wanted to feel nothing but the pleasure of him inside her.

"Please, Drithan," she asked, tears pricking the corner of her eyes. "Please don't stop." His hand reached up to wrap around her throat, his thumb paving pathways over the skin at her jaw. She moaned into his mouth, begging him silently not to be gentle.

He wasn't, and she was grateful for it.

They stayed tangled in each other's arms for some time. Drithan had surprised her. He was always tucked behind silence and stoicism. She hadn't expected him to be quite so rough as he'd been. She'd enjoyed it, but the moment they'd finished, his gentle nature had returned. She shivered as his coarse hands ran over her bare skin, and for a time, they remained silent.

"You still haven't told me why you want to come with us," Helai said finally, unable to contain her curiosity any longer. He'd seemed so certain of his position of becoming a rhun priest the last time she'd seen him. What had changed?

Drithan shook his head and pulled away to look at her, his mouth set in a grim line. "I cannot deny my feelings any longer, Helai." He brushed a hand through his hair, his gaze darting away from her to stare beyond her shoulder. He seemed wracked with indecision, and Helai pulled away to stand, her heart thudding in her throat.

She wanted him again. There was no denying that part. It ached low in her belly. But the thought of being with him, the thought of devoting herself to him when she had a mountain of worries to entertain, left her to dance with uncertainty.

"I belong with the Misfits far more than I belong in Kaldrom. I belong by *your* side." He spoke with a fierce determination as if convincing himself of the words that left his lips, and Helai reached forward for Drithan's hands. She wanted him to leave, to go back home, to long for him from afar almost as much as she hoped he would stay. He was a rock that tethered her to the ground, but he was also a distraction.

"I will not be the cause of that choice. Drithan, my heart belongs to my home. I cannot ask you to forsake yours for a dream."

"You did not ask me of anything. The dwarves are content with their stubborn whims, and I cannot sit around and defend a home against evil when I know there is also evil out here." He squeezed her hands, and Helai's cheeks flushed.

"The mountain shakes in the deepest parts of its bowels. Something is stirring. I believe you and the other Misfits are the only ones trying to do something about what's lurking. Please," he begged. "Let me come with you."

Helai nodded. Who was she to deny Drithan's aid when he'd proven himself tenfold? Even if his confession waged war on her emotions, she couldn't turn him away. "Okay," she said softly, pulling away to reach for her clothes. "I don't see why it would be a problem."

After they had both dressed, a small awkward tension settled between them. Other than Aryan, Helai had never been with someone more than one night. Being with Drithan felt different than what her relationship had been with Aryan, more stable but still confusing. She avoided Drithan's eyes. "We should make our way back to the general."

She began to turn away, only for Drithan to tug her closer, their lips meeting once more as he crashed into her. He kissed sweetly like he might break her now if he pressed too hard. Heat coiled in her belly, urging her to slip her fingers into his trousers, but he innocently kissed her in a way that made Helai's heart rebel. The emotions were conflicting and confusing, and she wasn't sure what to make of them. Still, she kissed him, relishing the warmth that rolled off him and chased away the chill the recent rain had brought. When he finally pulled away, his eyes were shining.

"I still have the card you gave me," he said, pulling away as he reached into his coat, pulling the partially ruined Elusive Shahara card from an inner pocket. The blood had dried, and the corner was still ripped, but it appeared Drithan had done his best to keep it from further ruin. "I do believe it keeps me safe," he grunted, his gaze darting away sheepishly.

"Like I said, they're magic," Helai said, smiling fondly at the card. "I'm glad it's keeping you safe."

As they fled the courtyard they'd tucked themselves in and made their way further into the city, Helai found herself comforted in Drithan's presence despite all of the hardship she'd just witnessed.

They found Angelika in the same spot they'd left her in, pouring over a map on the table. Her face was drawn with grief, and she pressed a hand to the swell of her belly as she sighed. Beside her was Massoud, who spoke quietly to her as Helai entered the home. Both quieted, only for Massoud to smile, though it never reached his eyes. There was grief there, too, and Helai's stomach twisted painfully as Zamir's death washed over her. Gods, she could use a drink or another fuck to distract her, but she urged her panic away and forced herself to approach the table.

"Massoud has informed me that General Sarem has been killed, and I've received word that the general your comrades were sent to take care of has died as well. The war efforts are far from over, but," she said with a tired smile, "the Shoman soldiers are reevaluating and have pulled back for the time being. I have no doubt Mohalis will reinforce his efforts for our lands, but we'll be ready."

"I wish we could stay and offer more aid," Helai said.

Angelika shook her head. "No doubt there are other things that require your attention. I can only be grateful you have provided the help that you gave. I wish to make a better life for the little one." She peered down at her belly, and Massoud moved forward but seemed to change his mind at the last minute and stopped.

"If there is anything we can do to help, name it."

Helai made a mental note to speak with Rooster about leaving Angelika with a hefty bag of skaels. It wasn't nearly all she wanted to do to make sure Zamir's wife and child were well cared for, but it was a start.

Angelika brightened, lowered her hands, and straightened her back. Behind Helai, a few people she did not recognize entered the house, and Helai stepped aside to give them room. Sadiki, Zamir's crow, perched nearby, and she stared at Helai with beady eyes. "Thank you both, for all that you've done. I would much like to keep in touch, if possible. Zamir spoke highly of both of you, and I would love for the little one to meet you both when the time comes. It's important for them to know their father's heritage, and what better teachers than the both of you?"

Helai nodded silently. There was much to do, and she hadn't the slightest idea on when they'd be able to return, but she hoped to. For the sake of Zamir's child. Helai didn't want him growing up loathing his father's culture. Not when there was much to celebrate when it came to the Shoman way.

"You're going to be a great mother," Helai said, sparing a glance in Massoud's direction. She wasn't certain of it, she'd only just met Angelika, but she was a fearless leader, and Helai admired her strength.

Angelika's eyes flooded with tears, and she stood tall, her lower lip trembling as she forced back her grief. "Thank you, Helai. I'm glad he had you there with him at the end."

Sadness ripped through her at the sentiment. *I could have saved him.* That knowledge would haunt her for the rest of her days, especially now that she had another lamp clasped to her side, but her gaze flickered to Massoud, to the tired but alive expressions crossing his face, and she settled into her decision to save him.

War was merciless, and Helai recalled something Cassius had said on their way to Halvdarc when he had panicked and fled the ship battle.

Have you ever had to raise your blade to end the life of a friend because they begged you to as they bled out on a battlefield?

Perhaps, for a moment, she grew a bit more understanding of the demons that Cassius battled every day. The bloodshed of war was so different than the horrors she'd seen growing up on the streets. She was no stranger to the violence of late nights in alleyways, of bloated and sickly corpses in dark places. Watching Zamir bleed out in her arms so close to safety, though, would haunt her far more than her childhood ever could.

"Here, take this." She reached into her pocket and pulled out what skaels she had on her. She had been prepared to find a shrine to Dalnor to donate them to, but Angelika and her unborn child needed them more.

"Oh, I couldn't—"

"Zamir would have wanted it," Helai said, closing Angelika's fingers over the skaels. "A gift. If anything, use it to help rebuild what has been lost, so your child can grow in the streets of a beautiful city, not one of ruin."

"*Graz*," Angelika whispered. "By your people's customs, we have located his body and are preparing him to be buried."

Helai's eyes shone with tears as she gripped Angelika's hand. She wanted to be there, but after all the death she'd been around, she didn't know if she had the strength. "Make sure his body is wrapped in a white cloth so that he may wash away this life and begin anew in the next one."

Angelika nodded.

"We should get to the Firebrand. Cassius and Rooster have been injured, and I'd very much like to check on their health," Helai said finally, ducking her head. "I wish you the best of luck in your war efforts. I know they're far from over."

Massoud uttered something quietly to Angelika as Helai slipped past the home and dodged around a soldier, moving slowly so Massoud could catch up with her. Drithan, who'd decided to wait outside, fell into place beside her, too. No one said anything as they made their way towards the beach.

TWENTY-TWO
HELAI

The docks were a flurry of commotion as they approached the Fire-brand. It wasn't until they'd gotten through the gate and out onto the other side of the wall that they noticed Delroy's ship next to the Fire-brand, and Helai's blood ran cold. The last time they'd run into Delroy's fleet hadn't been a pleasant one.

Drithan must have felt Helai stiffen beside him because he reached over to press a comforting hand to her arm. "What's a dead-walker's ship doing here?" Drithan asked darkly.

"Someone from Rooster's past. Turns out his memories showed up to haunt him," Helai said. It still made her mind spin, the notion that Rooster had grown up on a ship made up of pirates suffering from vampirism. How he hadn't come out a vampire himself was some miracle from the gods, surely.

"Helai!" Itale waved them over as he clung to the railing of the Firebrand, his hair tousled in a mess of curls as the rain plastered it to his face. "It's such a relief to see you're okay. Who's this?" His eyes darted between her and Drithan. Exhaustion cradled the young man's gaze, but he was uninjured, and Helai was relieved to see him so.

"This is Drithan, but Itale…" Helai trailed off, noting the horrifying look of his blackened fingers. They looked almost *rotten*. "What happened to your hands?"

Itale's expression turned sheepish. "Side effect of the necromancy…"

"You're a necromancer? Lad, that's very dangerous magic," Drithan said, taking a nervous step back.

"Sir Cassius is teaching me how to harness it," Itale said, tugging his hands away from the railing as Helai stepped up onto the ship. The Firebrand was a ghost, with no sailors tending to duties, and Delroy's ship looked to be the same. Where was everyone? Below decks, perhaps?

Drithan grunted but said nothing else as they both stepped onto the deck of the ship. The sails had been rolled up and tied, and the barest hint of Tantien's gryphon was seen flying through the clouds above. The rain made Helai shiver, but it seemed to be letting up.

Linda ascended from below decks, the gleam of their scales shining in the rain. Helai's head tilted to the side as she stared at Linda, trying to glean what appeared different about them. A soft hum radiated from them, like magic soaked their skin, but Linda had never displayed magic tendencies before.

"Cassius and Rooster downstairs resting. Rackjack too," Linda said. "Tantien said meeting happen when they wake." The implications forced

Helai's gaze over to Delroy's ship. Why was he here? Was he the reason for their meeting later? Helai's mind whirred, and exhaustion clung to her limbs from the aftermath of battle and grief. She wanted sleep, wanted it so badly it made her chest swell with emotion. Did they not all deserve a rest?

"Helai." It was Massoud who spoke, his hair drenched and his eyes knowing. "Come, let us find somewhere to sit and speak while we wait. My bones are weary, and now that the threat of immediate danger has passed, we may finally talk freely."

Helai's eyes darted to Drithan. "Go," he said, clasping Linda on the arm. "I have Linda here to keep me company."

"Have a drink with me later?" Helai asked.

Drithan nodded, and Helai turned, letting Massoud guide her towards the stairs that led down to the lower decks. They passed Intoh, his relief flickering across his features before he could hide it away. "Glad to see okay," he said, his voice tinged with awkwardness as he patted her arm and scurried up the stairs, followed closely by Sode and Khal.

"I keep thinking I've seen it all, and then someone from a distant land jumps out at me," Massoud said, laughter on his words.

"The Misfits are made up of a lot of...interesting characters."

"Misfits, huh?

Helai smiled despite the weight of everything. "A silly name the people of Volendam gave us after we rescued them from mermaids."

Massoud shook his head. "Not silly at all, little sister."

They wove through the halls until they got to the back of the ship, where the supplies were tucked away in boxes stacked and tied to the ship. Helai had made it a habit to find where the supplies were stored on each ship they found themselves on. It was the perfect little hiding spot when she needed time away from everything.

"Now tell me everything that's happened since I saw you last," Massoud said after they'd tucked themselves against one of the boxes. Helai sat cross-legged, where Massoud tugged one leg up to his chest, the other dangling over the edge of the crate.

Helai recounted everything, leaving nothing out. She told him of stealing the lamp, of her capture at the docks of Dalasae, of her time spent with the Shoma'kah. She recounted her time in the mountains, meeting the rakken, the brand, her time with the dwarves. She spoke until she was breathless, recalling everything from Volendam to Rhavna's ressurection and Cassius' rebirth. Silence encompassed them several moments after she finished, and Massoud raised his head towards the ceiling, as if deep in thought.

"This Cassius...is he easy on the eyes?"

Helai shoved Massoud, and he laughed as he slammed into a crate.

"Hey! It's a legitimate question."

Helai smiled, tugging her legs to her chest and resting her chin on her knees. "You'll think so. He's your type. Tall, brooding, protective."

Massoud's smile grew smug. "And what about this Rooster?"

Helai shook her head, her smile broadening. "Also your type...though I do not think you're *his*."

"And that dwarf? Is there something there?"

Helai's cheeks warmed at the notion. "I-I don't know." Breathless, embarrassed laughter breached her lips, her chest a maelstrom of conflicting emotions. A part of her wanted to deny it, but she couldn't deny Drithan's presence. It soothed her, chased away the chaos that consumed her. Her heart pounded every time she thought of him, but there was something souring it, a low expectation she didn't want to meet. She couldn't quite place it.

"Regardless, I'm happy to see you smiling again, *abibi*. After Aryan—" He pressed his fingers to the nape of his neck, quick to change the subject upon seeing the frown forming on Helai's face. "Ah, never mind. Come here." Reaching out, he enveloped Helai. He smelled of war, grime, sweat, and blood, but she nuzzled into him regardless, desperate for the comfort he always brought. She recalled when he'd found her and Aryan, dirty children barely surviving the streets of Dalasae. Helai had lashed out at him like a wild animal when he'd appeared in their dirt den, wide-eyed and uncertain. It had taken her weeks to trust him, but once she had, a bond had been forged stronger than anything Helai could properly express.

"I'm so glad you're okay," Helai sobbed. She hadn't thought she'd had any tears left to give, but they came regardless, soaking the front of Massoud's shirt as she curled her fingers into his back, loosening them only when he inhaled sharply. "If the jinn hadn't—"

"The what?"

She froze, realizing what she had done. She hadn't intended to tell Massoud about the seriousness of his wounds or how she'd gone about healing him. The undercurrent of shock in his tone made her shiver.

"I used a jinn wish to bring you back," she said, sullen over the absence of Massoud's warmth as he pulled away.

"Helai." He cursed in Shoman, his fingers darting over her arms and face as if to check her for wounds. She trembled as his fingers paved pathways across her skin, but she didn't *feel* injured from the jinn's wish. Not physically, at least. A weight sat inside her chest, one that hadn't been there before, but that could have been from the weight of the battle they'd just fought in or Zamir's death or nearly having lost Massoud.

"I'm fine." Helai had to swallow the anger that flourished in her throat. "You would have done the same for me."

"Jinn magic is sacred. It should not be used to bring back the dead. That's..." Massoud paused, a sharp exhale passing his lips. "They are to be respected, *abibi*."

"I know that." She pulled away too harshly, the hurt of his words singing through her. "What's done is done, big brother. Don't patronize me for doing what had to be done."

"What had to be done?" Massoud's laugh was mocking as he leaned back against a crate, his hand running down his face in exasperation. "You're always blaming obligation for your reckless actions. One day it's going to get you killed. Is that a new look or a warning for what you've done?" He said, gesturing to the strand of white that now bleached a small part of her hair.

Helai stumbled to her feet, her anger making her clumsy. "I couldn't lose you too." The pain ripped through her words as she choked on a sob. Her hand pressed against her chest as if it would lessen the ache that grew there. "I was right there, Massoud. *Right there* when Zamir died. He was going to be a father." Her voice cracked, and she sank. How much grief could one person handle? What had she done to the gods to deserve such brutal consequences?

Massoud reached out to comfort her, but she flinched away. "I'm sorry, Massoud. I just want to be alone."

He looked like he wanted to defy her but changed his mind. Lowering his head, he scooted off the crate. "I'm sorry too." The words stayed in the air long after he'd left.

TWENTY-THREE
CASSIUS

When Cassius woke, he was alone, unaware of how much time had passed or if Alavae still stood. He was in the same room he'd recovered in when he'd almost died during Volendam's siege. A dim flame flickered in a candle on the table across the room. His state of comfort hinted at his immediate safety, and the barest hint of conversation sounded from the hallway.

Cassius hissed as power thrummed through his arm, awakening the weapons that hid beneath his skin. It was a constant reminder that they were there, and his thoughts strayed to Ahma and the warning she had given him the last time she had shown herself.

Someone will test you. Someone from your past.

He shuddered at the possibility of what that could mean. Was he doomed to face Dmitry, the leader of the Order who'd exiled him? Or perhaps his sire, Vera? He loathed to think it would be anyone from his past.

"Glad to see you're doing better. We always seem to find you in this position."

Cassius' head rose at the sound of Rooster's voice at the door. He leaned heavily against the frame, but he seemed in good spirits. Cassius was relieved to see the jinn didn't seem to have left any lasting injury on Rooster.

"If you all would stop trying to get yourselves killed, it would make my job a lot easier." Cassius' smile quirked, and Rooster mirrored it, crossing his arms across his chest. He seemed distracted, his gaze darting to the hallway as he kicked off the door frame.

"Delroy's here," he said. "He and Tantien have called for a meeting once you woke."

Cassius' gaze darkened. "What is Delroy doing here?"

"That's what we're going to find out."

Pain flourished through Cassius as he attempted to push himself up. His vampirism healed him at quicker rates, but it was still a slow process, and he hissed through clenched teeth as he swung his legs over the side of the bed. Someone had removed his armor and left him in his undergarments, and Rooster shielded his gaze as Cassius stood and snagged some clothes left for him on the chair.

"Gods, hold still." Rooster must have gotten tired of watching Cassius struggle into the sleeves of his shirt because he drew forward, his hand outstretched to offer aid. Cassius accepted it gratefully, holding still as Rooster helped him pull the shirt on. His bones ached, and for the first time since his death and rebirth, he truly felt the scratch of bloodlust. It was strange and jarring to suddenly feel it again, and the surprise of it made his control slip, his fangs descending as he leaned towards Rooster's neck.

"Whoa, mate. Careful now." Rooster flinched back, his eyes flickering with a warning. His hand had gone out to push Cassius away, and his touch was just enough to drag Cassius back to the present.

"Fuck," Cassius growled, turning away and swallowing the bloodlust that festered in his throat. "I apologize, Rooster. It has been too long…"

"Plenty of dying out there to indulge. Or" –he winked– "a certain eldrasi might be willing to offer some assistance?"

Cassius' cheeks heated, his stomach rolling painfully. "That ship has sailed. I will be fine until after this meeting. Come." He left the room before Rooster could think to question him. He didn't want to talk about Tantien right now.

"I apologize," Rooster called quietly after him, the subtle nature of his steps not lost on the vampire as they headed towards the upper decks. "I won't bring it up again."

Cassius remained silent, and the conversation died there. He hadn't had time to think about Tantien's rejection before the battle, nor did he care to indulge in his friend's pity.

"Did Helai find Massoud?" he asked, reaching the stairs. The soft noise of voices could be heard above, and though it wasn't raining, it seemed to have just quit. Dusting of raindrops sparkled against the wood of the ship.

"Aye," Rooster said, dodging to the side to let an eldrasi pass. "And Drithan is here as well."

Cassius tossed a surprised glance over at Rooster. "The dwarf?" Rooster nodded, and Cassius' brow furrowed thoughtfully. Drithan had taken a liking to Helai as of late; perhaps she was the cause for his presence.

He paused at the stairwell, his fingers brushing the railing as he hesitated. His entire body screamed at him for rest, his chest still ragged from the healing process. By all means, he shouldn't be upright, and one step up the stairs caused pain to shoot up his legs and into his chest. He gritted his teeth together. Loose strands of hair fell onto his face as he clung to the railing. *You will straighten your spine and hold your head high. You soil our family name in such displays of weakness.*

"Cassius—"

"I'm fine," Cassius snapped at Rooster's concern, forcing his back erect and his chin up. No amount of pain, even as it coursed through him with each step, would stop him from making the climb himself. Shame already trailed through him for having let Rooster help him earlier, and Dominic Antonia's head shook disgustingly in his mind's eye. He was glad his father wasn't present to see such weakness.

Rooster left him alone after that, and though it took twice as long, Cassius made it up the stairs, grateful for the cloud cover that chased the sun away. Because of it, he was freed from the burden of a headache and left only with the persistent wail of his bloodlust in the hollow of his throat. That, he could ignore for now.

The deck was full of people. Helai, Drithan, and a young Shoman man stood nearest the stairs, their conversation dying at Cassius and Rooster's approach. Helai's relief was muted by the sudden presence of the Shoman man, who shoved her and Drithan out of the way to hold out a hand.

"Massoud," he purred, his smile radiant. "The pleasure is all mine." His eyes, dark and ripe with exhaustion, trailed over Cassius, taking their time to drink him in. "Rugged, broad, *extremely* handsome." He whirled around to give Helai a look that suggested betrayal. "She completely underplayed how handsome you were. You must be Cassius."

Cassius snorted, his smile half-cocked. "Nearly dying does little for one's looks, but I appreciate the compliment."

Massoud laughed, his shoulders shaking as his hair fell about his face. "Ah, but you see, I am *also* extremely handsome, and I also nearly died this day. It's all a matter of perspective. "He winked, and Cassius took one long look at him.

He was tall but nowhere near meeting Cassius eye to eye. He wore something free of the grime of war, loose-fitting and soft, much like Cassius', and low cut in the front. His hair was long and wavy, tied back in a loose ponytail that hung down to his shoulder blades, and his beard was long and untamed like it hadn't been kept for some time.

"Give him some room, Massoud," Helai said sharply, tugging Massoud away. "He's a handful; just ignore him." Helai's eyes were apologetic as Massoud laughed again, draping an arm across Helai's shoulders.

"Fine, fine, but you can't stop me from speaking with him later." He tossed the words over his shoulder at Cassius like a promise, and the two of them disappeared as Tantien approached with Delroy at his heels.

"Ah, da dead-walker still hides behind dem pretty face, hm?" Delroy clicked his tongue against the roof of his mouth in disapproval, and Cassius scowled. He cared little for what the vampire pirate thought of him, but the words clung bitterly to the air, souring between them.

"A relief to see you awake," Tantien said, offering a genuine smile. Cassius was relieved to find little tension between them. Perhaps he was simply exhausted from the fighting and the steady symphony of heartbeats that echoed in the air around him, drumming against his throat and distracting him from his embarrassment. Or perhaps it was simply easy to get over the rejection. Either way, Cassius returned the smile, if not a bit formally, and nodded.

"Indeed. Has anyone seen Rackjack? I need to thank him for keeping me safe in my state of unconsciousness."

Rackjack materialized in his dwarf form, the brass and auburn of his hair gleaming as the sun threatened to poke through the clouds. Shallow scrapes and bruises etched his skin, but he seemed in good spirits as he drew close to Cassius, his eyes glittering with wild, untamed emotion. He was still missing his prosthesis, but someone had crafted something for him to lean against, and he did so with good spirits.

"Glad to see you survive-live. Was worried you would not." Rackjack fiddled with his crutch, his restless energy affecting the air surrounding him. "Didn't manage to get bell, but Tantien-filth went with others to melt down part of it. Going to make me a new leg-leg." Cassius moved to clap a hand to his shoulder fondly.

"I do not think I would have survived without you."

Rackjack twitched. "You protect us-us. Only right to do the same for you-you."

Cassius blinked, and then his chest swelled with emotion. As a knight, all he ever wanted was to be the shield for the ones he cared for. He'd instilled it in himself ever since he'd failed to protect his brother in his human life. Sometimes, he wondered if he had failed in his knighthood, too. His exile had forged the notion, and he chased that regret away as Tantien waved the others over.

"We'll speak in the forge—just Delroy and the Misfits. Everyone else is welcome to make themselves comfortable anywhere else on the Firebrand." Tantien's smile was apologetic as Drithan moved to follow them inside. He huffed and gave Helai a lingering look before Massoud bumped shoulders with him.

"Come with me, Drithan. I'm sure there is a lot of trouble we could get into exploring the ship," Massoud said, pressing a hand to the middle of Drithan's back and leading him away. Cassius caught Itale's eye from where he stood near the figurehead, and he gave a firm nod. *I will find you after the meeting.*

Itale returned the nod with an understanding smile as Cassius turned and ducked into the forge, relishing in its natural warmth. Now that it had stopped raining, the ocean beyond the hole in the wall where Tantien's gryphon usually lay was bright and calm, with soft rolling waves that crested with white sea foam.

"I 'ave da best of news, Misfits," Delroy hummed the moment Tantien shut the door, his fangs gleaming against his dark skin. "I found somet'ing dat can put da big scaley beast in da west ta sleep again."

Alarm coursed through the room as Cassius and Rooster caught each other's eye.

"Even betta—" Delroy clasped his hands together, grinning widely. "Tantien has informed me dat you all intend ta make da trip to da eldrasi island of Míradan to liberate him sister out of da prison dere. The tome dat I need you to, ah, *obtain*, is on dat same island."

"Read about that tome," Intoh said suddenly, raising his head from where he'd been speaking softly to Khal and Sode in Drikoytian. "In Welker Estate. Spoke of tome that resides in heart of Osgol. Same tome?"

Delroy turned to Intoh and nodded. "Ah, yes. It is likely dat is da very same."

"Why have you not spoken of this tome before?" Rooster asked. Suspicion burned through Cassius as Intoh's brow furrowed. Intoh had been warming up to the Misfits a lot as of late, but that hadn't stopped the greka from abandoning his search for immortality.

"Happened upon it in the Welker Estate. There was a lot going on."

Also true. The weight of everything that had transpired came crashing down on Cassius—the Welker's ball, Rhavna's resurrection, Rembrandt's sacrifice, and his own rebirth. His wings shuddered behind him as Helai stepped forward, her brow furrowed in quiet rage.

"Are we supposed to just drop everything at your whim and collect this artifact for you to return to some tree in a distant land that may or may not have a dragon waking from its roots?"

Delroy slammed Helai against the door, his fingers curled around her neck before anyone could blink. The sound of her hitting the wood was jarring. Everyone moved forward, Linda roaring in anger before Delroy's fangs neared her neck. Cassius' hand had flung to his hip, only to realize that his sword was not strapped to his side. "I warned ya da last time, girl. Carter Wingman owes me. Either travel with him to meet da demands or don't. But I encourage you not to stand before me and talk to me in dat condescending way, hm? It would not end well for you." His warning was soft and seductive, cupped against Helai's ear but spoken loud enough for Cassius to hear it clear across the room.

Helai trembled and gave the barest of nods, and then Delroy released her, his hands held up in surrender. "Good," he said. "Now dat we're on da same page, it is important ta note dat time is not on our side."

Helai remained slumped against the door, her eyes blazing with rage as her fingers danced across her throat. Cassius heard the rapid beat of her heart from where he stood. The tension was so thick it was nearly tangible, and Rooster stepped forward, his eyes darting from Helai to Delroy.

"What information do you have on the whereabouts of this tome?" Tantien cut in before Rooster could, his mouth drawn in a thin line as he crossed his arms over his chest. The tension remained, but as Delroy turned to Tantien, Helai slumped ever so slightly, her face betraying her fear. She still looked at Cassius like that at times, though her fear of him had diminished in the years they had come to know each other. It made Cassius wonder what interactions she'd had with vampires in the past. He'd never thought to ask.

"I believe it was sold to da eldrasi for da pretty skaels, but I'm not too certain where on da island it is being kept. You will have to figure it out dere."

"I still know some people in Kelirium that I can reach out to, see if they know anything," Tantien said. Cassius joined Rooster standing in front of Helai, and Intoh edged forward, his fingers threaded together in contemplation.

The room fell into an uncomfortable silence. Helai's heartbeat was elevated, but so was Rooster's, and Delroy plucked a small dagger from a table and inspected it lightly as the blade's edge gleamed in the torchlight.

"I do not know how long we have ta keep da scaly beast from waking. So—" His smile was radiant. "Do not delay." Delroy's form faded as he transformed into a colony of bats that flung themselves out of the open back of the ship, and his departure released tension in the air as Helai turned, pried the door open, and saw herself out.

No one stopped her.

The room remained silent long after she had gone. A current of tension returned as the implications of Delroy's warning set in. They knew so little about the dragons of old. Much of the world thought them to be little more than myth, a way for the powerful to control their people through fear.

"I do not suppose we have a night to celebrate our continued existence with the men of this city?" Cassius pondered, breaking the tension.

"Want to drink until dizzy," Linda said.

"I do not think we can afford to delay. We do not know the state my sister is in." Tantien's face was twisted with worry. "With Delroy's instructions, we should leave the moment we can load up with provisions."

Exhaustion riddled the party, but Tantien was right. There was simply too much at stake to afford even a night of relaxation. "How long will it take to sail to Kelirium?" Cassius asked.

Tantien pondered the question. "If the winds favor our cause, only a few months. If they don't..." Worry lined his face. "Could take half a year."

Rooster whistled sharply as he clasped his hands behind the back of his head. "You're right then. No delays." His gaze was hard, his mouth set in a thin line. "Intoh can ensure the winds favor us, right, Intoh?"

Intoh blinked. "Will do my best."

TWENTY-FOUR
ROOSTER

Rooster found Cassius standing on the beach later that afternoon, tucked away from where the battle had taken place. There were no bodies, no bloodstained sands to sour the mood. Off in the distance Linda laid on their belly, sunbathing in their true state as waves rolled over their massive form. Rooster watched them fondly, envious of the way they settled into peace so soon after battle.

"I stood on the shores of this city many times long ago," Cassius said, his arms clasped behind his back, his eyes watching the ocean crashing against the shore. The sun had begun its descent below the horizon, casting the sky in brilliant colors of pinks and golds, and Rooster studied the side of

Cassius' face, attempting to gauge what the vampire was feeling. He was so difficult to read.

"My mother brought my brother and I here to meet with some other merchants. She led an empire of trade in Verenzia." Cassius gave a soft shake of his head, his face a slate of stone. No, not difficult to read. Impossible.

"Did you and your mother get along?" Rooster frowned, his own heart twinging painfully. He couldn't remember who his mother was, and yet thinking of the idea of her made him sad.

Cassius' smile was faint, so faint it only quirked at the corner of his mouth. "In a way. In a way she knew how. It was the only time Markus and I could be free from our duties to simply be brothers though. We would run up and down this beach, pretending we were knights in some far off kingdom."

Rooster tried to imagine a young Cassius. It seemed impossible, with his undead state. Perhaps a young boy with a head full of curls, not yet broad in the shoulders. "Was your brother younger or older?"

"Older." Rooster watched a shadow flicker over Cassius' face, but he couldn't tell if it was due to fondness or something else. "By a few years."

"Yeah, that makes sense." Rooster laughed at Cassius' withering stare. "In all seriousness, I would have thought you to be the eldest. Your sense of protective nature would have signified such."

"Markus would have agreed. He always thought me to take life too seriously. We were joyful children – for a time."

Rooster deadpanned, "You? Too serious? No." His sarcasm tugged a smile to his face. A brotherhood had forged between him and Cassius, a quiet sense of respect and honor. Rooster was confident that Cassius would be there for Rooster if he so much as asked. Rooster would if Cassius needed it.

"I have never been to Míradan," Cassius said, changing the subject. "I do not know what we face there. Eldrasi politics are not ones I am too familiar with outside of their trade agreements with some of the coast cities."

"My head still doesn't work too well. I'm sure I knew more once, but until we rescue Igraine, I'll be of no help." It was frustrating, sitting on the edge of memories that danced just out of reach.

"Let us hope for safe passage. It worries me…" Cassius paused, watching Linda slip into the ocean. "Drausmírtus may have sent Rhavna north, but we cannot pretend that we are safe. The cult in Halvdarc brought her back for a reason."

"We have more than just her to worry about, mate." Rooster reached out and pressed his hand to his friend's shoulder. "If what Delroy says is true, we may have a second dragon to contend with." Rooster shuddered at the thought. Rhavna had been horrifying, the presence of something far beyond his understanding, but the sliver of fear in Delroy's face when he'd spoken gave Rooster pause and the notion that they should take their task seriously.

Cassius' lips pursed. It was strange to see the vampire so worried; it made Rooster's skin crawl even more. "It is strange. I almost miss the burn of the brand."

Rooster's face must have displayed his shock because Cassius' mouth quirked into a grim smile. "At least we had some indication that danger was near."

Rooster shook his head. "Maybe, but at what cost?" The recognition that the brands had brought when the enemy had revolted against them had nearly cost the Misfits their lives. It *had* cost Cassius his and was only by the miracle of a literal god that he stood next to Rooster now. No, Cassius may miss their absence, but Rooster was grateful the brands were gone. No more burning. No more whispers in the dark.

After spending the better part of the afternoon provisioning and preparing to embark, they finally set sail as the sun began to set. Angelika had personally attended their send-off, instructing her men to provide them with anything they should need, and Helai and Massoud had grown silent in her presence, a gentle reminder of what they'd lost.

Helai had excused herself to her room after they'd set sail, and soon enough Alavae was but a distant, smoldering city behind them, the sounds of the waves crashing against the hull a welcomed noise. It meant they were well on their way to Míradan.

"It may be in poor taste to call it a celebration, so perhaps a distraction is in order, yeah?" Rooster suggested, turning to those who stood aboard the deck of the ship. His eyes met Tantien's, who responded with a grin and a nod, before handing the wheel off to his first mate.

"After we have our heading well under way, I see there to be little problem for the Misfits to share cheer and drink on top deck."

Rooster clapped his hands together. "Excellent." Now that they were on their way, his restless nature only grew, so he hailed down the first eldrasi sailor he could and offered his aid. The quicker things were done, the quicker they could fill their evening with distractions.

Many had turned up for the night of celebrations. Everyone from the Firebrand had settled around the deck, taking care to be out of the way for any sailors tending to their duties, but even Helai had come up from where she'd hidden away in her room to partake, settling down near Massoud and Drithan.

"Make sure to leave some for us, *ami*," Cassius called out as Rooster took another swig from his bottle. Itale and Tantien laughed from nearby, and Rooster held the bottle out in offering, his cheeks rosy from his inebriated state. The camaraderie was strong. Gods, it was good to get hammered after narrowly winning a battle.

"There's plenty to go around. It's not my fault if your tolerance is that of steel," Rooster protested. His mind was a glorious haze, and the soft soothing voices of those around him lulled him into a blissful complacency. The rum chased away the demons of war, and for once, his hands didn't shake, and he didn't worry over the threat of dragons.

"Has anyone seen Rackjack?" His absence was strange; since running into him initially in Halvdarc when Rackjack had saved him from a cultist, Rooster hadn't been able to pry Rackjack from his side.

"Saw him scurrying below decks when I was grabbing rum from the hull," Tantien said, leaning back against the railing of his ship as his skin gleamed in the torch's light. "Said he would not be partaking and not to worry about him."

"Hmm," Rooster hummed, nursing his bottle.

That only made him worry about Rackjack more. The rakken was always scheming or quietly muttering in his own native tongue. The Misfits' interactions with rakken had been less than pleasant up until they'd met Rackjack, and even with Rooster's gut screaming that he could trust him, there was something *sneaky* about the way Rackjack went about his life.

Rooster supposed he would learn more with Igraine's help. Assuming she'd be able to unlock his memories.

Thoughts of her sent an ache spiraling through him. Now that memories of her had resurfaced, now that he knew where she was, the restlessness in his bones did not tire. He feared for her safety, feared for his role in it by having left. Rooster's stomach rolled painfully, and he moved away from Cassius, murmuring excuses as he fled the peacefulness of the deck.

The vampire called out to him, but he ignored him. He walked until he was a good distance from the other Misfits before he sank to his knees at the back of the ship. The world was quiet, save for the gentle roar of waves crashing against the ship, which brushed him with sea foam.

Digging his fingers into the wood of the railing, he swayed, the pain making him dizzy. His mind was shackled behind his agony, screaming to be liberated and to steady his racing heart as panic clawed at his throat. Guilt forged fires in his veins. Igraine was locked away, shackled, and tortured because he wasn't there to stop them.

His shoulders shook as he fought back tears.

I'm coming, Igraine. Just hold on, he thought sullenly.

"Rooster?"

Tantien's voice carried out to him but Rooster's head swam, his stomach rejecting the food he'd eaten after the battle.

"I think—" He gasped, unable to finish his sentence as he lurched over and vomited, the bitter taste of alcohol and food drenching his tongue. A hand pressed to his back, and then his hair was being drawn back and tied loosely as he continued to empty his stomach, tears pricking the corners of his eyes. Gods, he hated this.

"Thank you." His voice was a whisper, his throat raw as he leaned back and wiped his mouth with the back of his hand. His head was clearer, but a headache was threatening to set in.

"I never had the pleasure of meeting your crew, but I know my sister." Tantien's gaze was a fire of determination and utter belief when Rooster's eyes met his. "They will not break her." Tantien spoke almost as if he were convincing himself as much as Rooster, and Rooster pressed his forehead to the rail.

"I'll never forgive myself for leaving her." The confession tugged at his vulnerability, a dark thought that had lingered within him since he'd learned of Igraine's capture.

"I'm sure you had your reasons."

"I don't even know what those reasons are!" Rooster's fingers balled into fists, his teeth grinding together in frustration as pain blossomed across his head. Memories tried to pour to the surface, but the harder he tried to draw on them, the more severe the pain was.

Tantien's silence was palpable, and Rooster's anger simmered. He felt like shit, his head throbbing, and he felt shackled to where he stood, unable to draw the courage to move, to face the other Misfits if he desired to return to the main deck. Perhaps he would just fling himself overboard, and the waves would carry him away to drown in the sea.

"Carter." Tantien held up a hand when Rooster's eyes flashed dangerously, his jaw pulsing. "Sometimes we cannot ignore the calls of our destiny. If yours was reaching out to you, no one can blame you for pursuing it. The Shoma'kah found you in the Daesthara Forest, right?" At Rooster's nod, Tantien's head lowered. He pondered for a few moments in silence. "The eldrasi god's tree resides in that forest. Its caretaker, Eirwyn, guards that tree. If that's what called out to you, it only makes sense why you left Igraine behind." It was too dark to truly see Tantien's expression, but what light there was from the moon showcased his pain.

"I don't understand," Rooster said.

Tantien gave a slight shake of his head as his gaze tilted up towards the stars. "As I said before, our god scorned our family. Returning to the home of our ancestors would be a danger to Igraine. I daresay it may even be more dangerous than the threat of the seas and of our people in Míradan. It is terrifying to think what they might be doing to her in Fraximus, but Daesthara is old. It remembers. No one can say how it would have reacted to Igraine's presence should she have gone with you."

Rooster's heart squeezed painfully, unwilling to admit that he might be free of the guilt for having left Igraine behind. So long as she was by his side, he could protect her from the evils of the world. Instead, he'd left her and hadn't been there to protect her when the eldrasi had come for her.

"Never again." Rooster wasn't sure if the promise he swore was directed at himself or towards Tantien, but he said it out loud regardless. It forged within him, strengthened in bitter determination. "It doesn't matter *why*." Rooster's gaze hardened. "It's never going to happen again."

There was something close to understanding that washed against Tantien's expression, a sad smile that pressed to his lips. "I believe you." His tone was genuine as he leaned forward and clapped Rooster on the back. "It is why I know you and the other Misfits will see this task through. I can trust no one else with this rescue mission."

Rooster hung his head. His headache was nearly unbearable now, a stake of pain wheedling its way through his brain. A year. It could take a year to get to Igraine. What torture would she be dealt? The guilt threatened him, but he shoved it aside. His guilt would only get in his way.

And nothing would get in the way of his path to Igraine.

TWENTY-FIVE
RACKJACK

Six hours earlier...

The sounds of soldier celebrations were far off as Rackjack skittered through the city, keeping to shadows and alleyways. Most of the city had spilled out onto the beaches to celebrate their close victory, but as a rakken, Rackjack knew he couldn't be too careful. The northern districts were still under threat of war, and the guards were on high alert. He'd shed the illusion of his dwarf form for his true one. He would need it where he was going.

The streets of Alavae were narrow and war-torn, with pockets of fire and rubble collecting against ruined buildings. Rackjack tasted the residual magic in the air from the Shoman having used the jinn, and he hurled himself against the wall of a building as a couple of soldiers strolled by, laughing and speaking in foreign tongues. One ruffled the other's hair, and Rackjack's heart felt like it was going to burst from his chest as they strolled by. He waited until long after their voices had faded in the distance to move again and, even then, took greater care to keep silent. He didn't want to be followed.

He ran into no one else as he found his way to the crypt once more, his ears twitching to and fro as he anxiously stared up at the yawning void of the entrance.

"Go-go and be quick," Rackjack uttered, scratching the backs of his ears as he sniffed the entrance. It smelled of rot, blood, and musky air, not at all a place that most would dare venture. It was tame compared to a rakken's normal home, so he darted inside quickly, tossing one more glance over his shoulder to make sure he was still alone. His crutch frustrated him, and his arm ached from having to depend on it for an extra leg, but he knew Tantien would prioritize making him a new one as soon as they set sail.

He tossed the thought away as he dove back into the crypt. Other rakken would underestimate him for his prosthesis, which would be good and well in the long run. If he wanted to bend the rakken to his will and honor Rat-King, he would need to be clever.

The dead Shoman soldier rotted at the front door, his eyes staring and unseeing. His skin had already begun to bloat and fester, and Rackjack failed to resist the urge to nibble a bit on his arm. The man tasted sweet, sickeningly so, so Rackjack spat out the small chunk of flesh he'd been chewing on. He eyed the corpse with suspicion and disgust. "No-no. Keep going-moving. No time."

He turned away, scurrying deeper into the crypt. Without Cassius, the tomb remained silent and absent of spirits, but the hair on Rackjack's back still stood on end, and he found himself looking over his shoulder more times than he cared to admit.

He made his way down to the bottom, where they had fought the general and his jinn. The torchlight had all gone out, but for Rackjack, it mattered little. He could see in the dark.

A rock scuttled across the floor somewhere in the distance, and Rackjack stilled, his breathing coming in quick waves as he cocked his head to the side. It was likely the rakken had gone, but Rackjack had to be sure. Rat-king had marked Hiss-rat for something, and Rackjack needed to know why. The scar he'd seen on Hiss' arm from the first time they'd been in the tomb overcame his mind, and he launched himself forward. *Must find him-him.*

He searched. And searched. And searched. After a while, he feared his absence would be noticed, and his frustrations came with several fits of him pulling out his fur. A small squeaking in the darkness pulled him from his despair, and he fell on all fours, his nose twitching as he sniffed the air.

"Hiss-rat?"

"Yes, I waited just as you asked." Hiss spoke in the rakken's tongue of Squeakspeech as he materialized from the darkness, his eyes dark and beady as he attempted to musk. Rackjack, offended, stood back up, his musk overwhelming the small, desecrated hallway.

Hiss lowered himself to the ground obediently, his eyes glaring up at Rackjack as silence injected the tomb. It hadn't been hard to force Hiss to submit the first time; Rackjack would do it again if he had to.

Hiss remained submissive, however, and Rackjack stopped musking, though he remained on guard, his arm with the fire contraption poised and at the ready should there be any other rakken around. Rackjack shuddered to think what he would do if that jinn had decided to remain. Now that it was free, it could do whatever it wanted.

No, he couldn't think about that right now.

"What news of the desert land?" Rackjack asked, switching to his native tongue. Words came easier to him then, the quickness of his mind able to keep up with the squeaky dialect.

"Something stirs in the sands," Hiss whispered, his voice low and hoarse. "Something ancient and wicked."

Rackjack bared his teeth at Hiss' words as they burrowed seeds of fear into his skin. The skeleton of a dead dragon lay in the sands of Shoma, its rib cage surrounding their holy city. "When did the stirrings start?" he asked.

"About six months ago."

Rackjack bristled. That was around the same time Rhavna's resurrection had occurred. If the two instances were correlated... Rackjack would have to pray to Rat-King later, see if he had anything to say on the matter. For now, he turned to Hiss.

"Muster with me. Time in sands only beginning. Must find a way to stay close to Sultan-filth."

Hiss hissed. "Do not want to tread with human-filth. What will other rakken think?"

Rackjack towered over Hiss, a shiver of satisfaction coursing through him when the other rakken trembled in fear. "Does not matter what other rakken think when you bow to Brass Rat. Will make them bend to my will. Come to you with Rat-King's promise. Build better world. Cannot build it if dragons return."

Drool slipped from Hiss' mouth as he nodded. "If Rat-King wills it, Hiss will follow." Hiss glanced around, leaning closer as the shadows tucked around him like a second skin. "Hiss knows that sultan of sands seeks to bring dragon god back. It is why he wants to claim this land. Wants to offer it to her when she returns."

Rackjack's fur bristled. "Cannot let that come to pass. Must muster forces. Growing army beneath Volendam. Need to seek rakken out in Lyvira."

Hiss nodded. "Will go where you ask."

"Is there anyone else down here that could be *persuaded*?" Rackjack asked.

Hiss shook his head. "Fled when jinn was released. Only stayed because you demanded it."

Rackjack's disappointment over the other rakken was washed away by Hiss' loyalty. For the moment, he would do.

His fingers twitched, and he longed for the magical strength of draugmin coursing through his veins. He would have to seek out more soon. He only had a small dusting of it left and could feel the tremors in his paws from it exiting his system.

"Come," he rasped, turning back towards the stairs. "Dark will come soon. Must have you out of city-streets before the sun sleeps."

TWENTY-SIX
LINDA

Linda ambled around on the Firebrand, enjoying the vibrant colors in the sky as they waited for the rest of the Misfits to wake. The city they'd just left was fresh from the devastation of the Shoman army, but a quiet peace had soaked the air, and Linda still felt it: a song of hope. They had heard it in the quiet singing of soldiers while they worked to collect the dead. They had felt it in the soft etch of magic that trailed through the air, chasing away the lingering aftermath of the jinns. They had seen it in the gentle interactions between soldiers and wounded and smelled it in the threat of rain that moved to clean the air of smoke. Linda had seen much war, and the aftermath always felt like a suspension of time, a strange step at the edge of a cliff.

"Linda, I've never met a krok'ida before, but it seems I have you to thanks for aiding Helai in saving my life." Massoud sidled up next to them, his face full and smiling. Despite having just survived the maw of death, Massoud had come back to this realm with high spirits. It was something to be admired, and Linda studied him with great interest. His face was still littered with bruises, his lip healing from where it had split, but his eyes sparkled with mirth as he rested his hands against the railing. Scars littered his skin, little stories that had etched themselves against his flesh. Linda bore many of those tales too, tales of times spent at war or punished by the greka that they'd served.

"Don't have to thank," Linda said, though their pride straightened their spine. "Would have done again." Seeing the Shoman soldiers do that to someone, let alone someone from their own homeland, filled Linda with a strange rage.

"Ah, regardless, I owe you a drink next time we're able. It seems like we are going to be stuck on this ship for quite some time, hm?"

Linda nodded, brimming with enthusiasm.

"I take my leave with that promise. I think my sister needs assistance getting her sea legs," Massoud said, laughter etching his tone as he gestured to Helai as she clung to the side of the ship.

"Give her week," Linda said. "Always like this at first."

Massoud flashed Linda a smile and waved in dismissal as he sauntered over to Helai; he laid a comforting hand on her back. Though the chill of winter had finally come, the sun shined, and everyone seemed to be in good spirits.

"Intoh, ask you question?" Linda asked as Intoh walked by, mumbling to himself. His hair stood up on one side as he'd never bothered to tame it after he'd woken, and he nodded, gesturing for Linda to follow him as he brushed past a couple of eldrasi sailors and towards the lower decks.

"Humans take forever to wake," Intoh mumbled irritably. His eyes kept flickering to the eldrasi, and Linda reached over to pat him on the head.

"Don't worry. Will wake soon, I'm sure. Know you will get us there fast, like you did when you carried us across big sea."

That earned a rare smile from Intoh, his chest swelling in pride as his gaze sought out Linda's. It was quick and brief, but it made Linda happy to see the greka smile for once.

They continued down the narrow hallway, and Linda peeked into each room they passed, where the officers' quarters were located. Tantien's higher-ups, his boatswain, first mate, and quartermaster all had exquisite rooms, if a bit small. The wood was dark and beautifully ornate like Tantien had taken great care in designing his ship. The builder in Linda was impressed.

"Linda," Intoh called in a chastising tone, and Linda followed, if a bit sheepish. Perhaps one day they would work on a boat. It felt natural being here.

The room Intoh stopped at was about half the size of an officer's quarter, with just enough room for a bed. It was too small for Linda, but it was better than sleeping on the ground. Small magical orbs darted about, filling the room with dim light, and Linda leaned *Volroth* in the corner of the room near the door.

"What did you want to talk about?" Intoh asked, scurrying in and peering out the window. The sun cast a soft glow over the ocean as Linda remained in the doorway.

"Think I saw a god." Linda was always certain of their emotions, always stormed forward without fear and uncertainty. But speaking of the vision they'd seen just before saving Drithan sent nervous energy coursing through them, and they found their eyes trailing towards the floor instead of meeting Intoh's gaze.

Silence filled the room between them for so long that Linda finally looked up to see Intoh staring at them with a peculiar expression. Linda couldn't discern whether that expression bore hints of jealousy, awe, or disbelief. Perhaps it was all three.

"Tell me," he finally said, and so Linda did. They told him of the sun dragon, of the fire that had burst from their mouth, of saving Drithan and the other dwarves from a gruesome fate. The memory of Ikotia was still so vivid that Linda could recall the immense heat rolling off the god's scales.

"Would be hesitant in believing you, but after what we've seen..." Intoh trailed off, pacing the small room with his hands clasped behind his back. "Remember you breathing fire at blood farm where we saved Rembrandt. Know you speak truth."

"Would not lie," Linda protested, offended that Intoh would think so lowly of them. "Should have gone to Rackjack. Talks about gods all the time."

Intoh waved his hands and shook his head. "Apologies. Did not mean to offend." His words felt genuine, and Linda paused from their retreat from the room. Intoh never apologized. "Trying to be better. Want—" Intoh hesitated, and now it was *him* who looked nervous. "Want to be part of family. A Misfit."

"What change? Thought you wanted to find way to live forever."

Intoh flinched. "Still the plan. Realized I can have both. Just like other Misfits."

Linda nodded, relieved that Intoh finally seemed to understand and that he'd finally stepped away from being haunted by whoever 'Ekalas' was. Linda had never gotten Intoh to speak about Ekalas in length, but Linda knew enough to know that her ghost was leading him down a path not good for him.

"Always been a Misfit," Linda said, reaching out to lay their hand on his head once more. A comforting gesture, Linda had come to realize. "Will always be a Misfit."

Intoh lowered his gaze. "Thank you." He cleared his throat, his cheeks warming in embarrassment. Linda often wondered why Intoh remained in his human form when he didn't need to. Linda had freed themself from the shackle of their ring for some time now and didn't even think of going back. The form they took when they put it on just did not feel right.

"You know, should talk to Rackjack. You're right, always talking about the gods," Intoh said, pulling Linda from their thoughts. He seemed thoughtful himself, the blue of his eyes glittering with interest. "Would like to accompany. See what Rackjack has to say."

"Do not think he is here. Have not seen him."

Just as the words left Linda, a noise shuffled from down the hall, and Linda turned around. Rackjack, looking frazzled, was moving something behind a series of barrels, towards the doors that led down to the hull.

"Rackjack," Linda called out, startling him. "Would like to speak."

"Oh? Yes-yes. Be right back-there!" He disappeared quickly down the stairs and only returned after a few moments, his gaze darting to and fro as he scurried towards them. He was in his rakken form, but Linda barely grew surprised at it anymore. If they were able to be in their true form, why couldn't Rackjack? No matter how much Linda enjoyed slaughtering his kind.

"Rackjack—" Intoh struggled to see past Linda from the room. "Linda just telling me something that might interest you."

Rackjack's head swung to Linda, his eyes glittering with interest, and Linda found it easier to relay the story of Ikotia to Rackjack, who stared at them with nothing but awe. He smelled like he had been somewhere dark and damp.

Rackjack drew forward. "You are Chosen. Yes-yes. I knew it." Drool clung to his buck teeth as he panted heavily, his armor thick and coated in mud and dried blood. Linda had never seen him take it off.

"Chosen? Mean I'm special?" Linda asked. They didn't feel any different, nor did they feel very special. Still, they'd lived a very long time and had never heard of a krok'ida being spoken to by Ikotia, even though most krok'ida worshiped him before battle.

Rackjack nodded. "Must consult with Rat-King. Much to discuss. Much to learn." His words dissolved into random mutterings, and Linda glanced down and met Intoh's gaze, their stomach a turmoil of confusion. They didn't feel like they'd learned anything more about *why* Ikotia had decided to speak with them. Perhaps it did not matter. All that mattered was that Linda's bite could light their enemies on fire.

"Why Linda? Why Misfits?" Intoh asked.

Rackjack shrugged. "The gods do not tell-speak of why. We just follow their word-command."

Linda didn't like the sound of that very much. They had never been a fan at following. Not recently. Not since they had learned how desperately they'd craved the taste of their own freedom.

No more.

No man or god would ever demand their blind loyalty ever again. No longer would they allow themself to be controlled. It was a liberating feeling, one that caused adrenaline to course through them every time they thought of it, and Rackjack looked at them with interest.

"Scales are different. Just around your mouth-teeth. Have orange around lips. Very interesting. You might try to reach out to your god soon, yes-yes. Only he can guide you along right walk-path."

Intoh pulled water from the surrounding wood to create a way for Linda to see themself, and Rackjack was right; the scales around their mouth were etched with orange now, like they were endlessly breathing fire. Their reflection shimmered in the water, and they stood straighter for it. If their god was going to choose them, they would do their best to make him proud.

"You three ready for departure?" Tantien's voice called down from the end of the hallway, the gleam of his hair lit up against the torchlight as he swung down the stairs. The eldrasi trailed down the hall towards them, an easy smile on his face. "I think we're due to set sail for Míradan soon."

Intoh let the water he'd been holding in the air drop to the floor. "Can assist with wind if need. Will help quicken this journey if I can."

Tantien nodded at Linda and Rackjack. "Prepare to set sail. If I have need of you two, I'll call." He paused, his smile widening as he clasped Linda's shoulder. "It's nice to see the both of you refusing to hide behind illusions. The world deserves to see you both as you are. Now, let's go get my sister."

TWENTY-SEVEN
CASSIUS

"Hmm, I don't think that's how it works, Linda." Cassius leaned back in his chair, a wine glass balanced delicately in his fingertips, and he swirled it mindlessly as Linda opened their mouth in protest. They'd been sailing for a month or two now. Thanks to Intoh, they had been keeping a steady pace with little trouble from the elements. Boredom had set in, but the Misfits were keeping themselves busy enough with each other's company. Even Intoh, when he needed a break from casting magic, would come down from the crow's nest to play Helai's card game with them some nights. Rackjack had been fitted with a new prosthesis made from the metal of the bell he'd gotten from the bell tower in Alavae, thanks to Tantien, and he'd just gotten done showing it off to everyone. Even Cassius was impressed.

"What do you mean? Beat you in arm wrestling contest means I get your sword. How it works. Asked Rooster, told me it true."

Laughter tugged at the back of Cassius' throat, but a scowl formed on his lips despite. "You have *Volroth*, Linda. What could you possibly want with my sword?"

Linda didn't have a chance to respond before Helai stumbled into the room, her eyes darting from Linda to Cassius. There was a certain gleam to her eye, one Cassius had not seen before Massoud had made his appearance again, and he lifted an eyebrow in question.

"Helai?"

"I, ah—" Her eyes darted to Cassius' bed. "Rooster wants us to meet up for dinner so that we may talk about breaking into the prison." She edged towards the bed, a bright smile on her face.

Cassius narrowed his eyes at her. Too bright.

"What are you doing, Helai?"

Linda nodded in response to Cassius' prodding. "Yeah, acting weird."

Helai shook her head, holding her hands up. "Nothing. Just informing you that we're needed in the mess hall when the sun starts to go down. Can't a friend inform a...friend?"

Linda's head cocked to the side as they pushed away from the table they sat at and ambled towards the door. "Going to find Intoh. Let him know."

Linda squeezed through the door, which was slightly too small for their broad frame, and disappeared down the hall. Cassius sipped his wine, his gaze not once leaving Helai's as he watched her with cool calculation. Exhaustion clung to her eyes despite her lighter demeanor. She lunged, grabbing the blankets from his bed. "I just need to borrow these. Don't ask questions."

"Absolutely not." Cassius reached forward and grabbed the other end of the blanket, his lips twitching as his wine threatened to spill over the lip of the glass. "If a *drop* of wine spills from this glass—" He left his warning hanging in the air, and Helai huffed, blowing a loose strand of hair out of her face as she let go of the blanket and turned on her heel.

"Honestly, ClassyAss. You haven't the slightest idea on how to have any *fun*."

Cassius caught the hint of someone peering into his room before Helai shut the door behind her and left him to his own monstrous thoughts. Ahma had been silent since her appearance at the bath house in Volendam, and her warning haunted his anxieties.

Someone would be coming for him.

Perhaps it would be better to let them come so he could willingly give them the two items of the Ebony Fang. He longed to know when they would arrive; the agony of waiting was near torture.

"Cassius?" Massoud popped his head in, his hair neatly tucked into a loose ponytail behind his head. "May I come in?"

Cassius' nostrils flared. He shouldn't have expected any alone time. The other Misfits were notorious for making sure he was never granted such privilege.

After Cassius nodded, Massoud sauntered in, his fingers grazing the door as he pushed it shut behind him. His shirt was unbuttoned halfway down his chest, his black pants loose as they hugged his hips. Cassius attempted but failed not to stare as Massoud moved closer, gesturing to his bottle of wine.

"Hmm, let me guess. Sophisticated man like you... that's gotta be a dry red from the heart of Hestia."

Cassius nodded. "I managed to gather as much as I could carry aboard the Firebrand before we left Alavae. You don't seem a wine drinker at all."

Massoud's eyes darkened as a mirthful smile tugged at his lips. "Ah, I'm a man that can be *persuaded*. What is it about red wine that you crave so much?" He edged closer, and Cassius' breath caught in his throat as he quickly raised his glass to his lips and did his best to appear nonchalant. He was trapped in his chair with nowhere to go, and he couldn't deny just how handsome Massoud was. He would have pursued him if he'd seen him at one of the parties he used to frequent during his younger years.

The truth? Red wine was the strongest when it came to stifling the cravings; the back of his throat didn't ache quite so much with the calling for blood. Since his transformation and the urges of it being dulled, however, he'd discovered his love for red wine had not been hindered. If anything, he was enjoying it far more now that he wasn't using it as a tool against his bloodlust.

"An acquired taste," he finally said. "My mother and father used to let my brother and I have it at dinner, and I suppose you never forget your first."

Massoud laughed, and Cassius' cheeks warmed. "No, no, you don't," Massoud said, picking up the bottle and taking a long sip. "Mm, Shoman reds are better," he said softly, stepping up between Cassius' legs.

How easy it would be to grab Massoud's hips and drag him closer. The temptation was there, especially after having been rejected by Tantien, and Cassius' free fingers begged to dart forward. Heat rolled off Massoud's skin from where his legs brushed against Cassius' thighs, and Cassius silently cursed the lack of wine now in his glass for he had nothing to distract him.

"I must agree. They come a bit sweeter than the dry grapes of Hestia," Cassius uttered. His cheeks warmed once more as he realized how hoarse his voice sounded. Massoud's grin turned wicked as he leaned forward, the smell of his spiced perfume wafting over Cassius' nose. It might have been too strong for some, but the scent mixed with Massoud's nearness made his cock twinge in excitement.

Pull yourself together, he thought, but whatever Massoud wanted, he knew just what to do to get it. He hadn't known the man for long, but Massoud was as gifted in his persuasion as he was in his shadow magic.

Cassius shuddered as Massoud's magic caressed the side of his cheek and slipped over his neck as if Massoud was pressing soft kisses there. Massoud's gaze pinned him to the chair, and he slowly set the bottle of wine down on the table as he curled one hand around the chair's arm while the other came up to trail over Cassius' shoulder.

"Helai tells me you were a soldier of the Sanguine Order, or, ah—White Dawn, as most of humanity knows it." His tone was hushed, his voice quiet against the cusp of Cassius' ear. "I've always had such admiration for those who swore an oath to protect those who don't deserve it."

"Who is to say they don't? It isn't our jobs as knights to judge who does and does not deserve to be protected."

Massoud pulled back slightly, his gaze searching Cassius' eyes. He wore a strange expression, one Cassius couldn't place, like a cross between anger and understanding. It sent Cassius' stomach rolling, and Massoud's smile widened, revealing the gleam of teeth.

"Such a knightly thing to say, *habti*. Is that why you left?"

A soft sigh passed Cassius' lips as Massoud's words dragged across the cusp of his ear, his mouth ghosting along the side of Cassius' neck. It was difficult to think, his own words always falling short as goosebumps rose against the skin of his arms. His erection was undeniable now, and the bloodlust in the back of his throat strengthened with the thought: *what does Massoud taste like?*

"Helai was way out of her league," Massoud whispered, pressing a kiss against Cassius' clavicle. Laughter danced over his tongue as the presence of his shadow magic disappeared, and he pulled away. "The secret to distracting a man is simple—all you have to do is get him horny." His laughter followed as he twirled on his heel.

"Wait—" Cassius' mind was a whirl of desire and confusion as he stood up, attempting to recover from the muddled mess he'd become in Massoud's hands before Massoud opened the door. "What do you mean—"

As Massoud pried the door open, an annoyed Helai appeared, her eyes darting from Cassius to Massoud. A hand was pressed to her hip, and she spoke quickly and softly to Massoud in Shoman. It had been so long since Cassius had learned the language that he only caught bits and pieces of her chastising.

"And *that's* how you do it, little sister," Massoud said through his grin, glancing back to wink at Cassius. "I do hope you can find it in your cold, dead heart to forgive me."

"Would never... That's ClassyAss... You cheated..." Helai said as their conversation faded. Cassius ran a shaky hand through his hair before he composed himself, allowing his desire to fade before he reached out and grabbed the bottle of wine. Massoud was not unique in his advances; Cassius had been victim to such manipulations before, had been on the other end of them from time to time too, but he scowled at the way he'd played into Massoud's trap without pause.

He'd be better next time.

Turning, he moved to grab something from under his bed before he headed to the mess hall. If there were plans to be made before they arrived in Míradan, he needed to be there. His hand stilled as his gaze found his bed, and he realized all his bedding had disappeared. It suddenly all made sense, and his scowl deepened as he turned back around and pried the now-closed door open, Helai and Massoud having left.

"Massoud!"

Massoud's laughter was heard down the hall. "My captain demanded it! You know better than I that we cannot ignore the commands of Rooster."

Cassius gritted his teeth and did not reply. He grabbed his sword from under the bed and then left his room. Shutting the door behind him, he headed to the mess hall.

Fucking. Mortals.

The mess hall was a flurry of conversation when he arrived. Tantien stood at the end of a long table, and Rooster, the three greka, and Linda sat nearby. Drithan was to the right of Linda, sharpening his knife on a smooth round stone, and Rooster was speaking to Tantien quietly.

The conversation quieted as Rooster and Tantien glanced over. Cassius gave a firm yet silent nod, slipping into the chair across from Drithan. The dwarf grunted in greeting, his gaze not leaving his blade, and Cassius could respect that focus. Once Helai entered with Massoud, both ghosting the edge of the room with silent steps, Tantien started.

"We were just talking about what needs to happen the moment we dock in Kelirium. The eldrasi have an enormous price on Car—ah..." Tantien paused, pressing his hand to the nape of his neck sheepishly as he glanced sideways at Rooster. "On *Rooster's* head. So arriving is going to be tricky as his, ah...association with my sister, among his general piracy, has caused Míradan to take a watchful eye for the Perseverance's flags, which they already have in their possession, and its witty captain."

Rooster stilled, a peculiar expression crossing his face.

"Then how are we going to dock?" Cassius asked. The odds were endlessly stacked against them. Not only were they to break into one of the most protected prisons in the world, but they had to locate the tome Delroy had requested, a tome that Cassius had a feeling would not be easy to locate.

"I have a contact from my time serving as a Thorn, the elite guard of Kelirium. We're going to meet and see, then she's going to transport you all there."

"And you're certain she can be trusted?" Helai asked, her voice uncertain. Suspicion was thick in the air. Only the drikoty seemed at ease with their travels to the eldrasi island, but it was common knowledge that the drikoty and eldrasi held good relations due to their trade agreements with one another.

Tantien nodded. "She's an old friend. I trust her with my life."

"We get inside the city, then what's our path?" Rooster's question made Tantien's brow furrow as he leaned forward and grabbed a tankard from the table. After drinking from it deeply, Tantien slammed it back down and sighed.

"We do not know the location of the tome Delroy seeks. My contact may have heard of it, but until I receive word from her about arranging a time to speak once we near the island, we're planning in the dark." He hesitated, his gaze shifting to Rooster. "We'll have to grab the tome before we rescue my sister."

Rooster's face grew haunted at the thought, and Cassius felt for him. He'd heard whispers of Fraxinus and the horrible methods the eldrasi used to extract information from their prisoners.

"What if we split up?"

The room turned to Intoh, who seemed uncomfortable about the sudden shift of attention. Red blossomed over his cheeks, and his eyes darted to his hands in his lap, as if his courage sat nestled there. No one pushed him to speak, but the room filled with the silence of expectation.

"If all go to prison, will make too much noise. Will likely get captured. What if some of us go, seek out tome, and then find a safe place to meet?"

Hesitation sat thick in the room. Splitting up would always come with certain risks, but Cassius could see the benefits of it too. Intoh was right; if they all went to the prison, they would be asking for capture.

"I could possibly have my contact get whoever obtains the tome off the island, but without knowing what the tome can do, it could be dangerous," Tantien said. "Magic with the power to put a god to sleep will call out to those who are magically inclined. We're going to have to figure out a way to smuggle you out of the city while you have it in your possession. That is –" Tantien cracked a smile. "If you're the one volunteering for such a heist."

Intoh nodded. "Will go. Magic could be useful."

"Khal and Sode will obviously accompany you." Rooster nodded towards the other greka. "I think that could work, so long as we're all careful. We don't want to alert the island about our presence too early, or they might reinforce the prison."

"Well, and if my memory stands, there is a tower near the prison that holds some of the island's best magical artifacts. There is a very good chance the tome is being kept there, which means we won't need to be separated for long."

"Helai, you should go with the greka," Massoud said, kicking off the wall and trailing around the table. His expression was thoughtful as he folded his arms and wiggled his fingers.

Helai's brow furrowed, and she shook her head. "I should stay with you."

"They'll need someone versed in shadow magic to aid them, and I am stronger when it comes to magic."

"I could assist as well." Itale's voice perked up from a side table, and Cassius' head raised. He hadn't even known Itale was here. "I'm growing more and more confident in my abilities since Sir Cassius is teaching me." His eyes flickered briefly to Cassius, his smile nervous.

"I will also go with the greka." Drithan's voice was gruff as his eyes landed on Helai, who still seemed uncertain as she watched Massoud move about the room. Massoud's fingers darted across Cassius' shoulders, and warmth seeped through him, reminding him of just earlier, when Massoud's mouth had darted across his skin. His mouth dried, and he shook the thoughts from his head before they could burrow. He was just a distraction.

"So, as it stands—Cassius, Massoud, Rackjack, and Linda will go with me into the prison," Rooster said, counting off his fingers. "Helai, Drithan, Khal, Sode, Intoh, and Itale will go and fetch the tome." His gaze shifted to Tantien. "Will you be accompanying us?"

"I wish I could," Tantien's smile was pained as he pressed his fingers to the side of the table. "My involvement with the Thorns will have me recognized too easily. It'll be too big of a risk, and we only get one chance at this."

Cassius understood that risk. It would be like him waltzing into Dragon Keep and expecting all of the other knights of the Sanguine Order to not recognize him. It would be impossible. Cassius was beginning to understand why Tantien had sought them out for such a task.

"We're honored you'd trust us with this, Tantien. We promise we'll get your sister out." Cassius' promise rang out through the room, and the Misfits seemed as determined as he felt to liberate Rooster's crew and Tantien's sister from Fraxinus.

"I appreciate it." Worry echoed in his gaze as he peered about the room. "With how long they've been in there, I'm not certain about what state they'll be in. Much of the crew will be in the inner cells due to their lack of command. Your officers and Igraine will be kept in the cages that hang from the tree branches, most likely at the top and most likely the most guarded."

"Ah, that's where my talents come in," Massoud mused, his tone tinged with amusement. "I can get us to the top, no problem."

"Excellent. We have the start of a plan then. We can discuss more as we get closer to the island. With Intoh's help and if we should continue to avoid the worst of weather, we should be there within the month. We'll have to make a stop in Saumur to restock supplies, but that shouldn't take more than a day." Tantien tapped his knuckles against the table and straightened. "Now if there's nothing more to discuss, I shall return to the wheel." No one stopped him as he disappeared from the room, leaving a quiet buzz of conversation to trail over the table. Helai and Drithan spoke in a heated argument under their breath, and Cassius' eyes met Rooster's from across the table.

Cassius gave a subtle nod. When they got to Míradan, he would be ready to do whatever was necessary to free Rooster's people.

TWENTY-EIGHT

CASSIUS

Saumur was a beautiful Nantiellian coastal town, and they arrived the next few days without any trouble. It was nice to get off the Firebrand for a time, to stretch his legs. He'd managed to get his bedding returned to him after the meeting and he needed a break from the other Misfits, even if it was just for a couple of hours. The world swayed a bit, Cassius having gotten accustomed to days at sea, as he trailed down the docks towards the small city laid before him.

"Be back here before nightfall," Tantien called out, and Cassius raised a hand in acknowledgment. The city was bustling with life, and Cassius was eager to explore. In his long life, he'd never been to many of Nantielle's cities despite one of the Sanguine Order's founders having been from Châtillon, Nantielle's capital. Nantielle was known for two things: their art and their bread, and while food no longer called to Cassius as it had done in his human life, he found a deep appreciation for art. Perhaps it called out to the boy in him who had loved to paint before his father had strangled it from him.

"Cassius, wait!"

Massoud caught up with him, falling into an easygoing step as they strolled through the city. He was looking way better than he had just after the battle in Alavae; his eyes were brighter, and his hair was clean and curled as he wore it back in a loose ponytail. His beard was now clean-shaven, save for a small dusting on his cheeks, and he wore a smile that oozed confidence. "You don't mind some company, do you?"

Cassius gave him a steady stare and then shook his head. "No, I suppose not. I do not have a destination in mind, so perhaps the company will be welcomed."

"You're so stoic, Cassius. Do you know that it's okay to smile? You have a pretty one," Massoud said, laughing as he bumped shoulders with Cassius before shoving his hands in the pockets of his loose pants.

"Have you been talking with Rooster?" Cassius scowled. "You two are like an echo chamber." Still, his cheeks warmed at the compliment. The city laid before them was beautiful; the buildings were decorated with flowers of various colors, and tables were lined outside, where people sat and ate. The low buzz of conversation wafted over Cassius in a language he did not know, but a certain comfort came with it, a lack of care as they strolled down the street.

"Let's stop here," Massoud said, ignoring Cassius' question. "The Shoman soldiers stole all of my rings when I was captured, and my fingers are too bare." He gestured as they passed by a store full of glittering gems and jewels. *L'dazel* was scribbled in elegant writing on the window, and Cassius eyed it for a moment before nodding. His own fingers were littered with rings of his own; he only wore them when he was confident about being out of his armor. Each of them carried one sentiment or another, and that alone made Cassius understand Massoud's grief.

"After you then."

He trailed in after Massoud as the warmth of the shop grazed his face. It felt strange after everything he'd faced in recent years: being stuck in his tomb, the brand, almost dying. A part of him felt undeserving of something so calming as *shopping*, and the notion left his skin crawling even as Massoud approached the burly man behind the counter, all smiles and batting eyes.

The owner of the shop was tall, with a thick mustache that curled at the edges, and he spoke to Massoud in Nantiellian, the words quick and fluid on his tongue.

"Ah, apologies, but do you speak Vilris?" Massoud asked, tapping a slender finger on the counter as he leaned against it.

"Erm, yes. A...a bit," the shop owner said, struggling over the words. "What...choose do you?"

"I can help with translation," Itale said, appearing at the door. He seemed at home in the city, his eyes bright as his curls sprang about his head as he entered the shop. He switched to Nantiellian to speak to the store owner, his words quick.

The owner nodded, and Itale looked at Massoud expectedly.

As Massoud conversed with the shop owner and Itale, Cassius meandered around. The shop wasn't very large, nothing like Cassius had seen in some of the larger cities, but it had its fair share of treasures. Some of the jewelry was piled in open boxes atop the counter. Cassius couldn't sense any magic coming from them. Instead, the magical pieces were tucked safely behind a thin layer of glass. Cassius was certain it was enchanted to prevent thievery. Glancing up, he noticed the runes carved into the four corners of the shop. They were beautifully carved and looked almost dwarven in nature. Another layer to prevent thievery.

"Cassius, what do you think?" Massoud turned, offering his hand. The ring sitting on his middle finger was large and over the top with a silver band and a yellow stone set in the middle. Non-magical. Cassius shook his head.

"No, that one does not suit you at all. The silver is fine, but you need something like—" Leaning around Massoud, he gestured to a smaller ring with a silver band and a purple amethyst set in the middle. A small amount of magic radiated from it, and Cassius nodded with a small smile simpering at his lips. "That one."

"I cannot afford that one." Massoud took it from the shop owner's offering hand regardless, holding it up to the light that filtered in through the open door. "I sense magic in it. What does it do?"

The shop owner struggled to find the words. "Make you ah...feel the lightness on your feet." Stones were perfect for holding minor weavings of magic like that. Something to make the wearer a little quicker or a little harder to hit in combat or completely silent when walking. One of Cassius' rings helped with his aversion to the sunlight. It had cost him a small fortune when he'd bought it off a low vampire in Fraheim.

"How much?" Cassius asked, shaking his coin purse at the owner.

"Seventy-two skaels."

"Cassius, don't." Massoud pressed a hand to Cassius'. "You don't have to do that."

"Nonsense." Cassius shook away Massoud's protest as he shuffled the skaels into the shop owner's palm. "I will spend my skaels however I want."

A peculiar look crossed Massoud's face as he turned back towards the shop owner, and a gut-wrenching pain pierced Cassius' arm. It trailed along his skin where the gun and lance from the Ebony Fang armory lay dormant, and Cassius gritted his teeth as he pulled his hand away and stepped back.

What?

An urge called to him, an urge to follow...

Massoud's laughter filled the shop, attempting to chase away the sudden darkness that had dampened it, but it was soured when Cassius turned and peered outside.

He felt the same as when Ahma had first presented herself to him and the urge to go to Volendam had plagued him. Or again, when he had been called to Halvdarc. He hadn't felt the pull since he'd scorned Ahma at the Walker's Estate, but there it was, clear as day radiating up to his chest from the spot in his arm.

"I have to go." He moved abruptly, ignoring Massoud's and Itale's questions as he stumbled slightly on the doorstep. Two women sat at a nearby table and eyed him wearily as he pushed past, following the call of magic that dragged him through the city. He barely noticed the people he passed, turning down streets until he found himself amid a beautiful garden tucked away in the center of the city. Cassius might have had time to marvel at its beauty had he not been so distracted by whatever had drawn him there.

He was nearing the massive fountain in the center when the magic forced him to halt in front of a stranger. He was the only one here. His back was to Cassius, but a sense of familiarity coursed through him, like a long-forgotten dream.

Someone from your past...

The stranger turned, and Cassius lowered his gaze as he realized he did not recognize him. He nodded in respect as the stranger brushed past him, and Cassius stepped up to the fountain, exhaling slowly and attempting to still his shaking hands. The thrum of magic that had pulled him here was still so overwhelming, he was nearly losing his mind to it, so he stared into the fountain and steeled himself against its will.

"Cassius." A familiar voice brought him from his mind. He turned as someone crashed into him and sent them both tumbling into the fountain.

The cold of the water was jarring, and he hit the bottom of the fountain, wrangling with whoever had tackled him. He was thankful in that moment for his lack of armor weighing him down. He snarled, his illusion bleeding away. Wrapping his arms around the person, he shoved them back towards the surface.

They broke free of the water, and Cassius buffeted his wings to fling them forward. His lips peeled back, and his fangs descended. They crashed into the ground with Cassius pinning the stranger onto his back.

The stranger's hood fell back, and Cassius recoiled, his chest heaving as horror flourished through him. He shook his hair out of his face. "Markus?"

Cassius' older brother stared up at him. He bore sharper lines and darker eyes than Cassius. His face was more angular and tucked behind a beard similar to his brother's. He was slightly thinner, still broad in the shoulder but taller than Cassius.

He was supposed to be long dead.

Red tinged the brown in his eyes as he stared angrily up at Cassius, his own mouth peeled back with fangs of his own. He was a vampire just like Cassius, with wings and talons to match as his monstrosity pushed through his illusion.

"You have something I need." He spoke in their native tongue, their Hestian roots gleaming between them, and there was no warmth in his tone. Using Cassius' surprise as leverage, he wiggled out from beneath him and moved away. He stopped a few feet away and Cassius' gaze darted around. If anyone were to see two high vampires in the middle of the city, they could draw the wrath of any nearby Blödragrs, those of the organization that hunted his kind. That was the last thing Cassius needed.

"How?" Still, the question poised itself upon his lips as he stared at Markus. He could scarcely believe it, his mind unraveling at the possibility. Markus looked older, middle aged perhaps when he had been turned, but how had Cassius been blissfully unaware of his brother's survival for all of these years?

"It matters little." Markus' laughter was bitter as he shot close. His fingers gripped Cassius' forearm. "When she told me you had two of the pieces, I didn't believe her at first. I thought you were still tucked away in that tomb your Order had trapped you in."

Cassius hissed in pain as he looked down to see dark blood pulling itself from his skin as the weapons that lay dormant there began to rise. Markus was attempting to pry them from Cassius' arm, and it was then that Cassius realized that Markus wore the cuirass from the Ebony Fang Armory, the same one that Cassius had failed to retrieve from the Welker Estate.

Someone from your past.

Rage coursed through him, swift as an untamed river, but Cassius' focus was pulled by a woman coming out of one of the alleys. He grabbed her and laced his words with the drip of his compulsion magic. "Tell anyone you pass that the center gardens are poisoned with some sort of magical plague and must be avoided." He shoved her away, and she stumbled before taking off down one of the paths. Right before Markus rammed into him, the shadow of his own wings raised behind him.

Cassius staggered back, then ducked as Markus swung out his arm to strike him. "Markus, wait."

But it was as if Markus could not hear him, and unlike when they had been children, where they'd been forced day after day to train against one another, his brother had grown stronger and faster than him. It was more difficult for Cassius to overpower him as Markus threw himself at him with reckless abandon.

Cassius' mind shuttered between past and present. *Two young boys sparred under their father's watchful gaze.* Markus shoved Cassius against the trunk of a tree, his hand once more reaching for the weapons tucked away in Cassius' blood. *Blood trailed down Markus' face where Cassius had struck him too hard on accident, his eyes full of betrayal.* Cassius struggled against him, his mind fractured. All he knew was that he could not let Markus get the weapons, even as they sought to join the one who wore the cuirass. He would not doom his brother to the fate of the Ebony Fang. *Two boys cried while tucked away in a room where they hid from the wrath of their scorned father, his footsteps thundering down the hall.* Markus' face peppered with decay, his fangs gleaming as he reached up to strangle Cassius, who lashed out and headbutted him. He recoiled, and Cassius swung out from underneath him, twisting to press Markus' front against the same tree trunk. *Markus' laughter danced out across the water. The sea rolled against the shore, where they plucked fayre stars from the sand.*

"Brother, please." Cassius' pleading was met with silence as he twisted his brother's arm against his back and pushed him harder up against the tree. "I do not understand."

Markus stilled, his lack of breath jarring. "You never understood, little brother. Your honor made you a monster." His words were slick with hurt, and Cassius recoiled. "You stripped my power away when we were young under the guise of protecting me when, in all reality, Father's wrath was instilled into you. I dare claim you grew to like its power. The woman whispering in our bloodline, the one seeking the Ebony Fang, she's promised me the same power you and Father denied me."

Markus' words struck Cassius deeply with their implications. Their father had been a cruel man, his eye on forging two great warriors that would make the Antonia bloodline proud. He'd seen Markus as a failure who had never quite been able to live up to the natural gift for combat that Cassius had, and thus, had been treated poorly because of it. Cassius had done his best to shield his brother from their father's wrath, but children weren't meant to see danger from their parents.

"Markus, I am so sorry." The words stuck in Cassius' throat like poison, knowing they would do little to soothe a century-long festering wound.

If anything, they poked and prodded at it, and Markus snarled against the tree, his wings kicking back and shoving Cassius away. Even most high vampires did not have wings; seeing them on Markus struck questions in Cassius he knew he wouldn't get the answers to.

"Give me the gun and the lance, brother."

"I cannot. It will make you crave unspeakable power."

Markus' eyes glazed over with rage at Cassius' defiance. His movement was a blur, and he slammed Cassius into the ground. His ears rang as his head hit the ground, and the air was knocked from his lungs. Markus' eyes were wide with manic glee.

"Then I will rip them out of you."

There was no pain as blood secreted from his skin once more, the weapons responding to Markus' touch as he pinned Cassius' arm to the ground at the crook of his elbow.

By the blood of the dragon.

Cassius howled, but Markus was strong and had pinned him more effectively this time. He could not free himself. His words were lost upon deaf ears as Markus' fingers wrapped around the hilt of the lance, which had just begun to appear from his skin.

The air thickened and then grew dark as shadows curled around him, and he was ripped away from Markus. He became weightless as someone wrapped their arm around his waist and tugged him close. Markus' frustrated scream was cut off when Cassius disappeared fully into the darkness, the void opening its gaping maw and swallowing him whole.

He went tumbling as he hit the deck of a ship hard, his head a maelstrom of panic and confusion. His stomach rolled as the world righted itself, and he rolled over onto his stomach and pushed himself up, preparing to launch himself at whoever came at him.

But there was no more danger. He stood on the Firebrand with Massoud a few feet away, on his hands and knees, his back heaving violently as he vomited dark curls of shadow magic. It slipped from his mouth, his nose, and ears, and Cassius rushed over to him, ignoring the wide stares of what eldrasi sailors had remained onboard as he pressed a hand to Massoud's back.

"Shade stepped—" He gasped, tears pricking the corners of his eyes as smoke rolled down to the deck and dispersed. "Too far."

"You should not have." Cassius' mind was fractured, still dragging up the darkness from his past, and the sudden appearance of his older brother and the pieces of the Ebony Fang he carried left him trembling. There was no way Markus couldn't feel the pull of the weapons nestled in Cassius' arm. He could feel the cuirass now, burrowed in the city, a quiet call. He harbored so many questions: how was Markus a vampire? How did he get his wings when it had taken Cassius dying as a vampire to receive his own? Would Markus continue hunting him? The notion left a bitter taste in Cassius' mouth.

Would he have to kill his own brother?

"Don't be silly," Massoud whispered, his face clearing up as the magical backlash softened. He turned and waved Cassius away, leaning against the mast nearby as his face caught the sun. "That asshole was trying to murder you. What pretty thing would I get to stare at all the time if you died?"

"There is no lacking of pretty on this ship," Cassius said.

A smile tugged against Massoud's lips, and he shrugged. "I suppose you're right. Go on then. Get out of my sight."

Cassius lowered his head, eager to retreat, to find solace somewhere dark and alone where he could mull over what had just transpired, but Massoud reached out and grabbed his hand before he could leave. Massoud's fingers were warm, and Cassius stared down to where their hands were joined.

"Are you okay?"

Cassius' heart thundered against his rib cage. *No.* "Yes." *My own brother, who is supposed to be very much dead, just tried to kill me.* "I am fine."

"Who was that? Someone to be worried about?"

"No."

Massoud's head tilted as if he didn't believe him.

A bubble of madness threatened to claw from the depths of his belly all the way to his throat, and he sighed, pressing his free fingers to the bridge of his nose as he collapsed next to Massoud. "That was my brother."

Massoud's eyes flashed in alarm as he pulled his hand away from Cassius'. He sat down next to him and laid his hands in his own lap. "Oh, so it's family drama." He held up his hands at Cassius' withering stare, and Cassius was interested to note that both the silver *and* gold rings were shining brightly on Massoud's fingers. "I do not need to know details, but if it's any consolation, sometimes I would also like to kill Helai for preying on my patience, and she's not even my blood sister."

Laughter edged his tone, and he looked better than he had just moments before. The evidence of his recent torture and the magical backlash he'd just forced his body through was fading, and Cassius felt himself being tugged away from the edge of his own trauma-induced panic.

"Helai has a talent for plucking the strings of one's irritation," Cassius agreed. "Still, she is a good woman. My brother—I am not sure..." He trailed off as shame curdled in his belly. Gods, he hated being vulnerable. "It matters little. I need to find Tantien. If Markus is in the city, it is unlikely he will leave me alone. We need to leave."

"I agree. We have too much on our plate to deal with the scorn of an angry brother. Come, we'll go and find him together." As they both stood, a chill rolled down Cassius' back, and his stomach rolled, like he was standing on the edge of a precipice.

Perhaps it was time to have a conversation with Ahma...

TWENTY-NINE
INTOH

Tantien demanded Intoh take a break a fortnight out from Míradan, insisting he'd need to be at his full strength for the island. "The wind is perfectly capable of getting us there, Intoh," he said after ignoring Intoh's several moments of insisting he was fine. "Go, have fun. Relax. If I see you up in the crow's nest again, the consequences will be severe."

Something in the eldrasi's eye told him he needn't defy him, so he spent a lot of his time getting to know Sode and Khal. Before, he'd just recognized them as bodyguards, sent to protect what they believed was a prophet of Axolli. Now, he was eager to hear their stories.

"Came from small village in the southern lands," Khal said, sharpening his spearhead with a whetstone. "Spent a lot of time at Straeva Tower, learning the power of the stars. Axolli speak to me often there. Would love for you to visit sometime. Think other prophets would benefit from your knowledge."

Intoh nodded. For some reason, his heart longed for it, like perhaps he had missed out on an entire community of people who would've understood him. If he and Ekalas had managed to free themselves properly, he somehow knew they would have granted them sanctuary.

Ekalas had not shown herself for some time. He was closer than ever to finding the answer to immortality with the tome, and yet Ekalas was silent. He tried not to despair, to see her silence as a sign of failure, but a small part of him screamed in guilt at having let the Misfits in, at having turned his back on his only friend to seek familial ties with those he'd been traveling with only for the last couple of years.

"What about you, Sode? Also from coastal town?" Intoh asked, turning to Sode as he watched the eldrasi sailors work. They sat on the ground near the bow, tucked away so they would be out of the way should the sailors need to adjust the sails, and Sode's tail slapped against the wood of the deck as he shook his head.

"No, my village was closer to the swampland. Small village, you probably never heard of it. I traveled up to Axcala to become a guard five summers ago." His gaze slid to Intoh. "Only left when Axolli came to me in a dream. Khal and I found each other and traveled to find you."

"Did Axolli speak to you directly?" Intoh found himself asking. Linda confiding in him some months ago had rattled him. Krok'ida weren't known for conversing with their god, and Ikotia was a rather quiet god in terms of his meddling. If he was speaking to Linda, it was for an important reason, one Intoh didn't want to speak to Linda about until he knew more.

Still, while he had never asked for his god's guidance, it was a bit of a slight to his pride for Axolli to have named him prophet and then refused to speak to him.

"In dreams," Khal and Sode said together. "Axolli is quiet god. Does not speak directly. It's usually through signs in sky or in dreams."

Khal leaned forward. "Sometimes meditating before sleep can help. Would recommend if you're trying to open yourself up to her."

Intoh waved his hand in dismissal. "Was merely curious. Will not question it."

As silence encompassed them, Intoh watched Cassius and Itale practice necromancy. His own magic shifted uncomfortably under his skin as they pulled at the air, but Intoh was pleased to see how successful Itale had been in picking up the craft. He'd never touch necromancy himself, not unless it was the only way to live forever, but the young human seemed to have a knack for it. Cassius even looked impressed, and it was hard to pull emotion from the vampire. The tips of Itale's fingers had blackened during the siege on Alavae and had never seemed to heal. When Intoh had asked Cassius about it, he'd said it was permanent damage from the necromancy magic eating away at its host.

"It is why it is imperative that I teach him and quickly," Cassius had said. "Necromancy is the wildest form of magic. It will take a person's life quicker than they can blink should they not learn to wield it properly. Itale performed powerful necromancy, bringing life back from the dead. His fingers will never be the same."

Still, the determinedness set in Itale's expression from across the ship made Intoh feel for the boy. He carried that same drive to succeed. The other Misfits teased him, but it was why he sought so much time to read.

His human illusion kept himself looking young, but he could feel the pulls of age beginning to grip him. He'd been six when he'd found himself captured by the Shoma'kah, and two and a half years had passed since then. His bones ached often, his eyes were unable to see as far as they'd used to, and it was more painful to molt than it had been when he'd been younger. He knew he was running out of time, but he'd found himself thinking about it less as of late even though he was closer than ever to finding answers.

The tome. He could feel it in his bones. It was the answer.

"Going to stretch my legs." He tossed out his hand as the others prepared to follow. "No need. Will find you later."

A frustrated groan echoed from one of the rooms as Intoh descended the stairs into the lower decks. At first, Intoh was content to ignore it, but then he peeked into the room and noticed Rooster's head in his hands, and despite his own awkward nature, he found himself pushing into the room and clearing his throat.

"Wh— Oh, hello, Intoh." Rooster sighed, pushing his hair out of his face as he straightened up in the chair he was sitting in. The day was paving the way to dusk outside the round window behind him, and the sky was full of brilliant colors of gold and pink. Intoh stared at it for several moments before he gained the courage to push past his awkwardness and ask, "Doing okay?"

Rooster hummed, giving Intoh a peculiar look. His laughter was soft, a jest as he waved a hand in Intoh's direction. "Just frustrated, is all. I grow tired of having my memories stuffed behind doors. I don't even know if they'll ever return, even after we rescue Igraine."

Intoh shrugged. "Who cares?"

Rooster flinched, an offended expression crossing his face.

"What I mean is, doesn't change anything. Past is past. We go forward, not back. Might as well focus on that."

Rooster's face softened slightly at that, but there was still a war going on in his expression, two conflicting emotions, anguish and understanding, fought in his eyes. "That, my friend, is easier said than done. I don't want to liberate my people from this prison and have them remembering a version of me that I cannot. What if—" He choked back emotion, his eyes shining. "What if I see her, and I remember nothing?"

Human emotions were so strange. Intoh could not understand their obsession with one another. The term they used, the 'love' they felt for the people they mated with, was a concept Intoh wasn't sure he'd ever be familiar with. He had comforted himself with the notion. Still, seeing Rooster so distraught *did* tug something inside him. Something in him wanted to reach out and comfort Rooster somehow.

"Wish I knew mind magic. Could perhaps try to see what's blocking. Rackjack said it might be dangerous—"

"Don't worry about it, Intoh." Rooster smiled, his turmoil tucked back behind tall walls. "I know you would do something if you could. This was merely me venting my frustrations, is all." Still, there was something sad in his smile, and Intoh wasn't sure whether to remain or flee.

"Perhaps..." He hesitated. He'd read all his books front to back and couldn't remember seeing anything about magical amnesia. Still... "Perhaps find something in one of my books. Could ease things. Just until you see Igraine again."

Rooster leaned back in his chair until the front two legs were kicked off the ground, and he dangled, his fingers clasping a mug in his hand. "If it doesn't take up too much of your time, then that would be wonderful. I know Tantien's been running you ragged, keeping the wind in our sails."

"No," Intoh protested with a small shake of his head. "Always offered. Like to help." He paused. "Will see if I missed anything in readings. If not, might be something in the tome that can help."

Rooster shrugged. "Maybe."

Intoh gave a faint nod and turned to go, nearly barreling into Massoud and Drithan as he did so. Massoud was carrying a significant amount of bedding. Massoud's smile danced on the edge of an ornery tone, while Drithan looked sheepish, like he'd been caught doing something terrible.

"Don't mind us, Intoh. Just gotta talk to Rooster about something if you two are done," Massoud said, peeking into Rooster's room as Rooster straightened his chair and offered a lopsided grin.

"Fort Kickass is coming along nicely. I see you've managed to snag more bedding for the blanket fort..." Their voices faded as Intoh scurried away, his mind whirling with the possibility of helping Rooster with his ailment. He'd never cared before because Rooster had never expressed such distress over it, but now that Intoh was aware, he'd pull out all his books and get to work.

THIRTY
HELAI

The nightmares had begun a few weeks into the journey. Helai had spent the majority of the first two weeks fighting vomiting spells and dizzy fatigue as her body struggled to get its sea legs, and, once again, she'd promised herself that this would be the last time she spent a long period of time on a boat.

She'd spent much of those two weeks locked away in her room, hoping that sleep would save her from the nausea. It had gotten so bad at one point that she'd wondered if she might trade her bed with a hammock, having heard the swaying would help. But with tensions and unease being so high now that they were on their way to Míradan, Helai hadn't wanted to be a burden. But she had finally been relieved of some of her worst seasickness symptoms at the end of the second week, only to then be plagued with nightmares that had yet to stop.

A jinn reached out with sharp claws in the dark, its voice all-encompassing and softer than a whisper as it caressed her ear. *Your wish bears a heavy burden. Are you willing to shoulder its weight?* A dragon replaced it, a long, thin dragon with whiskers and no wings. It trailed through a dusting of colors and stars. Its scales were blue as they shifted in shades of vibrancy through the night sky, and Helai watched it as it snaked towards her, knowing exactly who it was.

Qevayla, the dragon of dreams.

Something begged her to look away. A whisper in her other ear, his voice pleading for recognition though she couldn't for the life of her remember who it was. Rooted in place, she could not move as Qevayla snaked around the void of nothingness above. She flicked her tail, and trails of purple fire shot across the sky.

Your wish bears a heavy burden. An echo. Qevayla's gaze turned to Helai, her eyes large, round, and white, luminescent like the moon. It was no wonder Helai's people believed the moon to be Qevayla watching over them.

The weight of the dragon's stare hit her all at once, and her knees buckled. She plummeted; a sob lodged in her throat. *Are you willing to shoulder its weight?*

Yes, she longed to cry out. *Anything for the people I love.* No words left her lips, and tears rolled down her cheeks as Qevayla dove down from the sky, her maw open wide to swallow Helai whole.

Helai gasped as she woke, slick with sweat as she shot up in bed. For a moment, she couldn't recall where she was. Her muscles ached, as if the weight she'd been shouldering in her dream had crossed over to the waking world, and she pushed herself up against the wall, pulling her knees to her chest as she sobbed. The bedroom she shared with Massoud was empty, and she was glad about it. Massoud had enough demons to battle. He would try to bear hers too, and he woke up enough from his own nightmares to worry about hers.

A hesitating knock came at her door, and she lifted her head from her arms as Drithan's gruff voice sounded through the thick wood of the door. "Helai? Are you alright?"

A need burrowed in her chest, a flurry of panic and guilt that swam up and clawed at her throat, threatening to suffocate her. She rose to her feet and padded over to the door, opening it quickly to a surprised and sheepish Drithan.

"I heard—I uh, I just wanted to make sure—" He stumbled over his words, but Helai ignored them. Curling her fingers into his shirt, she tugged him into the room. She didn't want to think about the implications of the jinn's warning right now. She didn't want to think about how it might be tied to Qevayla or whether she was strong enough to shoulder the weight of the wish of bringing Massoud back. She didn't want to think of anything, so she pressed Drithan up against the door after slamming it shut and pressed her lips to his, her urgency building in her chest.

Drithan made a noise of surprise and pulled away, his hands clasping her arms. "Helai, do you want to talk about it?"

Helai shook her head, her eyes shining in the dimness of the room. Tantien's magical orbs flitted about, providing a soft glow of light, and Helai read the concern in Drithan's expression. But she didn't care. She didn't want his pity or his questions. She only wanted a *distraction*.

"I just want you," she begged, her fingers trailing down his chest towards his pant line. "Please."

His gaze searched hers for a moment before he conceded and rose up to kiss her again. His nearness chased away the panic. His fingers darted down her arms before tugging her shirt over her head and then his mouth lowered to pave pathways of kisses over her neck to her breasts, where his mouth closed over one of her nipples. She sighed, a soft moan curling against the back of her teeth as her hand slipped into his pants, and she let go.

They had found their way back to the bed, and Helai gasped, coming down from her climax as Drithan laid beside her, naked and staring up at the ceiling. Helai immediately danced away at his offering of cuddles by pushing herself up and finding her clothes on the floor. She could tell her lack of intimacy post fuck hurt him, but he didn't say anything, and she didn't explain. She couldn't explain the awkward, uncomfortable feeling in her chest every time he wanted to cuddle or just kiss or hold hands.

She needed to stop having sex with him.

And yet, she *did* enjoy his company. She enjoyed it very much, in the same way she enjoyed spending time with the other Misfits, with Massoud. She really enjoyed having sex with him too. It was the romance side of it she wasn't sure about, and she avoided his gaze as she pulled her shirt back over her head.

"Thanks for the distraction. Had a nightmare," she said, flashing him a quick smile as she made her way over to the small table nestled into the corner. A small basin rest there, and she cupped a small handful of water and pressed it to her face, relishing the coolness as she turned to sit in one of the chairs.

"Anything for you, Helai. You—" He hesitated, he always hesitated, his hand coming up to cover his face. "You need only ask," he finally said. There was a strange edge to his tone, covered by a soft adoration that sent a flurry of guilt coursing through Helai. She didn't want to hurt him, and the wood of the chair she sat in bit into her fingers as she finally forced her gaze to him.

"Drithan...I am sorry if I can't be what you want. I don't know what's wrong with me..." She swallowed a lump in her throat, and she prayed silently to Dalnor for strength. *Dalnor...Dalnor.* She realized with startling clarity that it had been Dalnor whispering in her ear in her nightmare. Tears threatened her again; how could she have forgotten her beloved god?

Drithan shot to his feet, his brow furrowed. "There's nothing wrong with you, Helai. If it's not what you want, there's no sense in me pushin' it." He studied her face for a moment, searching for something there, and then he stood, looking for his pants. Tugging them on, he turned back.

"I enjoy our time together even if it is just as a distraction. We move at your pace until you figure everything out. In the meantime, I'm here as a friend. Even if we, as friends, do that," he said, waving his hand towards the bed. There was a certain pain in Drithan's eyes as he smiled, and Helai's heart leapt to her throat. She knew he spoke against his own wishes, but her gut flopped at the thought of that sort of intimacy. It had been her and Aryan's undoing too, though Aryan had never been a man of romantic intimacy in the first place. Perhaps he had fucked her up in more ways than one.

Helai nodded, her lips pursed. She didn't trust herself to speak. Her mind was a whirl of confusion. Her life had been a state of survival growing up; she'd never had time to think about herself and what kind of relationship she'd wanted from other people. Her and Aryan had started much the same—fucking as a distraction from the fucked up life they'd shared on the streets together, and they'd spent so much time surviving as children that she'd never questioned their closeness.

"I—" She opened her mouth to confess about her nightmare. Now that the stress from it had ebbed from her body (Drithan was a selfless lover, always making sure she was taken care of before he was), her head was clear, and she felt unburdened by the thought of sharing. Still, she wasn't even sure why the dream scared her so, so she nodded, her smile warming. "Thank you for checking on me. I don't know where Massoud is, but I'm glad I wasn't alone."

Drithan gestured with his thumb towards the door. "Massoud was sitting with Linda, top deck. Nestled together under that bear pelt Linda wears and talking about old stories."

Helai nodded. Massoud's insomnia was no new development. The man fled sleep like it was the plague, and Helai was only beginning to understand why. Massoud shouldered his own darkness, much like she did—silently and in the distraction of another's bed. She only just realized recently how similar they were in that manner, and it brought a soft smile to her lips.

"Wanna go and join them?" she asked, standing. "I don't think I can go back to sleep just yet."

Drithan nodded, and she led them from her room.

THIRTY-ONE
ROOSTER

"Are you ready for this?" Tantien's voice pulled Rooster from his thoughts as they sailed towards an eldrasi ship, smaller than the Firebrand, with a figurehead of thorns and roses. It was Tantien's contact, the one who would take them the rest of the way to the island, and now that they were so close, Rooster's restlessness had only gotten worse. He'd tried to drown it with alcohol the last few nights, but that had only served to bring blinding migraines and irritable mood swings when anyone had drawn too close. He knew he was cleaving the other Misfits with it, and a part of him drowned in the guilt over that. The other part simply did not care. Nothing mattered when the thought of Igraine getting tortured in that prison replayed in his head over and over and over again.

He dreamed of her almost nightly now. Sometimes it was simply *her*, nothing but the endless sea of her blue eyes, the deep red of her hair. Her radiant smile. The smile that danced at her fingertips.

Other times it wasn't so nice. The world was burning, her cries came from a tree prison above him, but no matter how high he climbed, she sat in a golden cage just out of reach. The branches would grow thorns as he climbed, piercing his flesh, or the tree would grow, carrying her cage higher and higher until he could no longer see it. Each time he would wake, gasping for air and unable to return to sleep. He'd often find Massoud wandering the top deck, and sometimes Helai. Nightmares ran aplenty, it seemed.

"Yes," Rooster said, eyeing Tantien. The eldrasi seemed well rested, but it was difficult to tell. Eldrasi always looked the same, unbothered by human ailments. His eyes were haunted though, and he grew restless the closer they got to Míradan's shores. They'd been so lucky; between mild weather and Intoh's magical abilities, the trip had only taken them five months with some days. "As ready as I'll ever be, going into enemy territory, not even remembering the crimes I committed."

"If the stories are to be believed, there were many." A smile cracked against Tantien's face. One of Tantien's arms rested loosely against the wheel as Rooster leaned against the railing beside him, staring out at the sailors as they worked or lounged. Helai was teaching two eldrasi how to play her card game. Cassius laughed, *actually* threw back his head and laughed, at something Massoud had said, a radiant and satisfied smile on his lips. It was good to see the vampire laugh, when just a month before he'd been troubled with the knowledge that his *own brother* was hunting him. Rooster had frowned at the news, knowing that yet another enemy was proving troublesome, but the Misfits had decided that they would worry over it only once they liberated Rooster's crew.

The other Misfits were nowhere to be found, but Linda had been helping Tantien with quartermaster duties since he had fallen ill on the journey, and Intoh was likely up in the crow's nest. Rackjack had been a constant at Rooster's side, but even he was absent today, tucked away below deck.

Off in the distance, the other eldrasi ship was rapidly approaching. There was no reason for there to be tension, with her being Tantien's old friend, and yet, Rooster felt it, settling gently against his shoulders. Tantien was nervous even though he didn't appear to be.

"This contact of yours, who is she?" Rooster asked.

Tantien peered sideways at Rooster. "Naela is a high ranking Thorn."

"Thorn?"

Tantien's smile was grim. "City guard. I haven't spoken to her in quite some time. I hope she is still loyal."

"You're not certain?" Rooster's tone was exasperated. They couldn't afford any complications.

Tantien gave a slight shake of his head. "You must understand—I did not leave my home on good terms. Naela risks a lot by meeting me, and even more so by smuggling you onto the island. Your bounty is for three hundred thousand skaels."

Rooster flinched. "Three hundred thousand?" Disbelief rooted itself in his tone. He couldn't even fathom that many skaels.

"I know. I'm quite offended," Tantien said in a joking tone. "You'd think they'd pay more for my head, but I'm only at a hundred thousand skaels." While his tone stayed teasing, there was a sadness that tinged Tantien's expression, and Rooster felt for him. He couldn't imagine his own people turning against him.

Tantien must have seen the look on Rooster's face because he held a hand up. "Do not worry about me, Rooster. I made peace with my actions long ago. My home is here, with my ship and my crew. Something I know you will agree with once we break yours out of prison."

"I already know," Rooster said, watching the other Misfits interact below them. "The Misfits might have come later, but they're just as much a family as her. As my crew." It felt right, and the thought of thinking otherwise would have made him a cruel man. He would do anything for the other Misfits; that much was certain.

Tantien's smile was full of understanding as he nodded. "Of course." They fell into a comfortable silence after that, watching the lingering ship in the distance grow closer. The eldrasi soldiers knew what to do without Tantien's command, and they flitted about the ship as they prepared the sails and tugged them up, preparing to slow the Firebrand. Itale padded out from below deck, whispering something to Cassius as they pulled up alongside Naela's ship. Her crew was like Tantien's, only less sea weary, as if they'd gotten on their ship only this morning.

Rooster fell into step beside Cassius as the Misfits collected near the railing. Naela herself was a tall, willowy eldrasi, with long pointed ears that poked out of her inky, black hair. She wore no helm, but her armor was a shiny white gold plate, its metal gleaming with black and gold, a mixture of thorns and roses just like her ship's figurehead.

As sailors threw ropes to the other ship and they tugged the two together, a walkway was magicked between them. Naela crossed first, the very air of her breathing authority. It was only when she drew closer that Rooster noted the alienness of her skin. Like Tantien's, there was a faint green sheen to the undertone, a reminder that despite their closeness in appearance, eldrasi were not human at all.

"Naela, my—"

A crack resounded across the ship as Naela slapped Tantien across the face. He made no noise even as his head rolled to the side, and then she was fisting his shirt, tugging him close, and pressing a possessive kiss to his lips.

Cassius shifted beside Rooster. A soft breathy laughter came from Massoud on the vampire's other side.

Naela spoke in a wispy, billowing language, a slightly different dialect than Rooster had heard the sailors speak on the Firebrand, and Tantien nurtured his reddening cheek as he responded in the same language. A small, sheepish smile graced his lips, and he gestured to the Misfits.

"Tantien failed to mention there were so many of you," Naela said, switching to Vilris as she studied all of them. "Which one of you is Carter Wingman?"

Rooster's eyes shifted and met Tantien's, but Naela plucked him out of the crowd, approaching until she was standing right in front of him. He offered her a toothy grin, one she did not return, and his stomach plummeted nervously. What if she meant to turn him in after all?

"You will be recognized going in like that. Every Thorn in Míradan knows your face." Her gaze tore away from his to peer back at Tantien. "I'm good, but I'm not *that* good."

"Have plan for that," Intoh said, stepping down from a crate he'd been standing on. Weaving through the crew, he stopped in front of Rooster and produced a ring. Being in his human form, it could only mean it was Linda's. "Linda doesn't plan to use anymore. Could shield you from curious eyes."

Linda's ring was cool as Intoh dropped it into Rooster's palm, and as he slipped it onto his finger, he shivered from the magic washing over him. He thought it would be painful—he'd imagined so after having watched Linda and Intoh shift from their true forms into their human ones, the way their bones snapped and their skin reformed. There was no pain though, not as he grew taller, broader, and stockier.

"Holy shit, Rooster. You look just like Linda." Helai's voice betrayed her disbelief, and Cassius' brows furrowed.

"It is most curious. Some illusion rings will change depending on the person who wears it, but it appears that this one remains the same despite its wielder," Tantien said, studying Rooster closely.

"It feels strange, like I'm wearing skin over my skin." Rooster shuddered, hearing how his voice had deepened, how much he sounded like Linda when they'd first met and they had hidden behind their illusion.

"How many of them have rings like this?" Naela's voice was imploring. "Rings like these are rare and powerful. They may not pass against the strength of the wards."

"We'll have to hope they do," was all Tantien said.

"Warding?" Intoh asked.

Naela nodded. "The whole island is warded. Eldrasi are some of the best magic users in the world. There isn't much magic in the world stronger than theirs, unless you are stupid or powerful enough to find dragon magic." Naela's expression darkened. "There is much for my people to protect."

That was troubling. If that were the case, it wouldn't be easy to obtain the tome Delroy had requested they retrieve. Not that Rooster thought it was going to be easy in the first place. Rooster couldn't imagine how expensive his bounty would be if they managed to pull off both the heist and the prison break.

"Regardless, you are on your own once I get you inside. You will do as my first mate Jal says. Failure to do so will result in your inevitable arrest for I have a guise to keep."

Jal stepped forward, an androgynous eldrasi with twigs growing out of their scalp instead of hair and a deeper green tint to their skin. Their eyes swam with gold, and when they grinned, it was wicked, their teeth all sharpened to points.

"Tantien, we have private matters to discuss," Naela said.

Tantien's grin turned arrogant, and he gestured to his forge. "We can speak in my private quarters. He spared a glance at the Misfits. "It shouldn't take long and then we can get things underway. It's still a few days to Kelirium from here if the weather remains fair." As Tantien and Naela disappeared into Tantien's forge, Rooster turned to Cassius, Massoud, and Rackjack.

"We need a plan." Waving Linda, Intoh, and Helai over, they drew close together. "Let us not speak of it here though. We don't know who may be listening." Not that he didn't trust Tantien and his crew, but a ball of anxiety had formed in the pit of his stomach. He knew he was walking into terrible danger, and failure wasn't an option.

"Do not worry, Rooster," Cassius said quietly, clasping Rooster on the shoulder. "We'll get her out."

Rooster nodded firmly, as if it would will Cassius' words into truth. They had to.

THIRTY-TWO

ROOSTER

Tantien and Naela returned not much later. It was obvious that they had done more than *just* talk, with Tantien's hair being ruffled and Naela's gaze shiny, but no one said anything as they bid Tantien farewell. Still, something on Tantien's face was troubled, but he merely shook his head as he drew close.

"Naela had troubling information for me. I need to travel north." He stopped Itale as he drew close to Cassius, preparing to leave. "If I may borrow you for the time everyone is on the island? I have use of your services, should you agree."

Itale glanced at Cassius, his face wrought with worry, but Cassius shrugged as he tightened one of his pauldrons. "Less of us trying to break into a prison unnoticed is no bad thing."

Itale thought about it for a moment, then retreated to Tantien's side. The eldrasi captain gave a satisfied nod. "Excellent. I have promised to keep Delroy up to date as things progress, but since we won't be together, I want you to take this, Rooster." He dropped a ring into his offered palm. Rooster stared at it curiously. It was nothing more than a simple silver band, but a quiet thrum vibrated from the metal, betraying its magical nature.

"Wear it. I have one just like it. If the ring grows cold, something terrible has happened to you or I. Tell Rackjack to take you to Vitreuse when you've freed them. That's where we'll meet in a month."

"What if he dies? We need a place familiar to us." Rooster's words were blunt, but Tantien only blinked and nodded. "I'll show you the coordinates after we've concluded this conversation back in my study."

Rooster nodded and slipped the ring on his finger. It pulsed faintly, like a heartbeat but not so strong that it would be bothersome. It weighed down his hand though, a magical resistance he would have to get used to. For that reason alone, he switched it to his left hand in case he would need his right hand to wield his blade.

"Once you get in the city, be on guard. The drikoty and humans should be safe, but you two will stick out. Eldrasi don't have the best dealings with dwarves," Tantien warned, glancing at Rackjack and Drithan." His gaze softened. "Be safe. Be well. We'll see each other on the other side."

Rooster nodded. "'Course we will, mate. Next time we see you, you'll be able to hug your sister."

Tantien's face cracked in a grin. "That's assuming she doesn't slap me instead."

Naela transported them to a smaller ship with trade goods and a greka captain a day's sail out from the city, marking them under the guise that they were simple sailors working for the greka.

The greka captain was slender with white scales and a pink scar that ran over where his right arm should have been had it not been amputated at the shoulder. It didn't seem to slow him down any as he drew forward, accepting the skaels Naela shook into his waiting palm. "Just see to it that it's done," she said firmly. "And then our debt is cleared." She met the greka's gaze. "I won't save you from Fraxinus again, greka. That I can promise you." After that, she turned to Rooster and the others.

"In two week's time, I will be at Fraxinus' harbor when the moon is highest in the sky. There, I will wait for one hour. If you aren't there in that time, I will leave, and you will be on your own."

Intoh gave a firm nod. "Will be there."

The captain hissed but ushered them all on, his tail flickering in as he spoke quickly in Drikotyian. Intoh was drenched in tension as he stepped onto the ship, and the greka captain stared at Linda with interest.

"What krok'ida doing so far from home with no greka to watch it, hm?" His eyes gleamed as he looked back at Intoh. "Krok'ida look strong, good for combat. Good for carrying crates. Maybe I keep them?"

Cassius moved first, a blur of motion passing across the ship before he was standing in front of Linda. His illusion melted away to decay and monstrosity, his eyes a dark red. "You will not touch them," he seethed, his voice low. "You will not look at them."

The ship had gone quiet, the greka crew members whispering in their language in low voices. A couple of the krok'ida that worked aboard eyed Linda with interest, like Linda was strange and they weren't sure how to feel about them.

Still, Linda reached forward, placing a hand on Cassius' shoulder to calm him as the rest of the Misfits watched on, uncertain about what would happen.

"It okay, Cassius. Can take from here." Cassius settled, though his illusion remained broken, his eyes gleaming as Linda stepped around him and loomed over the captain, who cowered against Linda's sheer size.

"Will not be spoken to like that," they said. "Not a slave." They reached up to lightly clasp at their tooth necklace, their jaw splitting open to reveal rows of sharp teeth. "Won these honorably. Free from the chains your people put on me. No more." They rumbled something in Drikotyian, and the greka nodded in quick succession, though he looked less than pleased.

After that, it was smooth sailing to Kelirium.

The greka pulled his ship into the docks with ease, his trading ship small compared to the extravagance of the eldrasi ships. Some of them were trading ships, ready to set sail for trading cities. Others were large battle ships, their decks lined with beautifully decorated canons embellished with roses and thorns of white gold. Many of the battle ships looked comparable to the Firebrand, and Rooster thought about how much skaels had been put on his head for having stolen an eldrasi war vessel. He shuddered to think what *he'd* done to outweigh Tantien's bounty in skaels.

"It's beautiful," Helai said, her voice drenched in awe. "I've never seen anything like it."

Rooster hummed in agreement. He couldn't deny the island's beauty. Rooster had thought it to be tropical in nature, it being an island, but that wasn't the case, with its tall pines and massive oaks. Their cities were built straight out of trees and cliff sides, like woven treehouses with endless wooden bridges and grassy roads. Tall glass spires reached up into the heavens in the distance, their innards sparkling with swirling green magic.

"Don't let it deceive you," Drithan said, grunting in disgust. "The most beautiful things often deceive."

Rooster didn't get a chance to ask Drithan about his aversion to the eldrasi as they pulled up against the dock, and the drikoty scrambled about to get the trade goods unloaded. It was warmer here than it had been in Alavae, and Rooster relished the sun as he took an unsteady step off the ship. They'd spent many months on a boat; it was going to take him the better part of the week just to get his land legs back. He hated it. He never felt so at home as when he was at sea.

"Wonder if those spires are fueling that ward Naela spoke of?" Rooster uttered to Intoh. The power they wrought spoke to the magic swirling inside Rooster like a heartbeat. He'd gotten quite good during his time on the ship with his healing magic, per Intoh's instructions, when he hadn't been aiding the sails, and he was now confident he could heal in a combative setting should it come to it.

"Definitely feel them. Have strong magical power if not," Intoh agreed, staring at the spires off in the distance. "They're fascinating. Wonder if they take visitors." His eyes gleamed at the thought, and Rooster laughed beneath his breath, a meaty hand coming up to ruffle through his hair. He still wasn't used to looking like Linda, and many times over the last couple of days, the other Misfits had gotten confused by it.

"We do not have time for distractions," Rooster warned, weaving around a greka as they spoke with an eldrasi. The docks were bustling with life, such a jarring thing when Rooster was used to the war-torn shores of Alavae and Volendam. The eldrasi moved with a grace and fluidity that spoke of their ties to nature. Rooster had seen it a bit in Tantien, but Tantien had spent so much time on the sea, he'd lost some of it, and it looked alien now as they walked, as if they were a panther or a wolf stalking their prey.

Intoh waved him away, but Rooster trusted the greka to do what was necessary. Intoh had become easier to be around in the time since they'd left Alavae, like he was finally warming up to being around the Misfits. He was reading less, and on his rest days, he'd even joined Massoud, Drithan, and Rooster in their childish games of what Rooster had deemed as Fort Kickass. A smile threatened his lips at the memory of Massoud returning with Cassius' bedding shortly after Drithan returned with his own. Helai had been with Massoud, and when they hadn't let her join in building the blanket fort, she'd huffed and stormed off, muttering something about making her own club with Linda.

"Halt." An eldrasi guard in the same armor as Naela had been wearing approached. This one had his helm on and looked less than pleased at the company he was staring at. "You lot don't look like simple trading merchants or sailors. I'm going to need names and businesses in Kelirium."

Massoud stepped forward, his smile drenched in mischievous deceit. "Ah, my good sir, my comrades and I are merely weary travelers that seek shelter in your nearest tavern."

The eldrasi's gaze was molten, and he did not smile. "And your names?"

They gave him fake names, but the eldrasi stared at them in steady contemplation. Rooster refused to back down from his stare even though he worried the eldrasi could see through the illusions of those who wore them.

Finally, the eldrasi stepped aside and granted them passage. "Welcome to Kelirium. Your nearest inn will be near the ferry. It has no name, but you'll know it from the white flowers that litter the roof. All inns have white flowers. General stores have red flowers. The forge has green."

Rooster nodded, eager to get away from the eldrasi. There were so many of them, he wondered if it had been a bad idea, leaving the ship together...

THIRTY-THREE

LINDA

Kelirium was beautiful, full of buildings akin to some of the large drikotyian cities. It was strange, though; there was no sign of cultists here, no sign of uneasy magic floating in the air. It was as if the world of the eldrasi people were free of such mortal qualms, like the Misfits had walked into a different world entirely. Eldrasi worked the docks with grace, aiding the drikoty ships in their wares, and Linda flinched away from any wandering eyes of the greka or krok'ida that watched Linda travel with the Misfits.

They had never felt so alien from their own people. Since their growing awareness of the shackles that had chained them to the greka, Linda looked at the way the krok'ida were treated with disgust. Just because something was the way it had always been didn't mean there wasn't room to change. Perhaps Linda would ask the Misfits to aid them in liberating other krok'ida from their chains.

Massoud walked ahead of them with his hands clasped behind his head, an easygoing whistle trailing a tune through the air. Helai walked closely beside him, as if she thought he would disappear if she weren't watching him closely enough, and Drithan remained nearer her, his eyes trained to the ground.

"I do not know how I feel about this place yet," Cassius admitted under his breath. "I am beginning to think my undead nature does not like all of the life magic of this place." He glanced sideways at Linda as a grim smile wormed its way onto his lips. "Perhaps I should have stayed behind with Itale and Tantien."

Linda shook their head. "Know we will need you. Glad you are here. Stronger than life magic. Know it to be true." They would have smiled had they ever figured out how to do so, as they'd seen the others do when they'd wanted to be encouraging. "Also want to thank."

Cassius eyed them for a moment. "For what?"

"Standing up for me." They gestured behind them as if the ship that had brought them to shore was still at the docks. "Can stand up for myself but thank anyway."

"I meant what I said on the way to Halvdarc all that time ago, Linda. Anyone who has a problem with who you are, I will rip their tongue out of their mouth." His tone was filled with such promise that Linda believed him immediately, and they nodded in silent gratitude as they neared a building with a living roof, white flowers growing from it.

The building itself was carved out of a massive weeping willow tree, the wisps of branches curling over to brush the ground and dance gently in the wind. The white flowers wove through the leaves, glowing lightly as if magical in nature, and Linda halted to stare at its beauty for a moment before Cassius urged them along again.

"I'm going to familiarize myself with the city," Rooster said as they bunched around the front of the inn. "It's best we know our surroundings and get to know the natives."

"Will go with you," Intoh said. "Maybe find an apothecary or library? Khal, stay with them. Sode will come with me."

Khal seemed less than pleased by the demand, but Linda drew forward. "Can teach you how to drink."

Khal seemed interested by the notion, but Rooster shook his head. "No drinking. We have seen the chaos that sows from our drunken shenanigans. Lay low. Rackjack, you stay here too. Dwarves stick out too much here."

Rackjack seemed even more disappointed than Khal, but no one argued as Rooster, Intoh, and Sode split off to venture further into the city. Linda watched them go. It was still strange to see Rooster wearing their ring and donning the illusion they had tucked themself behind for so long. They were glad to be rid of it. Seeing the appearance on Rooster still made the prickle of unease shift on their skin as it had when they had worn it, and they tore their gaze away before that tight feeling in their chest could return.

You never have to wear it again, they reminded themself.

A ferry prepared to leave the shores not far off, heading towards the other part of the island, and no one paid them any mind as they walked by.

"You know what I'm most excited for?" Massoud said, stretching his arms above his head as they walked towards the tavern. "Trying their ale. I've never had eldrasi ale before."

"Massoud." Helai's tone was disapproving. "Rooster just said no drinking."

Massoud waved a hand at her in dismissal. "One drink won't harm, Helai."

The tavern was thick with the smell of rich soil and moss, and Linda inhaled deeply as they walked inside. Eldrasi flitted about the room, weaving around drikoty who nearly outnumbered the eldrasi in attendance. It was strange seeing Linda's people after not having seen them for so long, aside from Intoh and his devotees. Many of the drikoty were greka, but there were some krok'ida among them, and one with several teeth missing and a nasty scar discoloring their dark scales eyed Linda with interest. An urge to fight them overcame Linda, but they swallowed it, turning their attention towards the others as they wandered towards the tavern keeper.

The tavern was large and circular in nature, with large round glass windows that seemed to reflect color as the light shone through. Two eldrasi women laughed as they danced with each other near a creature Linda had never seen before—it was a woman, only her face bore characteristics of a deer, with large goat-like ears that hung from her head, and two large circular horns were nestled above her ears. One of the horns was broken near her hair, which was white and flowing and contrasted against her dark skin. Her waist changed into the lower half of a deer, where she swayed from side to side on two cloven feet, a deer tail flickering as she played a melodic tune on a wooden pan flute. The music filled the inn with its magical influence, and it tugged at Linda, beckoning them to join in on the fun, to let go. They made eye contact with the strange creature, and she winked, shaking away a few loose strands of her hair as they fell in her face.

Linda began walking towards her when someone bumped into them, breaking the spell. The eldrasi that had bumped into them murmured their apologies, and Linda shook their head and met the other Misfits at the bar, where Massoud already had a drink in his hand.

"Ahhh, this is dangerously good." He sighed, taking another long draw from his tankard, and Helai held her hand out.

"Let me try." She frowned, her face twisting in disgust as she took a drink. "I'll leave you to it."

Massoud laughed at the same moment the tavern keeper did. The eldrasi behind the counter was tall and curvy, her skin bark-like with small yellow flowers growing along her clavicles. Her smile was radiant, dimpled in one cheek, and her ears were long and tapered to points.

"Welcome, welcome! *Adal'as sileae.*" The second sentence flowed out of her in her native tongue, but Linda found themself able to understand it as the amulet hanging from their necklace whispered softly, *Well met.* Linda had been wearing the amulet for over half a year now, but they still weren't used to the way it translated for them.

They touched it lightly as Cassius leaned forward, resting an arm on the counter. "Do you have rooms here, or is this just a place to eat and be merry?"

The tavern keeper nodded. "We're not a full inn, but there are a few rooms upstairs. None to fit the size of your company, I'm afraid." Her eyes flickered to everyone, resting briefly on Rackjack and Drithan, both of whom looked terribly uncomfortable and out of their element. "Each room comes with two beds, but we could offer more blankets and feather pillows if some of you don't mind sleeping on the floor."

"We will make due," Cassius said, knocking his fist against the wood of the counter. "How much for three days?"

"Since you're being so kind for the lack of accommodation, three days will only be fifteen skaels." More expensive than it had been in Halvdarc, but Cassius barely blinked as he pulled out his bag of skaels and shook them into the tavern keeper's hand.

"Do not worry," Massoud uttered as the tavern keeper gave Cassius a key. "Cassius is welcome to keep my bed warm." The tone of his voice was strange, a playfulness that Linda didn't quite understand, and Helai shook her head and pressed her fingers to her nose as she looked at Linda and gestured to a nearby table.

"Please save me from his flirting and sit with me while we wait for the others to return?"

"Don't fret, dear sister. The long journey has tired me greatly. I mean to make use of our new room and retire for a time. Now that we are on solid ground, I hope to sleep a bit better." Massoud's smile did not quite mask the weariness in his expression, one Linda had seen often in many of the Misfits since they had left Alavae, and he took the key from Cassius and retreated up the stairs as they sat themselves around a large rectangular table. Nature thrived in this inn, something Linda hadn't seen in any of the inns they had been in on the eastern continent, and grass tickled their feet as they sat. Flowers and vines grew straight out of the wood of the table.

"I have been giving some thought to our reason here," Cassius said, lowering his voice. "A reason for us to stay together for its entirety."

"Best speak of it when Carter-filth gets back," Rackjack said, trailing his fingers over the grain of the table as if he were unable to sit still. "And best-good if not speak-talk it here."

Cassius gave a firm nod.

The tavern continued its lively nature as they conversed amongst themselves. Linda began to grow hungry and was pleased to find that the tavern supplied drikotyian dishes and, after borrowing some skaels from Helaì with the promise to pay her back once Intoh returned, ordered some raw spearfish and fresh prína, a sweet and tangy fruit native to Lyvira. It was Linda's favorite, and they hadn't had any since leaving their homeland.

Linda's food was dropped off not too much later, and they devoured it much too quickly. It was gone in three bites, and Linda eyed their plate sadly as the tangy sting of the prína bit at the back of their throat. There was never enough on their plate.

"The guard has been overwhelmed trying to fend off the north." Linda perked as an eldrasi spoke to another across the table next to them. "I hear the vykra are no longer locked in battle with Kreznov."

"Strange," the other eldrasi said as she took a sip of her drink. "I would have thought them to be at war for years yet. Little humans," she scoffed with a twisted smile, "and their silly little fights over land that isn't even theirs to begin with."

"Truly so," the first eldrasi mused, running a hand through his dark hair. "I wonder what has changed?"

"I have heard one of them wakens." The tavern seemed to darken at the words, and Linda suppressed the urge to shiver.

"You cannot be serious." The dark-haired eldrasi scoffed, leaning back in his chair.

The second eldrasi nodded, glancing up at a greka that scuttled by. She waited until the greka had passed before speaking again, lowering her voice. Linda had to strain to hear her over the conversation of the tavern surrounding them. "In Halvdarc. The trade ships have stopped going there."

"That doesn't mean one has woken."

The second eldrasi shrugged. "You cannot feel it, Fyr? I know neither of us were alive in those times when the dragons were awake, but my soul recalls it. Daesthara's trees shiver with anticipation. I have heard that Volendam was sieged by a dyrvak army. It would be foolish to ignore the signs."

"You worry too much. It is why our people left the old forest. Too worried about coming darkness, too stuck in the old ways; we are safe here. The wrath of the north cannot touch our shores."

Linda pulled away after that, noting that the other Misfits didn't seem to have heard them. Drithan and Massoud had defied Rooster's orders and were seeing which of them could chug eldrasi ale the quickest, and Helai was laughing as ale dribbled down into Drithan's beard. A part of Linda wanted to confide in the others about what they had heard, but Helai's laughter was so infectious that they leaned forward, growling happily as Cassius choked on his drink.

"Don't give up," Linda said as Khal watched on with interest. "Should try sometime," they told Khal. "Drink until dizzy."

"Don't want to get dizzy. Not sure if good idea," Khal said, uncertain.

"If dizzy, just take break." Linda shrugged. "No big deal."

"If dizzy, just take break," Khal reaffirmed. "Will maybe try when Intoh and Sode get back."

The afternoon paved way to the evening, and the eldrasi began to trail out as the tavern quieted. Massoud and Drithan slowed way down on their ale intake, not wanting to meet Rooster's ire when he returned. Only a few patrons now remained, some of those who had rooms above. After dinner was brought out, Massoud retired.

Intoh returned with new robes and several new books, which Sode carried for him. One of the books had several eyes that blinked lazily against their leather-bound cover, and Linda stared, wondering how Intoh had afforded such a book. Magical books like that were never cheap.

"The bookkeeper was telling us that they keep highly valued magical items near Fraxinus Prison, which I thought was oddly convenient," Rooster said as he arrived, sitting next to Linda. "I managed to sweet talk the bookkeeper enough to get some information out of him, and after talking it over with Intoh, it may be best if we all stay together for both missions."

Helai's brow furrowed. "How are we going to pull that off?" She glanced around, leaning forward and lowering her face. There weren't too many patrons around, and the majority of them were greka, but Linda knew all too well how easy it was to eavesdrop on a conversation. "There are too many of us. It'll never work."

"Maybe we do not want it to," Cassius said, folding his arms over his broad chest. His expression was thoughtful, and he reached out to tap his finger against the table. "What if most of us get caught? It will give us an easier way inside to rescue Rooster's crew. So long as you or Massoud avoid capture, you can get us back out."

The thought of getting captured on purpose made Linda's mood sour. "So no fight?" They complained. "Don't want to do it if I can't fight."

"Don't worry, dear Linda," Rooster said, clasping Linda's shoulder and squeezing gently. "I do not think we will be able to pull this off without a fight or two."

That raised Linda's spirits considerably. They ached for a good fashion fight, and *Volroth* was eager to smash in a head or two. Their war hammer hadn't seen any combat since the siege in Alavae, and Linda felt it, like an uncomfortable crawl beneath their skin. They grew restless, and that always made them more irritable.

"Massoud is the better illusionist. If anyone should avoid arrest, it's him," Helai said, chewing slowly on a leftover carrot from her dinner. The strange woodland creature with the deer feet still played her pan flute in the corner, and occasionally, Linda found their gaze straying to her and the gentle way she swayed with her music. The melody filled Linda with some foreign feeling they could not explain, a quiet longing that sat near their lungs.

"Then I will stay with him just in case we need to fight off some guards," Cassius said.

"Are you sure the reason is so noble?" Rooster teased, an ornery smile working its way over his lips. "You two have become quite close. Massoud can't seem to keep his hands off you."

Cassius' silence thickened in the space at the table, and Linda couldn't figure out why he seemed so irritated by Rooster. Every time Linda had passed them together on the Firebrand on the way here, Massoud *had* been touching Cassius in some manner or another—a hand on the shoulder or the small of his back. Linda had thought nothing of it, figuring it to be a human thing they didn't understand.

Helai scowled. "I don't want to think about ClassyAss and Massoud."

"Regardless," Cassius said, biting the word out in a warning tone, "Rooster should stay with us, too. We cannot risk them discovering who you are, even tucked behind Linda's ring."

Rooster nodded. Linda was only beginning to get used to seeing him in their old human form, and a big part of them was glad to be rid of it. Seeing it on Rooster only reinforced how uncomfortable it had made them.

"Could Massoud shade step two of us?" Cassius asked Helai.

"Yes, but that's most likely the extent of it before he overexerts himself. Any more could have dire consequences."

Cassius hummed in response and leaned back in his chair.

"How are we going to get the tome? We will need to make sure one of you gets it out so they don't confiscate it when we are arrested," Helai mused. She didn't look too pleased at the thought of going to prison, but even Linda had to admit that the idea could work if executed properly.

"Linda will do what Linda does best." Rooster watched Rackjack as he shoved food in his mouth, stealing bits from other people's plates as he ignored his fork and ate with his hands. "Provide a distraction. Intoh will get the tome and use invisibility to run it to us."

Intoh shook his head, raising his eyes from behind the new book he was reading. "Won't work. Surely have magical wards in place to prevent invisible spells. Otherwise, things would go missing all the time."

"Massoud could shade step?" Cassius suggested.

"Perhaps." Helai agreed. "Though it would be best to make sure that's within his strength to do so. Shade stepping that often can also be taxing."

"Will help-aid Linda with distraction," Rackjack said between bites.

Rooster leaned back and stretched. "We can speak more about it tomorrow."

The conversation devolved after that. Everyone but Linda and Drithan retired to the room, and they both sat in comfortable silence. The bard continued to play soft melodies in the corner, lulling Linda into a state of complacency.

They were just glad to be on solid ground again.

THIRTY-FOUR
RACKJACK

As they settled down in the inn again on the evening of the next day, Rackjack couldn't help his restless nature. Massoud had already retired, still not fully recovered from his time spent as a prisoner of war, and the idle sitting the other Misfits craved was not something Rackjack could abide by. He twitched in a restless state, loathing his dwarven hands, and pushed away from the table.

"Going to go explore," he said, slipping towards the stairs. "Will not be gone long." Everyone ignored him save for Rooster, who waved a hand in acknowledgment. The longer time passed, the more the others seemed to trust him. A part of him reveled in it—*good-good, they should bow to me-me*—but a bigger part of him was relieved. No more wondering if Helai-filth was going to try to stab him in his sleep.

He scuttled up the stairs first, slipping into their room to grab a small pebble of draugmin from his sack. It glowed brightly in the dim light of the bedroom, and Rackjack's heart thundered with glee as he pressed it into his pocket. Just in case. Next, he pried the bead from his beard hair, and he became a rakken once more. It was liberating, and he shuddered as he shook the loose feeling of the dwarf form from his skin.

Faint squeaking came from the inside of his jacket pocket, and he tugged his jacket away, allowing a small rat to crawl out and up to his shoulder. "Keep quiet-silent," he whispered. "Kratch-rat still not safe."

Kratch stopped squeaking, his chest rising and falling rapidly as he scampered up to cling to the fur at Rackjack's shoulder. It had been easy to sneak Kratch onto the Firebrand and easier still to keep him hidden. The only one that had questioned it had been Tantien, who'd always had an uncanny ability to see through illusions. Rackjack wasn't one for honesty but had spoken the truth to Tantien, and Tantien had understood.

Turning, he stilled. He'd forgotten Massoud had retired for the evening and was passed out on one of the beds. Scooting closer, he eyed the human nervously, noting how his hair had torn its way out of his braid and how his eyes shuffled quickly beneath their lids.

"Rest now, sweet man-filth," Rackjack whispered, pressing his paw gently to Massoud's cheek. He'd grown fond of the Shoman man for reasons he couldn't explain, and he sat still and silent for a moment or two more before forcing himself away and towards the window on the opposite wall.

It would have been easier to go through the front door, but this way he wouldn't have to change back into a dwarf. He loathed the notion, so he pushed open the window and scampered out onto the roof, noting the magical orbs that flitted about the city, bathing it in light.

He sniffed the air. A familiar scent wafted through Kelirium, a scent he could follow with ease. He'd thought he'd sensed it when they'd first entered but had said nothing for fear of hitting a dead trail. He followed it now, scurrying down the side of the building, using old vines and keeping to the shadows.

The smell led him deep into the city, deeper than he was comfortable going, and he found himself at the mouth of an alley – or rather, a space between two trees carved into buildings. At the other end was a child, folded fabric blanketing his eyes, a hat pulled down over his hair. He looked to be young, perhaps no older than eight winters, his face as dirty as his tattered clothes. He was human, or so he appeared.

"Florence? Is that you-you?" Rackjack called out, uncertain. No, it was him. It had to be him. There was no way a human child could smell the same as Florence did. No way.

The child lifted his head, his covered eyes raised as he listened. "Ratty-jack?" the child rasped, and Rackjack scurried down the alley as the child pulled their hat away, and two massive ears bounced out from their hiding spot. Not a child. A myrlír. The spores from Daesthara collected to form the little creatures, their skin solidifying and their ears growing to massive sizes to hear all the predators of the forest. Rackjack had heard humans call them goblins. Florence was one of Carter-filth's crew members. The myrlír had always been slippery despite being blind, and Rackjack was not surprised to see he'd avoided capture.

"'S that really you?" Florence's voice was thick and accented, harsh and rolling as he hobbled to his feet and threw himself into Rackjack's arms. It was a relief to see one of his dearest friends alive and well, and he quivered, pulling Florence close, his nose twitching in distress.

"How did you avoid capture-kidnap?" he asked, pushing them deeper into the alley, deeper into the shadows. No one walked by, but he did not trust this city nor did he trust the eldrasi and their uncanny ability to see all.

"Slippery li'le fella I am, bu' you already knew that." Florence's laughter was hoarse as he drew away, pulling a small flask out from his pocket. It swirled with a green liquid–a healing concoction that Florence was always nursing to keep the sun's wrath from killing him. "Managed to get away when they got us 'ere. Promised Igraine-y I'd find ya, I would. Looks like me promise was all wrong an' you found me instead!"

"I found Carter-filth," Rackjack said gleefully. "We come-come to break everyone out."

"Excellent," Florence rasped. "Did not like havin' to hide behind me disguise. Can take Car'er an' you to the prison. Don' know how we'll get inside though. I tried an' nearly got meself caught." Healing juice dribbled down his chin as he drank deeply, shuddering from its side effects. Despite the blindfold covering his eyes, he stared at Rackjack as if he could actually see him, and Rackjack shook his head when he was offered some.

"Must wait until we are out of danger-fear. There are others with Carter-filth. Call themselves Misfits, yes-yes. Think we can trust-follow."

Florence frowned, a deceitful thing that played on the edges of pretend. "Thinks he can replace us, huh? Li'le ol' Florence ain't goin' anywhere. But Ratty-jack..." He leaned forward, his breath stinking of flowered herbs. "I be 'earing things in the magical void. Strange things. Talks of gods wakin' up. Don't suppose you know anything about t'at, do ya?"

Rackjack nodded, taking Florence's hand and dragging him down to the other end of the alley, where there was no chance of them being over-heard. They tucked themselves beneath a massive root that grew overhead, and Rackjack composed his thoughts before speaking, "Do not know why-how, but dragon gods are trying to wake up-up." A nervous squeak passed his lips, and he cursed himself for it. He'd have to whip himself later.

Perhaps it would bleed the fear from his veins. His blood felt tainted from it.

"Oh, that can't be good."

Rackjack shook his head. "Not good at all-all. Saw one rise. Not god but god's general. Dragon god in north. Will not speak-say his name. Especially here."

"How are you alive, Ratty-jack?" The fear spread, catching in Florence's throat, and Rackjack ran his paws over Florence's ears in an attempt to calm him.

"One of Misfits is a vampire-dead one. They used-killed him for his blood, but he returned, came back to life. Sent her away-way. Think she is in the north recovering." Rackjack's teeth chattered. "Must find way-way to stop her. Think she will bring army south."

"What does th' Cap'n think?"

Rackjack trembled again. "Have not said anything. Do not know for sure-certain. Want to find out more-more before I do."

The air around them thickened with disapproval, and Rackjack knew it wafted from Florence. He refused to flinch away, certain of his motives. Carter-filth had enough on his mind to worry about the threat of dragon gods, even though Rackjack was *certain* they were coming.

"Don't look at me like that," Rackjack said, ignoring the fact that Florence was blind. "Can sniff-smell your disapproval, but captain-Carter focused on breaking the crew out of Fraxinus Prison. Will force him to worry-ponder about dragon-gods after," he promised.

Florence's silence was only for a moment more before he nodded. "I believe ya, Ratty-jack." Both stilled as voices carried through the alley, and Rackjack pushed Florence further into the shadows, his heart roaring in his ears. He was lucky to have brought his illusion bead with him, so he slipped it on, shuddering as the sensation of change washed over him.

"Ya feel different, Ratty-jack, like some sort'uh magic clings to your skin."

"Illusion ring-bead," Rackjack whispered. Being a dwarf in eldrasi territory wouldn't be much better, but he wouldn't be stopped like he would if he were a rakken. "Igraine-filth made it for me before I left to find Carter-filth, remember?"

"Ah, yes, I remember. Is there sum'fin else with us?"

Rackjack leaned close, showing Florence his shoulder where Kratch clung on. "Other rakken-rat. Name is Kratch-rat. Found him on journey-path. Have something for you-you." Rackjack rummaged around his jacket until he found it—the nugget of draugmin.

Florence's demeanor perked as he sensed the draugmin. "'S that what I t'ink it is, Ratty-jack?"

Rackjack nodded and then offered it to Florence. "Was saving it for something special, yes-yes, but want you to have-take."

Florence's hand lashed out as he took it, then pressed it to his chest as he inhaled deeply. "So generous of you, Ratty-jack. I know how much you love these li'le nuggets."

Rackjack *was* saddened to see the draugmin go, but he was so relieved to see Florence alive and well that he found it easier to part from the magical scale than he'd thought. He hadn't planned on giving Florence the nugget, but it felt like the right thing to do. Perhaps it was Rat King telling him he had done the right thing.

"Going to save that fer what's ta come," Florence said, shuffling the draugmin into his own pocket. "Going to be tricky, it is, to get into the prison. Have that place full'a guards."

"Carter-captain has a plan for that. Involves stealing a tome."

Florence inhaled sharply with glee. "Ol' Florence loves the sound of that. Lead me back t' th' cap'n; it's time for Florence to lay me nonexistent eyes on 'im." He grinned and tapped at his blindfold before tugging his hat back down over his head to hide his ears. "You'd think the eldrasi here bein' from the woods, they'd give ol' Florence 'ere a better time, but I've been posing as a small child for the last year or so even though there aren't many children here."

"Been all by yourself?" Rackjack asked, peeking out from the alleyway. With it being the dead of night, the eldrasi had all gone home, and the grassy streets that hugged the cliff sides were deserted. Eldrasi were daytime creatures by nature. The few that ventured out at night where usually tucked away to enjoy the presence of the moon.

Florence shook his head. "There's a small myrlír group here, but they only come out at night an' it took me ages to get into their good graces."

Rackjack was glad for that, though his own anxieties were beginning to rise at the nape of his neck. Míradan was eldrasi territory, and though there was an unsettling evil in the east, there were also places for Rackjack to go and hide should he need to. Here, he was exposed, unable to flee anywhere should danger present itself. No other rakken had made a home here; he was alone.

Not alone. Have Misfits-filth.

He shook his loneliness from his fur as several pitches of chirping echoed through the trees above, nearly carried away by the waterfall that slipped over the cliff side nearby. Florence stilled, holding an arm out, and Rack-jack stilled with him.

"This ain't good, Ratty-jack," Florence muttered, his ears quivering.

"Thought you said-told me you were in their good graces," Rackjack whispered back as several myrlír fell from the treetops, brandishing small spears and slings. They were all differing shades of yellows and greens, and some were no larger than Rackjack's head, where others neared Florence's size. One with half of an ear missing cried out and jutted his spear near

Rackjack's neck, his golden eyes sparkling with mirth. Unlike Florence, who'd once stared at the sun too long and blinded himself in the process, these myrlír could see. Rackjack gathered they must only come out at night, as their kind were sensitive to the sun's rays.

"Florence didn't say he was friends with a *rat*. Can see right through you, we can."

Rackjack hissed and released his musk. It sank into the air, and the myrlír scowled, their movements quick and erratic. They were much like rakken in that manner, their nervous energy like a current in the air that preyed on Rackjack's.

"Think we takes his beard ring. Thinks we want to be a dwarf too," one squealed, her voice high and grating as she clung to the back of another. The group of myrlír cackled like she had told a hilarious joke, and Rackjack narrowed his eyes.

"Come near me-me, and I will light you on fire," he warned, raising his flame arm slowly. "Know myrlír-spores are very, *very* easy to light on fire."

"Just want to talk." The one that had half an ear missing lowered his spear, freeing Rackjack from his capture. "Hear whispers in the magic, hear eldrasi talk below us when they thinks we isn't listening."

"What could possibly want-need to talk to me about eldrasi talk-speak?" Rackjack asked. Suspicion riddled his tone. What news could the eldrasi possibly have that would interest Rackjack? How did the myrlír know he'd be interested at all?

"The magic tells us to seek out one called the Brass Rat." The leader's eyes gleamed as he stared at Rackjack's beard, wild, untamed, and brass-colored. "Tells us to warn you: she seeks to claim the city. The one you gather."

Rackjack went still. So still his nose didn't even twitch. So still it was almost maddening. He wasn't sure who *she* was, but they spoke of Volendam, where he was mustering his army beneath its streets.

"You're going to have to be more specific for Ratty-jack," Florence hissed from beside him. "Speak plainly."

"Cannot. You know as well as I that magic does not work that way."

The myrlír was right. Magic could be used as a tool to see things, but the images were usually confusing and unclear. Rackjack sometimes teased such visions when he drank Florence's special tea, but oftentimes he understood too little for it to be of any value.

"Why do eldrasi speak of it?" Rackjack asked. That part made little sense to him. Why did the troubles of man concern the eldrasi island?

"Trade," the old myrlír said simply as the others shuffled back into the trees. He began backing up as well, his eyes dancing with shifts of magic. "Few times they have attempted to take trade ships to Volendam, they have been intercepted by northmen."

Vykra. Rackjack refrained from shuddering but resumed his normal flicks and twitches as the myrlír disappeared back into the trees as quickly as they had appeared. Myrlír were strange folk; if it hadn't been for Florence, Rackjack might have never gotten along with one.

"What did that mean to ya, Ratty-jack?" Florence asked, gripping tightly to Rackjack's arm. The city suddenly seemed darker, like a weight had begun pressing down on the tall trees and were casting the buildings into eerie shadows. Rackjack kept Florence close, content to keep him near now that he'd found him again.

"Nothing good," was all he said as he hurried them back to the tavern.

The other Misfits needed to be warned.

THIRTY-FIVE
ROOSTER

"Rooster." Cassius' tone was tinged with warning, and Rooster stopped drumming his fingers against the table and leaned back. A sigh passed his lips as he shot an apologetic expression in the vampire's direction. His anxiety was at an all-time high. Sitting here was doing nothing for it but feed it, and he leaned forward to grab his mug. He hated the taste of eldrasi wine, but it was better than nothing. Still, he grimaced as he took a drink.

"I know you worry for them. At first light, we will go out and attempt to learn more."

Cassius' assurance fell upon deaf ears when it came to Rooster's worries, but he smiled and nodded regardless. He was foolish to think he could trick the vampire; more than likely, Cassius was able to sense his anxiety through the shallowness of his breath and the beating of his heart, but Rooster didn't care to vent his frustrations.

A moment later, Rackjack came through the door tucked behind his dwarf form, followed closely by what appeared to be a small child. They hovered at the door until Rackjack spotted Rooster and then hurried over.

"Don't think you remember, but this is Florence-spore. Part of your crew, yes-yes," Rackjack uttered quietly, tugging Florence closer. Rackjack's companion was no child at all. Rather, he was a creature with large ears tucked haphazardly inside a round hat and a blindfold tied over his eyes. The creature wore long clothes to cover his skin, and he tilted his head.

"The crew has missed ya somef'in fierce, cap'n. Igraine-y hasn't been right since ya left." Florence stilled. "An' then everyone was taken. It's bin a lonely time, cap'n. Only avoided capture because I'm a slippery li'l fella."

His stomach twisted with guilt. "I apologize. I don't seem to remember..." There was a familiarity there, a flicker of it that just danced out of reach, and Rooster frowned, his head bent over his drink in shame. The closer they got to his men, the closer they got to Igraine, the harder it was to fight the guilt that plagued him over his amnesia. It had been easy, at first, to be Rooster. His ties to his past were far off, a dream. Now? Now Carter Wingman haunted him.

"'S okay, cap'n. Ratty-jack told me your head is muddled. Might be able to take a looky if you want. Good in th' magics, I is."

As tempting as it was, Rooster shook his head. "Not here. How did the rest of the crew get captured?"

Florence's ears drooped as he tugged himself into a seat and lowered his voice. Rackjack moved over to speak in low tones to Cassius, who continued to sip at his drink and look entirely disinterested in everything surrounding him.

"Ambush. Igraine-y didn't wanna lead 'em to Vitreuse... it's your safe place, see. She was protectin' it from the wrong eyes. Doing so cost them their capture, though."

"We need to learn more about the prison if we are to break them out," Cassius muttered, careful to keep his voice low as his eyes trailed the patrons surrounding them. Lucky for them, no one seemed interested in eavesdropping, even though they were a strange company. Off in the distance, Linda and Helai drank with Khal, and Intoh sat at the counter, a book open in front of him as Sode remained at his side, ever vigilant.

"Thinking I have someone to help with that. Will take you to her. Can get you th' information you need without having to go to Fraxinus," Florence said, and Rooster's eyes trailed over to Rackjack, as if to ask: *can we trust him?*

Rackjack stared back without blinking. So much for the silent communication.

Rooster sighed. What other choice did they have? He didn't want to go to Fraxinus until they meant to make their move. There would be more guards stationed there, and the last thing they needed was to be recognized.

"We'll leave in the morning. I'll speak to Helai about going with us in case we need her skills to get back unseen. Everyone else is to stay here."

"Fine by me," Cassius said, tilting his glass against his lips and finishing his wine. "Just be careful."

Rooster bore an arrogant grin. "I'm always careful."

The following day, Florence led them through the bustling streets of Miradan. There was a pleasant aroma in the air as they walked, weaving around eldrasi carrying baskets atop their head or leading small cow-like creatures down grassy streets. The soft roar of waterfalls crashed over cliff-sides, and it was almost too much to take in, so foreign from the human cities Rooster had been in the last couple of years. Even the dwarves felt closer to humans than the eldrasi did, despite the human-like appearances these eldrasi shared.

Rooster found himself at peace with all the nature surrounding him, and he trailed away from Florence and Helai to stand at a cliff's edge. The eldrasi architecture was awe-inspiring; they had woven tree branches across the edges of the cliffs to form living railings, likely to prevent the wandering traveler from falling to their death. Rooster leaned against it, allowing his belly to plummet as he peered over the edge. It was strange how quickly they'd climbed from where the docks were, and for the first time in a long time, Rooster smiled. In another life, he might have settled here.

"It truly is beautiful here," Helai said, stepping beside him. "I have never seen so much green before in my entire life. The sands, they hold so much beauty of their own, and Shok'Alan, our holy city, has life there like this, but..." her voice caught, her head tilted upwards to stare at the trees that soared high above their heads. "so, incredibly beautiful."

"Not t' be hurryin' you along, Cap'n, but..." Florence glanced towards their ascent. "we still have a looooong way to climb." A gnarled finger trailed a path in the air until it landed on a small, wooden hut at the edge of a cliff forged straight out of the trunk of a tree.

Helai groaned. "Should have made Massoud join you. He's the better illusionist anyway," she grumbled as they began walking again. "Better at magic, better at talking."

"Your skill with a blade coupled with your magic is impressive, Helai," Rooster said, sidestepping an eldrasi as they passed by with a mooing cow. "Don't sell yourself short. Your loyalty speaks volumes. I know you speak praises of Massoud, but I've known you the longest of any of the Misfits. I wouldn't want anyone else to join me on this."

Helai laid a hand on Rooster's shoulder. "I wouldn't be anywhere else. You helped me find Massoud. I..." her voice wavered, accompanied by a shadowed expression before she steeled it behind a wall. "We'll find Igraine."

Rooster didn't say anything. He was tired of people telling him that. It was like a broken mantra people sang to comfort him so he didn't lose his mind. They'd forgotten it was already lost; the only key to recovering it was *her*. He was tired of people telling him what would happen when they could focus their energy on doing just that.

Eventually, Helai's hand slipped off his shoulder, and they began the trek up the cliffside. Kelirium was truly a gorgeous city, but half an hour into their trek left Rooster hot, sweaty, and irritable. The sun glared down on them mercilessly, ignoring the fact that the eastern continent was getting bombarded with snow. Rooster might have enjoyed the heat had he been on a ship with nothing but sea surrounding him. Eldrasi trailed around the city in slow, graceful movements, and many spoke in a language Rooster did not understand. There was culture drenched into the trees surrounding them, with depictions of differing eldrasi history carved into the bark.

"Oh, thank the gods," Helai huffed, breathing heavily as she pressed her hands to her knees and leaned forward. They'd finally reached their destination, and Rooster wasn't certain Florence had led them anywhere insightful.

"We sure this eldrasi can help us, mate?" he asked, staring out onto the branch where the small hut nestled against the cliffside. "I would have figured you knew a dirty guard or something..."

"She can help," Florence assured as he fiddled with the bandage around his eyes. "But it would, ah, be better for me t' go in first. She only trusts th' wee ones from the forest, you see." He tilted his head up. "I sense your hesitation, cap'n. You can trust me."

Could he? Rooster didn't know who to trust; he'd only just met the myrlir. Rackjack seemed to trust him, but Rackjack had also told Rooster specifically not to trust rakken, so could he trust a rakken's word? They'd come this far and didn't want to go into the prison blind.

Rooster nodded and flopped down on the ground. He still wasn't used to seeing pieces of Linda's ring illusion on himself, and he stared at the large mass of his hand for a second before he spoke. "Go on then. Come fetch us when she's ready to talk."

As Florence disappeared into the hut, Rooster let his head fall back. The tree above sheltered him from the worst of the sun, and the grass was soft and cool beneath him as Helai sat down next to him. Wind trailed through the air, and eventually, Rooster turned to look at Helai.

"I meant to ask sooner, now that Massoud has joined us: tell me about your Ghosts. How did you all form? What was everyone like?" Helai's Ghosts had always been a product of mystery, shrouded in the shadow of her past that she did not share. Rooster sensed a bond there, similar to his with Igraine, but Helai was aired on the side of silence, content with keeping herself locked away. Massoud had spent much time on their way from Alavae to Míradan teasing Helai about things that happened when they were children.

Several emotions flickered across Helai's face. Adoration. Grief. Joy. Regret.

"There were eight of us: Aryan, myself, Massoud, Ehsan, Misaka, Zahra, Hosni, and Kílae. It was Aryan and I's idea to form the Ghosts; we were tired of the oppression of our people by those who sought to forsake our old ways. The Sultan Mohalis believed Qevayla was destined to return to her mortal flesh, and only the worthy would be spared by her dragon fire."

"So your people spoke of the dragons before all of this?" Rooster waved his hand in no particular fashion. "Rhavna, Gorvayne..."

Helai nodded. "Mostly among the wealthy. The common folk held strong to their faith, to the One."

"But you worship Dalnor."

Helai gave him a withering stare. "A western god, yes." She didn't explain anything further, so Rooster didn't ask. It wasn't his place to pass judgment. Besides, no god held his allegiance, so who was he to wonder over Helai's faith?

"Anyway, we all believed in the same cause: cutting out the corruption of Shoma and returning it to the people whose land was robbed from them. It was a good cause. Strong too. We got up to all sorts of trouble. Breaking into the homes of the wealthy. Disrupting Mohalis' plans." A smile threatened Helai's lips. "Then one of us slipped. Or betrayed us. We're still not sure which that was. We were on a mission, and Mohalis knew we were coming. We lost Zahra, and then we were forced to scatter. I hadn't seen any Ghosts until we found Zamir in Halvdarc."

"It sounds like you cared for them a great deal."

Helai opened her mouth to respond as Florence exited the hut, the door remaining open behind him. He gestured.

"She'll see ya now."

Florence's contact sat at a table with a tea cup in her gnarled hand. Her hut was as if they had stepped into another forest, with moss growing over the wood of her counters and much greenery and plant life. A bed sat in the corner, and several herbs hung from ropes at the windows alongside several small stick-like structures bent and hung at the door. As they passed through, Rooster's ring burned, and Helai gasped softly behind him.

"Your illusion disappeared," she said.

Rooster glanced sharply at Florence, whose ears fell flat against his head.

"Sorry Cap'n. Forgot to tell ya that the witchy here doesn't allow magic within her home."

"You're a witch?" Helai asked, hovering near the door.

The woman at the table grinned, her teeth black and rotten. Her hair was unkempt, like she hadn't brushed it in quite some time, tamed beneath a small hat she wore.

"I need to leave. It's not safe for me to be here." Rooster said, turning towards the door. His skin crawled; he was vulnerable without Linda's ring, surrounded by those who would seek to lock him up. If the guards of this town caught wind of his arrival, he'd never see Igraine.

"The guards won't come here. Sit down. The little spore has told me you wish to talk about your sweet'um locked away in the prison." Her voice, while sweet, was laced with something, a compulsion to follow. Rooster recalled once, long ago, when Cassius had compelled him to follow, and he did so without question. Rooster wondered if the witch used such magic here.

Rooster sat. "You can tell us about the prison, I assume. Otherwise, this is a waste of my time."

The witch's grin stretched. Wrinkles spanned across the landscape of her face, and Florence climbed into a chair beside Rooster, reaching for a cup the witch offered. Helai remained firmly at the door, and Rooster couldn't blame her. The place reeked of discomfort as a chill rolled down his back.

"I can do more than that. Drink this tea, and it will take you inside the prison," the witch said, pushing a kettle to the middle of the table. Liquid sloshed inside.

"Drink special witchy tea with Ratty-jack all th' time, Cap'n. Safe enough and strong enough ta make ya *see*," Florence said as Rooster drew his hand towards the kettle after a moment of hesitation. The last thing he wanted was to alter his mind while the illusion in his ring wasn't working.

"Rooster, I don't think it's a good idea," Helai whispered as if hearing his hesitations. "What if you drink that and something happens?"

"It's the easiest way to scout out the prison without risking capture," the witch rasped. "It will be as if you are a spirit; no one will be able to see you. Unless you speak. Don't speak a single word, boy, or they'll catch you."

"If you're just willing to wait, Massoud and I—" Helai started.

"No, Helai. I'm tired of waiting. The quicker we figure out what we're up against, the quicker we can get Igraine," Rooster interrupted, ignoring the sharp look she gave him.

"If anything happens, do everything you can to make it back to the others so you can warn them. Even if that means leaving me behind." His words thickened the tension in the air as the witch watched him silently, her eyes dark and looming. He reached for the kettle and poured the tea into a tiny teacup chipped at the corner. The tea's aroma was less than pleasant, and Rooster wrinkled his nose in disgust as his stomach twisted painfully.

"Gods, couldn't we put this in some rum or something?" He laughed nervously, noting the tension in the room did not change, so he sighed and quieted, staring at the cup before raising it in the air. "Bottoms up, I guess." He pressed the cup to his mouth and tipped his head back, noting with disgust that the taste was as foul as the smell. No going back now.

THIRTY-SIX

ROOSTER

I t was strange. The tea hit him suddenly and without mercy, and he slumped in his chair as his eyes rolled into the back of his head. Helai's protest was heard far off, but he was no longer in the hut. He still felt the witch's chair beneath him, still sensed Helai and Florence's presence, but he sailed, a ghostly apparition, through the halls of a prison. It was a strange prison, like the inside was that of a hollowed-out tree, and after a moment of gathering his wits, Rooster began to scan the room.

Two guards stood at the prison's entrance, and, Rooster noted, two more stood outside when the door opened. A small magical ball bounced in the air beside one of the guards, glowing a soft blue as it floated near nearby. As people entered, the magical ball would trail around them. A tall, willowy eldrasi exclaimed as the ball seemed to grow distressed and turned an inky black, a soft piercing noise echoing throughout the prison as the eldrasi was led somewhere. Then the checks resumed.

Rooster hoped Massoud's illusion would hold through whatever magic that ball possessed.

The center of the room bore tables that inmates sat at, either eating or socializing. Guards trailed along the spaces between tables, their armor gleaming too brightly amid the tea's magic. Stairs spiraled at the wall, where cells were carved out of the wood of the tree. Something tugged at Rooster's belly, beckoning him to follow, so he let go, let the effects of the tea lead him up. And up they went, traveling for far too long before it beckoned him to a tree branch that led outside. Rooster's stomach threatened to plummet as the sky rushed up to meet him, and he realized he *was* inside a massive tree, the largest he'd ever seen. The branch he stood on allowed him to look out, where the forest stretched far, disappearing into the horizon. A city of seashells and coral sat nestled on the cliffsides below, the building glittering in the sunlight.

Rooster pressed his hand to the carved-out part of the branch, light-headed even in his ghostly state. Gods, they were even above the canopy of trees, some of the oldest in the world.

"You're a smart girl. I know how much he cares for you. It's only a matter of time before he comes." A voice caressed him, and he turned to see a tall and bulky eldrasi woman standing on the branch about ten feet away. She was facing a birdcage that hung over the side, where a woman sat inside.

Rooster's stomach lurched.

It couldn't *be*.

But it was.

Igraine, he wanted to call out, but his voice was lodged in his throat, silenced by the magic that had brought him here. The witch's warning sang through him: *don't speak a single word, boy, or they'll catch you.* Oh gods, she was here, glaring up at the eldrasi standing outside her prison, her teeth bared in rage. Rooster lurched forward, ignoring his nausea, ignoring everything, until he stood near the eldrasi woman interrogating Igraine.

Igraine looked relatively unharmed, more so than Rooster would have guessed, having been imprisoned for a couple of years. Her expression was haunted and rugged, and bruises covered her face, but she was *alive*, and that knowledge alone made Rooster want to weep with joy.

"Assuming he is alive, he wouldn't be stupid enough to risk capture. You're wasting your time," Igraine whispered, her voice laced with rage.

The other eldrasi woman laughed, leaning against the railing on her arms so that she could draw close to the birdcage. Rooster's heart squeezed painfully; *if that is a fool's errand to come save you, then I am a fool.*

"There is time to break you yet, Igraine. Make peace with that. And then," the woman's voice lowered, all amusement draining away. "When we have Carter Wingman in our clutches, I will personally see to it that he watches you suffer."

"It wasn't our fault the Daemor died, you know." Igraine kept the emotion from her face, all except her eyes. Her eyes mirrored that of a sea-storm. "It wasn't Carter's fault your brother perished to Delroy's wrath."

The sentence must have struck a nerve because the guard straightened and gestured to the rope tied to Igraine's prison. "It would take only one command. I am the warden of this prison, Igraine Kindrath. Perhaps it would be a bigger warning to your beloved if I scattered your body against the roots of his prison." Her hand raised, hovering, and Igraine's prison lurched. Her scream pierced the air.

"No!" Rooster cried out. "Stop!"

The prison halted as both eldrasi women turned. Both were shocked, but where the warden of Fraxinus Prison remained silent, Igraine's shock and horror echoed over to him.

"Carter?"

Rooster reached out to her, uncaring, at that moment, that they could see him, but when he blinked, a sharpness pierced his lower belly and tugged, and then he was sitting back in his chair at the witch's hut.

"No," Rooster said softly, ignoring the concern in Helai's gaze, ignoring the curiosity of the witch as she sat across from him. "Oh gods, no."

"Rooster, what is it?" Helai asked. "What did you see?"

A headache had begun to form behind Rooster's eyes, and he groaned, holding his face in his hands. He was too heavy in his body, and he was vaguely nauseous. "I know where we need to go once we get to the prison, and I saw her. I..." the words lodged in his throat, and he raised his head, his gaze flickering over to the witch. Shame plagued him. He had spoken when the witch's one instruction had been to keep silent. "We need to go. We've tarried here too long. Igraine and my crew have suffered that prison long enough." He stood, avoiding the witch's withering gaze.

"Florence, there is a ferry to carry us across to the other side of the island, yes?"

Florence cupped his tea, nodding slowly. "We wouldn't make it back in time, Cap'n. They do not row the ferry across after nightfall," he said, gesturing to the dusty window, where evidence of sundown drenched the sky in brilliant colors. "They begin at first light, though. Could take the first one across."

Rooster began to pace. He didn't want to wait until first light, but there was little other choice. Igraine's scream haunted him; her look of terror as the warden had led her to believe she was going to plummet to her death etched into his brain.

"Let us return to the others, then," he said finally. "We leave for Fraxinus at first light."

"Careful, dearie," the witch uttered as they turned to leave. "I sense poison in your heart. Best to not let it fester." She went silent after that, and they all hurried out the door.

Rooster's fingers curled into fists.

He was coming for everyone who had dared lay a finger on Igraine.

THIRTY-SEVEN
CASSIUS

Cassius put out some of the candles, dimming the room to a soft glow. Rackjack and Florence had already passed out in the corner of the room near the door, and Cassius turned towards the window, his eyes scanning the lush nature that surrounded them.

Rooster, Helai, and Florence had returned just before nightfall from wherever they'd gone to get more information on the prison. Rooster had been frazzled, immediately pushing his way over to the barkeep for a drink, and Helai explained in a low voice what she understood had happened.

"We should keep a wary eye on things tonight," she had whispered, watching as Rooster threw his head back and drank deeply from a goblet. "I do not believe things went unnoticed."

"You should not have trusted one of the old witches," Cassius had said simply, meeting Helai's curious gaze. "They are old, stemming from the wilds of Daesthara. It is surprising that she did not require a payment of blood, or something worse."

"Cassius." Massoud's voice carried him away from his earlier conversation, and he hesitated to turn from the window. The air was tense; his gut screamed at him that something was wrong.

"Come keep my bed warm," Massoud purred, his eyelashes fluttering. Cassius' eyes flickered to Rackjack and Florence, and Massoud laughed. "Fine, fine. If you won't indulge, at least come and sit with me. I promise I do not bite; not unless you want me to."

"It is better I stand. If something were to happen—"

"Cassius, please." All the humor had drained from Massoud's tone, his expression pleading. "Sleep has eluded me as of late. Talk with me until I fall asleep. Tell me stories of your childhood or serving as a knight. Then you can go back to being stoic and beautiful as you watch over us."

Cassius relented then. He knew all too well the demons that haunted one's sleep.

The bed dipped as Cassius settled with his back pressed against the headboard. It was strangely intimate as Massoud's hair spilled out over his pillow, and his gaze found Cassius as the vampire shifted uncomfortably.

"You want a story?" he asked.

Massoud nodded. "Anything you wish to share."

Cassius pondered for a moment. "When I was probably fourteen winters or so, I convinced my brother to steal a pair of mares and ride them to Alavae for a few days. Father was away with his naval fleet, and we didn't have to worry about his wrath. Winter was beginning to turn, and the city of Alavae was celebrating *Li Faima*. It is a springtime festival with vibrant colors and good eating."

"I think I've heard of it," Massoud said.

Cassius nodded. "It's one of the largest in Hestian culture. A massive bonfire is built at the center of the city using leftover wood from winter to say goodbye to winter and welcome spring. We ate, and drank, and danced a lot those days." Laughter etched Cassius' cheeks. "My brother wasn't paying attention, and somehow his shirt caught fire."

When Massoud's laughter did not join his, he peered over to see Massoud had fallen asleep. All of the lines of worry had disappeared from his face, and he truly looked so young, perhaps the same age Cassius had been when he was turned.

Cassius reached out and brushed Massoud's hair from his face, noting with a soft thrill of pleasure just how *soft* Massoud's skin was. His blood called out to him, but Cassius ignored the bloodlust easily these days, and he scooted as quietly as he could from the bed before reaching to grab for his shield and sword.

A Thorn crashed through the bedroom window, tearing Massoud from his sleep with a soft exclamation. Rackjack woke as well, his fur bristling. He hissed and flinched in the corner of the room as Florence also woke and pressed against Rackjack's side. Massoud scrambled against the headboard.

Cassius reacted without thought, throwing himself between the Thorn and Massoud on the bed, his lips parted in a wordless snarl. His heart thundered in his ears, his panic pulling his sword from its sheath as he raised his shield in defense. "I will kill you if you touch him."

The words he uttered left his lips in a low, guttural tone, making him sound half-man, half-monster. As a knight, it was his job to be the shield, to defend the defenseless, to fight against those who would see his end.

It felt different this time.

Massoud's heartbeat throbbed in Cassius' throat, a quiet reminder of his bloodlust, but he stared into the eyes of the Thorn beneath his hawk helm, his own sword raised to strike.

"I will *kill you* if you touch him," Cassius growled again, his rage a dizzying high as it sang through him. Monstrosity bled through his illusion as his control slipped, his fingers elongating into talons and two of his teeth sharpened into fangs. Nothing else mattered; nothing else could tear Cassius away from where he stood.

Only by his command.

The Thorn laughed darkly beneath his helm as another Thorn made her way through the window. Anger poured through Cassius as his wings splayed out, casting another protective layer between the Thorns and Massoud, who remained on the bed, frozen in place.

"Tell us, where is Carter Wingman? His dearly beloved has been eager to see him," the Thorn said, sneering from under his helm. Behind him, the other Thorn fought with Rackjack and Florence, who attacked the Thorn with reckless abandon. Another Thorn appeared at the door, and there was commotion in the hallway as Cassius heard Rooster shouting in alarm.

"Rackjack, find the others and aid them!"

Florence crawled onto Rackjack's shoulders and lashed out with his daggers, managing to pierce the Thorn in the neck. Blood rained down on Rackjack and Florence as they ran towards the door and pushed that Thorn back, leaving Cassius and Massoud alone in the room.

Cassius felt that touch of madness return, the panic of the Thorns getting through him to Massoud causing him to lose himself to the monster beneath his skin. It ripped free, wrangling itself from his control, and he fell to the darkness as his illusion disappeared entirely, giving itself over. All at once, the torch light in the room went away, snuffed out by the yowling of Cassius' necromancy. Massoud's panicked heartbeat was strong as it echoed in Cassius' head, but it was drowned out by his rage as he dropped his shield and sword and launched himself forward.

The Thorn might have been able to defend himself had Cassius not snuffed out all the lights in the room. His panicked breath hitched as Cassius found the soft skin between his pauldron and his helm and bit down, his fangs sinking into the eldrasi's neck.

A memory washed over him, a memory that wasn't his own. It was a quick and fleeting thing, the quiet, gentle sight of a home carved into a tree where an eldrasi woman bounced a crying babe on her hip. She reached out to kiss him, and Cassius tore away, disoriented as the memory faded away, and the Thorn fell limp to the floor. His memory, perhaps?

Cassius pressed a hand to his lips as the eldrasi's blood stained his mouth, and the other Thorn shouted in her own tongue as a magical light lit up the room. It temporarily blinded Cassius, who ducked beneath the swing of her blade to reach for his own once more. His vampirism was still proudly on display, so he tucked it back behind his illusion as the Thorn's lip curled maliciously.

"A vampire in Míradan? A new tomb awaits you in Fraxinus."

Cassius felt someone wrap their arms around his waist from behind before he could respond. Just as the Thorn moved to break through Cassius' defenses, Massoud shade stepped them, the uncomfortable crawl of the void ghosting his skin as they landed outside of the inn. The city was in a sea of panic as patrons fled the inn, and Cassius was so dazed that he didn't realize what Massoud was doing until he was pressed up against the wall of the inn, and Massoud was kissing him.

Massoud was shorter than Cassius but still somehow managed to assert his weight as he pressed Cassius against the wood wall, his hands coming up to weave his fingers through Cassius' hair. He tugged him down, demanding their lips meet. He was warm, and Cassius leaned into him as he wrapped his arms around Massoud's back and pulled him close. If Massoud minded the eldrasi blood that still tinged Cassius' lips, he did not say anything.

Hunger clung to the back of Cassius' throat, an old hunger woken by his need, by habit. He wanted to draw his mouth over the skin of Massoud's neck, to bite, to draw blood. Once more, he wondered, *What did Massoud taste like?* It was almost insistent now, and he forgot the world as Massoud pulled him under, as his tongue darted out to tease Cassius' bottom lip. Too quickly, he was gone, his eyes half shut. He peered up at Cassius with a sly expression as several Thorns ran by and entered the tavern. Massoud and Cassius were so far in the shadows that they hadn't been noticed by the guards, and understanding graced Cassius' features as he met Massoud's gaze.

"The guards would have recognized us if we hadn't sprung into action." Massoud's eyes hardened, and all the desire was tucked away by his ire. "What the *fuck* were you thinking, stepping in front of that guard like that?"

Cassius opened his mouth to retort, his brow furrowed, when the other Misfits burst out of the front of the inn. Among the flurry of panic, Cassius locked eyes with Rooster and nodded. It was time to go. His argument with Massoud could wait.

His mind was still a haze from the kiss, but he chased that away as more guards appeared. "Run," Rooster called out in a panic. "Get the fuck to the ferry!"

His command fed the chaos, and they ran towards the boat that led to the other side of the island as the Thorns gave chase, their white fire landing in small bursts beside them. The ferry looked like it was getting ready to leave; the dock the eldrasi used to board was already being pulled back onto the boat. Cassius' heart was in his throat. They weren't going to make it.

"No!" Someone cried out as a bolt of magic sped through the air towards Intoh. Before it could hit him, however, Khal flung himself in front of Intoh and took the brunt of the magic square in the chest. He crumbled, and Intoh cried out, his own hand lashing out in retaliation as wind knocked the Thorns over and prevented them from coming any closer.

"Liiiiiinda!" he called, and Linda came, *Volroth* swinging in their hands as they roared. Intoh put out the flames in frantic gestures, and Cassius was relieved to hear that Khal still yet lived, though his heartbeat slowed considerably.

"Linda, to me!"

Linda's head whipped around. They scooped Khal into their arm and charged forward to Cassius' side.

"Will aid too," Intoh called out as Cassius' wings unfurled from his back, and he launched himself over onto the ferry, which was little more than a longboat with several oars to carry it through the water. One sail sat in the middle, and it was hauled up to catch the wind. He landed heavily, and the eldrasi near him cried out in surprise. They were lucky; most of the ferry was quiet. Besides the ferry master, there were only a handful of other eldrasi crossing to the right side of the island.

"Get back," he snarled at the eldrasi. His illusion faded away as he turned to the ferry master, whose mouth had opened to protest. "I am going to need you to stop this boat so that my comrades can board. You understand."

"I cannot. We have already begun to leave. I have a schedule to keep—"

The ferry lurched violently. Had Cassius not used his wings to buffer himself, he might have fallen, as nearly all the eldrasi did. Cassius spared a glance at shore. Linda had laid Khal down and grabbed hold of the back of the ferry, keeping it from moving forward. Intoh threw his hands out to create a current of wind that pressed against the back of Cassius' head.

Turning back around, Cassius cupped the ferry master's chin and tugged his eyes up to meet his. He was a young eldrasi (it was difficult to tell their age exactly), and his eyes bore stubbornness and subtle fear as they met Cassius'.

"You and your men jump over and swim to shore. Tell no one what you have seen here." His voice dripped with compulsion magic, and though the eldrasi resisted the magic at first, his eyes fell prey to it as his expression slackened, and he nodded. Without a word, he turned, climbed over the small lip of the boat, and crashed into the water.

Cassius turned, his lips peeled back into a snarl. "If you wish to live, I suggest you follow your captain into the water and swim to shore."

His compulsion was not needed, for everyone else, in their panic, followed his command and jumped over the side of the boat.

He hurried to the back of the ship, where Linda groaned. "Linda strong."

It was impressive, the way Linda was holding the ferry, keeping it from leaving. The wind still pressed against Cassius' back, but even still. He looked up to see the others holding back the Thorns, with Sode protecting Khal.

"Everyone on the boat. Now!" Cassius shouted.

Massoud rushed forward and tugged Khal into his arms. "Helai," he called out, and Helai hurried to his side, where they both disappeared in a plume of smoke only to reappear on the ship.

"Hurry. Getting too heavy," Linda whined, the muscles of their arms straining against the weight of holding the ferry in place.

Florence also disappeared, leaving a trail of pollen clinging to the air as he stumbled to the side to avoid Drithan, who jumped across the small ravine between land and the ferry. Everyone's panic was palpable in the air, with those who had been aboard the ferry previously crawling to shore and rushing off. Cassius' tongue darted out as the elevated heartbeats of everyone sang in a symphony around him.

There were only a few Thorns that pursued them, but they fought with unmatched skill and poise. Rooster was going to be overwhelmed if no one aided him.

"Stay here," Cassius instructed the others. "Intoh, Sode. Get on board. Linda, you too, when they're safe. I'll make sure Rooster and I are right behind you."

Linda nodded as Cassius leaped over them onto shore, where he rushed to Rooster's aid.

Unsheathing his sword, he crossed his blade with that of a Thorn's as Rooster was preoccupied with another, and the snarl of his growl met the silent rage of the Thorn as they locked together in combat.

It was evenly matched. Cassius hadn't fought with someone who nearly out-skilled him with a blade since he fought the vampire knight Sivgald in the opera house in Volendam. The Thorn calculated his movements with every turn as if he'd studied the way of the Sanguine Order, and Cassius ground his teeth in frustration as the Thorn blocked another of his attacks.

"What's the matter, Dead Walker?" The Thorn sneered. "Scared to die permanently this time? I'm surprised you can walk these streets."

Cassius didn't honor him with a response. Eldrasi magic was combative with vampiric magic; that much was true. The innate magic here dug into his skin and made his lungs wheeze. He wasn't supposed to be anywhere brimming with so much *life*, but it did not stop him from fighting it at every turn.

Cassius came to find out that patience was the key to destroying these guards. Eventually, the Thorn made a critical mistake, and Cassius cut him down. It was strange; they hadn't seemed to call for any backup, and the stillness of the city made Cassius' skin crawl as he hurried to Rooster's side.

"Carter Wingman," one Thorn said, his lips peeled back in a wordless sneer. "Your beloved's screams have been particularly delectable, but I have to say, I'm impressed. Her will is stronger than the prison guards give her credit for. We couldn't pry your whereabouts from her no matter what we tried."

The wordless fury that peeled across Rooster's face was nothing sort of breathtaking. Cassius fought alongside him, swinging his sword around and pivoting to avoid the slash of the Thorn's blade. Then he lowered his sword and darted forward, sinking his teeth into his neck.

The taste was instantaneous as his mind flooded with ecstasy. It tasted as Tantien's had, sweet and thick, with a flicker of some spice that made the edges of Cassius' tongue tingle. He drank deeply, snagging the Thorn's wrist as he reached up to pry Cassius from his neck. He tugged it away. As the Thorn went limp, he let the guard fall. The world was vibrant and a swirl of colors despite it being nighttime. Rooster sank his sword into the neck of the guard he fought and seeing the splash of yellow nearly made Cassius sway.

When Cassius looked him in the eye, he could have sworn he saw the ignition of amber fire in his gaze, like a luminescent glow of magic. It quickly faded as Rooster pried his sword free of the guard's neck. Massoud came back to grab them, but he looked too exhausted to do two trips. Cassius gestured to Rackjack and Linda. "Take them." He grabbed Rooster. "I'll bring him."

His back shuddered as his wings slipped out. He would never get used to the feel of them or how liberating it was to seek the freedom of the sky.

Cassius slid his sword into his sheath. As Rooster's arms slung around Cassius' neck, he pushed off from the ground with the beat of his wings and took off towards the sailing ferry. Rooster's heartbeat pressed against Cassius, his nearness weighing on his bloodlust. He'd thought he'd left it behind him when he'd ascended, but it was coming back slowly as if it had only been put to sleep for a time. He would have to feed soon.

Cassius didn't allow himself to think of it, though, until he and Rooster touched the deck of the ferry. His fangs ached to descend, his hunger a tickle at the base of his throat. He ignored it as he caught sight of the others' faces.

He'd never seen Intoh cry, not as he did now. No tears fell from Intoh's eyes, but the pain was so raw and palpable as it flowed from Intoh that Cassius flinched away from it. The wail that pierced the greka's lips was unnatural. He clung to Khal's burned body with reckless abandon, and Cassius realized he no longer heard Khal's heartbeat.

The greka was dead.

"Ekalas dead. All my fault. Khal dead. All my fault," Intoh wailed, and silence encompassed the ferry as it sailed towards the other side of the island. Sode stood behind Intoh, and his face was a wall of stone; no emotion passed through, but grief was heavy in the air, much like it had been when Helai lost Zamir.

"Intoh, I'm so sorry," Helai uttered, clinging to Massoud as tears of her own welled in her eyes. "He was too far gone."

Intoh did not respond.

Everyone stood in silence after that.

THIRTY-EIGHT

INTOH

Intoh was familiar with this kind of pain. He'd felt it the moment Ekalas had slipped through his fingers, as soon as she had returned to the sky and left him, all alone in the world. Her death all those years ago had brought his walls up, and he'd sworn to himself never to let anyone in again. Never again.

So why was he here now, wailing over the burnt body of Khal? Why did it feel as if his heart was cracking in two? *Stupid, stupid, fool.*

He stumbled to his feet to see the others mourning. Rooster stood at the end of the ferry, his jaw pulsating as he stared on in silence. Anger brushed off him in waves, whereas the others were more plain in their grief. Helai openly wept, and it was Cassius who drew forward, his face drawn in a hard line.

"How does your kind honor the dead?"

It took a moment for Intoh to answer, to steel his sadness behind a weak wall. Balling his fingers into fists, he met Cassius' gaze.

"Burn them. Welcome them back to sky. It is greka way."

"Then that is what we will do."

"First, we need to figure out how we're going to get off this boat undetected," Massoud said, drawing forward. He seemed to be the only one with his emotions intact, and even then, there was a splattering of sympathy across his expression. "They will have notified the guards on the other side."

"We could sail somewhere else, but it might take longer to get to Fraxinus if we do," Cassius pondered, slipping into his knightly role as he clasped his hands behind his back and shook the sadness from his face. "Though we wouldn't need to go far, just enough to where they can't see us, and then..."

"I shade step us to shore," Massoud finished, wagging his finger in thought. "Not a bad idea, but I can only do a couple of people at a time."

"Don't be meanin' to eavesdrop, but I can get meself to shore jus' fine," Florence said.

Rackjack trembled. "I can get some of us across too, yes-yes."

Intoh steeled himself and shoved his grief down. No time. There was simply no time, and Khal's death had all but reforged his determination to seek out his immortality. He turned, noting Linda and Drithan had sat down to row the ferry forward.

"Too dangerous to burn Khal's body. Smoke might attract guards." His gaze hardened. "We'll bury him when we get to shore. Return him to earth. Next best way."

They weren't followed, and Linda and Drithan sailed them slightly off course so they weren't greeted with more Thorns at the docks on the other side of the island. The moment they got close to shore, Massoud and Rackjack took them to shore using their own forms of teleportation. Intoh went with Rackjack and shuddered as the sensation of his magic felt like a small army of rats crawling over him. The moment he landed on the beach, he decided he never wanted to do that with Rackjack again.

Grief still struck Intoh in a way he couldn't describe. A part of him was desperate to shove it away, to push it so far down into the dark void of his mind that he could not see it, where it could not hurt him. The other part of him, the part that had lost Ekalas in much the same manner, refused to let him do so. But he couldn't cry; tears never came to him as they had to Linda once or twice, but the hollowness that forged in his chest begged him to do something to release the maelstrom of pain swelling in his throat. Sode kept beside him, but he didn't say anything. He didn't cry either, much as Intoh expected him to. He'd been much closer to Khal.

"Ekalas," he whispered beneath his breath. "Ekalas, I need you." He hadn't seen Ekalas for quite some time, and he despaired that she had abandoned him. He missed the sound of her voice, missed her quiet mutterings of reason when his mind would not stop swirling with information. Khal's death had re-opened the wound that he'd suffered when Ekalas had died, and he clawed at his own scales in a desperate attempt to liberate the overwhelming amount of emotions cradling his heart.

"Intoh, if you need to talk, it might help," Sode said softly in Drikotyian. "Not really good at talking but good at listening." Tension formed between them, and Intoh shook his head as he forced his breathing to steady. After a moment, his heart stopped racing, and the well of sadness that had built up against him lessened its hold.

"Thank you, Sode, but I don't want to talk."

He hadn't wanted to talk about losing Ekalas either. It had taken Linda a long time to even know who Ekalas was, and Intoh fidgeted with the ring on his finger, ignoring the sensation of magic as he alternated between greka and human. In a way, the sensation was soothing, a way to ground himself against being carried away by the river of grief in his veins.

"Just want to be more careful next time."

Sode nodded firmly. Something had formed from the ashes of Khal's death between Intoh and Sode, a sense of protectiveness that Intoh had dismissed before. Khal and Sode had sworn their life to protect Intoh, but a flame had been lit in Intoh in turn: he would do anything to stop the world from taking another Misfit from him.

"Life is bloody and cruel. You cannot shoulder the burden of his death. He served his purpose and protected you with his life. His duty was fulfilled. The halls of his ancestors will welcome him as a hero," Drithan said, watching Sode and Linda dig a hole big enough for Khal's body.

"Greka believe he will walk among the sky. Will become one of the lights above when nighttime is to watch over us," Sode said, his gaze turned up towards the sky. Dawn had broken, and the starlight of nighttime had slipped away. "With our goddess now."

Intoh nodded sadly. "Final Sleep Walk."

"Khal's death will not be for nothing."

Intoh's face forged into hard determination. "Never for nothing."

THIRTY-NINE
ROOSTER

Exhaustion and rage had swallowed Rooster beneath their gaping maws, their hungry teeth carving meanness into his bones. The Thorns were after them, and now that they knew Rooster was here, they'd likely post more guards at the prison.

Linda approached as Sode and Intoh buried Khal, their hand reaching out to rest atop his head, as they did when they meant to comfort. "Will be okay, Rooster."

"How do you know?" The words left Rooster's lips harsher than he intended, but he jerked away from Linda's comfort, a sneer curling at his mouth. "We were caught, we thought we got away, and then we got too comfortable at that tavern."

Helai's face twisted defensively while Linda's jaw fell open in protest. "Did not think—"

"No, Linda, you *didn't* think. None of us did." Guilt wiggled in his belly at Linda's hurt expression. "Khal is dead because of our lack of vigilance."

Helai stepped in front of Linda, her hand held out across their stomach protectively. "Rooster, walk away," she warned, as the silence of the party thickened in the air. "Before you say something else."

Rooster glared at her before turning abruptly on his heel and disappearing into the trees, away from the party, away from the reminders of what they'd just lost. He and Khal were never close, but the Greka's death served as a reminder of what dangers lay ahead and that they were not safe from those who hunted them.

He sank to his knees, his head in his hands. Lashing out at Linda had been a symptom of his fear and guilt. Igraine could be dead. He knew that now, seeing the ruthless nature of the Thorns. His stomach twisted painfully, fed to by his anxiety. He wanted her so desperately to be alive, to have her back by his side. What if this was all for naught, and he had put his found family in danger?

The prison would be more fortified, now that they knew Rooster was coming. Getting in would prove trickier, but Rooster had always known it would be a challenge. He'd rip the tree down with his bare fucking hands if he had to. Nothing else, no one else, would stand in his way.

He stayed crouched in the brush until his legs grew numb, his fingers pressed into the earthy soil beneath him. He stayed until someone called out to him, as Cassius' hand came to rest down on his shoulder.

"We mean to give Intoh and the other drikoty a moment to grieve before we move forward."

"I'm going to stay here for a moment," Rooster said softly. He continued to stare at the ground long after Cassius' hand fell from his shoulder, the retreating of his boots a relief. Rooster didn't want to explain himself, didn't want to nurture the tangle of panic that remained rooted in his chest. Had he led his new family to their doom? Had he forged that of his old one by leaving?

He just wanted to be alone.

Rooster returned to the others as Cassius helped Massoud to his feet. "Hey," Rooster said, capturing Cassius' attention. "Thanks for your aid on this journey. I could not hope to do any of this without you...without any of you."

"It is the knightly thing to do. Plus—" Cassius reached forward to clasp Rooster's shoulder. "You are my brother, Rooster, in all but blood. I would do it again." He gave a firm nod as if to reinforce his words as warmth poured through Rooster. "Now go and apologize to Linda and Helai. It was only a matter of time before someone recognized us. Eldrasi have some of the strongest magic in the world. I am surprised we made it through with our illusions intact at all." Then, as if to sense Rooster's hesitation, his face softened. "They will understand, but you should go to them. We are about to go into the trickiest of situations, and we have already lost people. It would be a shame to lose more and have not settled any hurts."

"You're right." Rooster would never forgive himself if they got into Fraxinus and one of them died without mending whatever offense had lodged itself between them. "Thank you again, Cassius."

As he turned away, he stepped up to Linda, who was shuffling loudly through the brush. The trees of Míradan were lush and full, its trees tall and foreboding. It was nothing like the trees Rooster had stumbled out of, their trunks massive and thousands of years old, but it was still impressive as they wove through them, silent and solemn.

"Linda, can I speak with you for a moment?"

Linda ignored him at first and the tension thickened between them so much that it wrapped around him and threatened to strangle the air from his lungs. He persisted, and after a moment, Linda's shoulders slumped, and they nodded.

"Can speak."

"I apologize for my behavior earlier. It wasn't fair to pin the blame on you, not when I am the reason we were in danger in the first place. I reacted because of my anger and fear, which does not make it right. I am sorry to both of you for the way I handled it," he said, looking to Linda, and then to Helai, who walked beside them.

"Because of me, Khal is dead." Linda despaired, the sadness in their words so heavy it stripped the air from Rooster's lungs. "Did not mean for us to drink so much, make so much noise."

Rooster shook his head. "I turned the guard's eye on us, not you. And besides, Khal made the conscious choice to partake in the festivities. It isn't your fault, Linda. Sode and Intoh's path through this life will carry his memory with them. It's alright to feel sad about it, though." All this time, Rooster had never really grown to know Khal; perhaps his death had opened his eyes, and he made a note to sit down with Sode the next chance he got.

That evening, they set up camp with no fire. Rooster was too anxious about being discovered by Thorns on the road even though they had made sure to travel a good way away from it. On foot and based on Tantien's knowledge, they were still a day or two out from Fraxinus. The trees protected them from the wind, and Rooster was glad for no rain as they all settled between the massive, gnarled roots of the trees. The island seemed untouched by the chill of winter despite how frigid and snowy Volendam had been when they'd left, but the warmth here was almost magical in nature, wrapping around Rooster as he nestled into a spot on his own, and he allowed it to lull him into a state of content.

Rackjack and Florence joined him, their quiet mutterings ignored as they conversed among themselves. A small rift felt forged between him and the other Misfits as Linda managed to draw a laugh out of Cassius, and Helai sat near Intoh and Drithan as they talked softly about the plan to retrieve the tome.

It was the first time since he had woken on the edge of Daesthara that he felt lost and alone, like the rope that tethered him to Igraine was strangling his brotherhood with the Misfits. It darkened his thoughts. *They are your family*, he reminded himself, *just as much as those of your past are.*

He had to believe it so. He watched as Massoud plucked a leaf from Cassius' hair, his smile curling slyly when Cassius glanced over. Massoud had slipped into the group with ease, and Helai was no lesser a Misfit for having introduced her past to them, so why couldn't it be the same for him and those from his past?

His eyes flickered over to Helai and then to Drithan, whose brow was furrowed as if in deep thought. The sight of them, the sight of him and Sode and Rackjack and Florence, lifted the darkness tangling in his heart slightly, the notion that the past *could* mingle with the present softening his anxiety.

"Can sense fear-musk," Rackjack rasped, pulling Rooster from his spiral. Rackjack was eyeing him with concern while Florence's head tilted, the cover of his blindfold fading in the growing darkness. Rooster longed for the light of a fire. Eldrasi woods, even the young Míradan ones, were ripe with strange creatures and even stranger flora.

Rooster shook his head and forced a smile. "Will just be glad to be off this godsforsaken island, Rackjack. As much as I love running from guards, we're a little too close for comfort."

"We'll get 'er out, Cap'n," Florence said. "We'll get 'em all out."

That was what everyone kept saying, but if Rooster had learned anything about life, he'd learned never to put too much hope in anything. It could so easily get strangled, caught on the sharp edges of the world.

FORTY

INTOH

They reached Fraxinus and saw it was very different from Kelirium in appearance, though it shared its ties to nature with its sister city. Fraxinus sat nestled between towering cliffs and the rolling sea, exuding its own form of natural beauty. Elaborate vines twisted to massive bridges that connected tall spiraling buildings made of seashells and crystal, their rooftops glittering as the sun hit them. Waterfalls cascaded over the cliff sides, pooling into clear ponds ripe with fish and other sea life.

It looked just like the coastal greka cities that Intoh had grown up in. As they drew closer, the air became fresher, with deep fragrances permeating off cascading gardens clinging to the sides of the cliffs, which were filled with vibrant flowers and fruit that some of the eldrasi were pulling off and collecting in baskets.

The city was magnificent in its own right, but it wasn't what captured the attention of the Misfits.

Off in the distance sat a magnificent tree so large it stood tall above all the other trees before its branches stretched out. Golden-yellow leaves covered the branches, and things hung from them like bird cages. A building was built around the tree, woven through its trunk, and Intoh stared at it in shocked awe as Rooster inhaled sharply beside him.

"That's the prison."

The tree pulsed with a magical energy, felt even as they stood at the edge of town. It whispered through the trees and settled over the roar of the waterfalls. Cassius pointed to a thin pointed spire beside the prison. "That appears magical in nature. Perhaps it is where the tome is?"

"Not to discredit you, dear Cassius," Massoud said, tossing his hand outward, "but the eldrasi are ripe with magic. *Everything* appears magical in nature."

"Massoud is right. We'll go in and see if we can't find the tome. It was…" Helai's voice caught as she met Massoud's gaze, and her lower lip trembled as she composed herself. "It was Zamir's specialty, but Massoud and I are capable of being persuasive when it comes to gathering information."

Helai and Massoud were gone, disappearing into shadows before Intoh could blink. It was almost eerie how quickly they melted away and were swallowed by the city. His stomach lurched as he kicked a rock and it skipped across the ground and lunged over the edge of the cliff they were near. He steeled himself, gathering the courage to peer over the edge. Far below were craggy rocks and the brush of the sea as the water crashed against the cliff sides. Intoh swallowed the nervous lump in his throat and scurried backwards, asserting himself closer to Sode. With Khal gone,

Intoh found his sense of mortality especially present, and that fear alone made him desperate for the protection of those around him.

"Should get off road," he said nervously, watching some eldrasi carry a basket full of some small, red fruit through the streets of the city. Eldrasi had always made him nervous. They were ancient beyond measure, the history of their people carved into the ruins of their cities. The greka had found some of those ruins in the forests of Lyvira and built their own cities around them. An old greka had told him the two continents had once been one, and that was why eldrasi ruins dotted the coastline of Lyvira. Said the dragon wars of old had caused a slumbering dragon to drag its claws through the earth and rip the continents asunder. The size of a dragon capable of doing such a thing had been lost on Intoh, and he'd never been sure if he believed the old stories or in the existence of dragons.

Perhaps he believed them a little now.

He even saw evidence of the tale here if he looked hard enough. He was uncertain where the islands that made up Míradan would have resided had they been a part of one continent in the past, but the jagged edges of the cliffs *could* have been from a dragon dragging its claws across the ground, splitting land apart, and forging the new world...

"Intoh." Liberated from his trance, he looked up at Rooster, who gestured back the way they came. "We're going to take a moment to rest just there. You alright, mate?"

Intoh nodded quickly as he moved past Rooster, unwilling to let the man see how out of his skin he felt in this city. It was strange; he hadn't felt this way in Kelirium. Perhaps it was the thrum of magic that sailed through this city, setting Intoh's own magic on edge. His insides vibrated, and he quivered from his restless nature.

He looked at Cassius, at the haunted look in his eye, and wondered what had the vampire seen the times he had died? Had he been born with more courage?

Cassius stood tall now, ever the rigid knight as he stared out between the trees at the city of Fraxinus. Linda fell onto their belly, their legs tucked against their body as they watched Drithan pace anxiously.

"We should not have let them go," Drithan said, his eyes shining with some emotion lost to Intoh. "Not after we just fled the dangers we did."

"If anyone is equipped to remain unseen, it is those who worship the path of Dalnor," Rooster said quietly. Intoh had to agree; even his magical invisibility paled in comparison to the way Helai and Massoud wove through shadow as if it were their home.

Drithan clenched his fist, a hand rising to grasp his beard, but he said nothing more as they used the trees to shield themselves from the rising sun.

"It is strange," Cassius muttered. "To see so much nature woven around a city."

"Don't think so," Intoh said. "Lyvira like this too." Only instead of being carved into tall trees or cliff sides, their city had been built upon the ruins of old eldrasi civilizations in the center of a vast forest.

Intoh's heart ached. Despite the way he'd left it, there were parts of home he missed, such as the sweet fruit that grew in abundance on the trees. Sometimes, Intoh had afforded himself a break from his constant research to merely sit beneath the large trees and split apart the large round kaunuts to feast on the fruit's delightful innards. He'd seen some being imported in when they'd arrived in Kelirium, and it had taken all his self-control to stop himself from taking some off the trader's hands when they hadn't been looking.

Old ghosts haunted him, but he shook them away as he settled against a tree, content to simply sit and wait for a while. He watched as several butterflies drifted over to Linda, their wings a soft gold color as they landed on Linda's head and back. Linda looked so at peace then that Intoh was suddenly jealous. It hadn't taken the krok'ida long at all to find themself, to feel comfortable among those they would call family. Intoh still found himself finding his footing, trying to decide if he belonged.

I want to, he thought.

Traitor, Ekalas seethed, the cusp of her whisper etching his ear. He ignored her, even as his belly twisted with merciless guilt. He didn't want to forget her, did not want to forget their goals, but the Misfits had been there for him in many ways, even when he tried to push them away.

Who was to say he couldn't have both?

Helai and Massoud returned not long after dark. It was strange, seeing Helai so full of life. She looked at Massoud strangely at times. Intoh was quiet and small, easily ignored, so it made it easier for him to observe. Cassius' ghosts came to bear in his eyes when he thought no one was looking. Rooster had a nervous tick where he'd tap his knee three times to calm himself. And Helai? Helai looked at Massoud like he was the only one that could lead her to safety. Her movements matched him as he led them confidently out of the shadows, his eyes as bright as his smile.

"We have found the tome," he said, tossing his arm across his chest as he bowed mockingly. "It is in the tower, a tower we've come to know as a lorekeep where the eldrasi store a plethora of information. I believe our best time to infiltrate would be now, under the cover of darkness."

"We'll talk more on the way. It may take us hours yet to weave through the city to get there," Rooster said.

Intoh shivered with anticipation. He knew they sought the tome for Delroy, but if he could just get his hands on it...

Perhaps it held the very answers he was searching for.

FORTY-ONE
HELAI

They traveled through the city quicker than Helai had thought they would, considering the size of their party. It wasn't the first time she wondered if some of them should have remained with Tantien on the Firebrand. Cassius was terrible at keeping quiet, the heaviness of his armor clanking every time he moved, and Helai gave him another sharp look as his boot came down on a loose shell, and the sound of it skittering cut through the air.

"It's impressive that Linda is able to be silent where a vampire cannot," she teased, delighting at his sour expression. Years ago, she wouldn't have had the courage to tease a vampire, but Cassius' constant presence had eased her of her initial fears.

Linda slunk out of the darkness, their jaw opened as if in pride. "Has become very good at being quiet," they said, the soft rumble of their voice vibrating through Helai's chest. "Have Helai to thank."

Satisfaction sang through Helai at the compliment. She had been working diligently with Linda, teaching them how to be quiet and utilize shadows or fog to surprise their enemies. Linda had picked up on it surprisingly quickly for being so large.

"We're close," Massoud said, gesturing in front of them and pulling Helai away from the smile she shot at Linda.

Silverleaf Lorekeep was massive, a tall and swirling building that reached up in a point towards the sky. It paled in comparison to the prison that stood tall behind it, but it was still impressive to look at, with shimmering translucent walls and swirling coral-like designs.

The Misfits stood near it under the blanket of darkness as they knew the vast majority of the eldrasi would be tucked away in their homes. Lights still dotted the pathways between trees and buildings, and the rush of waterfalls roared in Helai's ears. She could not deny the beauty of the place they were about to rob.

Her skin prickled with anticipation. She always felt giddy before missions like these. They had made up much of her adolescence, and a quick glance over at Massoud showed he felt the same. His shoulders were tense despite the sly and easy smile gracing his lips, and as he caught Helai's gaze in his own, he nodded. It was no different than the times they'd broken into the wealthy homes in Dalasae or Shok'Alan.

When they'd come here earlier, Massoud had suggested they stroll through the lorekeep under the guise of curious travelers. No one had suspected them, and Helai had been shocked to find the magnitude of artifacts kept within its walls. They'd even found a jinn lamp inside, tucked away behind several layers of magical barriers. It supposedly had belonged to the great Sultana Farrah, one of the few female sultanas of Shoma. She'd been sultana before Mohalis, before the corruption had taken root in Helai's people. It had taken them a better part of the day scouting out the lorekeep, where they could exit should they need a quick escape, what lorekeepers were there at night, and where the tome might be. Helai had been relieved to find it tucked away in a room heavy with magical influence, and the lorekeeper she spoke to explained that it held immense power and was one of their most protected pieces. It wouldn't be easy to take, but lucky for the Misfits, they weren't trying to escape the lorekeep so long as one of them was able to flee with the tome in hand.

"Convinced I can get it," Intoh said.

"If not 'im, I might be able to," Florence said, earning an irritated glance from Intoh. The sight almost made Helai laugh. Intoh was always one to be irritated but never one to be envious of someone else doing a job. It was almost comical.

"I actually have an important job for you, Florence," Rooster said.

Florence's eyes lit up. "Anything, Cap'n."

"You avoided capture once. If we all get captured with the tome, they will undoubtedly take it again. We need someone to slip away with it unseen and find a way onto my ship. I suppose you would be up for the task?"

Florence straightened, his ears quivering. "Course I can. Slippery li'l bugga I am. Will make sure the tome is tucked nice 'n safe in your drawers cabinet where no one can find it."

Laughter slipped from Massoud's lips.

"Not safe from me. No one's drawers' cabinet is safe from me," Massoud teased, a sly wink shot off in Rooster's direction.

"It is decided then," Cassius said, staring up at the twisted spire that would force their imprisonment. "We best get to it."

FORTY-TWO
HELAI

A lorekeeper met them at the door, just as Helai knew they would.

Intoh quivered beside Helai, perhaps in anticipation. Perhaps in fear. She didn't rightly know.

The lorekeeper gave everyone a long withering look. "If anyone has any questions, there are several lorekeepers throughout. Any of them would be happy to answer them." She eyed Drithan and Rackjack silently for a moment. "This will be the first time dwarves have entered a lorekeep. It is an honor to serve those who nurture the heart of the mountain." Her voice was lacking warmth despite what appeared to be a compliment, and Drithan stiffened beside Helai as he remained tight-lipped and silent.

Tension filled the air as the lorekeeper ushered them inside. It was just as grand as it had been the first time Helai had seen it. The rooms were round, with swirling staircases carved into the walls as they extended to higher floors. The circular stained-glass windows were dull at night, but she knew them to be vibrant in the day as they depicted nature in its rawest forms—falling green leaves and drips of sunbeams upon meadows of wildflowers. Magical instruments whizzed about, spinning around high up near the ceiling, and several large eyes stuck out of the walls, watching them as they walked.

"What happened back there?" Helai asked Drithan in a hushed whisper as they strode further inside.

"She spoke ill of Kurzda, the dragon that sleeps in the belly of the world." He looked troubled, his eyes darting about, his tension thickening in the air around them. "Many of my people revere him as a god, for he gifts us godly presents with the draugmin." Helai recalled Obrand having told them of such a dragon, and a chill rolled down her back. For the first time since they had been removed, the spot where her brand had used to be at her lower back burned.

"The eldrasi and the dragons were at war once," Drithan continued as if he did not notice Helai's discomfort, and she turned to him sharply.

"I didn't know that."

"It's kept hidden, but you could probably find information about it here," he said, waving his hand about the shelves of books and tomes that decorated the walls. It had taken her and Massoud some time to find the tome they were looking for, and they had scoured through this tomes as a result. Now that she thought about it, she recalled some titles bearing information about old wars. Artifacts behind glass doors and more hanging suspended on dias' were situated between shelves, and Helai stepped forward as Intoh gestured to the eyes watching them from the walls.

"Will keep a watchful eye on us. Will notice when we take tome. Must do this carefully." His eyes were far away and wistful as they passed by several rows of shelves. The lorekeeper that had let them in stopped to speak with another eldrasi in elegant green robes threaded with gold on his sleeves. He did not speak. Rather, he listened, and when he responded, it was through several quick and flowing hand motions that relayed emotion just as much as his face did. He didn't seem at all pleased, and when he glanced over, Helai quickly looked away.

He approached slowly with the other lorekeeper.

"This is Head Lorekeeper Jûmín. He was born without his hearing, so I will be translating for him. He is interested in knowing what brought you here." The tension in the air was nearly palpable.

Clear mind, clear soul.

The words Massoud had used to tell Helai as a child washed through her, keeping her from losing her wits. Sometimes she still felt like the wide-eyed child, frightened and dirty-cheeked.

"We were in Kelirium on a trade ship and overheard someone speaking of the lorekeep here." Jûmín's eyes flickered from Helai's to the female lorekeeper, his fingers darting in intricate patterns.

Some of the others had begun to wander. Intoh had found himself in front of some of the shelves of books and tomes, his brow slightly furrowed as Sode stood beside him, his tail trailing from side to side in a near lazy manner. The lorekeep was warm; the small magical orbs that darted about filled the room with a soft light.

Drithan remained tucked closely to Helai, his fingers grazing hers. It was a gentle gesture, one that grounded Helai even as she feared their path. They were all in way over their heads.

"It is one of the best of eldrasi lorekeeps, so if any of you have any knowledge you wish to seek, you will do so here," Jûmín signed.

"Ah, Mistuh lorekeeper sire." Florence bounced up. "Do you have any information on the old gods?"

Jûmín seemed surprised by Florence's presence.

"A myrlír? You keep strange company," the female lorekeeper translated for him. "We have only just begun seeing your kind here. Most myrlír dwell in Daesthara."

"Just because I don't have my eyes anymore doesn't mean I can't see the magic that surrounds you, lorekeeper," Florence rasped. "I've come here on my own curiosities—to see if this lorekeep has any knowledge of the north and what all might find their home in the snow there."

Rackjack nodded, speaking for the first time since they'd arrived. "Have much interest in Vykra culture."

The warning Rackjack had given them about the growing number of Vykra ships around Volendam was concerning, to say the least.

Jûmín turned and gestured to a little room tucked away from the main lorekeep.

"We don't have a lot on the people of the north or what settles there, but everything you find will be through that door." He gave them all a long withering look and then smiled as the woman translated. "Aerva and I will be walking around should you need any other assistance."

"Thank you," Helai said, relieved they would no longer be questioned. Her skin crawled like something unseen watched them. Everywhere she looked, the eyes that blinked against the wood of the walls pressed down on her, reminding her that their every move was being watched. It was a good thing they weren't trying to escape this place. They just needed to make sure Florence got out with the tome.

They could do that.

They weren't bothered again after that. Rackjack and Florence moved towards the door that led to the room where they could learn more about Volreya and the wild men that lived there, and Intoh tucked himself away with Sode in a corner of the room as he studied the tomes that lined the shelves. Going directly for the tome would be too suspicious.

"Is that from the lamp from Shoma?" Drithan's voice sent Helai's gaze towards the wall, where a lamp rested on a pillow of purple velvet. It was the same lamp that had captured her attention the evening before, with Sultana Farrah's likeness etched into a tapestry behind it. She had been murdered long before Helai's birth, but the streets of Dalasae still sometimes whispered of her rule, of her kindness and generosity.

So unlike Sultan Mohalis. So unlike the greed that had been sweeping through the sands after Sultana Farrah's assassination.

Helai nodded, unable to keep the bitterness from settling in her skin. She hated it, hated how hateful it made her. Massoud had used to scold her for her temper, saying it would make her do reckless things. A part of him had always been right for it, and a small part of her hated him for it.

Drithan reached his hand out and took hers, tangling their fingers together. A small part of her hated how grounded Drithan made her, how the anger seemed to wash away due to something so simple as a touch. *Pull away*, her brain begged, but her heart did not listen. She was tired of running. She squeezed his hand and drew closer, comforted by the warmth that radiated from him.

"They said she was a good sultana, but her assassination took place before I was born. She was good to the jinn too, as should be custom." A heaviness set about her shoulders, a reminder of the wish she had made to save Massoud's life. The jinn had warned her of its consequence. *Your wish bears a heavy burden.* She felt it in Dalnor's silence, saw it every time the bleached strands of her hair flew into her vision.

"Dwarves did not do many dealings with Shoma, but I remember her."

Helai turned to him sharply. "How?" She never stopped to consider how old Drithan might be. Her knowledge of dwarves was very small.

Drithan appeared sheepish. "We grow slowly, like the mountain we come from. I'm a little over a century old."

The news didn't strike Helai quite as harshly as she would have expected. "Just older than Cassius then." It had always been difficult to tell Drithan's age under the thickness of his beard, but dwarves and eldrasi were always safe from the tells of time.

Drithan nodded.

Helai hummed in response and turned back towards where Intoh was scurrying through the shelves. Despite his human illusion, there were greka-like movements to him, the way he moved as if to compensate for his tail, the way his eyes darted about. Linda looked bored behind him, Sode ever vigilant as his eyes swept the room.

"Are we going for it?" she whispered.

Intoh nodded.

"Then we go up," Helai said, peering at the archway tucked away in the corner, where a swirling set of stairs curled upwards.

"Go tell Rackjack and Florence," Linda said, ambling off. They moved with more grace and care than when Helai had first met them. She wondered if it was their eagerness to be sneakier or if it was their growing comfort in themself. Regardless, they returned not much later, gesturing to the room they'd just come from.

"Said they would stay here. Make it look more casual than if we all go up. Also keep watch down here."

Helai nodded, forcing her breathing to untangle the tight anxiety that had balled up in her chest. This had always been her least favorite part of any heists she was a part of. Planning? Fighting? Killing? She did those with ease. Keeping calm under the stress of sneaking through places to steal from underneath the owner's nose? Massoud had always teased her for her nervous nature.

"I'll lead the way," she said softly, chasing her fear away. There was no time for fear. She'd bear it because she must, because the lives of her friends depended on it.

FORTY-THREE
RACKJACK

As the other wandered up the stairs, Rackjack suppressed the urge to shudder and walked about the room. Tables were nestled in random parts of the room, empty now. Eldrasi were day creatures by nature, and evidence of it was shown in how quiet it was. Rackjack was grateful for it.

"Who's your wee friend?" Florence asked, pointing to Kratch. The rat ogre that Rackjack had magicked into a small rat sat perched on his shoulder, where he squeaked softly in response to Florence's question.

"Rat-filth," Rackjack whispered, prying Kratch off of his shoulder and pushing him into his beard. "Good for protection-fighting."

"I can see he's more than he seems," Florence mused, turning and disappearing into the small room that Jûmín had pointed out. If there was information on the old gods and their ties to the Vykra, a lorekeep would have it. Rackjack didn't expect to ever return; if he was going to check, now would be his only chance.

Rackjack scowled as Kratch dug further into his beard, his tiny nails scraping against the skin at his neck. An overwhelming compulsion to pry him away and squeeze him until he popped nearly overcame Rackjack, but he refrained, distracted as Florence poked his head out of the room and gestured to Rackjack.

"Think I found somef'in of interest, Ratty-jack." The room was intimate and round as Rackjack entered, with large, floor-to-ceiling windows overlooking the sea crashing up against the cliff side. Dragons were sculpted into wooden pillars that decorated the walls, and they stared down at Rackjack with jewel-encrusted eyes.

"Let me see-sniff," Rackjack said, scurrying over and pulling the tome from Florence's hands. Much of the room looked untouched, save for the cleaning and care that went into keeping the dust at bay, and the tome creaked in protest as Rackjack opened it. On page, a Vykra woman with deep red hair and kind eyes sat near a creek bed with two children clinging to her shoulders and her lap. The moment Rackjack had opened the tome, an uncomfortable feeling had pinched at his belly, and now it tugged, throwing him headfirst into the tome.

He blinked against the harsh light of the sun, so different from the dimly lit lorekeep he'd been in. On his hands and knees, he was a dwarf no more, his illusion stripped away as his rakken form bled through. Kratch squeaked in alarm, perched on Rackjack's shoulder, and he shivered violently as his paws pressed into the powder-like snow that covered the ground. Florence landed hard beside him, the light green of his skin a harsh contrast against all of the snow.

Rackjack grumbled. He hated the snow. Hated how stiff it made his limbs. He forced himself up, blinking rapidly against the light, and stilled.

The woman sat before him, her hair like fire as it wafted through the frigid wind. Her back faced him, and she hummed softly under her breath as she did something in the creek in front of her. Chunks of ice flowed with the water, and Rackjack spared a quick glance at Florence before finding his courage. He had heard of tomes sometimes drawing the reader into the text, but he had never experienced it before now. A part of him was still aware of the room in the lorekeep, but he felt the sun on his face, and his paws were growing numb beneath the cold.

"Rhavna."

Rackjack flinched as a voice called out from behind him, and he peered over his shoulder as a burly man with a thick beard and facial tattoos approached. He paid no mind to Rackjack or Florence, who had scuttled close to Rackjack in search of warmth and approached the red-haired woman.

Rhavna, Rackjack realized, horrified. *Rhavna will rise.* This wasn't the phoenix dragon that had risen from the depths of the Welker Estate, forged forth by Cassius' blood. This was just a woman, just a....

"Rhavna, what are you..." The man sucked in harshly as the woman called Rhavna turned, her fingers dripping blood. Her eyes unfocused, she swayed as the coppery scent hit Rackjack's tongue. In her lap was the corpse of a child, one of the children that had been in the sketch of the tome. One of her children? The other was nowhere to be seen.

The man looked to be full of rage. "What have you done?"

"They were hungry, sick... He said, he *said* he would liberate them from their suffering..." she mumbled, raising her bloody fingers to drag them diagonally down her face. Rackjack stiffened. That was his mark.

Gorvayne's mark.

"Rhavna, what have you done?" the man repeated, sad now. The visage before them slipped away like smoke, only to be replaced by a village center. They were still in snow, only now they were surrounded by small wooden buildings and tents made from animal skin. Villagers had tucked themselves away from the cold by brushing up against the sides of the buildings, and they watched on as Rhavna was tied to a stake atop a collection of sticks.

Rackjack had seen fabrications like this before. They were going to burn her.

His instincts screamed to flee, but something rooted him to where he stood. The fact he was reliving this memory, perhaps. He did not belong here. Where would he go?

"Ratty-jack, are they going to..." Florence's voice was raspy as he clung to Rackjack's paw. "I can smell her fear in the air, and there is strange magics about." It sang beneath Rackjack's skin, the same as draugmin. It drenched the air. It whispered softly through the breeze. He trembled from it.

The world was silent this time. No words were spoken as Rhavna glared out among the villagers, as her rage consumed her entire face. Children hid behind mothers or wooden fences, their eyes wide, and it was the burly man from before that lowered the torch to the wood in several places. The brush of heat from the flames etched Rackjack's cheeks, and he felt Kratch protest, nuzzling further into his fur.

Rhavna screamed when the flames touched her, the same as Rembrandt and his mother had screamed when she had burned them with her flames. It was bloodcurdling and made Rackjack's fur stand on end, and the villagers watched on, their faces void of emotion. Humans loved their children, could not fathom why Rhavna had murdered hers. It was different in rakken culture though. Rackjack had seen rakken eat their young if they were weak. Still, Rhavna burned and screamed as the fire peeled her skin away until she was naught but dust and bones. Her cries echoed throughout the village long after she died and still, Rackjack could not move.

A soft sigh shook the ground, so slight Rackjack thought he might be imagining it until Florence's ears twitched.

"Feel somef'in stirrin'."

Rackjack felt it too. It plucked at his blood like a finely tuned weapon, sending a thrilling hum down his spine. He loathed the way he shivered, the way the magic rubbed up against him like a lover. He resisted the urge to lean into it as the villagers spoke, their voices low and warped, like the dream or tome or whatever magic had drawn Rackjack and Florence into here could not translate it into their language. Rackjack knew that wasn't true though, not when they had understood the burly man and Rhavna from before.

A low growl trembled beneath the ground, like a slumbering beast annoyed to be woken from its long sleep. Rackjack's nervousness pattered against his chest as the village grew quiet and still. The stench of burnt flesh still cradled the air from where Rhavna had burned to death.

"Can you see that, Ratty-jack?" Florence trembled in fear as he drew close and gestured to behind the smoldering pyre. "Oh gods, it's one of 'em *scaly beasts*."

Rackjack looked but saw nothing, nothing but smoke and the endless white of the snow. "No-no," Rackjack whispered. "Magic, perhaps?"

"Oh gods, Ratty-jack," Florence cried, tucking himself against Rackjack's side. "It's *him*."

Rackjack didn't have time to ask who he meant before the pyre burst into flames once more. The village cried out in fear as a phoenix dragon rose from the fire. It was Rhavna, born anew, like she had been when they'd bathed her bone in Cassius' blood.

It was a blood bath after that.

As she had done to the cultists in the Welker Estate, Rhavna lashed forward and murdered without mercy. Instead of fleeing, like Rackjack would have expected from humans, the Vykra held their ground, snarling in harsh tongues and brandishing their weapons. It didn't matter. Rhavna ripped through them or lit them on fire and did not stop until the world was silenced and everyone was dead.

Or at least, that was what Rackjack thought until he noticed a stirring. Several children, all girls, huddled together against one of the buildings. One girl stood in front of them, one hand held out as if to protect the girls from Rhavna's rage. Her eyes were pools of liquid rage, her long dark hair tossed wildly behind her shaking shoulders. Rackjack tasted her fear from where he was, but she stood tall against Rhavna even as she approached, the visage of the phoenix dragon melting away as her human form appeared.

"Sígrun, come here."

Rackjack studied the young girl and realized with startling clarity that he knew her. Sígrun was Carter-filth's gunnery sergeant. Could be a coincidence, but Rackjack saw the same fire in the girl's eyes that he'd seen many times in the Sígrun he knew. Rackjack had never asked Sígrun about her past, but he recalled Carter having found her washed up on shore when she'd joined the Perseverance, and she was clearly Vykra, as this young girl was.

Sígrun clenched her fist and stared up at Rhavna with a stubborn expression. Rackjack admired her courage. It was a strength he fought for every day as rakken were prone to cowardice.

"Sígrun." Rhavna's tone darkened, and Sígrun finally complied, approaching until she stood in front of Rhavna. They wore the same expression, and that was the way the memory ended, and Rackjack and Florence were tugged back into the lorekeep.

FORTY-FOUR

INTOH

As Helai led them quickly up the stairs, the magic that tugged him up grew steadily stronger. Despite it being nighttime, the walls of the lorekeep pulled the light of the moon and reflected it, drenching the place in a tangible glow. Magical orbs of soft light also clung between windows. Linda grumbled as they tripped on a stair.

"Too big," they complained, and they weren't wrong. The eldrasi had not fabricated this place with any krok'ida in mind. Linda's massive shoulders almost touched the walls on each side of the stairwell, and it was a good thing they were the last to ascend in case they got stuck.

"That might come in handy if we need to bar the way," Helai joked quietly. "Just have to make sure they're not coming at you from behind, where you can't defend yourself."

Linda grumbled as they continued up the stairs until they all came to a floor that seemed to be humming with energy. The thrum of magical energy sat tucked behind a closed door as they all poured in front of it.

"Hear that?" Intoh asked, unable to keep the excitement from his voice. "Know it's in there." He didn't know how he knew, just that he did. It was like a shift in the wind or the warmth of newly forged spring telling him that summer was around the corner. He just *knew*.

"It feels foul," Helai said in a hushed tone, shuffling away from the door. Her hand flung to a place where she had one of her daggers hidden, and Intoh waved her anxieties away with a flick of his hand before he reached forward to open the door.

His fingers were inches from the door when he felt it—the same crackling magic that had surrounded the lamp in the Welker Estate. So it had been eldrasi magic at work? Strange. He urged his fingers a bit further through the magic despite his instincts screaming at him not to, despite knowing the injury he had gotten by messing with the magic in Emir Welker's library.

He hissed as the magic lashed out, as his scales peeled back on his fingers beneath his illusion, and blood dribbled down his arm until there was naught but the shine of bone. Just like at the Welker Estate. Most strange, indeed.

"You are harmed," Sode hissed, tugging Intoh away. The room curled in on itself as Intoh was overcome with a dizzy spell, and his attempt to push Sode away was met with great resistance. His gaze settled on his wound and only then did the pain set in, and he whimpered. The pain was sharp, so sharp he went nearly blind from it. It was much stronger than it had been before, and as Sode attempted to heal it, nothing happened.

"Not good at healing. Was Khal's…" He grunted as the magic slid and slipped around Intoh's fingers, unable to latch onto them to heal. Perhaps it had been incredibly stupid of him to make the mistake not once but twice, but he'd had to know if it was the same. How far had Emir Welker's influence spread if he'd been able to get his hands on an eldrasi warding? What lies had he weaved to gain eldrasi favor? The eldrasi would not have been fond of anyone trying to free the dragons from their earthly prison.

"Use this," Intoh said, impatiently pulling the necklace Tantien had made him from around his neck and shoving it at Helai. "Better at it than Sode. Use it quickly, so I can try again."

"Try again?" Sode asked as Helai took the necklace from Intoh and clasped it in her palm. Intoh would have done it himself, but he knew better than to test magic that much. Performing healing magic while in pain would only worsen the wound. He didn't want to lose his fingers altogether.

"Yes. Need to get beyond this door. Need to quickly before lorekeepers come."

Helai worked quickly and efficiently. Blue tendrils of magic manifested like water as they seeped into the bones of Intoh's fingers. He was dismayed to see they did not heal; his muscles and scales did not reforge, but his pain ebbed away until it was completely gone. He opened and closed his hand several times, relieved that it no longer hurt. He did not know if his scales would grow back on these fingers or if the pain would come back, but now that he knew for certain it was the same magic, he could disarm it the same way he had before.

"Keep back," he warned. "Know this magic. Convinced I can disarm it." This time, when he lashed out with his own magic, he knew where the edge of the eldrasi's magic began and did not tempt its wrath, edging along until he found the barest hair of a fracture in its strength. He nearly didn't catch it as the magic threatened to seep all his strength, but he blinked back exhaustion as it presented itself to him. Finally.

Lashing forward like the vipers of his homeland, he wormed his magic into the fissure until it widened and broke, the magic shuddering away like fog disappearing. He slumped as the tired nature of the magic hit him all at once, and he accepted Sode's shoulder to lean against when it was offered to him.

"Can go inside now but must move quickly. Eyes have watched us, and lorekeepers would have felt their magic breaking," Intoh said, fighting the urge to look over his shoulder. They would only have a few minutes. Helai whispered magic into her palm, and a shadowy fox formed and disappeared down the stairs, presumably to go retrieve Rackjack and Florence.

FORTY-FIVE
RACKJACK

They landed roughly back in the room of the lorekeep. Rackjack groaned, his heart leaping to his throat as he looked down and noted he was very much in his rakken form. He scrambled back, hitting his head on the bookcase behind him.

Florence immediately vomited, and Rackjack held his own head, his teeth chattering as he refused to unload his stomach on the floor. The tome had fallen from his grasp. It lay with its spine up as its pages spilled over the floor. A strange noise pierced the air, a soft metallic taste on his tongue. He loathed the symptoms of magical use, and yet, his body betrayed him by craving more. He noted with some relief that his ring was still clung to the

351

fur at his neck, so he twisted it, shuddering as magic washed over him and he turned back into a dwarf.

"Wos that *our* Síggy-run?" Florence rasped once his stomach had emptied all it could.

"Think so," Rackjack said, breathing quickly through the wave of nausea until his stomach settled and the room stopped spinning. "Which means we have question-things to ask her-her when we find her, yes-yes." His mind whirred with the possibilities. Sígrun had been loyal to Carter since the moment he had saved her from the sea, but the tome's contents troubled Rackjack. After everything he'd seen in the Welker Estate, he knew not to trust anyone tied to that phoenix dragon.

Rackjack had little time to gather his bearings before a shadowy visage of a desert fox appeared, its tail trailing away to a smoke trail that led off into the main room. Rackjack had seen Helai use such magic before once or twice and knew it was time to go find them.

"That's the others, yes-yes." Rackjack hummed, gesturing to the shadowy fox as it turned to bound away, its ears twitching much in the same manner that Florence's liked to do. "Must go find-seek them now. Must be ready to go."

Florence groaned, stepping away from the mess he'd made on the floor. "Don't think them lorekeepers will notice, do ya?" he asked, eyeing the vomit. "Don't usually have a reaction like that t' magic, but Rattyjack..." He heard the worry enter Florence's voice. "I don't like this. Whoever that phoenix was... it means nothing good."

Rackjack didn't have time to fill Florence in on how he already knew, how the implications of Rhavna's return was more than just "nothing good," but he nodded silently as they left the small room and followed the shadow fox towards the stairs.

It could only mean nothing good at all.

FORTY-SIX

INTOH

A soft thrum echoed through the door housing the tome as Helai pushed it open, and they all entered. The room was dark, and Linda retreated to wrangle one of the light orbs from the wall in the other room. When they returned, they brought a soft glow of light with them, bathing the room, and Helai pointed immediately to a tome that sat nestled atop a pedestal. A few moments later, Rackjack and Florence entered the room.

"There," she said.

He nearly shivered from the excitement, all exhaustion tossed away and replaced with anticipation. He didn't know how, but he *knew* it contained the answers he sought. A way to immortality.

Take it. The thought festered within him as the others drew closer to it. It fueled the darkness inside him, reminded him of all the trials he had faced to get to this point. *Take it and flee.*

"I do not sense any magic surrounding it," Florence said, his head tilted as if he were listening. "Someone grab it an' hand it t' me. They are *coming.*"

This will be your only chance. He darted forward. Eager. Desperate. Uncertain. As he plucked it from its pedestal, a whisper etched through the room, like an exhale of breath, and it made the hairs on his nape stand on end.

"Excellent job, greka," Florence said, holding his hand out. "I will make sure this gets to the Percy-verence safe and sound-like."

Rackjack scurried back towards the door, pushing it closed as the sound of eldrasi approached. It would only take a moment for the lorekeepers to figure out the magic was gone on the door, and that knowledge had Intoh handing the tome over to Florence despite not wanting to part from it. He would find a chance to study it later. If it fell back into the lorekeeper's possession, he'd never see it again.

Florence blinked out of existence the moment his fingers slipped around the tome, with yellow pollen and spores infecting the air where he once stood. The spores still danced about the room as the lorekeepers burst in, with Thorns following behind them, their spears poised in threatening stance.

"Thank you for informing us of your guests, Lorekeeper Jûmín. We have been searching for this group since they fled Kelirium." One of the Thorns turned to the Misfits, smiling beneath his helm. "Though there are some of you missing."

"We won't talk." Helai said, defiance burning pathways in her eyes as she tilted her chin up. "You'll never find Carter Wingman."

The Thorn laughed, a bitter sound that echoed long after he stopped as his comrades came forward and began shackling them all in chains.

"We shall see."

FORTY-SEVEN
ROOSTER

The wait outside was agonizing. They needed to wait nearby to know that the heist had succeeded before making their way to the prison, and the three of them sat in the blanket of trees where they could still see the entrance of the lorekeep. Rooster was glad for the island's warmth—so different from the eastern continent's chill of winter.

"So, Massoud..." Rooster's voice was soft as Massoud's head turned, a shadow in the darkness. "Your magic. What is it capable of? I have seen Helai wield a bit of the shadows, but she speaks highly of your illusions. Can you change appearances? Or is it more a manipulation for others?"

Massoud flashed a toothy smile and leaned back, pressing against a tree as he thought. "I am not like our dear, sweet Cassius here, whose vampirism casts out an illusion. My magic is more like the rings our friends wear on their fingers to shift them from drikoty to human. I had a very good teacher from Amajin."

Cassius seemed uncomfortable at the notion, his shoulders tense. "The people of Amajin are not who they say they are and guard their secrets with severity. It comes as a surprise to me that one of them would share it with you."

"I am *very* persuasive," Massoud drawled, his voice lowering into a purr as he batted his eyes at Cassius. "As I said, Takao was an incredible illusionist. It is because of him that I was able to keep Helai and Aryan alive on the streets in our adolescence."

Massoud waved his hand in an almost lazy fashion, and a skael slipped between his fingers, only to fall into his other palm as a small chestnut. He offered it to Rooster. As Rooster reached out to take it, the chestnut was a skael once more.

"Every illusion has a flaw. A good illusionist will make the flaw difficult to find, but if you find it, the illusion will break."

Rooster turned the skael over in his hand. It was difficult to see with only the moon to light the forest, but no matter how many times Rooster turned it over in his hand, the skael looked like nothing other than the shimmering likeness of the real thing.

"I can illusion anything if the strain isn't too much, but smaller things I can keep an illusion going for longer." As the skael faded away and the chestnut appeared once more, night paved the way to day, and Rooster glanced up with a startled expression. The three of them no longer stood in the forests of the eldrasi. Before them stood the sandy streets of a city

Rooster did not recognize. Overhead was the massive ribcage of a god, hazy beneath the sun.

"Is this Shoma?" Rooster asked, unable to tame the awe in his voice. Helai had not been exaggerating when it came to Massoud's talent with magic.

"Shok'Alan, the holy city. That," Massoud said, gesturing up to the skeletal remains above, "is Qevayla, the Dragon of Dreams. Much of Shoma look to her as their god, forsaking the Old Ways." People bustled by in silks and covered scarves, pulling donkeys and camels behind them, which in turn pulled carts overflowing with goods—incense, silks, wine. Rooster met Cassius' gaze, where he could see the vampire's impressed nature as well.

"This is amazing, Massoud," Cassius breathed, pressing his hand to his brow to peer up at the sand-colored buildings wrapped with vibrant colors. "Truly, I cannot find a flaw in the design."

Massoud bowed, his hair falling into his face as he chased away a vibrant smile. A bead of sweat ran down his brow, but otherwise, there was no indication the magic was straining him. "I have had a little over a decade to master my craft, and when two others depend on your success for their survival, it adds weight."

A young girl with two braids in her hair passed by, holding the hand of a young boy with short dark hair and dirty cheeks. They were both barefoot, and when Rooster met the gaze of the young girl's, his stomach plummeted. He saw the resemblance of Helai in her face as she darted around the corner of a building, tugging the young boy after her. He had never asked Helai about her childhood, but he knew it to be something she cared little to talk about.

The illusion bled away, and they were back in the forest. Rooster shivered suddenly. He hadn't even realized that Massoud had managed to illusion the warmth of the sun as well until it was gone.

"I'm afraid the rest of the demonstrations will have to wait until we enter the prison," Massoud said, a slight labor to his breathing. "But I can assure you, we will be able to walk in as if we belong there."

"It is reassuring to have you and your illusions. Without them…" Rooster glanced Cassius' way once more. "We've managed before, but it will make things easier."

Silence fell between them after that, a silence that left Rooster to his restlessness. It was nearing dawn when the Thorns entered the building, and Rooster knew it was time.

Cassius gave a faint nod, his lips paving way to sharpened canines as the Thorns left the lorekeep moments later with the other Misfits in tow. Rooster was pleased to see that Florence was not among them. He had to have faith that the myrlír had gotten out with the tome.

"We'll wait an hour before we follow," Rooster said quietly, watching the Thorns lead everyone towards the prison. "Just to be safe."

"Whatever you say… captain." Rooster's head turned at Massoud's words as a foreign feeling flooded through him. He still didn't feel much like a captain, still felt very much the drunken fool that had gotten himself captured by shoma'kah outside of the forest of the old eldrasi. Something sang in his bones though, a quiet reminder that he was meant for the role.

The trip to the prison was accomplished without trouble. The eldrasi had yet to rise from their nightly slumber, and with Massoud's help, they made it through the city unseen. Rooster ignored temptation to stop and marvel at how truly beautiful the city was, darkened by the ever-looming presence of the prison overhead. The closer they got, the bigger the cages hanging from the branches became. The main part of the prison was carved into the tree, woven inside it like it meant to choke the life from the tree itself. Still, the tree thrived, reaching out over the city with reckless abandon.

Rooster loathed to think what sort of unspeakable evil took place inside.

"Come," Cassius said, eyeing the tree. "The less we linger, the quicker we find your beloved."

Rooster nodded, drawing close. Massoud approached the bridge that crossed the ravine separating the city from the prison. He whistled as he peered over the edge. "I do not want to think about how far of a fall that is. I've never been a fan of heights."

"Don't worry. Cassius has wings. If you fall, I'm certain he'll catch you." Rooster grinned at the glower shot his way by the vampire and offered him an arrogant wink. He was not ignorant of the way Cassius and Massoud looked at each other.

Massoud pressed a dramatic hand to his brow. "My knight in shining armor."

Cassius groaned, earning a laugh from both Massoud and Rooster.

"Thankfully this bridge seems sturdy. I do not fear the threat of falling." Still, Rooster's stomach plummeted to his feet as he took his first step onto the bridge. It was wide enough, it seemed, to carry across carriages of trade goods and seemed to be carved flat out of one of the tree's roots. Now that they were so near to their goal, Rooster's nerves felt raw, like if anything rubbed up against him, it would set him off.

"Before we go across, we should, ah, let me illusion us." Massoud gestured to a cluster of trees nestled against the cliff's edge just before the bridge, and a sense of relief passed through Rooster as he stepped back to where he was safe from falling.

"Is there anything we can do to make this easier on you?" Cassius asked, peering out into the city as eldrasi began to leave their homes. A lone gryphon flew overhead, reminding Rooster of Tantien. The ring Tantien had given him was still warm against his finger, meaning Tantien, at the very least, was alive.

"I will have to remain focused on the illusion, so you two will have to do the talking." Black inky smoke unfurled from Massoud's fingers. He made it look so easy. The magic made Rooster shiver as it pressed up against his skin, wrapping around his clothes and arms and face.

"I suppose we can manage," Rooster joked as he watched his fingers elongate and take on a slightly green hue, like Tantien's. Reaching up, he felt his ears taper to points, his hair fill out and draped down his back. Cassius' transformation was much of the same. His skin remained its olive tone, but his face was more angled, tucked behind an eagle helm like the Thorns wore. A deep-green cloak billowed from his back, and silver thorns twisted against his gauntlets. They all looked like they belonged.

"Amazing," Cassius breathed, staring down at his gauntlets. "Truly. This rivals the magic of the rings Linda and Intoh wear."

Massoud grinned, obviously pleased, and winked at Cassius. He remained focused and said nothing as they turned, staring up at the tree prison that loomed before them.

It was time.

FORTY-EIGHT
CASSIUS

"Halt!" They made it across the bridge before they were finally stopped by an eldrasi guard. He was tall and lanky, with simple leather armor and a spear that he had staked to the ground in front of him. There was only one guard, and Cassius wondered fleetingly if that meant this guard was more than capable should something go wrong or if it was a foolish mistake on the prison's part. He'd seen what the Thorns were capable of and was moved to think it was the former.

"State your business," the eldrasi said.

"We've been sent from Kelirium to offer more aid to the prison in whatever way the warden sees fit," Rooster said, offering a smile. "We responded to trouble in Kelirium, and our commanding officer has reason to believe the misfits that caused trouble at one of our taverns might have traveled here."

The guard nodded and stepped aside. "Report to the warden immediately."

They didn't waste any time, brushing past the guard and entering the prison. Cassius held his breath as the scent of the eldrasi's blood wafted over him, tempting him to feed. Luckily for him, it was easy enough to ignore.

The inside of the prison was one to be admired. As they stepped inside, they found the tree was hollowed out, with the middle serving as a feeding quarter for the prison's inmates. The ceiling was so high, Cassius only managed to see it with his heightened senses, and prison cells were carved straight into the walls of the trunk, where inmates clung to metal bars faceted to the wood. They came from all walks of life, and Cassius saw red eyes peering out from the shadows of one cell. What had the vampire done to garner the wrath of the eldrasi?

They were stopped just inside the door, where a small, magical orb bobbed and wove around the two guards just inside. It was a luminescent blue, and it trembled as it sat, suspended, in the air. The guards looked to it for several moments before they nodded and gestured them through.

"It is going to take us forever to find everyone," Rooster said, peering up at the swirling cells. Anxiety rolled off him in waves, and Cassius pressed a hand to his shoulder as he led them over to the stairs.

"Every prison is the same. You always keep the most dangerous inmates either at the very center or deep within the earth, so that if they manage to escape their cell, it's more difficult for them to flee the prison. My guess..." He gestured upwards. "We will find your crew and the other Misfits at the top. Unfortunately for us, that is likely where the warden will be as well."

The prison hummed with life magic that pried at Cassius' limbs, like a tingling sensation that refused to settle. He knew it wasn't right for someone like him to be here, knew that vampiric magic did not mingle well with the nature of eldrasi magic, and he was eager to find Rooster's crew so they could flee this place.

He peered over his shoulder at Massoud, who met his gaze. There was a flicker of shadow in his eyes, an indicator that the magic that washed over them was still working, and Massoud gave the faintest of nods.

"Then up we go," Rooster said, taking the first step towards the top.

"Please, I beg. A break." Massoud spoke for the first time since they'd entered the prison, his chest heaving. "My legs are going to fall off and then you'll have to carry me." He pondered the idea for a moment. "Perhaps it wouldn't be so bad."

Cassius halted, and looking over at Rooster, he noted he looked just as winded, with a small bead of sweat coating his brow.

"No, no, we can't stop." Rooster pressed a hand to his chest, but he stared up the stairs with a burning expression. "Not until we find them."

"We can spare five minutes," Cassius said as Massoud collapsed to the floor. They were between cells, but Cassius felt eyes on them from the inmates as the illusion faded away, leaving them to be vampire and humans once more.

"I am sorry," Massoud said, his tone burdened with apology. "I did not realize this climb would be so...strenuous."

"You have gotten us inside. That is *more* than enough," Rooster assured. He remained standing, his gaze flickering anxiously above them. A railing kept the stairs from a straight drop, but Cassius peered over it anyhow, noting that they'd perhaps made it about halfway.

"We still have a way to go yet," he commented, turning. He noted some paths veered off from the stairs now that they'd gotten high enough. They carved between cells and lead to ornate doors.

"I—" Rooster trailed off as several voices started to sing several floors up. "Do you hear that?" he asked. When Cassius nodded, he started forward, ignoring Massoud's protests. Cassius offered Massoud his hand and pulled him to his feet, ignoring the way his heart skipped as their fingers touched.

Massoud's gaze turned heated as they hurried after Rooster. The singing began to grow louder until Cassius could understand the words.

It was a shanty of some kind, sung by a multitude of people.

Hoist the sails and let them flap,
For Captain Wingman leads the map.
With hope in sight, we'll never stray,
Through wind and wave, we'll find our way.

Through the darkest night, he guides our course,
With a steady hand and unwavering force.
Though the tempests rage, we stand tall,
For Captain Wingman, we give our all.

When doubt creeps in and shadows loom,
Captain Wingman dispels the gloom.
With a song of hope upon his lips,
He steers us through the storm's eclipse.

A strange look crossed Rooster's face. "That's them. I know it."

"What gave it away? Surely not their singing about 'Captain Wingman'?" Cassius' sarcasm was scathing, and the sharp look Rooster gave him was not unkind.

"Sarcasm? From you? I'm wounded." He frowned and then continued towards the singing. "No... the song is...familiar."

Cassius met the expression of an eldrasi in one of the cells, their brow raised in interest. "Curious," they said, and Cassius drew forward, his tongue laced with compulsion magic.

"You heard nothing. If the guards pass, you saw nothing."

To Cassius' dismay, the eldrasi's eyes did not glaze over in compliance. They hardened instead, their mouth twisting in a bitter line, and then they were shouting.

"Guards! Intruders."

Cassius' lips peeled back over sharpened fangs. The brown of his eyes melted away to red, and anger sang through him so quickly, it tempted him to pull the eldrasi against the bars and bang his head against them. He turned instead as commotion and the sound of guards rose up from below.

"Hurry."

They moved quicker then, following the singing until it pulled them nearly to the top. The song came from several cells at the end of a hallway. It stopped abruptly when Rooster halted outside of them.

"Captain?" Someone drew forward—a skinny dark-skinned man with long locs and golden teeth. His eyes were round with shock as his fingers curled around the bars of the cell. "'s that really you?"

"Would seem that way." There was a flicker of disappointment in Rooster's tone as he drew forward, only to be replaced by soft determination. "Where is Igraine?"

"She 'as been detained outside with da gunnery sergeant." A woman leaned out of the shadows, her smile bearing fangs. She was also dark-skinned, her braids thick, twisted, and long, pulled back and tied to showcase her pointed ears.

That had to be Araetha Greaves, Delroy's sister. Cassius saw the resemblance in her expression and the shape of her face.

She nodded at Rooster. "It's nice ta see ya again, Carta Wingman."

"Took you long enough."

Helai shuffled through the crew as she gestured to the other Misfits, her eyes shining. "They've spoken about taking us to interrogation. I loathe to think what that could mean."

Cassius could not imagine anything pleasant coming from an eldrasi interrogation, especially after having seen the way they'd mercilessly killed Khal. "We need to figure out a way to get them out," Cassius said as the soft patter of eldrasi heartbeats etched his throat. "I sense guards coming."

"Allow me," Massoud whispered. "Glad to see you're alright, little sister." He winked at Helai and then took a moment to steady himself, exhaling slowly. "Stand very still until I tell you otherwise," he said and then he wove shadows through his fingers. "You're all going to become invisible, and movement will make this harder on me."

As guards flew up the stairs, their eyes wild and their weapons drawn, a wave of magic rolled over the group. Cassius couldn't tell they were invisible, but the guards didn't appear to see them.

"Span out. They cannot be far." Their eyes fell against Cassius only to pass over, and as they drew close, Cassius was the first to lash out, followed closely by Rooster. They all moved with quick precision, working together to take down the guards before they could cause too much noise. One guard managed to cry out in surprise before Cassius knocked him out, and then the hallway fell to silence as they laid the guards on the floor.

"Think I can open door. Cannot be more difficult than shoma'kah enchantments," Intoh said, pushing his way forward. He studied the door to the cell for a moment, his eyes flickering to and fro as his fingers moved in intricate patterns. Soon, the doors to all the cells in the hallway opened and freed every prisoner. Across the hall, a massive krok'ida stumbled out, his scales a blend of black and red, and a giant scar blinded his right eye. Rooster pried a bag of skaels from his hip and offered it to the krok'ida.

"One hundred skaels in here if you'll keep the guards of this place distracted."

The krok'ida snarled. "Will do without. No need skaels. Glorious combat." He ambled off, and after a moment, more commotion was heard.

Linda grumbled, staring out where the krok'ida had disappeared. "Wish I could join. Want to fight something," they said. "Took my hammer away. Need to get it back."

"We will," Rooster promised. "Just have to find Igraine first."

"Her and Sígrun should be out beyond that door." The skinny man from before gestured. The rest of the crew had crowded near the front of the cell, eager to get close to their captain. There was nothing but adoration in their expressions, and Cassius' heart swelled for them. He'd felt that way once about his Order and his maker, Vera. He felt that way now about the Misfits.

"Figure out a way to get to the docks," Rooster said. "We're not leaving without the Perseverance."

The crew drew a palm over their hearts in salute, and then the Misfits headed further up the prison tree after pulling the unconscious guards into the prison cell and relocking the door. Rackjack wrangled his way to be next to Rooster; he was in his dwarf form and as anxious as ever. Glancing back, Cassius noted that everyone was accounted for: Helai stood next to Massoud and Drithan, and Linda took up the back with Intoh and Sode.

"Florence's absence is according to plan, I hope?" he asked, and Helai nodded.

"He fled the lorekeep with the tome. The rest is up to him."

All that was left was rescuing the final two of Rooster's crew and then escaping.

FORTY-NINE
ROOSTER

As Massoud masked their presence and Helai's magic unlocked the door, Rooster prepared himself. A part of him was full of giddy, nervous energy. He had spent so long being a slave to his amnesia that the thought of getting those memories back was strange. He'd grown comfortable in the man he'd become post-amnesia, and a large part of him feared he would loathe the man he'd used to be.

He shook off his insecurities. If someone like Igraine could love him, how truly evil could he have been?

As the door opened to the outside, Rooster's stomach flopped over itself, and he grabbed onto the wooden rail that rose out of the branch they stood on. They were easily hundreds of feet up in the air, and despite his comfort with heights, he refused to look down. The wind swayed the branches, and like the sea, he was able to keep his footing relatively easily. His heart fled to his throat as he noted the bird cages. Each one of them was filled with prisoners.

He marched forward, and each time he peered in and didn't see Igraine, his panic swelled, an ugly thing that burned at the pit of his belly. He had to find her. If he didn't find her...

"Carter?"

It was strange hearing his name. He hadn't heard it since Igraine had uttered it when he visited the prison during his tea trip. This time, when it was spoken, it was like a dream. His heart thundered against his chest as he turned to the next cage and locked eyes with impossible blue.

It was like the sea was trapped within her gaze, a swirling of dark-blue and grey. Her hair, dark red, shone brightly against the pale glow of the luminescent orbs that danced around the cages. Her fingers slipped through and curled around the wooden bars, as if the very will of her could break the cage. She sat on the ground of her imprisonment, and though she looked physically unharmed, her cheeks were dirty, and she moved slowly, as if she were too weak to move.

The moment their eyes connected, something inside him snapped into place. It was more than regaining his memories; it was like he finally remembered how to breathe. He didn't notice the tears streaming down his face until he moved forward, a sob of relief rattling his throat. He'd half expected them to torture her to death. He had refused to think of it until now, but seeing her alive allowed the thought to fester and rise.

"Igraine." Her name flowed from his mouth like it belonged there, and he reached towards the cage to tug it closer to the walkway.

"Wait!"

He halted at her command, quieted by her weakened state, and her gaze turned upwards. "Mine has been warded. I do not know what lengths they've gone to ensure I do not escape, but I know I cannot use my magic and I know the warden knows what goes on in this place at all times. It's by some miracle you got up here without being noticed in the first place."

Intoh eyed the cage with interest. "Looks like cage shoma'kah used to bind me. Very excellent warding. Does not contain all magic. Looks like just fire magic." He moved his fingers in a series of patterns, and the cage hummed as if aggravated. Frustration furrowed his brow as his fingers continued to move.

"Think I made poor calculation," Intoh said finally, slumping back as his hands fell to his sides. "Cannot break lock."

Igraine eyed the others warily. "Who are your new friends?"

Rooster could hardly tear his eyes away from her, but he did. After he introduced everyone, Massoud stepped forward, studying the cage intently. "I believe that if Helai and I work together, we can use shadow magic to unlock your cage. I don't think it will set off the wards." He glanced at Helai. "I could also shade step into the cage, provided it can hold both of our weights." He shuddered as he peered over the edge. "The last thing I want is to fall at this height."

Igraine shook her head. "I don't think it can. These cages were only ever meant to hold one person."

"Do whatever you need to to get her out of there. Hurry." Rooster didn't mean for his voice to sound so harsh, but the words bit the air with impatience as he stared at Igraine. He was afraid that if he looked away, she'd disappear.

If Massoud or Helai were offended by Rooster's brass commands, they didn't say anything. Both quietly went to work, and the entire time Rooster looked only to Igraine. He'd never leave her side again. He'd never be so foolish.

After what felt like an agonizingly long time, the lock fizzled and crackled, and the door to her cage swung open. The cage danced dangerously in the wind, and Rooster couldn't stop the noise of alarm from breaching his lips. *Don't fall, don't fall, don't fall.*

With Massoud and Helai's help, Igraine slipped from the cage and swayed, falling where Rooster could catch her. "Carter, my love," she said softly, tears shining in her eyes. "I knew you would come."

Rooster swiped his thumbs across her cheeks, chasing the tears away, and pulled her close. Her skin was gaunt, like they hadn't been feeding her, and there were small weeping wounds healing on her arms and legs. She seemed sound of mind though, her smile echoing her exhaustion as he curled protectively around her.

"I'm sorry I took so long." A tear of his own slipped unbidden down his cheek. Seeing her did not unlock his memories as he had hoped, but it was *her*. He couldn't get close enough to her. He ignored the others as he tucked her hair behind her ear and lifted her up.

"We need to go," Cassius said. "Does she know where your gunnery sergeant is?"

"Sígrun?" Igraine's voice was soft, like she teetered on the edge of passing out. She lifted a shaking finger further down the branch, towards another bird cage. "She's just there around the corner."

Anger simmered behind her eyes as she pushed away from Rooster and forced herself to stand. "They were far less kind to her than they were to me." Her gaze turned haunted, feeding Rooster's rage.

"What did they do?"

Igraine opened her mouth to speak but decided better of it and shook her head. "All I can say is that they wished to keep me, for the most part, uninjured in case they managed to capture you. The rest is up to Sígrun to share. Come, Carter. We need to get our family to safety." She glanced around at the Misfits, her eyes softening. "It seems our family has grown since we were separated. I cannot wait to have a chance to meet you all properly. Rackjack..." Her face softened. "Your illusion is holding up nicely."

"Illusion?" Drithan's voice thickened the tension in the air as Rooster turned to the dwarf, who had his brow furrowed. "Rackjack's illusioned?"

Igraine stilled. "Oops."

Rackjack fidgeted nervously, and Rooster straightened, stepping up and placing a hand protectively on Rackjack's shoulder. "We'll explain when we're not in the middle of a fucking eldrasi prison. Rackjack, Massoud, Helai, and Igraine: follow me. The rest of you stay here."

Drithan appeared less than pleased by the reprimand, but Rooster was already turning away, followed closely by Massoud and Helai. He kept Igraine tucked to his side, but her strength seemed to be returning the longer she was out of that cage they'd kept her in. Rooster wondered if the wards they had placed on her cage had been used to keep her weak.

As they rounded a corner, Rooster halted just before another wood cage. The woman inside had her hands bound far apart, each finger peeled open so she could not clench her fists. Her eyes, ice blue, raged as they stared out above a leather muzzle that covered her mouth.

"I can break her chains if we find a way in," Igraine uttered, her own anger a blistering heat that suffocated the air in her vicinity.

Massoud glanced over at Helai, who nodded. They had the cage unlocked in no time, just as they had with Igraine's, and Rooster's stomach lurched as Igraine climbed onto the railing and leapt over to the cage. It swung precariously, and Rooster was reminded only of the vision the witch's tea had granted him, where the warden threatened to drop Igraine to her death.

"Igraine," Rooster said quietly, his fingers curling against the railing so tightly his knuckled turned white. "Please—"

"We're okay," she said, peering back at Rooster and giving an encouraging smile. She refocused on the small chains that kept Sígrun's fingers from curling, breaking them with ease. The moment she did so, Sígrun clenched her fist as a few metal cages hanging nearby melted and reformed into a small bridge that connected her cage to the branch, granting them a safer way across.

"It is good to see you again, Captain." Sígrun's voice was rough and heavily accented as they returned to the safety of the branch path, her northern roots displayed proudly in the braids in her hair and the muscle in her arms. She was breathing heavily as she curled her fingers again. This time, when a nearby cage melted, it reforged into a battle-ax that appeared in her grasp. Rooster watched on with a minor sense of awe. He had never seen anyone wield metal magic before. "Forgive me if I do not show displays of mercy to any of this eldrasi *filth*," she said, spitting at the ground. "No offense, Igraine."

A simpering smile pressed against Igraine's lips. "None taken. This hasn't been my home for a very long time."

As they made their way back towards the others, Linda said,

"Find armory. Need to get *Volroth* back."

"I know where it is," Sígrun said, pushing past everyone and heading back the way they had come. "I also know where to go to get to the Perseverance." Twirling the battle-ax in her hands, she glanced back over her shoulder.

"Follow me."

FIFTY

LINDA

The urge to fight the Sígrun was strong. Power radiated from her that was intoxicating and difficult to ignore, and Linda openly stared as the Vykra moved forward and led the party back towards the door leading into the prison.

"Come, Linda," Intoh hissed, pulling Linda from their trance. Shouts could be heard from below, and Linda knew they were fighting against time. Soon, the prison would be swarmed with guards, and maybe *Volroth* would be able to taste their blood once more. They still hadn't forgiven the Thorns for killing Khal.

"Get ready. I can sense them behind the door," Cassius warned, pulling his sword from his sheathe. Rooster did the same as Igraine's palm lit up in flames, her eyes blazing. Magic soaked the air, and Linda was startled to realize it didn't bother them quite as much as it used to.

Guards burst through the door before Sígrun reached it, but she was ready, her fist coming around to strike one of the guards in the side. Another one slammed into his temple. The bridge quickly fell into chaos. There wasn't enough room for everyone to fight, but it mattered little. Sígrun struck down everyone in her path, and soon, they were able to make it back inside.

"We must go all the way down," she said, ignoring the protesting cries of the prisoners still trapped in their cells. "They will know it's us and will most likely fortify the Perseverance, so we need to go quickly."

"I'm going to make it look like there are less of us than there actually are," Massoud said, shadows dripping from his fingers. "Perhaps we can still maintain an element of surprise."

"Can make it easier—go invisible," Intoh said, disappearing in a blink.

"I can help too," Helai said, her own shadow magic manifesting.

"Your magic has improved, Helai. I'm impressed," Massoud said. Several of the Misfits disappeared as if they had never been there at all. Linda looked down and was pleased to see they could still see themself.

"Good," Linda said. "Want enemy to see I'm coming. Want them to fear me when they die." Normally, Linda would have reveled in the idea of catching their enemy by surprise, but Khal's death had lit a fire in their soul, and they wanted the guards to see them when they robbed them of their life like they had robbed Khal of his.

They moved quickly down the tree. Any guards they came across were either struck down by Sígrun or Linda, who led the spearhead of the group. The prison had fallen to chaos, with the prisoners all shouting. One managed to snag Rooster as he passed by, her eyes snaked with red veins that ran from her eyes. She snarled, her fingers curling around the fabric of his shirt as she slammed him against her bars.

"Rhavna musters in the north. They whisper of their return. They do not fear you, Misfits. Whispers of you have traveled throughout Vilanthris, and you will do well to tread carefully, Chosen."

Igraine lashed forward the same moment Cassius did. As Rooster started to pull away, fire burned the woman and Cassius cut her hand off at the wrist. Her howls of pain echoed long after they continued to flee down the stairs. Rooster murmured soft words of gratitude.

"Here," Sígrun murmured quietly as they traveled down a hall further into the tree. There were no prisoners here, no cells. Rooms lined the walls, and Sígrun halted at one with a door. "Further down is the way to the docks. Give me two minutes inside, and I'll have freed your things."

She pulled the door open and slipped into the room. Muffled shouting was heard, followed by the quick clang of metal against metal, and then silence. It took Sígrun all but a few minutes to return, holding the door open to show three guards had been slaughtered; their corpses lay scattered across the floor.

"Hurry."

They piled inside the room, save for Intoh and Massoud, who remained outside invisible in case they could have company. Chests and crates were scattered about in an organized fashion, full of weapons and other things the prisoners might have brought in, and Linda sought out *Volroth* immediately where it hung on a wall, eager to have the war hammer back in their hands. It was like a friend returning home, and Linda clutched the hilt with ease, eager to use it to fight their way to the docks.

"Excellent, Carter. You're here," a voice called out from the hallway, and Linda turned as a broad-shouldered eldrasi woman stood in the doorframe, her hands clasped behind her back. She wore heavy plate armor, like Cassius', with a swirling golden design in silver metal, depicting a tree across the chest. Her head was free of any helm, and her hair was cropped short on the side, much like Rooster's had been before it had grown out.

Behind her stood more guards, the gleam of their helms sharp in the flickering torchlight.

Igraine inhaled sharply beside Rooster. "The warden," she said darkly, and the warden smiled wickedly, the dark green of her eyes twinkling as she nodded.

"It did not take long to know which little birds had gotten free of their cages," she said, taking a step into the room. "The tree spoke of your liberation, and that just won't do," she cooed, shutting the door behind her. The moment the door clicked shut, the room became alive, and vines shot out in all directions, tugging them down to the surface. Some of them slammed against the wall, while others, like Linda, were dragged to the floor. Linda roared in anger, ripping the vines from the ground only for bigger, thicker ones to take their place. Outside, the guards shouted, followed quickly by silence. Linda could only hope Intoh and Massoud had taken care of them.

Soon, the room was still with everyone trapped, and the warden strode forward until she stood in front of Rooster, who clung to the wall next to Igraine. "Carter Wingman," the warden said, her voice devoid of any warmth. "We have been searching for you for a very long time." Linda couldn't see the warden's face with her back facing them, but Rooster's was full of rage. "Kaero will enjoy interrogating you." Her finger rose up to trail slowly down Rooster's cheek, but the vines held him so tightly, he could do nothing about it.

Try as they might, Linda could not find a way to break free of the vines that curled around them, but it didn't appear as if they'd have to as the vines trapping Igraine withered and died, her fingers forging flames that burned away the greenery.

"You forgot to trap my hand," she snarled as she slipped down the wall and hit the ground. She wasted no time launching herself forward, her fire winding around her arm like a whip waiting to be unleashed. The warden was quick, though, and avoided Igraine with ease, unsheathing the sword at her side quicker than Linda could follow.

"Touch him again and I'll take my time cutting every finger from each of your hands," Igraine hissed, her eyes a blaze of blue as she ducked beneath the warden's blade. The room was large, but not so much that it was easy to fight in, and Linda felt the warmth radiate off Igraine's fire as she pushed the warden back towards the desk in a corner of the room. The warden hit the side of the desk, clipping it with her hip, and she snarled in frustration and pain as Igraine's fire licked her side.

Igraine didn't relent there, didn't lessen her attack, and Linda watched on with awe as she grabbed the warden around the neck and heated her palm. The warden's screams drenched the room as Igraine burned her to death. The stench of burning flesh reached Linda as the vines that bound them lessened, and they ripped themself free. Everyone else did the same, and Rooster immediately stumbled over to Igraine, tugged her close, and kissed her deeply.

"That was incredible," he breathed after he pulled away. Linda had never seen Rooster look at anyone the way he looked at Igraine.

"Come on. We don't have time to delay," Sígrun said, tossing Linda *Volroth* with ease. Linda caught it, and Sígrun studied the war hammer with appreciation. "Nice weapon," she said, and Linda's chest brimmed with warmth.

"I know," they told her, twirling *Volroth* in their hands. "Kill many with it."

Sígrun nodded. "I do not doubt that."

They nodded at the battle ax in the Vykra's hands. "Like yours too."

Sígrun stilled as guards shouted from the hallway. "We are going to have a fight on our hands. I hope you all are ready." Linda glanced about at their family – at Intoh's fingers tingling with lightning, at Cassius with his sword and knightly grace, at Helai with her daggers flush against her arms.

"Let's go," Linda said; the Misfits were always ready for a fight.

FIFTY-ONE

CASSIUS

They rushed around a corner as guards flew past, shouting orders. Cassius dragged Massoud further into one of the open cells. The shadows seemed to cling to them, curling against Cassius' skin, and he shuddered as Massoud batted his eyes up at him, his fingers twisting with magic.

"This is so exciting," he whispered, and Cassius couldn't stop the smile from forming on his face. For the first time in his very long life, as Massoud peered around the corner, as the Misfits moved down the hall as one with Rooster's crew alongside them, Cassius truly felt free.

Linda fought some guards at the front. *Volroth* swung wildly, blood splattering across the walls as it struck true. Rackjack pressed beside Linda, his fire splaying out across the narrow hall to light guards on fire. Sígrun manipulated the metal of her battle ax, sending slithers of barbs flying through the air to kill those too far away from her swings, and the air was filled with the heart of exhilaration.

Massoud laughed, and Cassius wondered if the sound could be stitched into hymns he could worship. They locked eyes, and a seed of emotion burrowed into Cassius' chest. It was something he had not felt before, a great reckoning that could bring about his downfall, should he nurture it. Cassius had never been good at such things, but something about Massoud made him want to try.

"You do seem to be enjoying yourself. One for danger, no?" he asked, and Massoud's eyes lit up as he reached out to tug Cassius closer.

"Hmmm," he mused but did not answer. Instead, he seemed to forget they were running from a prison full of angry guards and that distractions could prove their capture. Dark lashes shielded his expression as he glanced up at Cassius through them. His fingers curled around Cassius' chin, and he tugged him close before crashing his lips to his.

This dance they'd been doing had been so agonizing that when Massoud began to kiss him, a soft noise of content etched in the hollows of Cassius' cheeks, and then he, too, forgot where he was. Affection had always been sharp teeth and hard touches. Affection had never been the gentle way Massoud's fingers slipped through his hair, nor the way the grasp on Cassius' chin softened. A low growl echoed in the halls of Cassius' throat and then he was pulling Massoud, demanding him closer.

Someone shouted, but that only seemed to make Massoud all the more determined to get closer. He anchored himself to Cassius as he parted his mouth to deepen the kiss. Cassius' fingers untangled the bun that Massoud often kept his hair in. Massoud's laughter danced across his lips, his eyes shining and dilated as he pulled away.

"Having fun?" Rooster shouted. "Linda has kept the guards busy so you could have your moment, but we have to go." Sígrun stood beside him, her mouth drawn in a hard line, and she looked less than pleased and eager to leave.

Cassius was unaffected by embarrassment. He pulled away from Massoud despite his heart and body screaming at him to do the opposite. Massoud's heartbeat was a melody in Cassius' ear, elevated from their kiss, and he nodded. "Of course. The air is starting to taste less stale, and I hear sea birds. We must be near a way out."

As they made their way through the twisting halls of the prison, Massoud darted forward and rested his hand on Cassius' shoulder. His lips pressed against the cusp of Cassius' ear. "Soon as we get out of here, soon as we find ourselves a moment of reprieve, come and find me. We have unfinished business, *abibi*." The weight of his promise heated Cassius' expression. As it settled like a kindling fire in his belly, he nodded.

"First, we have to make it out of here alive."

Massoud laughed again. At the sound of guards shouting, heading their way, he turned forward and blew into his palm. Shadows twisted into a plethora of smoky desert foxes that hit the ground and ran towards the guards, stretching up to coat them in darkness. When they reappeared and the shadows dissipated, the guards were unconscious and strung across the floor as everyone rushed down the hall. They hurried down the twisted roots with Linda, Rackjack, and Florence paving the way at the front. Soon enough they reached the bottom of the tree, where a small dock system was woven into its root.

"There she is," Sígrun said, pointing. "The Perseverance."

There were other ships in the docks, but the ship Sígrun pointed to was easily the largest. Naela was nowhere in sight, but it didn't surprise Cassius that Tantien's contact had not arrived. It would have been simply too dangerous for her to do so.

"That's *your* ship?" Cassius used to admire Hestian ships for their sleek light wood and white sails, but the ship in the water before them was massive, much larger than any ship Cassius had ever seen. It looked custom built by human hands but elevated by eldrasi influence, with swirling vine designs that decorated the three mast posts and the railings. The figurehead was that of an treeling, a wizened old face carved into a tree-like figure. The ship bobbed in the water, and Rooster's men rushed forward to meet the guards stationed there.

There weren't many, thankfully, but they put up a good fight, managing to deal a shallow wound to Helai's shoulder as she swung close to stab them between their armor. Igraine lashed out, a whip of fire snapping against the guard's sword hand, and he dropped it with a cry of pain as Massoud choked him with shadows. The illusionist stumbled, and Cassius caught him as Massoud laughed with a tired expression.

"Might have overworked myself a bit. Don't know how much magic I have left in me."

"We should hurry, before the rest of the prison arrives," Sígrun said as she cut down the last of the guards.

"Best ship-boat the seas have ever seen, yes-yes," Rackjack hissed, hobbling his way to a ladder. There were some moments Cassius forgot about his prosthesis entirely as Rackjack walked with such ease. Other times, he put in less of an effort, and it was clear as day. "Never find a better captain than Carter-filth."

Rooster looked just as shocked as Cassius though, his gaze flickering over the ship as he helped Igraine to one of the ladders. She had become so weak up in her cage. "Is this really mine?" A peculiar look crossed his face, akin to confusion and rage, and Sígrun, already on the boat, began barking orders.

"Give her to me," Cassius said, gesturing to Igraine as Rooster contemplated how to get her onboard. The way he tightened his hold on her and hesitated gave insight into his anxiety, and Cassius' face softened. "I can fly her up. You can trust me, Rooster."

After a moment, Rooster gave a firm nod and relinquished Igraine into his arms. Like Tantien, she was warm for an eldrasi, and so light he had to be sure his grasp on her was secure before he called his wings from his back. He was incredibly thankful for Tantien's skill with a forge as his wings slipped through the two slits in his plate armor and stretched out. The sensation of freeing them made him shudder and then pushed off from the ground, pumping his wings until they flew to the top deck of the ship. He landed gracefully. Several people stared at Cassius, but he ignored them, ignored their heightened heartbeats and soft whispers. As soon as Rooster climbed up from the ladder, he delivered Igraine back into Rooster's arms.

He watched the adoration slink across Rooster's face when he looked at Igraine. He radiated with so much of that feeling that Cassius was tempted to shiver from it, and he understood now why Rooster had been the way he had been these last few months.

"Thank you, Cassius." Rooster's voice wavered slightly.

"Cap'n!" Florence's voice carried down from the crow's nest, where he poked his head over. "Be checkin' your dresser, where it's safe and sound-like." He nodded knowingly, and Rooster returned it with a firm one of his own as he aided Igraine into the captain's quarters below the wheel. "Rackjack, lead in my absence," he said just before disappearing into the room.

"Yes-yes." Rackjack scampered forward as Massoud moved out of the way, and it appeared as if Rooster's men did not require much instruction as the sails were lowered to half-mast and the ship began to move towards the space between two massive roots. Everyone settled into their tasks, and Cassius reluctantly pulled his wings back as he stepped towards the ship's bow. The sun was beginning to set, bathing the sky in brilliant colors, and an overwhelming emotion sank into Cassius as they sailed away from the eldrasi island.

They were free.

FIFTY-TWO
HELAI

There was no sea sickness this time, and Helai was grateful.

She stood at the back of the ship near the wheel as Rackjack sailed them away. Helai watched the island begin to grow distant and did not say anything as Rooster stepped up beside her. She knew it would be foolish to hope that the Thorns wouldn't pursue them. There were enough boats in that dock for a small fleet, but they'd fought at sea before. They could do so again. Especially with a ship as large as Rooster's.

They didn't say anything for a time, and then Rooster drew her close and pulled her into a hug.

She was surprised by it, but after a moment, she let it happen despite the way her skin crawled uncomfortably. She had never realized how much she loathed simple touches. Rooster had just gone through a lot though, so she wrapped her arms around him as he stared behind her at the distant island.

"She's safe from them now, Rooster," Helai said, watching the sailors work.

"I am grateful for your aid. I know you have gone through a lot, losing Zamir and nearly losing Massoud. You didn't have to come with me on such a perilous quest." There was tension in his voice, and as she tried to pull away, she found she could not.

"Rooster?"

His hold on her tightened for a moment. Then he pulled away. Her relief was brief as she noticed what he held in his hands: the lamp she'd swiped from the general. It looked almost foreign in his hands, just as foreign as the vengeful nature of his expression as the wind whipped his hair around his face.

"Rooster," Helai begged, drawing forward. "Don't—"

"Thank you, Helai. You are more than the Jewel of Shoma, you are the soul of the Freeman Misfits. I envy your morality as I am not a forgiving man." He stepped forward, rubbing the lamp. Helai's ears rang as the world went silent, and the jinn slipped from the swirling magic of the lamp's center. Rooster did not hesitate. "I wish for the Fraxinus Prison to burn by choking ash and smoldering ruin, and the land upon which it rests to forever remain scorched by my wrath."

Helai turned, horrified, as the wish's magic shot out in all directions. Everyone was pushed to the ground except Rackjack, who clung to the wheel. The wish danced across the ocean, and the moment it reached Fraxinus, the tree prison burst into flames. Helai felt the heat hit her cheeks, and she turned to Rooster, her eyes blazing.

"What the *fuck* have you done, Rooster?"

Rooster pushed himself to his feet, his mouth drawn as anger simmered in his gaze. He looked out at the burning tree, his fingers wrapping so tightly around the railing of his ship that his knuckles turned white.

"What I had to. They'll pay for the sin of hurting *my* family with their lives."

Pushing the hair from her face, Helai stood as well. Her blood sang hotly, so much so she was dizzy and sick with rage. "There were innocent people in that city, Rooster. There were probably innocent prisoners in that prison too. You can't just—"

"I can," Rooster snarled, his shoulders tense. "I did."

Linda ascended the stairs, looking between the two of them as tension formed in the air. "Think it good idea. Think it will stop them from chasing us. Think—"

"Shush, Linda," Helai snapped, instantly guilty when the hurt crossed over Linda and they flinched away. "Rooster doesn't need you fighting his battles for him."

"Don't cleave Linda with your anger, Helai. If you want to direct that anger, direct it at me." Rooster stepped forward, and Helai stumbled back, her back hitting the railing behind her. She sensed Massoud's eyes on her, but her heart was beating too quickly in her chest to feel the comfort of his presence; the roar of the ocean was too loud in her ears. Rooster's wish stitched its betrayal in her, and she knew deep down, it would take a miracle for her to trust him again.

"You should have asked. You shouldn't have just taken it from me," she said softly, her eyes burning with angry tears. "How dare you."

A flicker of some emotion Helai couldn't discern crossed Rooster's face, but Helai turned on her heel and fled before he could say another word. There was nothing else he could possibly say to her.

It was taking her a while to find a place she could tuck herself into and hide. She snapped at Drithan when he tried to stop her, and the growing wound of her guilt festered inside her as she left him, but she hadn't been able to help herself. All she could see was that tree burning. All she could hear were the prisoners' cries for help as she'd passed their cells that she'd ignored.

She made it to the hull of the ship and tucked herself away as Rooster had done after Delroy had revealed to him his true name. Pulling her legs up against her chest, she leaned against a wooden box and allowed her tears to spill. She cried for Rooster's betrayal, for the lives that had been lost due to his wish, and for her own strange sense of isolation.

"Helai," a voice called out to her quietly, and she hurriedly wiped her cheeks as Massoud materialized, his face full of concern. "Do not think you can chase me away with your mean words like you have the others. I have had a lifetime to grow hard against them."

Helai sniffed and then scooted over, granting Massoud room to sit beside her.

After he climbed atop the wooden crate, they sat in silence for a while. The wood of the ship creaked. Somewhere something dripped. The rope that held fruit and small kegs whined as they swung.

"I'm going to say something, and I want you to listen until I'm done," Massoud said finally, reaching out to take Helai's hand. "I do not excuse Rooster's actions. I have no right to. I don't know him. I barely know any of the friends you've made in my absence. But Helai—" He met the sharpness of her glare. "Don't. Not until I'm done." He waited for her to close her mouth to continue.

"I would have done the same thing had you been in there."

Her gut protested—*no, no, no*—but he would have. She recalled the time in Dalasae when a wealthy Shoman merchant had caught Helai stealing some food in a market. It hadn't even been his booth, but he had grabbed her by the hair and had her beaten, right on the streets. Massoud had been furious when she came home, battered and bruised with a few broken ribs and a hungry belly. He'd disappeared, only to return in the dead of night covered in blood. It had taken her days to realize Massoud had murdered not only the Shoman merchant, but his entire family, too. She would be foolish to disagree with Massoud now. Still, stubbornness stayed her tongue, and she wrapped her arms more tightly around her legs.

"Ah, but I didn't come down here to lecture you. I don't think I ever properly thanked you for saving me. Seeing that fire burning in Rooster's eyes when he pulled Igraine from her cage—I saw it in your eyes when I woke and the jinn was gone." An uneasy look crossed his face, and he rubbed his beard with his hand. "I was dead long enough to know that I shouldn't be here, that I took too much for granted before. No more. You gave me a second chance. I won't forget that." He squeezed Helai's hand, and she squeezed back, tears etching the corners of her eyes again. She didn't want to talk about this, didn't want to think about that blank look in Massoud's eyes right before the jinn had brought him back. She'd give anything to pluck that memory from her head.

"So..." she said, changing the subject. "Cassius, really?" She bumped his shoulder and smiled when he laughed. "Be careful with that one. When you're that grumpy all the time, there has to be a reason." She was mostly teasing but knew there was much they didn't know about Cassius' past. The last thing she wanted was for Massoud to get hurt. "And be *kind* to him. I know how you can get." She glowered jokingly as he pressed a hand to his chest, gasping dramatically.

"I am a perfect gentleman, Helai!"

It felt nice to laugh. She sensed the tension easing from her shoulders as she laid her head on Massoud's shoulder, and they fell back into a comfortable silence. She had fought to be reunited with Massoud for so long, she would do anything to keep it.

"I really like him, I think." Massoud's admission did not surprise Helai; he was falling in love with a different man every time they spoke of it. His flirtations and easy-going nature were always so harmless, and Massoud was always chasing someone he thought could provide him the love he so desperately sought. A part of Helai worried Cassius could not be that for Massoud, but she raised her head to smile at him.

"I see the way he looks at you. I'm glad for you. I really am."

Massoud's eyes turned knowing. "Tell me about Drithan."

Helai's cheeks warmed, and she lowered her gaze to her hands. She was still untangling her own feelings on the matter. Being around Drithan liberated her lungs from their chains and stopped her anxiety from carrying her into the clouds. They'd shared their fair share of intimate moments, but fear drew her away from him every time he opened himself up to her.

"Nothing to tell," she said.

Massoud scowled. "If *you* won't tell me, maybe he will."

"No. I'll *kill you again* if you bother him with this." Horror snaked through her at the thought. "Maybe I like him too. Is that what you want to hear?"

Massoud grinned, entirely too pleased with himself. "Yes." Leaning his head back against the wall of the ship, he sighed. "He's good for you, Helai. You need someone like Drithan. I can tell you two will take good care of each other if you'd just let him in."

"Letting people in only ends up in this mess," she said, gesturing to where they hid away. "People always betray you."

"Not everyone. That mindset will only deprive you of happiness." He waited until he caught her eye. "Drithan is smitten. I can see it in the way he acts when he's around you." He paused for a moment, then reached forward to press an affectionate kiss to her forehead.

"Rooster says we'll see the shores of Vitreuse in the coming weeks, where we'll be free to take a moment to breathe. Fret not, little sister."

As Massoud climbed off the crates and disappeared up the stairs, Helai curled in on herself.

She did nothing but fret.

FIFTY-THREE
CASSIUS

The last time they had made port near the eastern continent, it had been at the heart of battle, aiding a city devastated by siege. This time, however, Cassius did not taste such war in the wind and could not feel the heightened heartbeats of those who fought for their lives and their country. He felt only calm, and he could already hear Rooster's men setting up a bonfire and moving casks off the ship after they'd approached the shores of the island Rooster called Vitreuse. It was a lovely island, just large enough to suit their needs and provide a little solace from the years they'd been fighting. Cassius inhaled sharply, welcoming the relief of the promise of relaxation.

Helai was the first Misfit to flee the ship, her silence tense in the air. She hadn't spoken to Rooster or Linda since their big fight, and Cassius wondered if that wound would ever truly heal. He stood by Rooster's reasoning; he would have done the same had he been in Rooster's position, but he also knew that Rooster should have asked Helai to be on his side too.

"D'you mind?" a large man with a floppy hat and arms full of kegs balanced precariously on his leg said, and Cassius reached out to take one from him, eager to be off the ship himself. If he had to aid their unpacking, so be it.

"Thanks," the man grunted, flashing a toothy grin in Cassius' direction. One of his teeth was golden, and a thin layer of sweat collected at his brow, but his eyes were kind. "Name's Habal. 'S a pleasure to meet ya."

Cassius gave a stiff nod as he passed the keg down to another sailor, who set it on a rowboat.

"Ah, good ol' Habal, roping him into helpin' with your duties? Cap'n will have your head for skirtin' your work, mate." A slender man with thick locs and a bright smile trudged forward and wrapped his arm around Habal's neck, tugging him close. A dimple cratered his left cheek when he grinned. Habal shoved him away playfully.

"Come off it, Skinny Jim. You know the Cap'n don't care so long as the rum gets to the beach. Tonight will be a night of celebratin'. Not every day you escape one of the most fortified prisons in Vilanthris.

"We're lucky Araetha knows how to ward this place. Right, Araetha?" Habal called out to where Araetha stood, her thick braids dangling over her shoulders. Unlike her brother, she half-tucked her vampirism behind a faintly veiled illusion: only the sharpness of her fangs and the red of her eyes poked through. She smiled wickedly.

"Mmm, you know da eldrasi be worried more about dem own trifles we left dem with than finding Vitreuse. Da island 's safe from da wanderin' eye. At least for da moment." Leaning against the railing of the ship, she waved her hand. "Go. Have da celebration you are earned. I will watch da shores tonight."

Despite the intimidating nature of Araetha's aura, none of the crew seemed frightened of her, except for Drithan, perhaps, who kept a wary eye on the vampire the entire time he was on board.

Skinny Jim laughed. "An' we know you're good for it, Araetha. Feel safest when you're the one watching over us." He winked. "See you on the beach, yeah?" He disappeared down the ladder as Cassius and Habal nodded, resuming their work of getting the kegs to shore. He wasn't sure why. Maybe it was the lightness in the air or the way Rooster's crew joked and laughed around him. Maybe it was simply the break from danger. Regardless, he knew it was going to be a night to remember.

Cassius' stroll was a leisurely one as he walked down the beach with goblets of wine in his hands. The familiar sound of Massoud's heartbeat called to him. It had been the first night in a very long time that Cassius felt free, like he could undo the latches of his armor and be liberated of its weight...if he hadn't already left his armor on the ship. The water lapped up against the shore as the sound of waves overcame the receding noise of celebration behind him.

Massoud came into sight before too long, his head upturned as he threw an empty bottle into the sea. His hair was freed from its normal bun, and it sifted gently through the wind. His gaze caught Cassius' as he sidled up beside him.

"Ah, I wondered if you were ever going to catch up." Massoud laughed to himself, taking the goblet of wine as Cassius offered it to him. He was quiet, contemplative, and Cassius studied him silently, relishing how beautiful he looked in the light of the fading sun.

"I figured you'd be at the life of the party. Imagine my surprise to find you had slipped off with only yourself for company," Cassius said finally, gesturing to the lingering light of the bonfire behind them.

Massoud's gaze turned coy. "Ah, but I am not alone, am I?"

Cassius eyed him as the setting sun cast the rest of Massoud in a brilliant gold. *Where did you come from?* Cassius wanted to ask but held his tongue. Instead, he took a sip of wine, forcing his gaze to stare straight ahead.

Silence did not last long between them. "I see you found the wine, after all." Massoud hid his lips behind his glass, but Cassius could hear the amusement in his voice. "And here I thought you shared the last of it with the captain."

Cassius laughed. "I wouldn't have shared the last of the wine with Rooster. He's a good enough comrade, but I had plans for the rest. The less he drinks, the more for me."

"Some might say you would make a good cleric of Dalnor, with all your trickery and wit."

"Ah, but that would require any god to hold my allegiance." A lie. The weight of Drausmírtus' hold on him pressed against his back, where his wings lay tucked hidden behind his illusion. His allegiance to the goddess of death strengthened each day he took in borrowed breath.

Massoud openly laughed this time, throwing his head back. "Then what *does* hold your allegiance, dear Cassius?" He paused, growing serious as his fingers brushed against Cassius' shoulder. Underneath his shirt, the contact called out to something that had long slumbered in the bowels of Cassius' belly. "What commands your soul to go forward?"

Cassius stared down at Massoud's fingers, how gently they splayed across his shoulder. Ahma's ghost haunted him. *Power. The lust for power*, she begged him to say, but that's not the confession that poured from his lips. "I'm still trying to figure that out." The vulnerable confession urged him to flinch away, but Cassius stood strong, relieved to be honest with someone for once.

Massoud glanced up at him through lashes, then sighed. "Me too." A moment of thoughtful silence trapped itself between them. "I'm glad you caught up," he said, staring at the moon as it rose up into the sky, bathing them in its luminescent glow. "Now, I don't know if I have anything to steal from you, Cassius. For surely if you had a heart, I'd try to take that."

Hesitation furrowed Cassius' brow, his lips forming a thin line. As if to mock Massoud's words, his heart thundered in his ears. The sound of birds cawed softly in the sea breeze, and Cassius' expression softened. "Good thing we don't have to worry about that then." *You must think me so monstrous that I am incapable of love. Perhaps you are right. Perhaps I am not worthy.*

Cassius could not read Massoud's expression given he was turned away from him, but he heard the small hum flee his lips. "Hmm. Perhaps," was all that followed. Silence fell between them.

They walked for some time more until they reached a series of palm trees. Cassius placed his goblet on a rock in the sand. Cassius had never been a fan of sand. He could remember a time very long ago when he and Markus had run along the shores of his home as children. They'd used to go searching the shallow pools for fayre stars as they were rumored to bring good fortune to whoever found them. They had never been successful at it though.

"Cassius?" Massoud dragged Cassius from his thoughts as he stood close enough to the water that it brushed up around his bare ankles. Cassius didn't know when Massoud had taken off his shoes, but now he felt entirely overdressed. The weight of his promise when they'd been fleeing the prison washed over him. *Soon as we get out of here, soon as we find ourselves a moment of reprieve, come and find me. We have unfinished business, abibi.* His lower stomach clenched in anticipation of what might happen next.

"Yes?"

Massoud wasn't one to pause; his charm came as easily to him as Linda slipped through water. He paused for a moment now though. Cassius couldn't read him, only that his pulse was heightened, and he was staring at Cassius as if he hungered for something. "I will admit, there is..." He paused. "There is a certain charm about you, Cassius. And I will..." He sighed, nervous laughter dancing on the edge of his lips as he pressed his fingers to the nape of his neck. "Ah, Helai makes it look *so* easy." Cassius strode forward until he was only a few feet away as Massoud's confession slipped.

"It has been difficult not to worry about you." Massoud's vulnerability caught on Cassius and pried at something deep within him. He'd seen every member of the Misfits ready to save his life with no hesitation should he need it. Gods, they *had* saved his life more times than he would ever admit. Somehow it didn't feel the same as Massoud standing here right now, admitting his worries. Not for the first time, Cassius wondered what it was about Massoud that had had him staring down that eldrasi guard back in Kelirium and putting himself in harm's way to make sure Massoud didn't die. Cassius wanted to believe it was honor that had bound him, but no. It had been something else entirely. A selfish desire to keep Massoud safe. A need that had wormed his way into his chest and burrowed in his heart.

Cassius' gaze darkened as he closed his mind to those thoughts. It wasn't the time for that now. Not as warmth spread through him. Not as desire yawned awake in his belly. "Tonight, you need not worry. It is a night for celebration, no?" And with such declaration, Cassius made his move, stepping back as his fingers grazed his shirt's buttons, and he began to undress, holding Massoud's gaze.

Massoud's mouth parted as he drank in the sight of Cassius. His goblet slipped from his fingers, falling into the sand, forgotten. Normally, Cassius would have grieved the lost wine as it trailed through the sand towards the open sea, but his gaze was consumed by Massoud striding forward, moving at a speed that impressed even Cassius.

He managed to get his shirt off before Massoud reached him. His fingers threaded through Cassius' hair as he demanded their lips meet. Massoud tasted of wine, and Cassius sucked it off his lower lip with untamed greed. A low noise passed Massoud's lips as Cassius pulled him closer.

Massoud's pulse thundered against him, all-consuming as his fingers wandered over Cassius' skin, etching pathways of pleasure as they danced across the dips of his hips, up to his sides, around his neck, and through his hair.

As Cassius fell back into the sand, he tugged Massoud along with him. He barely noticed hitting the ground, too distracted by moving his hand between them to tug at the silk of Massoud's belt. The fire in his belly drowned out all else, and for tonight, Cassius freed himself from all the shackles that chained him. Duty, honor, hunger, greed—he sheathed them for the morrow. Tonight would be all shuddered breaths and shared bodies.

Cassius rolled so that Massoud was beneath him, his hair splayed about along the sand. Massoud's eyes were dilated, his cheeks rosy, and he was breathing hard, his eyes hazy with lust. Beneath him, Massoud's erection pressed against Cassius' belly. It took Cassius' breath away.

"You are so beautiful," Cassius murmured, his lips moving to brush against the pulse at his neck. How familiar the motion, how *easy* it would be to bite. He kissed instead as Massoud laughed, breathless.

"Ah, now you're stealing my lines. I'm losing my touch."

Massoud's hand wove through Cassius' hair as the vampire began to descend. He kissed Massoud's neck, his collarbone, and downward still. His movements were slow and deliberate despite the hunger that fueled him. It was a different hunger, one that lacked his vampirism or his taste for power.

Massoud's soft sighs drowned out all else.

The waves lapped up against the sand as the full moon bathed the beach in its soft, tangible glow. Cassius laid on his side facing Massoud, who was on his stomach, his cheek pressed against his arms, with his eyes closed. Cassius took this moment to let his gaze wander.

Massoud's inky dark hair spilled over his shoulders and lifted gently in the breeze. His back was uneven and scarred, and Cassius slowly reached out to trail his fingers over the puckered scar tissue, a quiet and unexplained rage settling quietly in his belly.

"Who did this to you? Did this happen in Alavae?"

Massoud's eyes opened as he shifted in the sand, pulling away from Cassius' touch. "My people think of me as a traitor. This is the result." His voice was bitter as he scooted closer, his lips pressing against Cassius' collarbone. Cassius' skin tingled wherever Massoud's lips touched. "They burned me over that pyre for who knows how long before Helai and Linda stormed in there and murdered them all. It would have been a better kindness to kill me, but ah! They thought this old street rat had information. Kept me just far enough away from the fire to keep me alive but close enough that I'm left with this reminder. Sometimes they'd drag me away just to lay the whip to my back." His lighthearted tone did not match the harsh implications of his words.

Cassius' fingers dipped under Massoud's chin to tug his face up so that his gaze met his. He stared at him silently for a moment before he pulled him in for a kiss. "Their death was too kind. I would have made them suffer as you had."

Massoud's gaze pinned Cassius to the ground when he pulled away, and Cassius struggled not to squirm from the vulnerable way Massoud looked at him. He wasn't a man deserving of such tender gentleness.

"Alas, seems you are stuck with me," Massoud said, sighing dramatically. "I could not think of a more wretched company than I." Splaying his fingers across Cassius' chest, he watched the steady rise and fall of his breathing. "Do not worry about me, Cassius. Linda and Helai did make sure they suffered. My home has been a festering wound in my side my whole life. I only wish to live here, as I am now."

With you. Cassius was desperate to hear those words, but they never came, even as Massoud pushed himself up so that he could straddle the vampire's waist.

There were still many worries. Now that they had retrieved the book from the prison, they would surely set out for Lyvira once the seas settled and Tantien arrived with Delroy to discuss their next plan. He couldn't think about any of that right now. Not while Massoud's face hovered above his, and his fingers wandered lightly over his skin.

Reaching up, he threaded his fingers through Massoud's hair, tugging him closer, and demanded their lips meet once more. He kissed Massoud until his lips were swollen, and eventually they made their way further into the forest, eager to seek more privacy.

FIFTY-FOUR

CARTER

Carter heaved a sigh, still coming down from the high of his climax as Igraine nuzzled into his side. Steam clung to the air above the hot springs, and exhaustion threatened to tug Carter under. He refrained, instead wrapping his arms around Igraine and pressing a soft kiss to her forehead. Now that he had her, it was so apparent how much his soul had longed to find her. The urge to hold on and never let go prodded his anxiety, but he forced it away. He wasn't going to let his fears chase away the calmness of this moment.

"Carter?"

"Hm?"

Igraine tilted her head so that she stared up at him. The water lapped around them as she shifted, and her fingers moved up to ghost across his face. "Did you find what you were looking for?" Her voice was soft, her expression almost sheepish.

He didn't answer her, not right away. His memories were still returning to him in fragments, but that one, the one that had caused his amnesia in the first place, had returned with perfect clarity.

"I didn't want to ask when we were at the prison, for obvious reasons. Then what happened after..." She trailed off, and Carter's heart squeezed painfully. He wasn't sure if Helai would ever forgive him for that. A harsh darkness within him didn't care. He didn't regret having used the wish on the prison nor in having deceived Helai to do it. He'd freed her of the burden of any guilt she might have felt by letting him do it.

"No," he answered truthfully, recalling the memories of Daesthara. "Some dyrvak chased me away from the grove before I could find out why I was called there. I–" He stared into her eyes, stared so long, he felt himself get lost within them. Now that he had her, he never felt more at home than when he stared into her eyes.

"I regret going at all. It was foolish to leave you, to leave the crew."

Igraine sat up, her hair like drenched fire as it draped around her shoulders. "Don't," she said, a fire burning in her expression. "Don't you dare blame yourself for our capture. It wasn't your fault."

The anger still sang through him like molten lava, like the maelstrom of a storm in the middle of the sea. He was lost to it, and his hands trembled, only being stilled when Igraine forced his attention to her.

Gods, she was beautiful.

"Gods, you're beautiful," he told her, reaching out to tuck a strand of hair behind her ear. He shivered in adoration as her eyes lit up at the compliment, and he threaded his hands through her hair. It was like liquid fire as it trailed through his fingers, and he drew her close to press a searing kiss to her lips.

Igraine laughed as she wrapped her arms around his neck. "Don't try to distract me from your guilt. I can feel it strangling you. What matters is now. Look at me."

How could he look away? By her command, he met her gaze, and his chest ached. He had been a hollow man before, a husk of his former self. Her gaze forged fire in his belly.

"I'm here to stay. Do you still feel the call to Daesthara?"

Her words swept him with indecision. It was a small thrum in the back of his mind, a soft urge that beckoned him back to the forest that had stolen his memories. Something had called him there, and it hadn't been until his memories had begun to return that he'd felt it once more.

Rooster nodded.

Igraine's gaze darkened. "Then one day we'll return, but—" Her finger trailed down Rooster's nose and over his lips before she gripped his chin roughly in her grasp. "This time I'm going with you."

Rooster's hesitation was shorter than it had been last time, and Igraine didn't give him the chance to speak, her fingers splaying over his mouth to silence him.

"I know the forest is ripe with danger, especially for someone like me. The forest will hunt us the moment we step foot inside, but Carter –" Her eyes shone with angry tears. "We are hunted everywhere. I am safer at your side and you at mine. In this life and the next."

He reached up. The hot water lapped around them as he gently curled his fingers around her wrist and pulled her hand away. Oh, how he *loved* her. "In this life and the next," he repeated softly. "A worry for another day, my love. We have more pressing things to attend."

"Yes," she agreed slowly, pushing away from him to wade in the middle of the springs. "The tome you stole. You have still failed to mention its significance."

Intoh had been pouring over it, muttering to himself and studying its contents. The magic that permeated off the tome had kept Rooster's distance. He didn't like the way it felt, the power it gave off.

"We believe it will aid in putting a god to sleep."

The news seemed to worry Igraine as she chewed her lower lip, her brow furrowed. "That is no small task, Carter. You know what my people say of the gods. Where—"

"Lyvira," Rooster said, raising his hand to cup her cheek. "I know. We watched one wake beneath the Welker Estate in Halvdarc. We watched Cassius *die* so the cults of this world could bring her back. It's too late to turn the other way. I fear they will stop at nothing until the dragons have been liberated from their earthy prisons and the gods walk among us once again."

"Then we go to Lyvira," Igraine said, turning to press a kiss to his palm. "Whatever happens, we'll do it together."

He nodded and then pulled her close to kiss her. Their little solace away from the festivities left Rooster hungry for Igraine's closeness, and his desire flooded through him as Igraine wrapped her arms around his neck and sucked water from his lower lip.

"We should really return to the bonfire," she uttered against his cheek, then gasped as his fingers slid over her nipples. "Celebrate with the crew."

"Hmmm," he hummed as he lowered his lips to press kisses against the curve of her neck. "I don't wanna. I'd much rather stay here and ravage you until the sun comes up."

Laughter echoed throughout the halls of the cave as Igraine swam closer, took Rooster's head in her hands, and tugged his gaze up to meet hers. He fell obediently into her gaze, enamored by how truly *blue* they were.

"Close your eyes," she whispered against his lips as her fingers drew small paths over his cheeks. "And count to ten."

Rooster obeyed, the world growing dark as he shut his eyes and began to count to ten. He did so slowly despite his impatience as he felt Igraine draw away from him, his space suddenly devoid of her. It made his heart ache painfully, a small flicker of fear that she would be taken from him again.

"Ten," he said, opening his eyes to see Igraine fully dressed, her hair dripping water over her white shirt, and her eyes twinkling mischievously. "Igraine, what are you..."

"Come, come, love. Come catch me," she said, laughter trailing behind her as she turned on her heels and bolted out of the cave. Rooster rose, the air cold against his bare skin, and it took him a moment too long to realize she had taken his clothes.

"Igraine," he shouted, but laughter of his own danced on his lips as he stumbled after her stark naked. He had never been a man uncomfortable without clothes on, but the thought of running through the forest without them was less than ideal. Still, he did, allowing the glare of the moon to guide him through the trees as he followed the sound of Igraine's laughter.

At one point, he passed something shuffling in the brush, but that proved only to be Cassius and Massoud in their own state of undress with Massoud on his knees.

"Hey, Captain," Massoud said, a simpering smirk crossing his lips. "Nice ass."

Rooster ignored him and ignored Cassius' agreeing hum as he continued his hunt through the forest, knowing that the moment he caught up to Igraine, he intended to make up for lost time.

FIFTY-FIVE

LINDA

Everyone was slow to wake up the next morning. The night of celebration had been a large one, so large that even Linda was feeling the slow draw of lethargy in their limbs as they woke. It was nearing sunrise, with the colors of the sky just beginning to shift, when Linda rose from their resting place and sought out Sígrun, who sat near the shore.

"Sit here?" they asked. Sígrun had been all but silent since they'd escaped the prison, and something about her intrigued Linda.

"So long as you promise not to speak so loud," Sígrun said, rubbing her temples. "I didn't mean to go quite so hard last night, but some of the crew are quite persuasive."

Linda dropped down next to Sígrun, the sand kicking up as their tail flicked through. They suffered a headache of their own, but it was nice to sit in a simple silence and watch the sun rise. The sound of the ocean lapping up against the shore was comforting, and Rackjack scurried over, the gleam of his new prosthesis offensive as the sun hit it. Now that everyone knew Rackjack's true nature, he'd gotten rid of the bead in his beard and assumed his rat form. Drithan had taken care to stay away from him, still weary for what Rackjack truly was, but the Misfits and Rooster's crew were so used to it that no one paid Rackjack any mind.

"Sígrun-filth. Must talk to you about your home-burrow in north."

Sígrun tensed beside Linda, her eyes trained to the sea as an unfamiliar expression crossed her face. "I don't like talking about that, Rackjack," she said, her voice low and tinged with warning. It gave off the same energy as when Linda hissed if something they didn't like came too close.

Rackjack's beady eyes glittered as he drew forward. He didn't appear frightened by Sígrun like the others were, and Linda's respect for Rackjack flourished. Even Linda was a little intimidated by Sígrun. Maybe Rackjack just had little regard to his own life.

"Important, Sígrun-filth. Saw Rhavna."

The name made the air thicken, and Sígrun stood. "Don't utter that name here," she hissed between gritted teeth. "Tell me everything." As Rackjack recounted what had happened to them in the Welker Estate, Linda drifted off mentally. They didn't want to think about Rhavna's resurrection or watching Cassius and Rembrandt die or the implications of that phoenix dragon returning.

"The Phoenix Mother was a member of one of the Vykra tribes in Volreya a long time ago," Sígrun said finally, pulling Linda from their dissociation. "I remember fleeing to her tribe when my entire village was slaughtered. Her tribe wasn't faring much better with the brutal winters and lack of food." She paused, forcing her jaw to relax. "She kept muttering about a dragon in the snow whispering to her about salvation, and she had to do what must be done. One day, one of the villagers found her at the river."

"Saw this part in memory-dream," Rackjack said, his voice hushed as if the Phoenix Mother herself could hear them. A chill had overcome them, and Linda shivered, annoyed. They were tired of feeling so cold.

Sígrun nodded. "She drowned her two sons in the river and her only offer of explanation was that she saved them from their suffering. When they burned her at the stake for her crimes, she was born anew from the flames. She slaughtered everyone." For a moment, it looked as if Sígrun might cry, and a soft feeling inside compelled Linda to reach out and somehow comfort her.

"Everyone except for the girl children." Sígrun's face hardened. "We were *chosen*."

Linda wanted to ask Sígrun what she meant by that, have been called 'chosen' by some of the cults themself, but they never got a chance to.

"That Tantien-filth?" Rackjack asked, his nose twitching in excitement as he limped forward, careful to stay away from the waves. Two ships approached the island, with a hydra trailing beside them, her scales sparkling in the sun.

"We'll talk more later," Sígrun promised. "It sounds like we have a long journey ahead of us if we're to set sail for Lyvira."

It took some time for Delroy and Tantien to weigh anchor and approach the beach. By that time, those that had disappeared the night before were filtering out from deeper inland. Cassius kept sneaking glances at Massoud as they stumbled out of the trees, and Rooster and Igraine arrived not much longer after Skinny Jim had been sent to retrieve them. Helai was still absent, had been since they'd arrived, and Intoh poured frantically over the tome as he sat at the bonfire, which had long since gone out.

"Itale," Linda said, eager to see their new friend. He looked exhausted, the underside of his eyes darkened with lack of sleep. The tips of his fingers were still black, and his lips were pale, but he seemed to be in good spirits as he climbed over the rowboat and smiled broadly at Linda.

"Oh, it is so good to see you, Linda. It's good to see solid ground too. I haven't even been able to enjoy my tea due to how rough the sea was."

"Have tea time soon?" Linda asked. As much as they hated the taste of tea, they'd missed the time they'd spent with Itale. Despite their aversion to his magic and the chill that permeated the air wherever Itale was now, Linda felt comforted by Itale's presence.

Itale's eyes brightened. "Of course!"

Off to the right, Araetha approached Delroy with a fanged smile. "A pleasure, as always, Delroy." They didn't embrace, but a look of fond affection and relief crossed Delroy's face from under his massive hat.

"I would offer a warm relief ta see you, but unfortunately der are important matters to discuss. There will be time later to catch up." Araetha nodded as Tantien strode forward, stopping a few feet from Igraine. Delroy's words seemed to have been lost to Tantien for he made no move to discuss things as he stared at his sister, who stared right back.

Tension bled into the air as Linda pushed themself to their feet, shaking the sand from their scales. The sun had fully risen, and the crew of the Perseverance was beginning to wake. Warmth soaked into Linda as Igraine finally stumbled forward and embraced Tantien, who slowly returned the hug.

"I have missed you, sister," he said, though the tension remained. "I know we left things on uncertain terms, but I am so glad to see you are safe." There was anger in Igraine's eyes when she pulled away, but there were tears too, shining as they refused to fall.

"We'll talk of old wounds later. For now, there are world-ending matters to discuss, as Delroy has said." She turned away, returning to Rooster's side; he draped an arm across her shoulders and tugged her close.

As Tantien composed himself behind a wide smile, he held his hand out towards where the bonfire had been. "Much to discuss indeed."

"If a dragon wakes in Lyvira, others are sure to follow," Sígrun said, her mouth pressed in a thin line. Since Rackjack's questioning, Sígrun had been tense and silent, even as the Misfits had filled everyone in on Rhavna's resurrection and Delroy's news of the tree in Lyvira. "They will all wake and then Mot is sure to follow."

"Mot?" Cassius questioned, drawing forward. "Do you mean Mo-taumr?"

Sígrun nodded. "He goes by many names. The dwarves might know him as Kurzda. My people simply call him Mot, the father of Vilanthris." Drithan frowned, an uneasy look crossing his face. "If he wakes..." Sígrun continued, her eyes blazing in the new fire they'd built, "the world will split apart. He is believed to sleep at the world's center, where Vilanthris is hottest."

"Mohalis has been trying to bring back Qevayla since he became sultan. What reason do we have to believe there will be any success in these schemes?" Massoud asked, his arms folded loosely across his chest. He rested on a log near Cassius and next to Helai, who remained still and silent. A flicker of sadness and hurt ran through Linda, who still hadn't spoken with Helai since she'd lashed out at them after Rooster's wish. They missed their friend, but Helai hadn't expressed interest in speaking, having tucked herself away with Drithan somewhere the moment they'd gotten to Vitreuse.

"Because der are already signs," Delroy said. "Wicked creatures drawn to da tree of Osgol. Stirrings in da magics. The sea be unsettled, and Sollatso has expressed her concern when we be near da shores of Lyvira." Gesturing to the Misfits, his expression turned grim. "With da news of Rhavna's return, der is no time to question whether it's going to happen. Not when we should be asking ourselves *when* it will happen unless we can stop it. Da scaly one dere." He pointed at Intoh, who hugged the tome to his chest. "He holds a magical tome powerful enough ta put da god back to sleep."

"Shouldn't we worry about Rhavna and stopping her from whatever it is she's doing in the north?" Rooster asked.

Delroy nodded. "I'll be sending my fleet to da north to hunt her while Carter takes his men west to Lyvira to return da tome to da tree."

"I'll accompany you," Tantien said, straightening. His hair gleamed in the firelight, his expression thoughtful. "I am hunting someone who I believe might be mustering up in the north."

"You aren't still on that silly venture," Igraine said.

Tantien nodded, not meeting Igraine's eyes. "Of course I am."

Igraine frowned but said nothing else despite the curiosity that burned in Linda's chest. They usually cared little for listening to the trifles of the others, but the tension between Tantien and Igraine was great, great enough to take notice of.

"We would welcome da help, Tantien," Delroy said, his eyes glowing as he offered a fanged smile. "We're going ta need it."

"I'll go with you too," Itale said suddenly, then looked sheepish when all eyes turned to him. "I mean, i-if you'll have me. I...ah, quite liked being on the Firebrand, and I think Sir Cassius has taught me what he can." Uncertainty burned into his expression as his eyes flickered to Cassius, who nodded firmly. "I think I would be more use than braving Lyvira, as much as I don't want to separate again."

"Your skills are always welcome on the Firebrand, Itale," Tantien said gently. "Just know I cannot promise your safety." A shiver passed through the small group. Rooster had sent the rest of his crew to the Perseverance to heal from their hangovers, with a promise of at least a week more of relaxation before they set sail again.

"I understand," Itale said.

"Will we know what to do once we arrive?" Rooster asked. "Where is this tree?"

"Know the location. Deep in Lyviran forest. Old forest. Old secrets. Will be dangerous. Might..." Intoh shuddered. He was in his greka form for once, and it felt almost unnatural now that he had spent so long tucked away behind his human illusion. Linda thought he might have been content to remain a human forever, but he seemed just as comfortable being a greka again, with Sode relaxing beside him. He took a deep breath, then continued, "Might have to go to one of the cities. Speak to leader."

A thrum passed through Linda, a sudden current of warmth that seeped into their bones. Somehow, they knew Intoh's words rang true, like a purpose that suddenly made sense.

Ikotia's words flowed through Linda once more. *"You will be tested."*

It seemed like Linda was going home.

The idea was terrifying, something that Linda could not seem to comprehend. It had been years since Intoh had plucked them from their spot and commanded them to aid him on his quest. Would it feel like home anymore?

"I fear da war for dis world is only beginning, Misfits, and we've been deemed pieces on da board. Time to play our part," Delroy said with a reaffirming nod from his sister.

As what they needed to do next became clear and the meeting devolved, Linda watched Florence pick over Rackjack's new prosthesis, feeling the intricate and magical grooves Tantien had carved into it to ease his ability to walk. They watched Rooster place a loving kiss to Igraine's temple, the way Massoud's eyes burned when he glanced over at Cassius. They watched Itale and Tantien softly discuss with Delroy as Araetha slipped away. Intoh resumed fussing over the tome, with Sode watching on with mild interest. Helai and Drithan had disappeared, but Linda hadn't seen much of them since they made landfall.

No, they decided. They weren't going home. They were already home.

ACKNOWLEDGEMENTS

First and foremost, I would like to thank each and every reader who has stuck with the Misfits this far. I feel like this community is its own little D&D party, set along to attend the Misfits' journey with them. I wouldn't be here without the support of the people who have continued to pick up, read, and love every story in the *Whispered Tales* series. I am but the bard, recounting the tales of their quest. Miranda, my editor, is the blacksmith, forging and whiddling this story into the best version of itself. My readers are fellow Misfits, each of their own class, ready to fight against the cults of the story and the dragons of old. We're getting to the real exciting parts of the story now (in my humble opinion), and those who have stuck around get the reward of enjoying the true reason I wanted to write this story in the first place. The relationships, the heart of the conflict, the Misfits' bond with one another: it's just going to get better and better.

Thank you for being a Misfit. Thank you for making the start of my author journey a special one. I'm forever grateful. To many more of the Misfits' journey. To many more other stories too. We're in the thick of it now. □

WHERE TO NEXT?

If you enjoyed *A Song of Hope*, please consider leaving a review wherever you're most comfortable. If you would like to stay updated with Dugdale's publishing journey, consider following them on Instagram and/or TikTok: @jordandugdaleauthor. The Misfits' journey is far from over; I cannot wait to take you along for their next adventure.

https://www.instagram.com/jordandugdaleauthor/
https://www.tiktok.com/@jordandugdaleauthor